# THE WICKED WEST

BOOKS 1-5 IN THE CAPITAL CITY MURDERS SERIES

TROY LAMBERT

STUART GUSTAFSON

Published by
CCMbooks
P.O. Box 45091
Boise, ID 83711 USA
www.capitalcitymurders.com

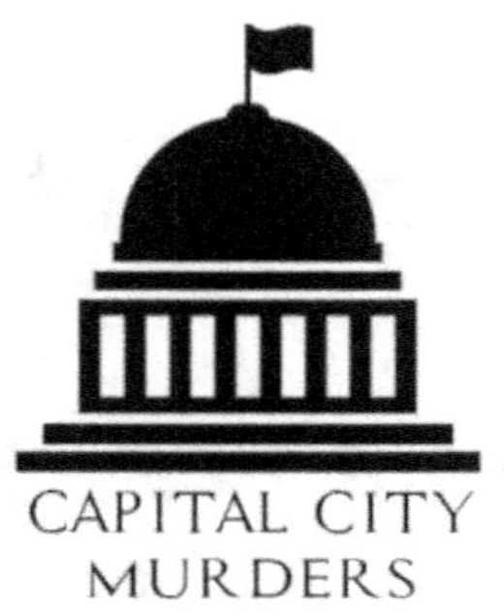




First Printing October 2019
This is a work of fiction. Names, characters, businesses, places, events and incidents are either the products of the authors' imaginations or used in a fictitious manner. Any resemblance to actual persons, living or dead, or actual events is purely coincidental

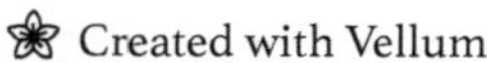 Created with Vellum

# AUTHORS' NOTE: THE ORIGINS OF CAPITAL CITY MURDERS

From Troy:

In March of 2019, two authors sat down in a café for coffee. One of them, Stuart Gustafson, travel and mystery writer, and "America's International Travel Expert®" pulled out a stack of paper filled with ideas, and presented it to me, Troy Lambert, thriller and mystery writer, freelancer, ghostwriter and publisher, and said the words that set all of this in motion: "I have an idea. It might sound crazy, but..."

Then, after looking over his plan to take a character, Nick O'Flannigan and send him on a journey of mysteries around the country, a year-long photography assignment to take photos of every single state capitol building for a magazine, a journey where he would find mystery everywhere he went, I was intrigued. Then when he suggested the timeline: that we release one novella a month for fifty months, I said the next words that gave birth to this entire thing: "Let's do it."

Thus, the fifty in fifty project now five books in and here with our first print compilation, was born.

It's been fun, educational, and at moments a little stressful as we try to coordinate writing, editing, covers, and formatting for not only fifty eBooks, but also one compilation every five, meaning print and eBooks means actually an additional ten books. That's actually sixty books in 50 short months.

Does that sound crazy to you? It did to us too, but here we are, well on our way to an entirely new series that we hope will bring enjoyment to everyone who reads it.

I'd like to thank a few people, even at this early stage. I'd like to thank my co-author, Stuart for the idea and for sticking with this thing. It's already been a wild ride for us and for Nick.

I'd like to thank Elle J. Rossi for the great covers. Evernight Designs is the best for logos, promotional materials, and more. When I told her I would need fifty covers in fifty months, plus the other stuff I have her doing, she said "yes" too.

So did Dana Long, our amazing editor. We've hit her with some short deadlines, and she's said '"yes"' every single time.

I'd also like to thank my wife Shannon for helping with marketing, e-mail lists, ARC (Advance Review Copies), and all kinds of little tasks in the background. She's the best partner a writer could hope for.

I hope you enjoy this first of many compilations and that you follow the entire series. We hope you'll have just as good a time as we are.

**From Stuart:**

My name is Stuart Gustafson, and I'd had fifteen books published before approaching Troy Lambert with THIS crazy idea. But unlike Troy, I haven't been writing as a full-time career. My career was in Marketing and High-Tech, taking early retirement in 2007 to spend more time writing, traveling, and with my Mom, then age 90.

I have leveraged my U.S. Registered Trademark *America's International Travel Expert*® to travel the world as a cruise ship speaker and to write full-length mystery novels set in places such as Los Cabos, Mexico; Sydney, NSW, Australia; the Mediterranean Sea, and Paris, France.

The idea for this series came to me many years as our family was camping by a lake in Northern California. We were on our way home from a vacation in Santa Barbara, California, the setting for Sue Grafton's novels *A is for Alibi*, etc. A thought came to me as we roasted marshmallows, *"She can only do twenty-six; I can do fifty."* The idea was to write novels set in each U.S. state capital. I got started on the first one, and then I realized how hard it was to write a full-length novel. And to do fifty of them!?!

I set that idea aside and moved on. Many, many years later—March 2019 precisely—my wife and I were driving home from visiting our first grandbaby when it hit me. They don't have to be full-length novels. They can be novellas. And the idea was back under-way. I wrote notes as my wife was driving. The idea: A series of novellas featuring a photographer visiting each U.S. state capital and using his keen eye for detail to help solve a murder case. Alliterative titles were a must!

To write fifty novellas in a series, or to write fifty of anything, takes discipline. That word is not used frequently in describing me, so I knew I needed someone with writing discipline. As a successful full-time writer, Troy Lambert was that person with discipline. We'd met through mutual writers, and even though we'd never worked together, I knew he was, AND IS, the person who can work best with me on this project. And so, as Troy says above, I contacted him with a "crazy idea."

And here we are, releasing our first one in June 2019, and a new one the second Wednesday of each month!

I'd like to thank Troy for his trust in me, and for sharing his amazing talent and wealth of writing knowledge and contacts. I am constantly learning from a professional, and it's fun. Thanks, Troy!

My wife Darlene has put up with my crazy for our forty-five years of marriage. She knows that retirement is not just sitting in a rocking chair. That doesn't work for either of us, so it's a good working rela-tionship.

I'd like to thank the readers and reviewers of our first books, espe-cially those who have volunteered to be minor characters in a capital city of their choosing. It's quite enjoyable to see their reviews and their remarks.

# INTRODUCTION TO NICK: THE BEGINNING

Nicholas Christian O'Flannigan was born into a strong Irish family in Boston, Massachusetts. As a skinny kid growing up, he was constantly teased about his name and his reddish-orange hair. Other kids would taunt him with things like, *"You will never be like Saint Nicholas because you're too skinny and you look like a carrot."* Or *"Hey there, bean pole Nicholas."* He hated his name and vowed to change it as soon as he could. As he entered high school, he insisted that people call him "Nick," and he would ignore anyone who used his given name. His frame began to fill out and he continued to gain height. He was 6'3" as he entered tenth grade, and the basketball coach sought him out and convinced him to try out for Varsity Basketball (*"The girl cheerleaders prefer the basketball players over the football jocks."*). He made the team in spite of his initial awkwardness; everyone, especially the cheerleaders, now called him 'Nick.'

So where did his name come from? His dad served in the Navy, did his twenty years and then retired. He was a Warrant Officer, a Non-Commissioned Officer, an NCO. And so when his first son was born he told his wife that he wanted to give him a name that honored his role in the military. Thus, "NCO" was born, in more ways than one.

During his senior year, Nick was a 6'5" State All-Star, earning him a basketball scholarship to Boston College. His hair maintained its orangish hue, but now it was more of an asset, attracting attention and getting him noticed. One thing Nick really liked was the road trips the team would make, particularly when they took a bus. He would sit next to a window and gaze out at the scenery. The buildings, especially the historical ones, fascinated him. Nick didn't have a regular camera, an SLR, but his cell phone took good enough pictures for him. He would occasionally post some of the building photos on social media sites, gaining him a loyal following.

Nick was a good student while in college, and he was a rather consistent player on the court. He had dreams of entering the NBA, but a freak accident during an early season game in Atlanta, Georgia, left him sidelined for the rest of his senior year. His right fibula was broken in two places, shattering any hopes he had of playing professional ball. His "Plan B" (being an accountant) now became Nick's "Plan A."

Hoping to lift Nick's spirits, his dad bought him a nice camera, an Olympus E-M1X, and a set of lenses that would make many professional photographers jealous. Nick appreciated the lightweight nature of the Olympus gear, and he could easily carry it around with him even as he went around on his crutches. He was snapping photos everywhere he went.

One of his online followers posted a comment under a photo that said, *"These are great pictures, why don't you make a calendar of them and sell it?"* Nick had more spare time now that he didn't have to go to basketball practice, so he assembled twelve of his photographs of Boston buildings, and with a little computer work, he had a calendar.

Nick didn't know it at the time, but he had just started his career as a professional photographer.

By time graduation came around in May, Nick no longer needed his crutches, but he did walk with a slight limp. His "Plan A" was still to become an accountant (he had several local offers already), but his "side gig" of photography was more fun. He wasn't making a lot of money from the jobs he would pick up from time to time, but he saw that there was a future in being a photographer. He definitely stood out in a crowd; he was now a little over 6'6", and his full head of orangish hair made him visible from anywhere.

Two years after graduation, Nick married Susie, one of the former cheerleaders, and they lived in a relatively nice apartment in downtown Boston. He plunged headlong into a photography career, and she was an elementary school teacher. His right leg limp was almost gone, but he would occasionally notice the old injury going up and down stairs, so he would take an elevator whenever he could. Since almost everything to do with photography was now digital, Nick could work at home without the need for an outside office where he would have to pay rent—he was smart that way. Working out the apartment also gave him time to read. His favorite authors were Agatha Christie, John le Carré, and Arthur Conan Doyle. He never tired of re-reading one of their books because he would uncover some new detail each time, something he hadn't noticed previously.

Nick's eye for details was getting stronger; as he would take pictures of various designs on buildings and in nature, he would occasionally see something that most people wouldn't see or they would just ignore. One of his more interesting "finds" was when he was looking at some photos he'd taken of the Rose window at the Cathedral of the Holy Cross, the largest Roman Catholic church in New England. The images looked great, but there was something about the window's symmetry that seemed odd. He began to study the minute details of each section, and he noticed that the color sequencing in the bottom right part of the window (looking from the inside) was different from all the rest. Nick posted his finding online along with the question, *"why is this one pattern different?"*

There were many responses to Nick's question; the newspaper even ran an article about it. The church's historian was perplexed as he couldn't find anything in the archives dating back to its dedication in 1875 that mentioned the color differences. Finally, the Archbishop responded, *"The window is a reminder that while we are all beautiful in our own ways, we are not meant to be like everyone else."* Nick's online fan base grew tremendously after that, and his reputation as a detail-oriented photographer increased along with the demand for his services. He was once again very popular, just as he had been when he was a college basketball star. He created and moderated a social media site on Macro Photography where some of the photographic details were no larger than a half inch square.

Susie felt insecure in their relationship. Used to being the center of attention, her star stopped shining when she became an elementary school teacher. Nick was a good husband, and a faithful one, but he just couldn't provide the nurturing Susie desired. They separated shortly after Nick's twenty-fifth birthday and were divorced a year later.

While he had a very good business in the Boston area, Nick was ready for a change. After two more years in Boston where he had spent his entire life, he wanted to experience something different. He sold all of his possessions except for his clothes, his beloved mystery novels, his computer, and his camera gear. He packed up his car and drove west, headed to Seattle, Washington.

There was nothing waiting for him in Seattle except possibilities. He did have a few ongoing streams of revenue based on licensing some of his photographs, but he left most of his business behind in Boston. His first choice for an apartment was in a great location, but the rental price reflected that greatness. He chose a less desirable, yet pleasant area, to rent his first place in the Pacific Northwest. He hit the streets hard right away, talking to businesses, organizations, government entities, anyone he could pitch. Business slowly started coming his way, and by the end of his first year in Settle, he had rebuilt his income to the level it had been when he left Boston. He chose to stay in the same apartment rather than move downtown; he would be able to sock away some money as well as do some traveling —all while taking photographs, of course.

A year later on one of his trips into the mountains he met Gerry Grainger, a social media manager for *Travel USA* magazine. Gerry let Nick know right away that she was gay, but that didn't dissuade Nick from pursuing a friendship with her. She was attractive and fun; she was smart and well-connected in the high-end photography business. Their times together, definitely not "dates," were typically spent sharing photographs, talking about social media, and comparing the latest camera gear. Nick, now twenty-nine, asked Gerry if he could submit some photographs for publication to her magazine, and if there were any projects that he might be able to apply for.

"There is one project, a long-term one, which might be a good fit for you. The book printing and marketing arm wants to create a coffee table book containing each of the state capitals. You would have to visit each state capital, take the typical photographs, but also get some very unique shots of the capitol building, the highlights of that city, and maybe even the state bird, the flower, et cetera. You'd be on the road full-time for at least a year to do all that. I can't promise anything, but would that interest you?" Gerry picked up the cup and took the last swig of her coffee.

Nick closed his eyes and nodded his head slightly as he processed the information. A slight smile lit his face. "Wow. Yes. I could do that; it would be fun."

"I'll get you more details tomorrow; maybe I can get you in with the right people before it's made public."

Gerry didn't get the details to Nick the next day as there were some political games being played inside the magazine headquarters. But she was able to pitch him to the decision makers before there were any other applicants. It was almost two more months before Nick got the phone call. "Of course, I still love the concept of the project," Nick gushed when the magazine's Executive Editor asked him if he was still interested. He was then invited to present his approach for the job in person.

"We have a tight timetable, Nick," the editor said as she explained the details. "We have outlined a route for you to take, starting here in Washington, then down to Oregon and California before heading over to Nevada and Idaho. You should travel on weekends so you have Monday through Friday to take your photographs, conduct interviews, and look for the special angles that make that state capital stand out. You will have one week to cover each, so that means you will be on the road for almost a full year." She continued to reiterate the financial aspects of the freelance project, including how to charge gas for his car, which hotels to use, his per diem allowance for food, what and when he would be paid, and the schedule for submitting his work. "So you can start in three weeks?" the editor asked.

"I could start anytime you want," Nick replied. A date was set for Nick to go to the magazine's headquarters to sign the necessary papers, get the electronic reimbursement forms, and take a bouquet of roses to Gerry.

# OVERDOSES IN OLYMPIA

BOOK #1 IN THE CAPITAL CITY MURDERS
SERIES

# PROLOGUE — ANOTHER OVERDOSE

Mary slipped her arms into the white sweater, the one with the name tag Mary Lawson, RN attached. She took one final sip of her coffee, poured out the rest, and paused. *What did I miss? The patient had come in with a shattered right leg and an arm broken in two places. Thank God he was wearing a helmet, or he might have been taken to the morgue instead of to the hospital. He seemed healthy other than the injuries from the motorcycle accident.*

She'd been racking her brain for the past two days trying to figure out what happened, why the accident victim overdosed. He was under her care, and she did everything that any nurse would do in the same situation. The odd part was, the patient had been almost ready to go home.

Sure, he seemed a bit melancholy, but who wouldn't be after that kind of accident? It seemed odd.

There would be an autopsy, of course, and that would show exactly what caused his death. That would take at least two weeks.

Mary looked at her watch. She should be heading to work. The drive to Mercy Hospital took her past the location on the freeway where the motorcycle had been sideswiped, and she grimaced as she passed the spot. There was a piece of shiny metal on the right shoulder she hadn't seen before. Was it from the accident?

"Good morning, Mary," the guard said as Mary pulled into the employees' secure parking area and lowered her window.

"Good morning, John," she replied. "How's it going?"

"Pretty quiet so far," he answered as he pushed the button to raise the gate. "Have a good day."

"You, too." Mary raised her window and drove to her favorite parking spot. Close to an entrance, it was shaded in the afternoon. She disliked getting into a hot car, but even worse she hated leaving the windows down and having the elm leaves blow inside. There was something in those leaves that set off her allergies and made her sneeze uncontrollably.

Once inside, Mary put her purse in her locker and took the staff elevator to the fourth floor.

"Good morning, Pat," Mary said as she approached the nurses' area.

Pat looked up from her paperwork. "Hi, Mary. You know I am always glad to see you, and not just because you're taking over."

"I know. I see a new name on the board. What's he in for?"

"Mainly observation," the departing nurse said. "He works at a lumber mill and was hit in the head with more than just the proverbial two by four. A CT scan didn't show any abnormalities, but the ER doc wanted to hold him for twenty-four hours just to make sure. He will probably go home sometime during your shift, so you'll give him his instructions and meds to go home with."

"Well, let's go over the shift handoff report so you can go home and get some rest," Mary said as she pulled a chair.

Mary started her own rounds thirty minutes later. She entered room 414, the one with the new patient. The woman who'd been in there for the last few days had gone home last night. The room was now Robert's, and his alone at least for the next few hours. A putrid smell hit her as she stepped further inside.

*Flatulence. The kitchen needs to stop serving so much beans and broccoli.*

She cleared her throat as she stepped around the curtain to see her new patient, who completely filled the length of the standard hospital bed.

Robert looked up at her and smiled.

"Good morning, Robert. My name is Mary Lawson, and I'm the RN on duty, so you'll be seeing a lot of me today." She caught his eyes checking her out. Her face flushed slightly as she tried to maintain her composure.

She cleared her throat.

"How are you feeling? I see in your chart that you took quite a blow to the head." Mary glanced up from the screen that held his electronic patient chart.

Robert extended his right hand over his reclining body as Mary awkwardly reached across the space separating them and shook his hand. He could probably fit both her hands inside one of his. "Nice to meet you, Mrs. Lawson," he said in a deep voice.

"It's Miss Lawson, but that's okay. Actually, Mary is fine."

What was this awkward feeling coming over her?

Mary gently pulled her hand back. "Your hand seems a bit cool," she said as she looked at his vitals that had been taken just about an hour ago. "Are you in any pain right now?"

"I do have a headache, but the doc last night said I probably would for a few days. It's pretty normal considering. He also said I might be able to go home today?"

"That's up to him," Mary said and looked back at the chart. "You've had enough acetaminophen that it should've taken care of your pain, but I can get you something stronger if you'd like."

"Sure," he said. "That would be great. If the doc could send me home with something just in case, that would be good too."

"I'll get some prescription naproxen for you. Like Aleve, only a little stronger. Have you had that before?"

Robert shrugged. "I think so."

"Okay. I'll bring some in a bit and see if I can get you a bottle to go, so to speak. Need anything else at the moment?"

He just smiled and looked up at her through his arched bushy eyebrows. "No, ma'am. Thank you."

Mary felt warm. She unconsciously grabbed the front of her sweater and flapped it to try to cool herself down. "You're welcome, Robert, but you don't have to thank me. That's what we're here for, to help you get better. I should be back within a few moments with something for that pain." Mary turned and left the room. She sensed Robert's eyes following her until the curtain blocked his view.

A few minutes later, Mary made it back into room 414, carrying a small dispensing cup holding two capsules. "Knock, knock," she said as she entered the room. Some sports station was on the television. The same odor hit her as she stepped past the curtain. "Who's winning?"

"They are just replaying old games," Robert said as he used his bulging arms to push his body into a more upright position.

"Thank you," Robert said as he tossed the capsules to the back of his mouth and swallowed them without any water.

"If you drink something, it will help them get into your system faster."

"Yes, ma'am," he replied as he took the cup of water from the tray and emptied it in three huge gulps.

"I'll be back later to check on you. Maybe even to send you home. Need anything else?"

"No, ma'am," Robert said as he let his long, well-muscled body slide back down into the bed. Her eyes instinctively watched his movements as if in slow motion.

"I'll close the door, but you can always press your call button if you need anything." Mary pulled the door closed behind her. The cool air in the hall felt really good.

A few hours passed quickly, and around the time for her noon rounds, Mary got the discharge papers for room 414. She gathered up the prescription bottle of capsules the pharmacy had sent up. Pulling up the forms for him to sign on her tablet, she made her way to his room.

Since her hands were full, she knocked softly and went in. The room was now very quiet, and the odor that previously plagued the room was gone.

Robert was laying on his side, sleeping, and she woke him gently.

"Robert?"

He sat up, still seeming to be a bit groggy. Not a great sign for a guy who might have had a concussion. "I'm awake," he managed to say.

"Let me check a few things really quick," Mary said, a bit concerned.

She took out her penlight and shined it in each eye. Pupils were reactive. She felt the pulse on his neck, and it felt strong and normal.

"You seem to be okay. I'm going to have you sign these discharge papers. We do it on these tablets now, and then I can print it out for you. But I am going to have the doctor check you out before you leave."

Robert smiled, seeming to be coming back from his impromptu nap. "Sounds good. I guess those pills really did help with the headache."

"Here are your ones to take home," she told him. "No more than one every twelve hours. You can get dressed now, and I will be right back."

Mary walked down the hall to the nurses' station, hitting the print button as she went.

She grabbed Robert's paperwork as it spat out of the printer. Reaching for the phone to page the doctor on call, she saw the call light came on above his door and heard the chime at the desk.

Without hesitating, Mary sprinted down the hall back to the room. She heard a crash as she opened the door.

Robert was on the floor, face red as if he was choking. Lying beside him on the floor was an open pill bottle.

For a moment, she caught a whiff of almonds.

Mary knelt beside him and felt his neck for a pulse. There wasn't one.

She dropped his arm and pressed the call button again, yelling into the speaker: "Crash cart! Stat. Four fourteen. Now!"

Immediately she started CPR. Help seemed to take an eternity to arrive, even though she knew it was only seconds. Her arms already felt heavy as she continued compressions on his chest.

A doctor arrived followed closely by another nurse pushing a cart. Mary moved aside as the doctor put his stethoscope to the man's hairy chest.

"Still no pulse," he said.

The other nurse turned on the fully charged defibrillator. "Ready," she said.

The doc grabbed the paddles and placed them on the patient's chest. "Clear," he said, and the nurse flipped the switch. Mary watched in haunted silence as Robert's body shook from the electric charge coursing through him. The doctor listened again for a heartbeat. There was none. He applied the paddles again. Another shock. Still nothing.

He threw the paddles aside and resumed CPR, pressing down hard on the chest and counting aloud, "One, two, three." Doc counted to ten and placed his ear near the patient's mouth. Still no breath. After several futile attempts, he stood back.

"He's gone, I'm sorry." The doc looked at the bottle and capsules on the table. "He must've overdosed."

"Why would he do that?" Mary said. "He was on his way out."

"I have no idea," the doctor said.

*No!* Mary's mind churned in anguish. *Not another overdose! And both of them had occurred when she was on duty.*

# 1

# THE DRIVE

Nick looked at the map he'd downloaded for the short drive from Seattle to Olympia. *Straight down I-5; that's simple enough.* He looked at his cell phone to see if there were any new messages. None.

He selected the phone icon, then the Recent Calls menu. He saw the number he wanted, and he pressed it. The phone on the other end rang. It rang four more times before it went to voicemail and the ensuing beep. *Rats.* "Hello, Mr. Lam. This is Nick O'Flannigan calling on Sunday afternoon about two thirty. I was hoping to have an answer from you about sub-letting my apartment while I'm out of town. Please give me a call. My number is 7 8 1 ... 5 5 5 ... 8 4 2 3. Thank you." He ended the call and returned the phone to his pocket.

Nick looked around the front room of his apartment. He picked up the folder he'd labeled "The Assignment," opened it, and started reading the top sheet, a short one-page letter. He'd read it many times before, and a smile came across his face as he began reading it again.

Dear Nick,

Per our recent phone conversation, we at *Travel USA* magazine are delighted to offer you a one-year contract to provide us with unique and interesting photographs of each U.S. state capitol building and surrounding areas. You were selected for this prestigious assignment because of your excellent photographic background and skills, your keen attention to detail, and a very strong recommendation from one of our most valued employees, Gerry Grainger. Attached is the sequence that you are to follow for visiting each state capital. Please do not deviate from that schedule.

As a reminder, time is essential, and you are expected to spend no more than one week in each city, while traveling on weekends. You are to submit your photographs no later than Saturday for that week's capital city, and email that week's expense report, including lodging, gas, and per diem allowance no later than Sunday. Your timely submissions will enable us to prepare and remit the electronic payment to your bank account within five days.

Should you have any questions, now or while you're on the road, do not hesitate to contact me.

Respectfully yours,

THE LETTER WAS SIGNED Emily Gorham, Executive Editor, *Travel USA* magazine.

He looked at his checklist; he'd checked everything off. It took several elevator trips for Nick to get everything loaded into his car. He made one last pass through the apartment, switched off all the lights, and locked the door as he left.

*Goodbye, apartment. See you in a year.*

Nick had picked a good time for the drive south to Olympia. Traffic was very light through Seattle. His hands-free phone in the dashboard cradle rang. "Hello," he said as he pressed the flashing icon.

"Hello, Nicholas. This is your mother calling." She was only one besides his father who called him by his given name.

"Hi, Mom. How's everything in Boston?"

"We're fine. We were just ready to sit down for supper, and your father suggested we call and see how your new job is going."

"It's just starting today, and it's not actually a job. I'm on a contract assignment for the magazine, and I'm in the car right now driving down to Olympia, Washington's state capital."

"It's not a job, Patrick," she yelled away from the phone to Nick's dad who was in another room. "He says it's a contract."

"The difference, Mom, is that I'm not an employee of the magazine. They're just paying me to take photographs for them. It's kind of like what Dad did when he got out of the Navy. Remember when he worked for that electronics firm? He was a contractor for them, not an employee who got benefits from them besides a paycheck."

"I don't really understand it, but that's okay," she said. "So, how long are you going to be gone?"

"I told you before, Mom. I'll be gone for a year. I'll spend a week at most in each capital city, and it'll be about ten to eleven months before I'm there in Boston. They have a set schedule for me to follow. It's actually a pretty good route even though the cities are farther apart here on the west coast than they are out East."

"If you're gone for a year, what's going to happen to your business you worked so hard to re-establish after you left here? Isn't that a waste to just throw all that away?"

Nick exhaled deeply. He hesitated slightly before answering. "No, Mom, I'm not throwing it all away. I do most my business online, and I can do that from anywhere."

"What about your apartment? Who's going to take care of it?"

He spoke slower. "I'm hoping to be able to sub-let it while I'm gone. But even if I can't, I have enough savings to cover it. I'll be fine, Mom. I'm not a little kid anymore."

"I know, big shot. You're a six-foot-six former college basketball star, but that doesn't mean your Mother still doesn't worry about you."

"I know, Mom. I didn't mean it that way. I'm sorry." He paused. "There's some traffic up ahead. I'd better go focus on the road. I love you, Mom. Tell Dad I love him too."

"I love you, too, Nicholas. Drive carefully."

"I will, Mom. Bye," he said as he disconnected the call.

*She'll never understand.*

Nick's bushy orange hair almost touched the roof of his car. His height had a few disadvantages, but a definite advantage when driving into the sun. He glanced down at the odometer and saw that he'd already driven twenty-six miles.

*Almost half-way there. It'd be nice if all the weekend travels were this short.*

On long drives, Nick usually listened to audio books, but in this case with such a short drive, he listened to podcasts. He especially liked this one, a couple of ex-policemen talking about murders they had seen and solved, and how. He was fascinated by how they made connections between things that seemed random but were not.

He had selected a hotel in Olympia that was not only a short distance off the freeway but was also within walking distance of the capitol. The nightly rate was within his lodging budget, and there was no parking fee.

The podcast ended, and Nick clicked off cruise control as he neared Olympia. There was some traffic congestion, and he wasn't familiar with the area, so he cut off the next episode so he could concentrate.

His map showed the freeway would make a sweeping curve to the right, and his exit would be before the turn back to the left. He watched the exit signs; his was next, Exit 105A.

Slowing as he left the freeway, Nick continued on Plum Street Southeast. A half mile farther, he took a left on Union Avenue Southeast. He'd seen on Google Maps that all the road names in this area were suffixed with "SE." Four blocks later he made a right turn on Franklin, and he saw his hotel up on the left at the next corner. The Capital City Inn was located on the northeast corner of Franklin Street and Tenth Avenue, both suffixed Southeast, of course.

Nick slipped his backpack on and grabbed two large rolling bags from the trunk. One bag contained clothing and the other bag was full of camera gear. As he walked into the office, the clerk glanced up from her work. Then she looked up even more, titling her head back to be able to look Nick in the face. "Welcome to the Capital City Inn, sir. Checking in?"

"Yes, I am. The last name is O'Flannigan."

"Certainly, Mr. O'Flannigan." The keys on her keyboard clicked for a short minute. "We have you here for six nights in a King room. Do you prefer ground floor or higher up?"

"Higher up would be nice, and one that faces south if possible. I'm here to take photographs of the capitol, and I think I just might be able to see down the North Diagonal to it, if I'm lucky."

"Let's see," the clerk said. "Ah, yes. Room 306 should be perfect. How many keys, Mr. O'Flannigan?" she asked as she once again leaned her head back to look at Nick.

"Just one, please. And do call me Nick. It's much easier."

"Certainly, Nick," she said as she put the key packet on the counter along with the pre-completed registration form. "If you'll just sign right there. Also add your car make and model and the plate number, here ... here ... and here. Still the same Visa card?"

Nick completed the form and set the pen down. "Yes, same card. Breakfast?"

"In the room right behind you from six until nine thirty. Someone's here twenty-four hours a day, so just dial zero if you need anything. Oh, the elevator's down the hall on your left."

"Thank you, Cindy," Nick said as he bent his head down to see her name tag.

"You're welcome, Nick. Hope you have a good stay."

"Thanks, I'm sure I will," Nick answered as he pulled his bags toward the elevator.

# 2

# MORNING PAPER

The early morning crowd was gone, and the late group was meandering in and out of the breakfast room as Nick entered. He wasn't in a rush to get going this morning. He would focus on special effect photos of the Capitol Building later in the week. Today was a day to take the "standard pictures" and get acquainted with the area. Even though he'd lived in Seattle for a few years and driven down I-5 to historic Astoria on the Oregon side of the Columbia River, Nick hadn't spent any time in Olympia. He had five more days here, plenty of time to check out the city of fifty-some-thousand.

Newspaper folded and tucked under his left arm, Nick headed first to the coffee station. *Hmm. Sabor Bravo Coffee. Wonder what they had to do to keep Starbucks out of this place?* He poured himself a full cup of steaming Dark Roast and took it to an empty table next to the window. He sat the cup down, then the paper, still folded in half, and made his way around the small buffet area to survey what was available.

Returning to the table with a plate of scrambled eggs, sausage, along with a banana and a yogurt cup, Nick sat down and took a sip of the hot coffee. *Good.* He took a bite of the scrambled eggs as he unfolded the newspaper with his left hand. He'd picked *The Capital Daily* instead of *USA Today* because he was interested in local news. His phone fed him national and international news on a regular basis. "Another Mercy Hospital Overdose" blared the headline along with a recent photo of the young victim accompanying the lead article. Nick read the article as he ate. *What luck. One poor guy's in a motorcycle accident and goes to the hospital with some broken bones. Then he overdoses the next day as he is being discharged. But then there's a second similar overdose at that hospital in just a week, both men about to leave. What's with the young people these days? They're both about my age. What could possibly drive them to overdose? What a waste.*

Nick went back for another plate of eggs and sausage, plus a glass of orange juice this time. It took a lot of energy to fuel his six-six frame. He skimmed through the paper, noticing an article about the Governor's reception for the media on Thursday evening. *I wonder if I can get invited to that.* He took out his pocket notebook and wrote a note: "Gov's office; get invite to Thurs. reception." The Sports section was mostly the local teams and leagues along with a few final scores from around the country. He grabbed the paper, put it back under his left arm and cleared the table.

There were a couple and a businessman checking out as he passed by the front desk on the way to the elevator. He got to his room, brushed his teeth, got his camera bag, and put the front section of the newspaper into the side pouch. He took the stairs down the lobby level and saw there was a new person at the front desk.

"Good morning," Nick said to the young man. "I'm in 306 for the week, and I don't know the area. Any suggestions close by for a really tasty lunch?"

The clerk's eyes scanned higher and his jaw opened wider at the sight of this "big man" standing there. "It all depends on what you like. Mexican, Italian, steak and potatoes, Chinese, Japanese, we have all kinds of restaurants close by," he said as he reached for a tourist map of downtown. "They're all listed on here."

The clerk took his pen and drew several continuous circles around the one at the northeast corner of Cherry and Twelfth. "This one's my favorite; it's a small Vietnamese place that has the best spring rolls. Plus, their lemon chicken is totally awesome."

"Thanks," Nick said as he smiled, took the map, and slid it into his bag next to the newspaper. "Have a great day." Nick turned, and strode out of the lobby, camera bag looped over his left shoulder. Once outside, he headed south on Franklin.

Centennial Park was on the opposite side of Union Street, the next block down. *Some interesting possibilities for photos,* he thought as he looked at the block-wide park. Ten minutes and two turns later, Nick was heading southwest on the North Diagonal leading to the Winged Victory statue. He stopped short, brought his camera out of the bag, and took a few shots with the Capitol Building in the background. He slung the camera around his neck.

*Not exactly like the one in the Louvre,* Nick thought as he got closer, *but it's still a nice representation.*

Taking pictures as he walked along, Nick's head brushed the bottom of a pine branch overhanging the sidewalk. He reached up with his left hand to rub the top of his bushy mane, much to the delight of a group of school children playing in the grass. Nick heard their giggles, so he turned, waved, and flashed a big smile at them. He snapped a few photos as they waved back at him.

Standing halfway between the Temple of Justice and the Legislative Building, aka, the Capitol Building, Nick couldn't get the proper focus on the capitol. *The sun is too high in the sky for this southerly shot,* he thought to himself. *The front's more important, anyway.* He put the camera away, walked around to the South Entrance, and went inside. "Where's the Governor's office?" he asked the security guard.

"He's out of town for the next couple of days," the guard volunteered.

"That's okay; it's his secretary I wanted to talk to," Nick responded as he retrieved his camera bag from the screening belt.

The guard, six feet tall himself, looked up at Nick. "Second floor, all the way down on your right," he said.

"Thanks," Nick said as he headed to the wide marble staircase and took the steps two at a time.

"Show off," Nick heard the guard mumble, and he grinned to himself.

"Back at 10:30," announced the printed sheet taped on the glass door leading to The Office of the Governor.

Nick looked at his watch, 10:20. He sat on the tufted velvet bench and pulled out the newspaper. He scanned the lead article again and looked at the photograph of the latest overdose victim. Nick's eyebrows furrowed as he squinted to focus on a small area of the picture. On the young man's neck, just below his left ear was a small tattoo. *I didn't see that earlier, but it looks like one I've seen online before. Too bad it's not a sharper photo.* Nick read the article again, folded the paper, and put it back in his camera bag. He looked at his watch, 10:38. *Oh, well. I'll check back with her.*

He grabbed his camera bag, slung it over the left shoulder, and headed back to the hotel.

# 3

# THE TATTOO

Nick walked into his room and saw that it was the same as when he'd left it not long ago. *That's okay. I don't really need anything,* he thought. He took the "Do Not Disturb" sign, slipped it around the door's front handle, closed it, and flipped the dead bolt. He picked up the desk phone and pressed the "Front Desk" button.

"Front Desk. How may I help you?"

"Yes, I'm in 306, and I plan to be working in my room today, so I put the 'Do Not Disturb' sign out. Will you please tell Housekeeping that I don't need anything today?"

"Of course, Mr. O'Flannigan. Is there anything else I can help you with?"

"No, thanks."

"Have a good day, sir."

"You, too," Nick said as he put the phone back down. He pulled the laptop out of his backpack, set it on the desk, opened it, and pressed the power button. As it was powering up, Nick went to the window and looked southwest toward the Capitol Building. He saw the North Diagonal he'd walked down, and the impressive—though not the same—Winged Victory statue.

He pulled the paper from the camera bag, sat down, opened the browser, and entered "tattoo images" in the Search field. Almost a billion results popped up. *Okay, let's try again.* He opened the paper and looked at the grainy photograph again.

Back to the browser. He typed in "thecapitoldaily.com" and hit the Enter key. There it was, front and center—the same photograph in the print newspaper, but a much sharper digital image. Nick right-clicked on the photo and selected "Save Image As..." opened the file, zoomed in on the tattoo, and immediately recognized it. There had been several postings on his "MacroPhotography4U.com" website of that same tattoo.

Nick went back to the newspaper's webpage. He clicked on the Contact Us tab, found their phone number and called it.

"The Capital Daily, how may I direct your call?"

"Local News Editor, please," Nick answered.

"Hold on, please."

"Local News Desk, how may I help you?"

"Hi. I'm a photographer who's here in town on a completely different assignment, but I think I might have something for your overdoses story."

"May I ask your name, please?"

"Sure. I'm Nick O'Flannigan. I'm from Seattle, but I'm on assignment from a major magazine to visit each U.S. state capital. That's why I'm here in Olympia."

"How do you spell that last name, sir?"

"Capital-O-apostrophe-Capital F-l-a-n-n-i-g-a-n."

"Thank you, sir. And what is it that you have?" the beleaguered voice continued.

"As I said, I'm a photographer, and I host a macro photography website that's focused on the small details in photographs." Nick continued. "I noticed the photograph in the paper this morning of the overdose victim, and he had a small tattoo on the left side of his neck. It's one I've seen several times before."

"Oh?" The voice sounded more interested.

"Unfortunately, it's a tattoo that represents a cult that likens itself to the Jonestown group. They often commit group or individual suicides as part of a strange pact using nightshades and other poisons. You know who they are, right?"

"Of course. So, what's the connection?"

"Your story said this was the second overdose victim at that hospital. Do you have any photographs of the first overdose victim? Did he have any tattoos, perhaps one like this?"

"Mister, uh, O'Flannigan, we can look into that. Is there a way we can reach you?"

"There is," Nick answered in a frustrated voice. "But we're talking about overdoses here. What is your paper going to say the next time a young person is admitted to the hospital and overdoses? What if the connection between the two victims is some kind of suicide pact?"

"Hold a minute while I get the editor on the phone."

"Thank you," Nick replied. *That's who I was trying to reach in the first place.* He glanced out the third-floor window; sitting tall in the chair he could see the very tip of Capitol Lake at the end of the Puget Sound.

"Hello," the new voice finally came on. "My name is Mark, the Local News Editor. You think the overdoses have something to do with a Jonestown copycat group?"

"I'm not saying that for sure, Mark. What I'm saying is that the tattoo on the young man in today's front page article is from a cult that is known to engage in suicide pacts. My question to you is if you have a photograph of the first overdose victim, does he have a similar tattoo?"

"Just a minute, please."

Nick got out of the chair and walked over to the window. The lake was in view, although it wasn't the best angle to see much of it. The view down the North Diagonal, past Winged Victory, to the Capitol was nice though. Cindy had given him a good room. *I need to get something for her.*

"Sorry for taking so long," the news editor said as he came back on. "We do have photos of the first victim, and he had no tattoos at all. They're still waiting for the autopsy report. But Mr. O'Flannigan, is it?"

"Yes?" Nick said.

"I can't share details with you anyway, of an ongoing police investigation or anything we are doing here at the paper. I do appreciate the call, and your concern though."

Nick thanked the editor, and hung up, disappointed. He really thought he'd been on to something for a minute there.

*You're not a detective, and you do have work to do*, he told himself as he put his phone down. *The editor told you as much just now.*

Maybe he should go get some lunch, come back and start fresh when his stomach wasn't growling so loudly.

# 4

# THE APARTMENT

Nick left the "Do Not Disturb" sign on his door as he left for lunch. He didn't grab his camera, just a notebook, pen, and his cell phone. He headed for that small Vietnamese restaurant about six blocks away. His cell phone vibrated and then played the opening bars of "For Boston." Even though he'd been away for a few years and hadn't been back to alma mater Boston College since his graduation, he liked hearing the B.C. fight song.

"Hello, this is Nick." He squinted his eyes, not recognizing the voice at first. Then the caller identified himself.

"Oh, yes, Mr. Lam. Thank you for calling. Of course, I will still be responsible for paying the rent and covering any damages if there's a problem. The rent is on auto-pay, so it'll be in your account the first of every month just like it's been for the past year."

Nick stopped under the shade of a large oak as he listened to his landlord.

"Thank you, Mr. Lam. I know the lease said no sub-letting, and I really appreciate your making this accommodation for me. There is a renter who was very interested. I'll send you his contact information just as soon as I finalize the details with him. That is, unless he's found a different place by now."

"Yes, sir." Pause. "Yes, Mr. Lam. Thank you again." Pause. "You, too. Good bye for now," Nick said as he ended the call. *I hope Ben is still interested,* he thought.

He reached the restaurant a few moments later and went in to eat.

"YES, I'll have the spring rolls and the lemon chicken, please," Nick said as the waiter approached. "And a large iced tea," he added. Nick pulled out his phone and checked his email messages. He put away his phone, took a sip of water, and then he heard a loud crash behind him. He turned around and saw a young man on his knees hurriedly picking up the broken dishes and bowls that had just fallen from his tray.

"Sorry about that noise," Nick's waiter said as he delivered a small plate of spring rolls, a large plate of white rice topped with lemon chicken, and the glass of iced tea. "Anything else for now?"

Nick looked over the two plates, and then to the waiter. "No, thanks."

Nick cut into one of the spring rolls and a line of steam rose toward the ceiling. He picked up a piece with chopsticks, dipped it into the sauce, and ate it. He smiled as he enjoyed the flavor combination of the vegetables and the tangy sauce. He leaned over slightly to catch the aroma of the thick lemon sauce on the chicken. *Hmmm.* He worked his chopsticks on the chicken and the rice, occasionally alternating with part of a spring roll until both plates were fairly empty. A few pieces of rice were left on the large plate, but that was all.

"Excellent," Nick said as the waiter came by and left the tray with the bill and a wrapped fortune cookie. He took the wrapper off the fortune cookie, cracked it open, and chuckled as he read his "fortune." He got up, paid the bill, left the restaurant and headed back to the hotel. He stopped in Centennial Park and sat on a bench in the shade. He pulled out his phone. "Call Ben," he commanded the phone.

"Calling Ben," the phone responded as he put it up to his ear.

"This is Ben."

"Hey Ben, it's Nick O'Flannigan. I just got off the phone with my landlord, and he said I could sub-let the apartment to you. Still want it?"

"Heck, yes," Ben replied. "I've been looking for a place like yours. What a perfect location near so many software houses. Want me to bring the paperwork and a check over?"

"Well," Nick sighed into the phone. "I'm already out of town. I'm down in Olympia actually on my first stop. Can you scan the paperwork and send me the PDF?"

"Sure," Ben replied.

"Once I get it, I'll call the apartment manager, a Mr. Lam, and tell him you're coming by for the key. I already told him about you."

"Sounds good!" Ben said. "I can't wait."

"Once you're inside, you'll find an envelope on the kitchen counter. It has the wi-fi network id and logon information. And there're a dozen deposit slips for you to pay the rent. Utilities and the rest are on auto-pay and in my name, so everything should run smoothly for you."

"I really appreciate it," Ben said. "Thank you."

"No, thank you. This keeps me from having to dig too deeply into my savings."

"It's great to get away from my old roommates and into my own place. I don't know when those other guys slept. They stay up all night, almost every night, playing and commenting on video games. It's like they didn't get enough screen time at work. I'll have the papers to you in an hour or so; I've got a design review meeting that starts in about ten minutes."

"That's fine. Thanks again, Ben."

"My thanks to you, and don't worry. I'll take good care of the place."

"Appreciate it. Later, man."

"Take care, Nick."

Nick ended the call, let out a big sigh, and walked even taller than his already six-six height back to the hotel.

# 5

## LOCAL FLAVOR

Nick stopped at the front desk on his way to breakfast the next morning. "Oh, hi, Cindy. You were right, my room has a great view to the entire capitol complex."

Cindy smiled up at him. "I'm glad you like it," she responded. "Is there anything you need today?"

"Yes, thanks." Nick pulled on the lanyard that was sticking out of his shirt pocket, bringing a thumb drive out with it. "Is there someplace I can print out a couple files?"

"Of course," Cindy replied. "The Business Center is down that hall and to the right. You probably haven't seen it because you go left to the elevator. It's open twenty-fours a day. Just use your room key to get in. There's no charge for printing."

Nick looked to his left and saw the Business Center sign and the right arrow. "What about a florist? Any nearby?"

Cindy used her left hand to point out the front door. "Just a block and a half down Tenth on the right-hand side."

Nick looked at her left hand and saw that she wore no rings. "Thanks, Cindy."

"My pleasure, Mr. O'Flannigan."

"Nick," he replied.

"My pleasure, Nick," she countered with a slight smile.

Nick put the thumb drive and lanyard back into his pocket, picked up a copy of *The Capital Daily*, and ate breakfast. He got up, cleared his table, and went to the Business Center. The two computers were in Sleep mode as he sat down in front of one, shaking the mouse, then pressing the left key with his right index finger. The screen awoke.

He pulled the thumb drive out of his pocket, stuck it into the one open USB port, and waited for the dialogue box to open. It finally did, and he opened the folder to view the files. Nick had downloaded a map of the local area with highlights of interesting buildings. He'd also found a file that listed some of the state's symbols, such as the state bird, state tree, state flower, state fruit, and some other facts he found interesting. He selected and printed those two files, removed the thumb drive, took the printouts, and went back to his room.

Nick looped the camera bag over his left shoulder, grabbed the small notebook, his phone, and the two sheets he'd just printed. He'd let the maid come in today, so he took the 'Do Not Disturb' sign off the door and hung it on the back side. He pulled the door closed, walked down the stairs, and out the side entrance. He stopped and thought for a moment. He then headed toward Tenth Street. Thanks to two green lights and his long stride, Nick entered Tenth Street Floral in three minutes.

"Good morning, sir," an employee said. "How can I help you?"

"I need a bouquet with a vase that's says, 'Thank you.' I barely know this person, but she helped me, and I want to let her know that I appreciated it."

"Of course, sir," the florist replied. "Do you have a price range in mind?"

"Do you have something in the twenty to thirty-dollar range?" Nick asked.

"Well." The florist's halting voice told Nick he'd have to go a little higher.

"I guess I could go a little higher, but I don't want her to get the wrong idea. They're just to say, 'Thank you'; nothing more." Nick said.

The florist smiled as he opened a display case door, reached in, and pulled out a colorful assortment in a nine-inch vase. "This one is very nice, and it even includes a Rhododendron, our state flower. It's normally forty dollars, but I'll let you have it for thirty-five."

"And a small card to write a note on?" Nick responded.

"They're on the counter. Pick any one you want."

Nick wrote a short note on one of the cards, put it in the envelope, paid for the flowers, and headed back to the hotel.

"Nice flowers," a young woman said as he walked past her. "Lucky lady."

Nick slowed his pace slightly, smiled, but kept on going. He reached Franklin, turned left, and then right into the Capital City Inn lobby. He had the vase in his huge right hand as he approached the desk. "These are for you, Cindy. I love the room. Great views. Thanks."

Cindy's face flushed as she smiled. She tried to say something, but no words came out.

"I'll see you later," Nick said as he turned around and walked back outside.

Nick walked around the area for the rest of the morning, using the map he'd printed. *I didn't think I'd need an entire week just to take some photographs. But there's so much here. I'm glad the schedule isn't any tighter.*

His map showed him the location of several Western Hemlocks, the official state tree. He switched his camera lens to a fisheye one, turned the camera ninety degrees using the optional handle on the Olympus EMIX that he'd purchased just for such occasions, and snapped several photos of the broad-based tree. He turned and started north on Capitol Way when the aromas and the sounds of a food truck assaulted him. He reached the truck and bent his head down to see the chalkboard menu leaning against the side. The pulsating ten-note bass guitar riff of *Louie Louie* was hard to ignore. Nick nodded his head in time with the song's steady beat. *Dut-dut-dut Dut-dut Dut-dut-dut Dut-dut. Dut-dut-dut Dut-dut Dut-dut-dut Dut-dut.*

"Help you, amigo?" the friendly voice came from the truck's open window.

"Yes," Nick said slowly. "Okay. One Beef Chimichanga and a bottle of water."

"Hot, medium, or mild salsa?"

"Mild, please."

"Seven-fifty," the man said as he handed him a bottle of water.

Nick handed the old man a ten-dollar bill. "Keep the change," he said, priding himself on being a good tipper.

"Gracias, amigo." The man's eyes lit up and his broad smile showed a gap in his upper teeth and another one on the opposite side in his lower ones.

"What's with everyone playing *Louie Louie*?"

"The people in Washington have adopted it as the state's rock and roll song. It's not official, but once it got started, it just kept going. Did you know that the song was originally about a Jamaican sailor?"

"I didn't," Nick answered. "I was never able to figure out the words until I looked them up online." Nick saw the reflection in the truck's shiny chrome siding of a couple behind him. He turned around. "I'm sorry," he said. "I didn't hear you come up."

"The music is loud," the man said. "But at least it is as good as the food. This truck is always busy around lunch time."

"So you like it?" Nick said, salivating at the thought of his coming snack.

"No better Mexican in the city."

"Wow. Thanks," Nick said. "I'm glad I found the place then."

"You'll like it; that's for sure. But be careful of his hot salsa. It's a killer."

"Just mild for me," Nick said as the old man handed him a plate covered with aluminum foil. "Thank you," Nick turned back as the couple placed their lunch order. He saw an empty bench, sat down, and ate his Chimichanga.

*They're right; that food is good!* He tossed his trash into a bin, walked around, took more pictures, and then returned to the hotel.

Nick spent the rest of the afternoon sorting through the photos he'd taken so far, organizing them, and putting short, yet informative, labels on each one. He also created a document that named each photo, and he added a short description, such as the one for *Winged Victory*, that was built to commemorate World War I. The bronze statue on the granite pedestal created an impressive visual with the Capitol Building in the background. He uploaded a few to the Cloud folder that had been created for him, wanting to show Emily, his editor, that he was being both productive and proactive.

After a few hours staring at his screen, he decided to order in and then call it a night.

# 6

# THE DREADED "BLUE SCREEN"

The incessant buzzing of the alarm clock finally awakened Nick. He showered, shaved, and got dressed. He put a few shirts and other items into the hotel's laundry bag, filled out the slip, and set the bag on the bed. Downstairs, he grabbed the last copy of the paper, ate breakfast, and got a cup of coffee to take back upstairs. *Maybe I should try a local place for breakfast tomorrow.*

Back in his room, Nick set the coffee cup on the desk, sat down, and opened his laptop. He pressed the Power button and heard the machine's whirring as it went through its start-up cycles. Nick popped the lid off the coffee, took a sip, and look at his computer's screen.

It was blank.

The whirring continued.

A blue screen was all that was there.

The whirring continued. And then it stopped.

But the blue screen was still there.

No sound.

No activity.

Just a blue screen.

*I've got to get that checked out right away.* Nick was a bit stressed. Even though his stuff was backed up and on the cloud, he didn't want to buy a new machine this early in the trip.

7

_______

## DID SHE DO IT?

Nick closed the lid of his laptop and picked up the phone. "Front Desk."

"I need a computer repair shop, preferable one that's close by and opens early. I'd look it up myself but my laptop's dead."

"I've got a couple people checking out right now, but if you can come down here in ten minutes, I'll have a few names for you."

"Okay. Thanks," Nick said as he put down the phone, and got things ready to head out.

Nick approached the front desk and recognized the clerk as the one who'd given him the restaurant recommendations. "Great Vietnamese restaurant," Nick said as he licked his lips. "I called down about computer shops."

"Yes," the clerk said as he set a piece of paper on the counter. "This one's on Eleventh, just a block closer than the restaurant, and they're already open."

"Great. thanks," Nick said as he grabbed the slip of paper, scooped up his bags, and speed walked the four blocks to the repair shop.

He pushed the door open and walked up to the empty and shiny counter. He pulled his laptop out of his bag and set it on the counter.

"Hi, there. How can I help you?" the young man behind the counter asked. "Brian" said his name badge.

Nick opened the laptop lid. "I tried to power on this morning and all I got was a blue screen. Everything's backed up to the Cloud, but I need this for my work. The manager at the hotel said you guys are one of the best in the area. Can you look at it right away?"

"Sure," Brian said. "You want to wait?"

"Yes," Nick answered.

The young man closed the laptop, turned it over, and popped out the battery. "Let's check this first." He turned around and took the battery to a large area with numerous battery chargers. He slipped Nick's battery into one and flipped a switch. A green light came on, but just for a short time. The light changed to yellow. Both men watched for a minute. It stayed yellow. Brian turned the charger off and removed Nick's battery.

Brian turned back to Nick. "It still has some charge, so it's not completely dead. But if you're opening a lot of applications and processes during start up, then the battery just doesn't have enough charge to work on its own. It should work okay with a power cord because the battery isn't your laptop's primary energy source. But it won't work on its own."

Nick grimaced. "Do you have one in stock?"

"I'm sure we do," Brian said. "Let me check our inventory and see what we have that is compatible." He went to the computer and typed in the battery's specs. "Yes, we do. Actually, we have two. One's eighty-nine ninety-five and the other's ninety-five. As far I can see, either one should be fine."

"I'll take the one for ninety-five," Nick said.

"Sure," the young man said. "Let me get it and put it in just to make sure you do start up okay."

"Good idea," Nick answered.

Nick's laptop started up promptly with the new battery. "Thanks," he said.

"No problem," Brian said. "And I'd keep this old one as a spare to use with your power cord just in case something happens to this new one."

Nick paid for the battery and walked back to the hotel. "Thanks," he said to the desk clerk who'd given him the repair shop name.

"Everything okay?" the clerk responded.

"It is now," Nick replied as he went to his room.

He set his bag down and called *The Capital Daily*.

"The Capital Daily, how may I direct your call?"

"Local News Editor Mark, please. I'm returning his call." The last part wasn't exactly true.

"Who's calling?"

"My name is Nick, a photographer from Seattle. We spoke a couple days ago."

"Hold please."

"Local news; this is Mark."

"Mark, Nick O'Flannigan calling. We spoke on Monday about the overdose victims at Mercy Hospital. One had the tattoo and one didn't."

"Right, I remember," Mark said.

Nick continued. "I was wondering, actually I was hoping, if you had some time I could come to the paper and talk to you about a couple of things. I won't take up too much of your time."

"We're running up against a deadline, so I don't have much time," Mark said. "Can you be here in twenty minutes?"

"Sure, I can be there then. Thank you," Nick added as he closed the call.

He didn't grab his camera bag this time. He could always use his phone if he needed to take a picture.

Nick arrived at the newspaper's main office twenty minutes later. He signed in, and was escorted into the newsroom abuzz with conversations, some heated, and people typing away at their computers. "Nice to meet you, Mark. I'm Nick. Thanks for meeting with me," Nick said as the two men shook hands. "I thought a morning paper would be busy mostly at night," he continued.

"That's for the print edition. Our online editions are updated every six hours, so it's pretty much a non-stop effort around here. Not to be rude, but I don't have a lot of spare time," the editor said.

"I understand. I think I told you I'm into macro photography, and I was wondering if you had any other photos or other information about the overdoses that you could share with me. I'm not looking for anything confidential, just items I can look at."

"Why?" Mark asked.

"Because this really intrigues me." Nick paused. "These men were my age. It would really bother me if one my good friends did this."

"And why should I give you access to our photo library?" the editor asked. "You're not a cop or a P.I. are you? Or working on your own story?"

"No, I am on a completely different assignment. I've just found that many photographs hold minute details that most authorities don't see because they're looking for something obvious. It's your story, but I'd like to help any way I can," Nick said. "I didn't know the victims, but I know it had to have affected someone, and affected them deeply."

"That's one thing about working at the paper," Mark began. "You have to tell the story, the facts, just as they are. But deep inside, some of these stories really rip you apart. I do have a few photos that we've not released yet. They came to us from a confidential source, and I'm not at liberty to say who it was or to let you have copies of them."

"I understand," Nick said as the editor clicked on a few icons on his computer screen.

"Here is one from the first victim's room. This is a copy where I've covered the victim's face out of respect for him and his family." Mark clicked on another file. "And here's another one. There's nothing special about them."

"They look like everyday hospital rooms to me," Nick said.

"Exactly. That's partly what's baffling. Why would someone take photographs of everyday hospital rooms?" He then clicked another file and the image popped to the screen. It was similar to the first one he'd shown. "They almost look as if they were taken by a phone or a laptop."

"Wait a minute," Nick blurted. "Go back to the first photo, please."

Mark minimized the image and clicked on the first image.

"See that?" Nick asked. "It's the same nurse in both photos. Who would take pictures of the nurse?"

"I hadn't noticed that before," the news editor said as he went back to the most recent image. "Yes, it is," he added as he zoomed in on her name tag. "Mary Lawson," he read. "Let's go back to the first image, just to make sure."

Mark went back to the first image, zoomed in on the nurse's name tag. "Yep, Mary Lawson," he said. "Hmmm. Coincidence?" Mark asked as his eyebrows lifted, and his eyes widened.

"You've been in this game much longer than I have," Nick began. "But, two overdoses in the same week at the same hospital, and the same nurse is in the room with them. It seems a bit suspicious to me. Do you want to run a story on it, or call the police?"

"Slow down. I think I'd need a lot more information before I ran a story like that. I'd be putting the paper at risk for a lawsuit if it didn't pan out."

"I know. I'm sorry," Nick replied rather dejectedly." I thought I was on to something."

Mark chuckled. "Don't worry about it. It happens to all of us. You wouldn't believe how many stories I chased just to find they were dead ends or led to other rabbit holes I didn't have time to chase. Hey, but thanks for coming in. It never hurts to have another set of eyes on what we have."

"Sorry I wasted your time," Nick said as he rose from the chair.

"Not a problem," Mark said as he handed him a card. "How long are you in town?"

"Just to the weekend, and then down to Salem."

"Well, don't hesitate to contact me if you discover some real facts, or if you hear anything."

The two men shook hands, and Mark escorted Nick to the lobby.

Nick clicked the hotel address on his GPS device and headed back to the hotel. The flowers he'd given Cindy were on the back counter, but he didn't see her. He took the elevator to the third floor

*— I should be taking the stairs —* and went to his room. *Oh, good. Housekeeping has been here.*

Nick flopped down in the somewhat-comfortable chair in the corner. *Should I, or shouldn't I?* That thought persisted in his brain. Finally, *Yes, I should!*

He looked up the phone number for the Olympia Police Department and called them.

A recording greeted him, telling him if this was an emergency, to dial 9-1-1, and then an option to enter the extension of who you were calling, or dial zero to speak to the receptionist. Nick pressed "0."

"Olympia Police Department, how may I direct your call?"

"Homicide, please," Nick answered.

"Are you reporting a homicide, sir?"

"I'm not sure. I have information about some recent deaths that I think might be homicides."

"Alright. Hold for a moment, please."

"Homicide. Detective Parsons."

"Yes, Detective. I have some information about those recent overdoses at the hospital. I don't think they're overdoses; I think they're homicides."

"May I have your name, sir?"

"My name is," and Nick slowed his speech, "Nick O'Flannigan. That's Capital-O-apostrophe-Capital F-l-a-n-n-i-g-a-n. I'm a professional photographer from Seattle on assignment here in Olympia just for the week."

"Thank you, Mr. O'Flannigan," the detective responded. "And what makes you think those overdoses are homicides?"

"Well," Nick began. "I can't reveal my sources, but I've seen photographs of the hospital rooms where the two men died, and the same nurse was caring for both. Her name is Mary Lawson, and I think she should be looked into."

"Mr. O'Flannigan. We appreciate your interest. But we've already looked into her as we wait for the autopsy results on both men. She certainly had opportunity. But she did not have a motive, and until we see the definitive autopsy results, we don't know that she had means either."

"Maybe no apparent motive," Nick replied. "But think of this. If she was the last one to be with them and gave them meds, then she certainly had access and opportunity. Right?"

"Mr. O'Flannigan," the voice on the line said. "I think you've been watching too many shows on TV. Even if we did suspect her, and we don't," the detective responded. "I can't discuss an ongoing investigation with a journalist."

"Photographer," Nick countered.

"Whatever," the detective said. "I still can't discuss it."

"Was she the one who ordered the prescription for both men?" Nick persisted.

"I'd have to look back at my notes," Parsons answered. "But again..."

"Is she married?"

"I don't know that I'm at liberty to disclose that. What are you thinking?"

"Well," Nick began. "Married or not, what if she wanted revenge, let's say against some young stud who rejected her or maybe even just slighted her? What better opportunity than to pick some guy at random and let him be her victim? Or let them be her victims?"

"Honestly, I thought along the same line. But as I said, I can't really discuss it. That being said, if you do notice something or come across anything you think we missed, feel free to contact us. I do appreciate your call, and I hope you enjoy the rest of your stay here in the capital city."

"Okay. Thanks," Nick said as he disconnected the call. *Wrong again. He really wasn't much of a detective after all. He should just stick to taking photos.*

# 8

# RESTAURANT RECOMMENDATIONS

The slight opening in the drapes allowed some light to enter the room as Nick awoke and turned off the alarm. He showered, shaved, and dressed before opening the blinds completely to his view south and southeast toward the Capitol. He picked up his personalized map and saw where he'd noted a couple restaurants. He looked them up on Yelp and drew a circle around Linda's.

Nick put the "Do Not Disturb" sign on the door, went down the stairs, and headed down Tenth Avenue. He passed the flower shop and saw a line of people standing in front of Linda's for breakfast on the next block. He could smell breakfast as he approached the restaurant. "That good?" Nick asked the person in front of him as he joined the line.

"She's amazing," the old man said. "She only does breakfast six days a week, and then dinners one weekend a month."

"My first time here," Nick responded. "What should I have in case it's my only time?"

"Stuffed French Toast with Homemade Apple Sauce and a large glass of orange juice. The French Toast is so sweet you won't want to put any syrup on it. And the orange juice is mixed with other citrus for a flavor so distinctive you'll never forget it. You have those two, and I'll bet you'll be back." The man edged forward as the line slowly moved each time someone came out the door.

"Thanks for the recommendation," Nick said. "What about places for dinner?"

"Any place along Columbia Street that's got a view of Capitol Lake. That's if you're into seafood. Otherwise, I'd suggest The Chuckwagon Grille if you want steak or ribs. It's a couple blocks south of the capitol on Water Street. The food's really good and their prices are fairly reasonable. Don't go before five or you'll run into all the old folks like me who are there for the early bird specials."

"Thanks again. Hey, you're almost inside."

The old man chuckled. "Time is one thing I have plenty of."

"Thanks, Linda!" yelled someone who turned his head around as he was leaving the restaurant. Nick's height allowed him to see over the other people in line, and he saw someone in the kitchen waving. *That must be her.*

Nick ordered what the old man recommended, along with a bottomless cup of hot coffee. *I wonder if the paper would be interested in a story about Linda and her following. She's almost like a social media phenomenon without the social media, but in real life.*

"More delicious than I could have imagined," Nick said as the waitress came by.

"Glad you liked it. We're on TripAdvisor if you feel like leaving a review," she said as she handed him the check.

"Will do as soon as I get back to the room."

Nick did as he said he would. He returned to the hotel room, opened the laptop, and posted a five-star review on TripAdvisor for Linda's, the top-rated restaurant in Olympia. He opened his notebook to see where he would be staying in Salem and a few states beyond. He signed up for the hotel loyalty programs, and then for a couple gasoline programs. *Saving a few bucks on gas will help save my per diem allowance.*

After he posted a few more photographs in the Cloud for the magazine, Nick wrote an email to Emily. *"I'm making good progress,"* the email said. *"And I found out something I'd never heard about Washington. Did you know that 'Louie Louie' is the state's unofficial rock and roll song? How crazy is that?"* Nick completed the email, looked at his Inbox, and deleted most of the incoming mail. He went to his bank's site and saw that Ben had deposited the rent. He looked to see what activity was taking place on his macro photography website, and if there was anything for him to moderate or reply to. There was nothing new.

Nick shut down the laptop, grabbed his camera bag, and went back to the capitol campus for some mid-day photographs. He liked it when the sun was pretty much straight up; the shadows came down like holding an umbrella over your head. Nick attached the wide-angle lens to capture the full width of the main campus building, the Legislative Building. It was surrounded by other buildings on three sides plus lots of trees almost all the way around it, and so using the wide-angle lens was the only way Nick could capture the building's full width and height.

He made his way around all four sides of the building and used his telephoto lens to capture some stunning photos of its dome, the tallest self-supporting masonry dome in the U.S. at almost three hundred feet high. The sun was highlighting the Governor's Mansion just a few hundred feet away, and Nick used various filters to get different perspectives the four-story Georgian-style building.

Nick back-tracked to the North Entrance. He waited until a group of school children filed out two-by-two. Several of the youngsters waved to him and said, "Hi" as Nick waved back.

"Do you play basketball?" one of the young girls asked as she craned her head back.

"Not anymore," Nick said. "Do you?'

"No, silly," she replied as she giggled with her friend.

Once they were all out and headed toward the school bus parking area adjacent to the Winged Victory monument, Nick went in. He took a lot of photos in the Rotunda, including the roped-off state seal in the floor. He looked up and went to various locations to get pictures of the five-ton bronze Tiffany chandelier with over two hundred light bulbs. He moved to each corner in the Rotunda for photos of the firepots, similar to ones used to convene the Senate two thousand years ago. He zoomed in on the brass plate on each firepot, "Made by Tiffany & Company, New York."

*I think Emily will like these,* Nick thought as he left the building and returned to the hotel. He downloaded the pictures to his laptop, and also copied them to the thumb drive. He looked out the window and saw the long shadows from the right to the left. Nick retrieved his penciled map and plopped down into the comfortable corner chair. He looked at his map and found the location for the evening's dinner destination.

*I don't care if the old people are there for the early bird specials. The sun's setting, and I'm hungry.*

The old man was right again. The dinner at The Chuckwagon Grille was every bit as good as the breakfast at Linda's. After dinner, Nick returned to his hotel room, and pulled out his main map of the Western States. He saw that it was only about a three-hour drive to Salem, his next capital city. *I wonder if there are any swap meets this weekend where I can look for some old camera gear.* He opened his laptop, and began a search; he found some, but they weren't on the direct route to Salem.

*I've got plenty of time. Besides, I'm going to be on the main freeways for a long time. It'll be okay to have a few side-road trips.*

# 9

# THE GOVERNOR

"Governor Returns from Successful Trade Trip" read the headline of Thursday's paper. *The media reception this evening. Shoot.* Nick had forgotten to ask the governor's secretary for an invite. He quickly finished his breakfast, grabbed the paper, and returned to his room.

Nick brushed his teeth, got his camera bag, and headed to the Capitol. His long legs allowed him to maintain a quick pace without actually having to hurry. He entered the North Entrance. It was the same guard he'd seen before on the other side.

"Oh, hi there," the guard said. "Did you ever get to talk with the Governor's secretary?" He opened Nick's bag and did a cursory look inside.

"No," Nick replied. "She was out, and I had some other things to catch up on. But that's where I'm going right now."

"Good luck," the guard said as he handed Nick's bag to him. "The Governor just got back last night, and his office is typically very busy right after he returns." He paused and then offered, "If you'd like, I can call his secretary and tell her you've been here before and you just need two minutes with her. Then it's up to you."

"That's actually all the time I need, if even that. Thanks."

"No problem, man."

Nick went left, following "The Office of the Governor" signs to his left as he heard the guard talking to the secretary. Nick reached the office and saw the well-dressed secretary standing at the open doorway.

"You must be the photographer. The guard did a pretty good job of describing you. I'm sorry, but the Governor is extremely busy today as he just got home from an overseas trip last night. You could wait around and see if he has an opening to take some pictures, but I don't know how long that might be." She finally took a breath.

"Thank you, ma'am. No offense to the Governor, but you are the one I wanted to see. I'm Nick O'Flannigan, and I'm on assignment from *Travel USA* magazine to visit each capital city and take photographs. I saw in Monday's paper that there's a media reception this evening. I know it's last minute," Nick said as he turned on the Boston charm. "I was hoping I could get an invitation to it."

She looked up at Nick. "All the slots have been taken, but I might have an extra card in my desk. Let me take a look," she added as she turned and slowly walked back inside.

Nick crossed his fingers as he waited and watched.

She approached her desk, pulled down on the sides of her sleek dress, and opened the top desk drawer. She reached in and fumbled around for a moment. She closed the drawer and walked slowly back outside the main office door. "I couldn't find one. I'm sorry, Mr. O'Flannigan."

"Thank you, very much for looking," Nick said.

"You're welcome," the secretary replied. "Sorry I could not help more. Maybe another time?"

"I would if I were in town longer," Nick said as he smiled and gave her hand a slight squeeze. "Thanks again."

"Of course," she echoed as she slowly pulled her hand away. It was sweating. "Sharon," she added.

"Nick," he responded. "Thanks, Sharon." He turned and left the building.

# 10

# THE DISCOVERY

As he walked back to the hotel, Nick's mind wandered back to the alleged overdoses, the nurse, and the things the newspaper editor and the detective had said. Something was bothering him.

"The hospital photographs," Nick blurted out loud as he walked back to the hotel. "I've got to see them again." He picked up his pace, jaywalked across Union Avenue, and entered the hotel lobby. His eyes were focused straight ahead.

"Hi, Nick. Want a fresh cookie?" Cindy held a plate of chocolate chip cookies out and even a little upward toward him.

"Oh. Hi, Cindy. They smell great. Don't mind if I do." A slight smile came across Nick's face as he used a small napkin to select the warm, gooey cookie.

Cindy's eyes opened wider as she stared at Nick's smile.

"Thanks again. Sorry, I'm in a rush. I've got an idea I have to chase down," he said as he turned and went to his room. He set the camera bag on the bed, grabbed the car keys, left the room, and bounded down the back stairs. He pulled into the newspaper's parking lot fifteen minutes later.

*I probably should've called ahead. But then, he might have told me not to come.*

Nick strode confidently into the building and smiled at the receptionist. He spoke slowly. "Hello. I met with the local news editor, Mark, yesterday, and we had some unfinished business. Would you please let him know Nick O'Flannigan is here to see him?"

"Certainly," the receptionist said as she called the newsroom.

"Mark," she spoke quietly into the phone. "There's a tall guy out here to see you. His name is Nick something. Said you two spoke yesterday; something about some unfinished business."

She listened.

"That's what he said."

She listened some more.

"Okay, I'll tell him," she said as she ended the call. She cleared her throat as she looked up at Nick. "I'm sorry, but he's rather busy for the morning deadline. Could you come back this afternoon?"

"Will you do me one more favor?" Nick asked politely. "Would you call him back and tell him I only need two minutes of his time? I swear that's all."

"Well, okay," she replied.

"Thank you," Nick mouthed as she picked up the phone and called Mark again.

"He said just two minutes," she said into the phone as she glanced up at Nick and smiled.

"I'll tell him." She hung up the phone.

"He'll be right out," she said to Nick. She continued in a soft voice. "He can be rude, though, especially when it's deadline time."

"I won't take long. Thanks again." Nick pulled the Register over and signed in.

The newsroom door swung open wide as Nick rushed through.

Nick smiled and stepped forward with his large hand out to greet him. "Hi, Mark. Thanks. I promise. Just two minutes and then you can throw me out."

"Uh, I don't think that's possible," the News Editor said as his eyes scanned up the tall solid body in front of him. "What do you have now?"

"The photographs," Nick said in a whisper. "There's something about them that's been bugging me. Can we go take a quick look at them again?"

"Okay, but I really am on a tight deadline, and this is the last favor I do for you."

The two men stepped into the frenetic newsroom and went to Mark's desk. He opened the folder on his computer and clicked on the first image.

"No, not that one," Nick said.

Next image. "No."

Next one. "Yes, that one. The one with the pill bottle. Can you go close in on it?"

Mark zoomed in on the bottle; the one with the red and blue capsules spilling out on to the floor.

"Yes. Now can you rotate the image so I can read the label?"

Mark rotated the image; the label was 'upright.'

"Look at that," Nick began. "It's hard to tell for sure, but it looks like it says a quantity of twelve. Is that what it looks like to you?"

Mark lifted his glasses and squinted his eyes. "Yeah. It looks like twelve to me."

"Zoom back out and take it back to the original orientation."

Mark didn't seem like the kind of guy to take orders, but he did what Nick asked. The image was now back to its original position.

Nick began pointing to, and counting, the red and blue capsules. "One, two, three, four, five, six, seven, eight, nine, ten, eleven. There are eleven whole capsules still there."

"I'm not following. How is this new information?"

"Okay," Nick said slowly. "If there were twelve prescribed, and he took only one, he didn't take any more than had been prescribed. It wasn't an overdose, at least not from these pills."

Mark looked up at Nick. "Oh, wow," he said. "Let's find out if the police noticed that too."

He picked up his phone to call the Police Department. Nick stood up straight to stretch out his back from bending over. He looked around the newsroom as Mark spoke softly into the phone.

Mark hung up the phone and looked up at Nick. "They're going to get the remaining capsules from both deaths and send them to the lab for analysis." Mark pushed back his chair, stood up, and shook Nick's hand. "Good work. We might have some new headlines soon."

"Awesome," Nick said as they shook hands. *Maybe there was something to his detective skills after all.*

# 11

# REVENGE

Nick was already awake and dressed when his cell phone rang. He looked at the number, and recognized it as one he'd recently called. "This is Nick."

"Nick, this is Mark from the paper. I know it's early, but I just got a call from the police lab. How soon can you meet me at the paper?"

"It means skipping breakfast, but I can be there in fifteen minutes," Nick replied.

"I'll buy you breakfast. This is huge, and it's because of you."

"I'm on my way," Nick answered. He grabbed his camera bag, slipped his notebook into its side pocket, and pulled his cell phone off the charger. He picked up his keys and headed out of the room and down the stairs to the parking lot. *Slowly. A couple more minutes won't matter.*

He pulled into the mostly vacant parking lot at the paper and went into the empty lobby. He pulled out his cell phone just as Mark came through the door.

"Sorry. I should've told you no one would be here," Mark said as he moved forward to shake Nick's hand.

The two men went through the door into the newsroom. It was unusually quiet. Mark pulled up a chair for Nick to sit in. "So," Mark began. "I had a call from the police lab this morning. There was cyanide in all of the remaining capsules from both of the overdose victims. The police are getting a search warrant right now, and are planning to meet us at the hospital in twenty minutes. The nurse is a suspect again, and they're giving us an exclusive on the story, and I want you to go along as my photographer."

"I wasn't expecting this, but I'm ready," Nick replied.

"Okay," Mark responded. "You, my friend," he re-started as he looked directly at Mark, "have probably just solved a murder case. We might not solve it right now, depending on what the cops have a warrant for, but we will solve it."

"Wow," Nick remarked unabashedly. "Who's driving?"

"I will."

The two men arrived at the hospital and saw two police cars already parked there. Mark led the way as they headed to the Administration Building. "Human Resources 312," the sign said. Nick saw four suited detectives standing around as he and Mark exited the elevator on the third floor.

"So, what's the plan?" Mark asked.

"We've got a search warrant," one of the officers replied. "It only covers personnel records for now, but we have a judge on standby in case we find anything else and need another one."

"Okay if we follow you in?" Mark replied. "Oh, by the way, this is Nick O'Flannigan who noticed the pill count. He'll be taking photographs for me."

The officers nodded their heads at Nick.

"H.R. is that way," Mark said as he pointed the way down to 312. The door was open, and the senior officer led the way in.

"Good morning, ma'am," the officer said. "This is a search warrant authorized by a judge to access any and all records pertaining to your employee, Mary Lawson."

"But your people already said she had nothing to do with those deaths," the H.R. rep responded.

"Ma'am. I'm just doing what I'm told to do. You know how the bureaucracy can work sometimes. Believe me, I don't like this any more than you do."

"Let me see the warrant," she replied.

The woman took the warrant and read it. It wasn't the first one she'd read. "Let me give my boss a call," she said after reading it over.

"Of course," the officer said as the H.R. Rep picked up the phone and called the HR Manager.

"Okay," she said into the phone. "Thanks, I'll see you later," she said as she put the phone down. "It'll take me a couple minutes to pull up the records. Want to have a seat?"

"Thanks," the senior officer replied as he looked and saw five empty chairs.

"I'll stand," Nick said as he saw that there was one person more than chairs in the room.

The woman's fingers mis-typed a few letters as she attempted to open Mary Lawson's personnel records. "She's been here a long time. I can print out all the files, but that's a lot of paper."

"To save time and rather than having to pore through her personal papers here," the senior officer interjected, "did Ms. Lawson have any romantic interests or affairs with anyone at the hospital? Or did she ever file any complaints of harassment?"

"Yes," she answered. "It involved Dr. Reynolds, our staff pharmacist. They had an affair and apparently he promised to divorce his wife to marry Ms. Lawson, but she rejected his overture."

"Who would have the records of which pharmacists prepared the prescriptions that Nurse Lawson ordered for the two men who died of the overdoses?" the officer continued with his questions.

"That would actually be in the pharmacy, I assume," she answered.

"And who's in the pharmacy right now?"

She looked at her computer screen and clicked on a few icons. Her eyes widened. "Dr. Reynolds."

"You've already been so helpful," the officer soft-toned. "Any chance you would show us where that is?"

She looked at her watch. "I've got about twenty minutes until I really need to be back here."

"Thanks."

The seven—the four police officers, the H.R. Rep, the News Editor, and Nick—left the Administration Building and walked to the main hospital building. They entered the open elevator and the woman pushed the button for the basement. There was little down there other than a hallway leading to a locked door. PHARMACY it said. NO ADMITTANCE was the second sign. A security guard, who had been sitting in a chair next to the door, now stood.

"What's going on?" he said, directing his comments to the hospital official.

"These men have a warrant, and my badge won't open the door," she said. "Will you buzz us in?"

"Can I see the warrant?"

"If you must," Detective Parsons said. "But this matter is urgent."

The guard stared at the officer's badge for a moment, and then slid his keycard into the slot. The door buzzed.

The HR woman went to step inside first, but the detective moved her aside, and the six others walked in.

"What are you doing here?" the stunned pharmacist blurted.

Parsons stepped forward. "Sorry to startle you, Doctor." He looked at his name badge. "Doctor Reynolds. Do you have a few minutes so we could ask you a few questions?"

The doctor looked around. His eyes settled on the security guard.

"And you are?" the pharmacist asked.

"I'm sorry," the lead detective answered. "I'm Detective Parsons," he said as he pulled out his badge and displayed it. "We have just a couple quick questions to ask if you don't mind."

"I'm a little busy," Reynolds replied. "But okay."

"Thank you. Do you know Mary Lawson, a nurse here at the hospital?"

The pharmacist hesitated before answering. "Oh, yes. I've heard of her."

Parsons nodded his head as he looked down at the ring on the pharmacist's left hand. Looking back up, he asked, "Do you know if she's married?"

Reynolds shook his head. "No idea," he answered.

Detective Parsons looked at the mixing table and saw some open red and blue capsules and some powder on top of a small scale.

"Do you ever eat in here?"

The pharmacist's eyes closed slightly as he looked around. "I get breaks, of course. So I don't ever eat in here."

"No?" Parson responded. "Never? Right now, I think I smell almonds."

"I have no idea what you're talking about."

"Okay," the detective said as he nodded his head and stepped forward. "Did you ever have an affair with Nurse Lawson?"

The pharmacist looked at the H.R. Rep. "I don't have to answer that, do I?"

She shrugged.

"Let's try that again. Did you have an affair with Nurse Lawson?"

The pharmacist hesitated before answering. "Yes, I did. But we broke it off a while ago. So what?"

"Do you have any cyanide here in the pharmacy?"

"Why would I have cyanide in a hospital pharmacy?" Dr. Reynolds responded.

"I have no idea," the detective said. "I just asked if you do or you don't. It's that simple."

"I don't have to answer that," the pharmacist insisted.

"You don't. You're right. You can wait right here while we search if you want."

His eyes darted toward the scales.

"Do you have something you want to say?"

The pharmacist looked down at his hands and sighed. "She rejected me. I loved her. I would have given up everything for her."

"For who?"

"For her. Mary. I would have left my wife. We could have had a life together. But she—she was mean. Now—now I am ruined."

"So you decided to frame her?"

"If my life is over because of our affair, she should pay too." The pharmacist lunged for the counter, trying to reach the scales and the capsules.

One of the officers grabbed his collar, pulling him back, but the man was strong, and managed to knock the scale on its side, getting the powder there on his fingers. As another officer tackled him, the pharmacist tried to put his fingers in his own mouth.

The officer stopped him, and between the two, they rolled him over and cuffed his hands. Detective Parsons stepped forward and pulled a little baggie from his pocket. With his other hand, he opened a small pen knife.

He carefully scraped some of the residue from the pharmacist's hands into the little baggie.

"Dr. Reynolds," the detective said formally. "Dr. Reynolds, you are under arrest. You have the right to remain silent. Anything you say can and will be used against you…"

# 12

## TO SALEM

Nick stayed one more day at the hotel. It had rained in the morning. The rising sun shining on the wet dome of the Capitol building provided just the special photos that Nick wanted. He returned to the hotel, organized his photos, uploaded them to the Cloud, and then spent some time photographing the trees in Centennial Park. *Maybe the magazine doesn't want them, but I think they're pretty cool.*

He packed his bag before he headed down to breakfast on Sunday morning. He grabbed a newspaper as he headed into the room where the local TV news was broadcasting the arrest of Mercy Hospital's head pharmacist. The paper's headlines were the same: "Pharmacist Suspected in Recent Overdoses!"

"Dr. Reynold's wife has said that she stands by her husband and that there's no way he would commit any crime," the TV reporter said. Nick looked up at the TV and shook his head. He looked at the paper, and there was his name under the headline. Mark's was first, and Nick O'Flannigan's name was there also. *I wonder if anyone in Seattle reads this paper.*

Nick picked up the newspaper and headed to his room. He got his bags, headed downstairs, checked out, and looked at his new map. He'd found some swap meets selling old camera gear. So instead of heading straight down to Salem, he took I-5 to US-12 to Yakima. Then to Kennewick off of I-82. Then I-84 to Portland, back to I-5 to Salem.

*Maybe a few extra hours, but it's a piece of cake.*

# SOME FACTS ABOUT OLYMPIA AND THE STATE OF WASHINGTON

- Even though Olympia was named the state's capital city in 1853, it wasn't incorporated as a town until 1859, and a city in 1882.
- Washington became an official U.S. state in 1889, and the rivalry between two other cities (Ellensburg and North Yakima) split citizen votes, enabling Olympia to remain the capital.
- As the largest city and the seat for Thurston County, Olympia is only the 24th largest city in the state and 750th in the U.S.
- The state fruit is the apple; the state vegetable is the Walla Walla sweet onion; the state dance is the square dance; the state insect is the green darner dragonfly.
- Water from artesian wells in Olympia have long been called the reason for great tasting coffee.
- Washington State Patrol is responsible for security and law enforcement on the Capitol grounds as they are outside the normal jurisdiction of Olympia and Thurston County.
- The Legislative Building, aka the Capitol, has a dome that

is 287 feet high, the tallest self-supporting masonry dome
in the U.S., and the fifth tallest in the world.

- Some coffee houses in Olympia include Burial Grounds
  Coffee, Mud Bay Coffee Company, Dancing Goats
  Espresso Bar, Sizizis, Bar Francis, Maxim, Girls Espresso.
- The nose on the brass bust of George Washington in the
  Legislative Building has become shiny from visitors
  rubbing the nose, thinking that will bring them good luck.
- 9.5% of the surface area of the city of Olympia is water.
- Several monuments on the Capitol grounds include those
  dedicated to World War I, World War II, Korean Conflict,
  and a POW-MIA memorial.

# SLAYING IN SALEM

BOOK #2 IN THE CAPITAL CITY MURDERS
SERIES

# PROLOGUE: SLAYING

Steve needed the money, so he took the second job at the Oregon State Hospital doing security. During the day, he drove an armored truck, a pretty boring job most of the time, although he had fended off a couple of robbery attempts. On that job he was armed with his weapon of choice, a Ruger P97 .45 with ten rounds of "nope, I don't think so" loaded in the magazine.

At the Oregon State Hospital, he carried a baton and a radio, and although he was good with both, it wasn't much reassurance when patrolling the old tunnels under the building. People said areas of the place were still haunted even after the extensive renovations that removed the creepiest parts of the facility, including the old morgue and a room known as the "Library of Dust" which had contained thousands of copper canisters filled with the unclaimed cremated remains of former residents. There was also the story of those once buried in the cemetery. Many of the bodies had been moved, but others had never been recovered.

Not normally a superstitious guy, Steve believed those souls were probably still roaming these halls, waiting to be freed from this world to move on to the next. He had seen and heard things. Light and shadows. Footsteps. He even felt a chill from time to time when he patrolled those tunnels, and his rounds tonight were no exception.

Off limits to the public and current residents, the tunnels, now cleaned up, looked like simple hallways with no windows. Water dripped in various places every so often, but otherwise an empty silence indicated the complete lack of humanity down here. Earlier, the power had unexpectedly gone out in a particularly chilly section, so his flashlight was the only illumination, and he moved it constantly. His patrols down here were the part of the job he hated the most. He felt eyes crawl over him constantly as he walked, the ghosts of patients past staring at him from just beyond the darkness.

As he rounded a corner, Steve tensed. A former Marine, he could sense something off. Someone was there.

He considered himself to be in good shape, and even at a compact 5'9", there was little that scared him. He flashed his light ahead of himself in the tunnel, and there one of the residents stood, staring at what should be a closed wall.

"What's going on, Bill?" he asked. "You okay?"

Bill pointed at himself, and nodded, but didn't speak. He dropped his hands to his sides and looked at his paper slippers. Clad only in the blue scrubs all the current residents wore, he looked cold.

"You're not supposed to be down here," Steve told him. "What is going on?"

Bill looked up, and there were tears in his eyes. A second later, sobs destroyed his face.

"What is it?" Steve approached slowly jerking back as Bill's arm shot up from his side. His finger pointed to where the wall should be.

Steve felt a cold draft that should not be there. Not sure what to be ready for, he raised his baton with his left hand. As he approached Bill at an angle, he could see that what must have been in the wall was a hidden door. Now open, it was only a rectangle of darkness. "Back up slowly, Bill. You gotta let me by."

The resident did as he was told, his arm still straight out, pointing.

Steve took three deep breaths, trying to slow his racing heart, wishing for a weapon better than a stick. He ducked low, making himself a small target, and poked his head around the edge of the door for a quick glance. As he did, he felt cold breath on the back of his neck.

A body, motionless, lay on an old metal table. Blood dripped from the fingers of its right hand. At first glance, he had not seen anything but the body. He flashed his light around, trying to see if someone remained in the room.

There was no one. The cement walls and the metal table on wheels, the only things in the newly revealed room, offered no place to hide.

The body dressed in the medical whites worn by staff remained motionless. The light did nothing to disturb its wearer.

Slowly, Steve rose from his crouch and made his way toward the table, shining the light at his feet, careful not to step in any blood or something else that might be evidence.

He directed the light on the face of what he now knew to be a corpse.

"Doctor Hawkins," he breathed. "Damn."

Something touched his back, a gentle skittering down his spine. He spun, baton raised to strike.

"Bill!" The resident was right behind him and screamed into his face.

"Doctor dead! Doctor dead!"

Then Bill ran. Not knowing what else to do Steve followed, wanting to contain Bill, to protect him. At the same time, he dropped the baton back into its holster on his belt and grabbed for the radio.

He keyed the mic as he ran.

"Situation 7, unauthorized resident in the tunnel. Foot pursuit in progress."

"Roger that, responding," he heard the voice of his bored companion. He knew staff would be grabbing restraints and a jacket.

*Poor Bill.*

Keying the radio again, he said, "Need police." He just managed to keep Bill in sight. *Damn, he was fast.* "We have a situation down here."

Ahead, four large staff members dressed in white came around the corner flanked by one of his fellow security guards. He slowed as he saw Bill go down, but the resident kept shouting over and over.

"Doctor dead! Doctor dead!"

"You okay, Steve?" his coworker asked.

"Yeah," he said, catching his breath. "But we have a situation."

"What kind of situation? What happened back there? You look like you've seen a ghost."

"Not a ghost, not this time."

"What then?"

"Doctor Hawkins. He's dead. His body is in a room off one of the tunnels. One that should not be there."

"Hawkins? Are you sure?"

Steve nodded. He heard sirens in the distance. Bill had fallen silent, and hung, restrained, between two burly staff members. They were headed to a pair of steel doors, ones that led to the ward where Bill was assigned. Steve wondered how he had gotten out and managed to make his way to the tunnels.

"Did he do it?" the other security guard asked.

"I don't think so," Steve said.

"Then who did?"

"I have no idea."

First the police showed up and took his statement, closing off the corridors with yellow crime scene tape. Pretty quickly, they were followed by the press.

**1**

---

## SALEM

With some extra time on his hands, Nick O'Flannigan decided to take the long route from Olympia, Washington to Salem, Oregon. He planned to drive through Kennewick and Richland, and then take I-84 along the Columbia River and through Mt. Hood National Forest. At first, it felt pretty good. A photographer on assignment from *Travel USA* magazine, he could use the time to take some extra photos for his social media sites, and maybe even get a few good enough to make a few bucks selling on his website.

The day was cool, at least to start out, so he rolled his windows down and blasted the radio. By the time he got to Richland, it was noon, and he was getting hungry. Already four hours into what easily could have been a two-hour drive between Olympia and Salem, he needed to stop for gas and to stretch his long legs.

As he got close to the Columbia River, traffic got thicker, really slowing him down.

He stopped at a gas station, parked at the pumps, and walked inside. He needed a bathroom, snacks, and gas in that order.

The clerk looked up at him, literally. At well over six feet tall, Nick was used to the stares.

"Can I help you?"

"Where's your restroom?"

"Back corner." The clerk gestured over his shoulder toward a tiny hallway.

"Thanks. It's been a long drive."

"Where are you coming from?"

"Olympia last night, headed to Salem. Originally, Seattle."

"Kinda took the long way, didn't ya?"

"Yeah." Nick really had to pee, and while the clerk was friendly, he needed to get to the facilities before he had his first accident of the trip. "Be right back," he said, gesturing.

"Oh, sure, sure," the clerk said.

When Nick came out, he was relieved to see there were four people in line and the clerk was busy. He went over to the wall of drinks and snacks, looking for something at least marginally healthy. A star basketball player in high school and at Boston College, a leg injury his senior year had sidelined his plans to join the NBA. After a brief thought about working as an accountant, his photography hobby turned into a lucrative freelance career which led him to move to Seattle where he now lived.

He selected a bottle of Smart Water and some beef jerky with an organic label. He would need some lunch soon.

"This all for you?" the clerk asked when he reached the counter.

"Yep, thanks," Nick answered.

"You gonna stop and see the jet boat races?"

"Jet boat races?"

"Yep. That's why all the traffic."

Nick laughed. "Not sure I have time."

"Take care," the clerk said after throwing Nick's purchases in a plastic bag. "Safe travels."

After filling his tank, Nick slid behind the wheel and checked his navigation app. He still had four hours to drive. He had a reservation already at a great hotel for the week in Salem, and he could check in any time tonight. The early start from Olympia was paying off.

As he drove toward the river, the frequent stoppages caused by traffic allowed him to get some good shots of the races by rolling down both his windows and taking pictures with his zoom lens.

Action photos were not Nick's forte. Buildings and landscapes were his bread and butter, but he'd developed a taste and skill for macro photography, and it was his eye for extreme closeups and unusual angles that had landed him this gig.

While Nick made a very good living doing freelance work, he also had a significant following on social media, where he actually made some money selling prints and stock photos. Businesses, companies, brokers, realtors, shopping centers, hotels, and even tourist attractions were all things he had photographed for his livelihood.

Though many of those gigs were on hold while he was on this assignment, he loved the opportunity to travel, and this contract was a lucrative one. For a single guy with no real attachments, the opportunity was near-perfect.

So, he drove on, following the river and enjoying the beauty. His water consumption made frequent stops necessary, and he took a few photos each time, but kept going until he got to Mt. Hood National Forest.

Nick parked by a trailhead, one that looked promising, and grabbed his camera and bag. He exited the car and stretched, glad to be on his feet. Glancing at his watch, he decided he would give himself an hour to take photos before moving on.

As he brought his arms down to his side, his phone rang. It was Gerry, his friend and the social media manager for the magazine he was working for.

"Hey, Nick. How are things?" she asked.

"They're okay. I'm tired already," he told her.

"Where are you?"

"Mount Hood," he answered. "Stopping to take some pictures along the way."

"Mount Hood? That is a bit off the planned route, isn't it?"

"Yeah. I took the long way."

"I'd hate to see Emily's face when you submit those gas receipts."

Nick hadn't thought about that. "Eh. I'll cover the extra."

"You better. And don't tell her you're dallying around."

"It's the weekend, my travel time."

"Just the same, you don't want to fall behind."

"Tomorrow's Sunday. Maybe I'll get some exterior shots and even get ahead of the game."

"No worries, Nick. Just checking in. Making sure you're not too lonely on the road."

"Not at all."

Gerry was gay, so there was no chance of romance between them, but she and Nick had become great friends and often hung out together when they were both in town.

"Thanks," he said. "I'll call you tomorrow. I still have a little bit of a drive."

"You bet," she said, and hung up.

He snapped off several photos, kneeling to take some close ups of flowers and weeds, and even what he thought was a really cool shot of a fence post with Mount Hood blurred in the background.

Nick looked at his watch. *Dammit, time to move.* Otherwise, he'd be driving in the dark, something he preferred not to do on unfamiliar roads.

He headed out, looking again at his navigation app. Hopefully, he would just miss the Portland rush hour.

The miles fled under his tires. He finally reached the intersection of I-84 and I-5, and even though there was some traffic, the transition went smoothly. As he accelerated just north of the speed limit, Nick groaned as blue and red lights lit the interior of his car. He made his way to the right side of the road and pulled over.

"Evening, officer," he said as the Oregon State Patrolman reached his window.

"Evening. Where you headed tonight?"

"Salem."

"Can I see your license and registration, please?"

"Sure," Nick said, and pulled them out.

"Any idea how fast you were going?"

"Sixty-five?"

"Are you asking me or telling me, sir?"

"Honestly, I'm not sure. But close to that."

"A little faster, actually," the officer answered. "That's a nice camera," he said, gesturing to the EMIX sitting in his open case on the passenger seat. "You a photographer?"

"Freelance, yes, sir. Headed to take some photos of the capitol building."

"Very nice. I'll be right back."

The officer went back to his car and returned a few minutes later. He handed Nick a ticket and his paperwork.

"Had to give you a ticket. Drive safe and try to keep your speed down," he said. "You can pay it at the courthouse while you're in Salem."

"Thanks," Nick said. The officer tipped his hat and was gone.

*One-hundred and twenty dollars? For five over the limit?* Nick groaned. First, he was covering his own gas for detours, and now a ticket. He needed to be more careful.

As he started his car, the radio came on. "—strange events at the Oregon State Hospital in Salem today. One of the doctors was found murdered, his body located by a patient and a security guard in the old, unused autopsy room. There are no suspects at this time, but police say they are seeking a person of interest. We'll keep you updated here." The news transitioned into a pop song about blank spaces and writing names.

*I'll have to pick up a paper and read about that,* Nick thought. He carefully stayed one or two miles an hour under the speed limit as he drove to his hotel.

# 2

## CLOSED AND OPEN

The next morning Nick woke, tired, but knowing he had work to do anyway. Even though it was technically still a travel day, he wanted to get ahead of the game and keep his editor happy. At least his phone should be quiet.

After grabbing some of the free, but anemic breakfast at the hotel, he put his camera and his bag in the car and headed toward the capitol building. On the way, he stopped at a local grocery store and picked up a few things for lunch later. Riverfront City Park sat right on the Willamette River just down the street. He figured he could picnic there and take some photos for his social media and stock photo accounts between shooting at the capitol. He picked up a paper while he was at it, wanting to learn more about the murder he'd heard about on the radio the night before.

When he arrived at the capitol building, he discovered it was closed for cleaning. Outside one of the doors, he saw a security guard, a round, short man with a radio hanging on one side of his belt, a can of pepper spray hanging on the other. His silver badge read, "State of Oregon" and his name.

"Hi. Nick O'Flannigan," he said, introducing himself and holding out his hand. "I'm a photographer on assignment from *Travel USA* magazine. I'm here to take some photos of the capitol for a book they're working on."

"Name's Dale," the guard said, shaking Nick's offered hand. "Go ahead, but only outside. The interior will open on Tuesday."

"Is there any way I can get inside sooner?" Nick pressed, showing his freelance media badge. "I want to get ahead of my deadline."

"Nope, not unless the governor gives you permission. And he's out of town at the moment."

"Fair enough. I'll take a few daytime shots and probably come back tonight to catch some with the place all lit up."

"Sounds good. I'll pass it on to the next shift. You won't be hard to describe."

Nick laughed. "Thanks, I think."

"Hey, you have to be used to it. Tall guy, red hair, muscular but with a limp. Carrying a big-ass camera. No offense."

"None taken. Sometimes it opens doors for me, sometimes it closes them."

"I bet. You ever think about the NBA? The Blazers could use somebody like you."

"I did. The limp settled that for me."

"Oh, sorry man."

"No need. This is a great gig, working for myself. There are days though." Nick gestured at the closed sign.

"I hear you. Wish I could help."

Nick wandered the grounds, taking photos, but only a few he thought he actually might use. He was just getting a feel for the place. Other tourists wandered, too. After a while, his leg started to ache. He made his way back to his car but liked the parking spot he'd found. Shade still covered it and from the angle of the sun it looked like it might stay that way.

So, he grabbed his lunch in his little cooler, and walked down to the park, camera bag over one shoulder, newspaper tucked under his arm. When he reached the park, he found a picnic table under a tree and near the water. The reflection of light from the waves in the current was nearly blinding, and he was thankful for his sunglasses.

He set the camera bag in front of him, and after setting out his lunch, opened the paper.

On the front page, there was an astounding photo. The sky was dark, and an old stone building rose into the darkness. About half of it appeared to be lit.

"Doctor Murdered at the Oregon State Hospital," read the headline, and Nick looked over the story underneath. It was brief as the crime apparently occurred late the night before, and the reporter had probably snuck the story in past the print deadline.

Then he saw the byline. "What do you know about that?" He said aloud. "Ron Gibson."

Ron had been one of his classmates at Boston College, but Nick had not seen him since they graduated. It would be good to catch up, if he could find his number.

He opened a browser on his phone, typed in '*Statesman Journal*,' and got their phone number. Under the website heading was a staff list. Under Ron's name was an email address.

*What the hell, if he was a good reporter, he would check his email even on Sunday. If not, there was always tomorrow.*

He clicked on the email address, opened a message, and sent off a quick note: "Ron, it's Nick O'Flannigan. In town on an assignment. If you want to get together for drinks or just to chat, here is my number." He added his phone number, and figured Ron had his email address.

As he ate the rest of his lunch, Nick flipped through the photos he had taken so far. None of them stood out to him. He just wasn't feeling it today.

Maybe he'd head to the state hospital where the murder had happened. He could take some photos, just check the place out. It looked fascinating. He threw his lunch leavings in the trash and searched his map app for the location. It was about a four-minute drive, but a half-hour walk. His leg was tired from all of this morning's walking, so he went back to his car and took the short drive, parking on the street nearby.

The brick building was imposing from the front and a long sidewalk led to the entrance. A spire rose into the sky, and Nick snapped some wide-angle photos with his normal lens as he walked up. The red brick looked almost friendly in the daylight, a stark contrast from the photo in the paper.

A man sat in the grassy area outside the front with an easel set up in front of him. Next to him on a stool was a painter's palette and in his left hand he held a brush.

Nick wandered over behind him, and saw he was working on a rather abstract painting of the front of the building. Instead of red brick, the building was an unusual, almost mud colored brown, and the skies in the painting were dark with storm clouds, contrasting with the actual sun today.

"Hi, I'm Nick."

The painter started and nearly dropped his brush. "H-h-hi," he stammered. "I didn't hear you come up."

"You seemed pretty involved in your work," Nick indicated the easel. "It's good."

"Thanks. You're a photographer?" The artist indicated the camera around his neck.

"Yes," Nick said. "Freelance."

"You here about the murder?"

"Yep. That and curiosity about this place."

"It does have a pretty dark history. Tragic murder though."

"Seems to be. Did you know the—" Nick hesitated. "Victim?"

"Not really," the man said, his tone changing. "I need to get back to this."

"Of course," Nick said. "Have a good day."

The reason for the difference in photos came to him quickly. It wasn't just the time of day and lighting. One part of the complex was a Museum of Mental Health while the rest was an operating hospital. The photos had been taken from the angle of the entrance to the museum, not the actual hospital entrance. He snapped a couple of distant photos, including one of the painter and his easel, shot surreptitiously, since he really did not have permission.

He made his way to the door intending to visit the museum area first, only to find it was closed on Sundays and Mondays. As he turned to walk away, a short, round man in blue coveralls with an Oregon State patch on the sleeve stopped him.

"What can I do for you?' he asked.

"I'm a reporter," Nick told him, flashing his media badge, not wanting to explain that the real reason for his visit was curiosity. "I'm here about the murder that happened last night."

"What about it?"

"I'm looking into what happened. Doing a story."

"I think we've seen enough press," the man said. "They've been here all morning. But I'll show you to the main building, and they might be able to help you."

"Thanks."

"Don't thank me. It's my job."

"What do you do here?"

"Caretaker," came the short answer. "Follow me."

The walk continued in silence, as they made their way around one building and down a sidewalk toward the main office.

As they reached the door, Nick's phone rang. It was an Oregon number. Probably Ron. He'd call him back once he got inside.

The caretaker opened the door and ushered him inside. They approached the front desk and the receptionist, a woman of indeterminate age, sat behind a sign bearing the name Cathy. She looked up at them. What he assumed to be fake nails decorated the end of slender fingers attached to largish hands, and her hair was a brilliant red, a color not known in nature. Deep brown eyes were covered by equally unnatural fake lashes. This bracketed a sharp beak of a nose where tortoiseshell glasses rested. She looked over the rims.

"What are you doing in here, Chet?" she asked the caretaker.

"Found this guy wandering around. Another reporter."

"Thanks. Be with you in a minute," she said to Nick. "Can you sign this maintenance form while I have you here, Chet?"

"What's it for?"

"New plants for the front of the museum."

"I need to do this on a Sunday?"

"You think I want to be here? Just sign the form."

Chet picked up the pen with his left hand and scribbled a signature.

"Thanks, you're a dear," Cathy said.

Chet grunted and left.

"So, you're a reporter?" she asked Nick.

"Freelance photographer," he said, showing her his press credentials. "Hoping to get some shots I can sell."

"I see," she said. "Okay, fill this out. Completely. Read the fine print. No faces, no patients, no people. When you get close to the scene, listen to the police. They are in charge there."

"Yes, ma'am."

"Before you publish any photos you think might be questionable, email them to the media director for approval. Understood?"

"Of course," Nick said. "Thank—"

"Don't thank me," she said, echoing Chet's earlier sentiment. "I'm just doing my job. Remember the rules while you wander."

Nick handed the form back to her. "Which way?" He asked.

"Go out this door, take a left. You'll see where to go soon enough."

"Than—" Nick stopped himself. "Appreciate it," he said instead, and left.

*What was wrong with these people? I guess nobody wants to work on a Sunday, and a bunch of press sniffing around probably doesn't help either.*

As he stepped out of the door, he heard a shout.

"Nick!"

He looked over and walking down the sidewalk toward him was Ron Gibson.

# THE LOCAL NEWS

"Ron, it has been a day or two!"

"Yes, it has," Ron said. The two men shook hands, and Ron pulled Nick into a surprise embrace. "How are you doing?"

"Good. The freelance work is going well. How about you?"

"You know, good and bad. With all the online news, we journalists are struggling to keep up. What brings you to Salem?"

"A freelance assignment actually. I'm traveling around the country taking photos of all the state capitals for *Travel USA* magazine. I'll be on the road for a year."

"So, why are you here?"

"I saw some photos in the paper. Thought I would come check this place out. It's much different than it used to be."

"True. One newspaper story with a happy ending. *The Oregonian* investigation caused the legislature to turn this place around."

"I read about that online. So, what happened?"

"We're not sure yet. There are still some old tunnels under the place, and a patient found a doctor, a member of the staff, stabbed to death in one of them. There was apparently a room walled over in the tunnel, and whoever committed the murder knew about it and opened it up."

"Wow. That is scary. Are there any suspects?"

"So far, a person of interest. The security guard who found the patient knew the layout of the hospital, about the old tunnels, and he didn't like the doctor who was killed."

"Really? Didn't like him enough to kill him?"

"Of course, the cops are not sharing details, but they do say he had motive and opportunity."

"Mmm. I would love to see some more detailed photos of the scene."

"I have some. Ones we could not print, of course, and a few I got from the coroner's office. What's your interest?"

"Curiosity. Sometimes I notice things in photos that other people don't."

"Were you the tipster in Olympia?"

"Yeah, that was me. I was there taking photos. My editor just prefers that I stay on task and out of the news."

"I get that. Let's go grab some coffee and talk it over."

"Sure."

Ron led him to a nearby coffee shop, they ordered and found seats. Ron pulled a laptop from his bag. Nick did the same.

"See here?" Ron said. "How the wall has been broken in? But there aren't a lot of hammer or other marks around it. The person who did the cutting had to know where this was."

"Thus, the security guard? He would have had access to the plans?" Nick asked.

"Yeah, he would have known where to look at least. And although it is routine, some guards never go down to the old tunnels in a shift. Most think once a day, even less is plenty, at least that is what his coworkers say."

"But the resident who was down there?"

"Totally incapable."

"Who else had access?"

"Security staff. Hospital staff. Conceivably, a visitor visiting someone who had been there a while. I mean, technically the old building plans are available online, so nearly anyone who really wanted to kill the doctor. He seems pretty well liked by most of the staff and the patients, at least from reports so far."

"Is that the guard there?" Nick carefully studied the photo Ron had just brought up.

"Yeah, that's him."

"Can I see the morgue photos?"

"Sure." With a few clicks through the folder, Ron brought them up.

"Mind if I take over for a bit?" Nick asked.

"Why not?" Ron said, looking on with interest as Nick enlarged the photos so the doctor's wounds filled the screen, and zoomed out just a little bit.

He brought up the photo of the guard, Steve.

"They have the wrong guy," he said. "You should tell the local cops."

"What makes you say that?"

"Look at the guard, how he is wearing his baton on his belt. He's right handed."

"So?" Ron said.

"Look at the wounds here," Nick said. He turned the computer to Ron again, and zoomed out and back in. "See how they are on his right side, and you can see how they taper toward the top and toward his chin, this way?" He gestured to make his point.

"That means?" Ron asked, but Nick thought he saw a sparkle in the man's eyes.

"The killer was left handed."

"Wow," Ron said, sitting back. "I think you're right. But what if the killer just held the knife in his left hand?"

"The wounds would not be as deep or neat. And why would the guard use a knife, not his baton, or at least use it to knock the doctor out and immobilize him?"

"You spotted this. You should call the cops."

"No way, not unless you won't. My travel assignment editor will literally kill me if she finds out I got involved in another local case."

"Jeez, Nick, you sure you did not miss your calling? Maybe you should have been a detective instead of a photographer."

"Too much violence."

"So, who did it, if not the guard, Agatha Christie?"

Nick shrugged. "The guy I first saw when I came in seemed more upset about the press around than the doctor's passing. And he was left handed."

"I'll pass that along, too."

"Thanks, Ron. Why don't you call the local police? I'm sure you have connections. Then come back and check out the shots I got today at the capitol building. I didn't take many. I'll go back tomorrow to get some more, but I think a few of these might be keepers."

"You're that calm after you just told me the cops have the wrong guy in a murder case?"

"Why not?" Nick said. "I'm not going to go get him out of jail or arrest a new suspect."

Ron went to make the call and was only gone for a few moments.

"The detective told me thanks, and that he would check things out. He also told me not to print anything about this until they give me the green light."

"You going to listen to them?"

"Depends how long they take to get back to me."

Nick smiled, and they went over the photos he had taken for a little while. Ron gave him some pointers on places and angles to get some unique shots.

"Thanks," he said.

"Walk you back to your car?" Ron asked.

"Why not?"

They left the coffee shop and walked back toward the Oregon State Hospital. As they rounded the corner, they saw four police cars in the parking lot in front of the museum.

# 4

# PICTURE THIS

As they passed by, Nick saw the man who had shown him to the office in a heated discussion with two police officers.

"Where were you last night?"

"I was home with my wife, all night!" His face was red, his hands flying about with every word before settling into fists at his side.

"Just calm down. We are just asking, acting on a tip." The officer typed a note into his phone.

"A tip? A tip? From who?"

"We can't tell you that. Just stay here and give me a minute to call your wife," the officer said.

The man turned and saw Nick and Ron approaching. "Aha!" he said. "It was you, wasn't it?" A long, thin finger pointed at Nick.

"Me? What?"

"Did you tell these guys I might have done something to that doctor?"

"I—I—no," Nick said, since the statement wasn't entirely true.

"If they arrest me, you're done as a reporter, you understand me?"

Nick shrugged, and he and Ron turned away.

"Don't just walk away!" The man shouted after him.

As they made their way down the sidewalk, the cop returned to talk to the man, and Nick saw his face got even redder. Then the cop put him in cuffs. He could not read lips, but he assumed the cop was reading him his rights.

"That was fast," Nick told Ron.

"They must not have had much confidence in their other arrest," he said. "I have no idea."

"Do me a favor and keep me posted," Nick asked.

"Sure, and let's do dinner this week, before you take off."

"Sure," Nick said. "Shoot me a text or give me a call."

He slid into his car and drove to his hotel.

Technically, it was his day off, but Nick wanted to show his editor his good intentions to get ahead of schedule, so he decided to upload the raw images he had taken, at least some that might be keepers, to the cloud account they had set up for him.

First, he took the battery out of his camera and placed it into the charger. He had spares, but he liked to make sure they were all fully charged just in case.

He took the SD card out and plugged it into the adapter for his laptop. The computer was no slouch, with over 500 MB of solid-state hard drive, and loaded with the latest and best editing software.

Nick grabbed all of the photos on the memory card, and copied them over, but left them on the card for now. Even with the cloud, he kept a physical backup of his raw photos, especially after his computer scare in Olympia.

He loaded them all, raw, to the cloud. He knew this would take up a lot of space, and soon he would delete the ones he absolutely was not going to use.

He started to edit them, one at a time. He deleted a few right away, repeats or just poor shots.

As he was working his way through, his phone rang. It was his editor, Emily.

Ready for high praise at his head start on Salem, he answered in a cheery voice.

"This is Nick."

"What the hell, Nick? What did you just upload to the cloud file?"

"Some raw photos from today," he said, taken aback.

"These are not all from the capitol building, or even from the area around it," she said. "In fact, they are from the state hospital."

"Yes, they—"

"I read the news, Nick. In fact, I will be in every city you visit from now on."

"I can explain," he said.

"I am sure you can."

"No, really. I just heard about the murder on the radio, went to check it out, and took some personal photos. I ran into a friend who works for the local paper—"

"Nick, I know it is technically your day off. But try to keep your personal photos off the cloud drive we gave you. And stay focused. Whatever this is, don't get involved. When will you be able to get inside the capitol building for some photos?"

"It's closed the next couple of days, but as soon as it reopens, I'll be there."

"Good, Nick. Keep me posted and stay on task."

"Will do. I promise."

The call ended. It seemed Emily was keeping a close eye on things, not that Nick blamed her. He was getting paid a handsome sum to do this job.

He looked back at the photos, intending to edit them just a little and determine which ones he should keep. His Olympus EM1X took great photos, and although he was drooling over the newest edition, the $3,000 price tag kept him satisfied with his current option.

His phone rang again. It was Gerry.

"Hey," he said.

"How goes it?" she asked. "Did you sleep well?"

"Well enough. Did some exploring today, and even went and took some photos at the old Oregon State Hospital."

"Where that murder happened?"

"Yep. Ran into an old friend. I got some good shots, and before that, I did manage to get some outside shots of the capitol. I am looking through them now to see if there are any worth keeping. The interior is closed for a couple of days."

"Don't let Emily get word of you going too far off track."

"Too late. I accidentally uploaded some of the State Hospital photos to the cloud folder. She called right away."

"What did she say?"

"Told me to stay focused."

"Good advice. Be careful, Nick."

"I will. I'll be more cautious from now on."

"Good. Well, have a good one."

The call ended, and Nick hoped for some peace. He went to the cloud drive and downloaded the state hospital photos to his hard drive instead of the cloud and deleted them from that file. He'd move them to his personal cloud folder once he had a chance to look them over.

As he started to go through them, he realized why Emily may have been so frustrated with him. The photos from the hospital were much better than the ones of the capital.

*It's passion and interest,* he told himself. *I need to ignite that about the book photos as much as I do for the hospital photos.*

He clicked through them, deleting most, but keeping some of the front of the building. He found the shot of the painter to be oddly compelling, so he saved that one as well.

It had been a long day. He would start again in the morning, first with the capitol. Even if it was still closed, he would get some better exterior shots, something to show Emily how serious he was about the project.

He could wait until Tuesday to go back to the museum at the Oregon State Hospital. Maybe there was another travel story there, another freelance one he could either sell to *Travel USA* or to another publication. Maybe it would just be good stuff for his blog.

Just before he closed his computer for the night, he sent the photo of the painter to his phone and uploaded the edited version to his Instagram account.

He flopped his large frame onto the bed and turned on the television. The news came on automatically, but he quickly turned it to the internet input and signed into his Netflix account. He would stay logged in for the week while he was here.

As he lay there, he glanced at his phone from time to time, and saw several notifications from Instagram. People loved his photo. He'd have to post more tomorrow.

5

---

## WAKING UP

His alarm woke him early from a dead sleep, but Nick wanted to get some early shots of the capitol building, maybe around sunrise.

His stomach growled and, as he dressed, he thought about two things: breakfast and coffee. Both could wait but not too long, not if he wanted to function well.

The hotel was quiet as he left, the front desk monitored by a sleepy night clerk toward the end of his shift. Nick got a weak wave, a puzzled look, and nothing more.

The streets felt almost deserted, too. He was up ahead of the commuters, ahead of everyone it seemed.

As he got to the capitol building grounds, he stopped. Right there, on the edge of the lawn, was a rose bush. A pink rose flanked a white one, and both were just beginning to open.

Behind them, the capitol was lit from the inside through a few windows. The morning light was still gray and had yet to brighten into real daylight.

He put his macro lens on his camera and adjusted the settings. The roses were in perfect focus, the capitol blurry in the background, but still looking regal. He knew, as he took several shots in a row, that these were impressive. These were the kinds of shots his editor and the magazine were looking for in the book.

He took several similar shots as well. One of a parking meter, the edge of a park bench, all with the capitol in the background, blurred but still visible. As he took shots, the light got brighter. He only had a few moments to use this unique lighting.

Then he saw it. A shrub with the yellow flowers of the plant known as the Oregon Grape. The state flower. Nick knelt so he was almost looking up at the petals. In the background was the Oregon State flag, waving lightly in the morning breeze. He snapped a series of shots, each one brighter than the last, until the glare of the sun ruined the shot.

He quickly switched camera lenses and trotted around the building as much as his sore right leg would let him.

On the other side, he took some wider shots of the capitol from every angle he could think of. To get low, he had to kneel. To get higher and look down on the steps, he had to stand on various barriers.

He took one such shot and hopped off the concrete slab to the ground, favoring his bad leg as he did.

He was going to be sore and pay for this. But these were the golden shots, the ones that had earned him the editor's respect and, therefore, this assignment.

As he did, he saw a man wearing a cheap suit, staring at him.

Nick's phone rang, and he dug it from his pocket. It was Ron.

"What's up, Ron? Little early for you newspaper guys, isn't it?"

"Sorry, Nick. This is no joke."

"Oh, sorry. I have been up for a bit anyway. Down at the capitol."

"Remember where we had coffee yesterday? Meet me there in a few. The police suspect did not pan out. They are pissed and so is my editor. He's mad at me for wasting time and for getting the cops all up in our business."

"What's the big deal? They checked him out, he's innocent. At least they checked, right?"

Ron sighed. "Nick, I love you man, but you're not in the newspaper game. Ever since *The Oregonian* ran the story on the state hospital and the legislature made them clean it up, the place is a little sensitive about publicity and journalists. In fact, because there was a murder there, they are pretty on edge. They don't want people to even think things might be going back to the way they were before."

"I'm not sure I understand," Nick said. "But I guess I get it. I'll meet you in a few and we can talk it over."

"See you soon," Ron ended the call and Nick dropped his phone back in his pocket. He put his camera back in its bag, at least for the moment, and slung it over his left shoulder.

The man in the suit approached him.

"You Nick O'Flannigan?"

"That's me," Nick said, puzzled.

The man pulled out a badge. "Detective Martin, Salem Homicide."

"Pleased to meet you." Nick stuck out his hand to shake. "What can I do for you?"

The detective let his hand hang there, and eventually Nick let it drop.

"Are you a detective, O'Flannigan?"

"No, sir."

"Any experience with law enforcement? Investigations?"

"No, not really. I—"

"You stepped in and wasted our time on a case with a fruitless tip. You from around here, Mr. O'Flannigan?"

"Not really. Just here for a week taking photos of the capitol building."

"Good. Get that done and leave. In the meantime, keep your nose where it belongs."

The detective walked away and didn't look back.

"I was just trying to help," Nick mumbled, and headed down the street. He couldn't wait to tell Ron about this encounter.

When he arrived at the coffee shop, he found Ron seated at a table outside.

"You won't believe what just happened," he told him. "I had a detective come up to me and basically tell me to back off."

"I believe it. I'm not sure why they are so sensitive and ticked off at the moment."

"Yeah, tell me the whole hospital story thing. I know a little about it, but I don't remember details."

"Well, there were a lot of bad things happening there. Poor conditions for patients, patients not being monitored, and even kids in some pretty horrible circumstances, basically because they had nowhere else to go. *The Oregonian* got wind of it and did an investigative piece. As a result, the legislature put together some funding and made a plan to remodel it, which has been done."

"I get that."

"So, the hospital and the officials in Salem are really sensitive about the place. They don't like reports of anything bad that happens there getting out. This murder is a major blow to their public relations department. But it gets worse. There is a part of the story I can't print."

"What's that?"

"Dr. Hawkins was a holdover. When the renovations happened, many of the staff left, most pretty ashamed of what happened there. A few stayed though. Hawkins is one of them."

"So, maybe he is not well liked?"

"Not by everyone," Ron said. "And of course, there are former patients and their families, some of them don't like him at all."

"Lots of people with motive then?"

"Yes, but fewer with opportunity, and I think that is what has the police upset. Two of those who would have had opportunity have been cleared. I think they feel like they are at a dead end."

"Understandable." Nick paused. *What had he gotten himself into? Everything about this place seemed more complicated than he thought it would be at first. He'd just been a little curious, that's all.*

Intrigue was leading him places he had never expected to go.

"Curiosity killed the cat," his father had always said. "But satisfaction brought him back."

"What do you have on your plate the rest of the day?" Ron asked.

"Not much until tonight. I got some great shots this morning, ones I hope my editor will really love. I plan to go back around sunset, just before, to try and get some more."

"Good. I wonder if you could help me with something."

"Sure. What do you need?"

"My editor thinks to make nice, we should take some photos of the Oregon State Hospital Museum and write up a nice story. Would you be willing to take the photos for me?"

"Sure! I don't see why not."

"Okay, come with me."

The two friends walked towards the hospital, Nick limping a bit as they went. If he did go back to the capitol building tonight, today would be a long one.

And he'd have to get interior shots tomorrow.

"Stay focused," he heard Emily say in his head.

*No matter,* he thought. *This won't take long, and it is just a favor for a friend.*

# 6

# CAPITAL CITY

As they approached the hospital, Nick saw the same painter on the front lawn, still working. He walked up to him.

"Hey there, how's it coming?"

"Almost done," he said.

Despite the fact that it was another sunny day, the painting had gotten darker if anything, the storm more prominent.

"It's good," Ron said. "That is amazing. Can we take a photo of you with your painting?"

"I'd rather you didn't," the painter said. "Not until I'm finished and can unveil it officially."

Nick stayed quiet about the photo he had snapped before and how popular it was. "How about if we take one from a distance? Neither you nor the painting will be up close at all."

"I guess that would be okay," the painter said. "But don't get my face or details of the painting."

Nick nodded, and strolled off a ways to get the shot, Ron right behind him.

"Did he seem a little odd?" Ron asked.

"He's a painter. Artists are all a little odd, right?"

"Yeah, I guess," Ron said.

Nick opted for a handheld shot and snapped off a couple with the painter to one side or the other, never super clear.

"What was that color he was using for the building?"

"A dark brown, I guess. It must be what it used to look like," Nick answered. "He seemed to have a good eye for sure."

Ron just nodded but looked a little troubled.

As they approached, Nick snapped off some shots, and then froze.

"What is it?" Ron asked.

"Shh," Nick said, unslinging his camera bag and changing to his zoom lens.

He knelt low, hearing his knee crack as he did, and hoping the sound was not as loud as it seemed to be to him. The bird he had spotted flapped its wings but stayed put.

He laid flat, almost in a sniper shooting position, and aimed his camera carefully, using his elbows for support and hoping the image stabilization was as good as advertised. He switched to the auto-focus mode and fired off several shots in a row.

The Western Meadowlark, its breast a prominent yellow, sat and sang as he did so.

It wasn't at the capitol, but he thought he might just have gotten another great shot for the book.

As he stood to brush himself off, the bird took flight, winging its way across the grounds. Ron had been watching the whole time.

"You're an amazing photographer," Ron said. "Your editor should be really proud."

"I hope so," Nick said.

They walked up to the front door of the museum. The docent did not seem too happy to see them, Nick with his camera gear, now switched back to a regular lens, and Ron with his recorder and notebook. But when they simply said they were doing a story on the museum and asked for a tour, his eyes lit up.

"Right this way," he said. "I'll give you the personal tour."

As Ron talked and asked questions, Nick took photos while listening much of the time.

He found the place fascinating, and the museum filled with amazing light despite its dark past.

When the tour was complete, he turned to Ron.

"Lunch, somewhere nearby?"

"You buying?" Ron asked.

"Sure. I'm on a per diem anyway, and I skipped breakfast. I'm starving."

"I know just the spot," Ron said. "And it's not far. Give your leg a rest."

Nick had not been paying attention, but now that he was not taking photos, he realized his limp had become pretty pronounced. He was going to have to put his feet up before tonight.

Ron was right. The Sassy Onion Grill was not far and was on the way back to the capitol where Nick's car was parked.

They sat down, and Nick looked over the menu. This would be a great breakfast spot as well, but the burgers and wraps he saw looked divine.

The narrow restaurant was full.

"They're only open a few hours for breakfast and a few more for lunch," Ron told him. "It's great food though."

Nick ordered a burger after debating over the menu for a few moments.

"Can you send me the photos you took?" Ron asked.

"You bet," Nick said.

"Want me to byline you?"

"Sure," Nick said, sipping the iced tea he'd ordered. "Let me know which ones you use so I can use the rest on my website and social media."

"You'll have to let me know how that bird pic turns out," Ron said.

"That one you can't have," Nick said. "I need that."

"Deal," Ron said.

Their food came, and the conversation descended into talk about old times in school, who they still kept in touch with and where they were, and other simple topics.

When they were done, they walked back toward the capitol.

"Thanks, Nick, for your help," Ron said.

"No problem. I'm going to head back to the hotel, upload some of these photos, and get some rest."

"Watch the paper in the morning. I'll let you know this evening which shots we use."

"Thanks," Nick said. "See you soon."

"Before you leave for sure," Ron said.

Nick got into the car and sat for a second, taking a deep breath. He needed to get some work done but felt like he needed a nap, too.

He thought about a coffee. He'd be up late tonight anyway, probably. He was positive they had some at the hotel.

As he drove, he thought about how successful his morning had been.

He also thought about the cop and how angry he had seemed. Ron was right. Best to just leave this one alone.

# 7

## SELF-DOUBT

Nick popped two ibuprofen capsules in his mouth and chased them with a swig of water. Tonight, maybe the last of the exterior pictures, tomorrow the interior ones.

No more messing around with the hospital, with news stories, or with anything but his assignment. He'd get done here, have dinner with Ron, and then head on to Sacramento.

It was that simple. Stay focused. Keep on task. Just like Emily said.

His phone rang again.

"Hey, Gerry," he said.

"Hey, big guy," she answered. "How goes the battle?"

"Good. I got some great shots today. I think just what Emily wants."

"Staying out of trouble?"

"Trying to," he said. He filled her in on the slaying and the events of the last couple of days.

"Whew," she said. "Sounds like a lot. You're right. Probably just best to stay clear."

"Yeah, I figured Emily might see the pics in the paper in the morning, but since I got some great shots for the assignment, she won't be too upset. Including one of the state bird while I was there."

"Fair enough. Emily is a good person. She is just a little enthusiastic from time to time. Be patient with her."

"Of course," Nick said. "I'm sure it will all work out. She clearly loves my work."

"She can't stop talking about the photos from Olympia," Gerry said. "But don't tell her I said that."

"It's just between us."

"Good," she said. "I miss having you around here."

"I miss being there already," Nick said. "But being on the road is also a blast. I'm just headed out to get some sunset and night shots."

"Fantastic. Good luck. I'll talk to you this weekend?"

"Count on it," he said, and ended the call.

The coffee he'd had was already wearing off. But he'd done longer shoots before. Nick headed for the door to, once again, make the trek down to the state capitol building.

As he approached from the front, hoping to get some quick, long, and wide-angle shots in, Nick stopped and stared. There was a painter, sitting on a stool in front of an easel on the front lawn.

As he approached, he saw it was not the same painter he'd seen at the state hospital.

*How do you know?* he asked himself.

Then he answered just as quickly. This painter was painting with his right hand. The other painter had been using his left.

That wasn't unusual. Many artists were left handed. A higher percentage than the normal population.

This artist was doing a realistic painting of the capitol. The sun was shining in her picture, and Nick could tell as he got closer that the piece must almost be done.

"Nice painting," he said.

"Thanks," the painter answered.

"I'll leave you to it," Nick said. "Just going to grab some quick photos and hoping to capture some sunset shots."

"Good luck," she answered. "I'm about done here. I'll put on the finishing touches in the studio."

"That's great. Have a good night."

Nick moved forward, taking shots as he went, looking at angles, hoping to see something new or different.

As he did though, he thought of the painter at the hospital, the darkness of the painting.

The fact that the painter in question was left handed. The strange brown ink he used.

*Leave it alone, Nick,* he told himself. *Just like the cops and Ron said. You're no detective.*

But it bothered him.

A moment later he realized that to really catch the sunset, he needed to be on the north side of the building.

As he turned to go around, he looked back. The painter was packing up her things, preparing to leave.

He hurried around, finding that the light was beautiful, and he'd caught things at just the right moment. He snapped off several photos, and then sat in the park to wait for darkness. He wanted some night shots, just in case, and thought he could get a few macros, too, ones that even if they did not make it in the book would be great additions to his portfolio.

As he sat, he thought about the slaying, how he had spotted the problem with the suspect while looking at the photos.

*The killer is left handed,* he had concluded. And told everyone. And he was right.

He'd been wrong about the "who" though.

*Could it be the painter? Should he even suggest it?*

Maybe, just maybe, he should ask Ron before he did anything else. A call to the police, even a call to Ron at the paper might be seen as interference in the investigation.

On impulse, he pulled out his phone and called Ron.

"Nick! How are things?"

"Just down here at the capitol getting some night photos. Can I ask you a favor?"

"What's up, buddy?"

"Want to go for a drink when I'm done here? I could use a listening ear."

"I suppose. Trouble at home?"

"No. Just...we'll talk then okay?"

"Sounds good. I'll send you the address of a great pub. You're gonna love it. You need an hour to get your photos?"

"That should be plenty of time."

Nick wandered the grounds, getting some cool shots with the lights coming out of the capitol building windows and some of the exterior lights. A security guard approached him once but walked away with a wave once he recognized him.

The night was cool, and Nick shivered as he finished up about forty-five minutes later. He looked at a few previews on the screen of his camera, pretty satisfied with himself. He had good photos, both day and night, from all kinds of angles. The editor and publisher would have plenty to choose from. He'd done his job here. At least on the outside.

*Which was what?* To create an impression of the capitol building, one those who bought the book could learn from. An impression they would only get from just a few photos over a few pages, but his pictures should say more than just words could. He was creating art, communicating with people he would never see or know.

The same thing a painter did. Or a writer. Anyone who created, really.

That was where Nick struggled from time to time. Through his photos, he could communicate, but when it came to words, sometimes he was at a loss.

Then it came to him. That was it. Ron was good with words, but Nick had the pictures. Maybe there was a way they could put a story together, one that might pique the interest of the police, without coming outright and accusing anyone or pointing to any one suspect.

The address Ron had sent him was about a 10-minute drive, so Nick got in his car and headed that way. He turned left onto Grove Street and saw the name of the place. Unable to help himself, he burst out laughing.

"f/Stop Fitzgerald's Public House" the sign read. Perfect. It fit with both what he did and what he planned to say to Ron.

It took him a moment to find parking and then he made his way to the entrance. As soon as he walked in, Ron waved him over to a comfortable chair beside a small table in the corner.

He looked quickly over the beer list and gave the waitress his order.

"Nice," Nick said when they were alone.

"I thought you would like it."

"I love the name," Nick said. "Have you written your positive piece on the Oregon State Hospital yet?"

"Mostly. I'll finish it tomorrow. Why? What's on your mind?"

Nick shrugged. "I have been thinking about the slaying that took place there."

"Seriously? I thought you were at the point where you wanted to leave that one alone."

"I do." Nick paused. "I do. But something has been bothering me."

"That sentence in itself sounds like trouble."

"You know the painter we saw, right?"

"Yes. Pretty dark work, but I liked it."

"He was left handed."

"So are a lot of painters."

"He was using an odd, dark red paint." Nick paused and felt himself shudder just a little. "It might have been blood."

"And it might just have been paint."

He dipped his brush in something else before dipping it in that paint. Something clear. Maybe an anti-coagulant to keep it from clotting."

"Or maybe paint thinner."

"You're right, Ron, but what if—"

"What if nothing, Nick. I can't go to the cops with something like this. We have no proof of anything, just your overactive imagination."

"Calm down, Ron. Just hear me out. I have an idea."

"Okay. What is it?" Ron said. He appeared to be tiring of the conversation.

Nick pulled out his computer. "Look at this picture," he said.

He'd opened up the picture of the painter in front of the hospital, the one he had taken the first day. It was from a distance, and the painter's back was to him, but the resolution was high thanks to the EM1X and the advanced image stabilization it had, so he zoomed in.

"You can't read the label on the bottle, but you can read part of a word. 'Lithi.' Could be paint thinner, could be something else. Why don't we let the experts decide?"

"What do you have in mind?"

"In the article, let's not just mention the painter, let's focus on him as a backdrop for the rest of the story."

"How?" Ron asked, sitting forward.

"Contrast his dark painting, which you can see in the photo with how much better the State Hospital is now. Make that your lead photo, only cropped like this."

Nick pressed a few keys and turned the screen to Ron. The painter was now at the center of the screen. His brush was poised above the container of clear liquid. The name on the bottle was not clear, but the unusual reddish color of the paint was.

To the right was the dark painting, and to the left, the building he was painting, bathed in sunshine, stood in stark contrast.

"This is your idea?" Ron asked, and shook his head.

"Yes," Nick said. "Either the cops investigate it because it piques their interest, or they don't. Either way, you and I are out of it. We're not accusing anyone or even tipping the cops. You're writing the story. I'm giving them the photographs."

Ron stared at the wall for a minute and drained the rest of his beer. Nick did the same and signaled for a second for both of them. Tonight would not appear on his expense account but would come out of his personal funds. He usually did not spend his entire per diem anyway.

"What do you think?" Nick broke the silence, a little impatient.

"Okay," Ron said. "We can try. But this is it, buddy. It's time to put this to bed for good. I'm not even sure you're on to anything at all. But it will make a good story anyway, one everyone will appreciate."

"Thanks." Nick breathed a sigh of relief as their next round of beers arrived.

"No problem. For the record, even if you're not right, this story is a great idea. This type of contrast is just what people are looking for. Adds a little spice and controversy to a fluff story designed to placate the state. Know what I mean?"

Nick did.

Ron tilted back his second beer and drained it in one giant swig. "Thanks, amigo. I'm going to go finish this story, try to get it into the paper tomorrow morning and on the website."

"Thanks again," Nick said, sipping his beer. "Let me know when it is live."

"Send over your bio, too, for the photo byline. Talk to you tomorrow."

Nick sat there alone for a bit longer. A woman at the bar smiled and seemed to be flirting with him, but he wasn't in the mood.

A certain anxiety ate at him. His instincts screamed that the painter had something to do with the slaying or had seen something. There wasn't a rational reason for it, the clues were all circumstantial, but the feeling persisted.

He wondered if cops felt the same sometimes; that knowing feeling overriding all the logic in the world.

The question was, would the cops even look at the photo the same way he did at all? Would they read between the lines? He had no idea and no real direction to go if they didn't.

Nick paid the bill and when the woman at the bar waved at him, he waved back. He headed back to the hotel, hoping the alcohol would help him sleep.

# 8

## HELPING OUT

The ringing of a phone invaded his muddled head and Nick tried to force himself awake.

When he finally did, he realized it was the shrill ringing of the hotel phone, not his own. The red light blinked as it rang on the side table.

He looked at the clock beside it. Neon blue numbers read "6:30."

He fumbled the receiver from the cradle and put it to his ear.

"Hello," he said, trying to keep the sleep from his voice.

"Nick! Don't you pay attention to your cell phone?"

The tinny voice on the other end of the line belonged to Ron.

"Not at night. I have one of those do not disturb apps. It will send notifications again in twenty-five minutes or so."

"Well, I've been trying to text and call, but kept getting nothing, so I tried the hotel phone. The police are here."

"Where?"

"The newspaper. They want the raw photo we were going to run."

"What? How did they even hear about the story? The paper isn't out yet is it? Even online?"

"Nope. They actually flagged my editor to run every story we might have on the hospital by them. He sent it over about an hour ago. The detective showed up here 15 minutes later demanding the photo and to know the source."

Nick groaned. This couldn't be a positive development.

"Want me to drive down now?"

"The paper is sending a car for you. Bring your laptop and your camera. The police might want more than you gave me."

"Alright," Nick said, feeling far from it. "I'll be downstairs in ten minutes."

"Make it five. Skip brushing your teeth and grab a breath mint. My editor is as nervous as a long-tailed cat in a room full of rocking chairs with all these cops around."

"Fine," Nick said, hung up, and headed for the bathroom.

Five minutes later he was in the back of a Town Car, a baseball cap hiding his disheveled hair, and hoping he did not smell as bad as he thought he did. Beside him on the seat were two bags, one containing his laptop, the other his camera.

He felt a headache coming on. His leg ached even though he felt well rested.

The drive to the paper seemed like it took a lifetime. Stop lights at intersections, though empty of cars, took forever to change. Finally, the driver pulled up in front of the newspaper building and parked behind a cop car and what appeared to be an unmarked car parked in front of it.

Nick sat in the car for a minute.

"Sir?" the driver asked.

"I'm fine," Nick said, grabbed his bags, and walked what seemed like an incredible distance to the front door. Ron opened it before Nick could even reach it and directed him inside.

"Follow me," he said, his face looking somber as well.

They walked into a conference room. Two men in suits with badges on their chest pockets sat on the opposite side of a long table flanked by two police officers. At the head of the table, a man Nick recognized as the editor in chief of the paper sat, arms folded. He turned back to the detectives and recognized one of them.

"Have a seat," Detective Martin said.

Ron moved further into the room and chose a chair. Nick sat next to him. He had to reach down and adjust the seat height to accommodate his large frame.

"Did you take this photo?" the detective began.

"Yes, I did," Nick said.

"When?"

"Sunday, midday or so? I can check my computer for a time stamp if you want."

"Not yet," the detective said, turning to Ron. "And you got this photo from him?"

"Yes, sir," Ron said.

"Do you know this man, the one doing the painting?" the detective addressed both of them.

"No," they both replied in unison.

"You're sure? Where are you from again?" he asked Nick.

"Seattle," Nick answered. "Just—"

The detective held up his hand and stopped him. "Before that?"

"Boston. That's where I grew—"

The detective stopped him again. "Is this the painter in your photo?"

A picture spun at him across the table, and Nick stopped it with his large hand. "Yes."

"You're positive?"

"You keep asking me that. What is this about?"

Another photo followed. This time it looked kind of like a mug shot, but more like an employee badge. The next sheet of photos that flew at him were actually mug shots, the familiar black and white numbers under the face of a man turned first to the left, right, and then straight ahead.

"Who is he?"

"He is a former employee of the Oregon State Hospital. He was suspected of abusing patients but never convicted. Until during the cleanup, when he was fired. He stalked Dr. Hawkins, who apparently was instrumental in his dismissal. This is his arrest photo after an incident that led to the filing of a restraining order."

"So, he did it?"

"We don't know that. This photo is evidence that he was on the property the next day, but we have nothing that proves he was there the night before, nothing that proves he even could have gotten in without being detected."

"What do you want from me?" Nick asked.

"You want to help, really help?" Detective Martin said. "You come in here like you're some Sherlock or something, sending us first after the wrong guy, and then showing up with this photo?"

"I'm sorry I was wrong before. This time, I just wanted my friend to run a positive story..."

"We got your hint. The story is going to run, all right. After that, you're going to go see if you can meet with our artist here and get him to confess."

"I'm afraid I'm better with pictures than with words."

"We'll help with the words part. We've got all the gear we need right here."

"Do I have a choice?" Nick looked around the room.

He met Ron's eyes, but his friend just looked down at his hands folded on the table.

The editor sat, stone faced, and stared a point somewhere on the wall. Somewhere Nick wasn't.

Neither detective showed sympathy at all.

"Fine. What do you want me to do?"

9

**FINAL MOVES**

Nick raised his camera and took a distant shot. The painter was not where he had seen him before, but that made sense. His painting had looked pretty much done when Nick saw him last. Who was to say he would even come back here to paint again at all?

The detective, that's who. The reason Nick was out here, walking around taking photos, looking for him.

"He's not done," Detective Martin had told him. "He'll be back, especially after he sees the article."

Nick took a wide shot of the museum entrance, one of the more regal views of the building, and walked northwest, hoping the painter did not show, and he could just move on. He still needed to grab some interior photos of the capitol building, and his little detective sideline was getting in the way of his real work.

*Never again*, Nick told himself. *This magazine shoot is a simple, fun assignment. Stay out of the news. Stay away from the papers and the cops. Just take your photos and move on. That is the assignment.*

That might work for the rest of the cities, but right now he was in the center of the investigation of a slaying in Salem.

Nick saw the painter, sitting near the street, easel set up, on a stool with his pallet on a companion stand. The painter. The suspect.

Nick walked toward him but did not get far. The man rose from the stool and walked toward him.

Nick raised his hand to wave.

"You!" the painter shouted. His hand came up, holding a brush, pointing it angrily. "You!"

Nick stopped walking. "What did I do?"

"You took that photo of me, the one from a distance, but you sold it."

"I didn't—"

"You sold it, and that newspaper guy blew it up. Showed my work before it was done. How can I ever sell it now?"

"I'm sorry, I—"

"Shut up. Let me see your camera."

Nick stood nearly a foot taller than the artist, but he felt threatened. Intimidated even. He slung the camera over his left shoulder and turned his body to protect it.

"No," he said. "I'm not giving you anything."

"You know what this means, you—you—jerk?" Clearly the man wanted to use stronger language, but his voice quivered.

*He's intimidated, too,* Nick thought. *You can use that.*

"I don't know what it means."

"The cops here, they already don't like me. They think that just because Dr. Hawkins got me fired, I hold a grudge and can't move on."

"Do you? Hold a grudge, I mean?" Nick asked.

"Of course, I do. You know what he did to my life?"

"No, I don't," Nick replied.

"Keep him talking," a voice said into a hidden speaker in his ear.

"Of course not. You're not even from here. Just some puke photographer passing through who couldn't mind his own business."

"Honestly, I did not mean to cause any trouble, for anyone." As Nick said it, he knew he meant it, too. He suddenly sorry for the guy in front of him.

"He destroyed my life and my career. And your photos could do that all over again. So, I want your camera. Now."

"No," Nick said again. He took a step back as the painter stepped forward.

"Give it here, you puke."

"No," Nick said again. Another step back. This man looked small, but clearly, he was dangerous. He's stabbed a doctor after all.

*Allegedly*, Nick corrected himself.

The painter dropped the brush into his pocket and pulled out a knife. The blade looked incredibly long, incredibly sharp.

"Hang on just a second," Nick said. His voice shook, and he instantly hated that. He was bigger and stronger. Standing up to this guy should be easy, especially with an audience in his ear and cops nearby to back him up.

"Not unless you want to be cut, just like that doctor. Give me the camera, Red, or I'll take it."

Nick took a step back and nearly tripped. Then he looked down at the painter, red faced, brown eyes shooting flames from his fearsome face. His arms were skinny, skinnier than Nick's lanky limbs.

"Fine. You know what, I'll give it to you," Nick said. His temper flared, something that didn't happen often, but once his red-head switch was tripped, there was no 'off' option.

He pulled the camera from his shoulder, aimed and took a shot. "You want this? The camera with pictures of you threatening me with a knife?" He took another photo.

"Stop it," the painter said, but Nick stepped forward.

"There, I took another one," he said. "Are you sure that's your good side?"

The painter stepped back. "Stop taking pictures you big gorilla and give me the camera before I cut you."

"Is this how it happened with Doctor Hawkins?" Nick taunted. "Did you threaten him, too? Try to intimidate him?"

"No! It wasn't like that at all."

"Really?" Nick snapped another photo, the click of the shutter sounding like a gun shot. He flipped to action mode, pushed the button again, and the shutter clicked six times.

"Stop!" The painter swung the knife, but Nick was too far away. He held his camera at the man's eye level and pushed the button again.

Six clicks, right in a row.

"What was it like then? Did you ambush him from behind? No. You couldn't have. I could tell from the stab wounds. You were facing him. Was it like this? Did he fight back?"

"No," the man stopped and laughed. "It wasn't like this. You should have seen his face. I'm sure he thought he would never see me again after court. But I snuck in a couple of times. Once to break open the hidden room, but you knew that."

"Of course, you would know where it was."

"No one knows this hospital better than I do."

"Why was he down there anyway?" Nick genuinely wanted to know.

"He went down there almost every night, into the old hallways. He should have been the one they fired. He is the one who abused those patients, not me. Now, give me the camera. Or I do you the way I did him."

"No," Nick said, and stepped forward again. As he did, the painter lashed out with the knife. Nick saw it coming, saw it was going to hit his arm. Wondered what it would feel like.

The painter's arm stopped in mid-air, and suddenly he was on the ground, a burly police officer on top of him.

"Nice tackle," Detective Martin told the officer. His hand clapped Nick on the shoulder, although he had to reach up to do so.

"Great job, kid. We got what we needed."

"Thanks," Nick said.

"I don't know what you were thinking going after him like that."

It was then Nick noticed how fast his breathing was. How light headed he suddenly felt.

"You need to sit down?" the detective asked.

Nick nodded and folded himself onto the grass. Ron walked up. "Great job, Nick."

Nick just nodded and laid back. He closed his eyes, just for a moment, and felt the grass on his back, the breeze on his skin.

Then he got up, shook Ron's hand. He shook the detective's hand too and gave him his number. He promised to send any relevant photos to him and walked away.

"Give you a lift to your hotel?" Ron said as he came up beside him.

"Sure," Nick said.

"How about an exclusive interview?"

Nick looked at his friend for a moment, weighing the consequences.

Emily was going to kill him for this one. Oh well, maybe his actual assignment photos would calm her down.

# MOVING ON

Nick spent the majority of the next morning at the capitol building. The odd-shaped dome was even more spectacular on the inside. He learned that the capitol of Oregon had not even always been Salem. It had moved from Oregon City to Corvallis and back again. The current capitol building was young in comparison to others, only in use since 1938. The building was actually completed in the height of the Great Depression with the Federal government's help, providing much needed jobs in the area.

This trip was turning out to be educational as well as an adventure.

He snapped some close ups of wooden railings and took overhead shots of the legislative rooms. Some school groups on field trips wandered in and out while he was there, making capturing all the photos he wanted a little harder.

Nick spent the afternoon going over what had happened, first with Ron and then with the police. After that, he packed up his bags, planning for an early morning departure.

He also uploaded his photos to the cloud folder, editing the best of them first, and ensuring none of those from the Oregon State Hospital and recent events were among them. He'd have to create another folder for the non-assignment related photos, maybe even use a different memory card or camera.

*That's my excuse to get a new camera,* he told himself. I could have two. *One for my freelance work and one for my other work.* He'd need a bit more money before he could pull that off.

By the time the photos were uploaded, it was nearly ten o'clock.

He went back to f/Stop Fitzgerald's to grab a drink.

The woman he'd seen at the bar, the one who waved at him the night before, was there.

She caught his eye as he came in and waved him over. He went, taking a stool next to her with a smile on his face.

"You come here often?" she asked and giggled.

"No," he answered. "Just in town on business."

"Business? What kind?" she asked.

"I'm a freelance photographer. Nick O'Flannigan by the way, but just call me Nick."

"I'm Sandra. Nice to meet you, Nick. Did you get all the photos you came for?"

"And then some," he said. "Honestly, I'm looking forward to being on the road again."

"I'm a photographer, too," she said. "But strictly local."

"That was me not long ago," Nick said. "Only in Seattle, not here. I never imagined I would land an assignment like this one." He went on to explain his proposed year of travel.

"That's a pretty ambitious timeline," she said. "And a lot of driving to do on your own."

"It is," he said, ordering another beer. "Tomorrow will be a long day."

"Where are you headed?"

"Sacramento."

"Wow. That is a trek. You should divide it into a couple of days and stop along the way. There are some great photo ops along the coast."

"I might do just that," he said.

"What do you shoot with?" Sandra asked.

"Olympus EM1X, for now. I would love to get my hands on the new model," he said.

"Nice! I shoot with a Cannon myself, but I'd love a new one, too."

The conversation descended into one about cameras, photos, and trying to make it as a freelancer.

Nick glanced at his watch after slowly nursing two beers. It was 12:30.

"I need to turn in. Long drive tomorrow."

"I get that," she said. "It was nice talking to you tonight."

"You, too," he said.

Sandra handed him her card. "If you ever need anything, any help along the road, feel free to call. Or just call anyway, for whatever reason, or next time you're in town."

"Sure," he said, smiling as he pocketed her number. "See you in a year." He handed her a card of his own.

"I'll follow your blog. Maybe if we are in the same place at the same time, we can get together for another chat."

"I'd like that," Nick said. She seemed really nice, and he wished a couple of things. First, that he did not need to get an early start in the morning. The second, that he could stay in Salem a little longer. But for the next year, he was a man on the move.

As he laid down to sleep, he wondered what tomorrow's paper would bring from Emily and others and what she would think of his photos.

*I'll have to call Gerry and fill her in,* he thought, and drifted off to sleep.

# AUTHOR'S NOTE: BAD THINGS AND GOOD INTENTIONS

This story talks, briefly, about some things that happened at the Oregon State Hospital. Unfortunately, those things are true. And this isn't ancient history, but it does have a happy ending.

We talk in more detail on our blog about this story, but briefly: in 2004, a room was discovered in the old sections of the Oregon State Hospital and became known as the "Library of Dust" or "The Room of Forgotten Souls." That is where the unclaimed remains of around 3,400 former patients were stored.

The resulting outcry sparked an investigation by the Oregonian, which won them a Pulitzer prize, and the outrage of the Oregon legislature at the deplorable practices at the hospital over the years.

Funding was allocated, the buildings were removed in some cases and new ones were created. A museum on the site chronicles the dark history of the institution.

The thing is, many of the people who worked in that system had good intentions. They were not bad people.

Mental illness is a huge problem in this country, and unfortunately it is being handled poorly. State budgets for public mental health are decreasing, and studies show that there are more mentally ill individuals in jail than in formal institutions. There are a variety of reasons for this, but they all trace back to one thing: a lack of both awareness and empathy.

If you or someone you love struggles with mental health, get help. And even if you are one of the few not touched by this yourself, understand that the problems are huge, the solutions not simple or cheap ones, and that even today in many state systems, bad things happen even when we have the best of intentions.

# FACTS ABOUT THE OREGON STATE CAPITOL BUILDING

Oregon's State Capitol building has an amazing history. The state capital moved from Oregon City to Salem to Corvallis, and back again. Two capitol buildings have burned and been replaced, and the current building has only been in existence since 1938. Even then, it was small, and two wings were added in 1977 to increase the space for offices and legislators.

That makes this a young capitol building, and a fascinating one. The cylindrical dome is a unique feature, and is topped by a gilded brass statue of the Oregon pioneer. An observation deck offers amazing views of the city on a clear day.

The building was completed in 1938 during the height of the great depression, one of the construction jobs funded by the Federal government to bring much needed jobs to the west.

You can take a virtual tour of the Capitol Building here, or better yet, visit in person next time you are in Oregon.

# STRANGLED IN SACRAMENTO

BOOK #3 IN THE CAPITAL CITY MURDERS
SERIES

# PROLOGUE: STRANGLED

This early on Sunday, the paved running trails circling McKinley Park were empty. It was one of Andrea's favorite times to run. The sun was not yet up, the shadows cool and playful. Water droplets turned every leaf into a myriad of crystals in the gray morning light. Whether it came from dew or sprinklers, she didn't care.

There are only two reasonable times to run in Sacramento in the summer months: early in the morning or late at night, that is, unless you went to the jogging center and ran the indoor track. That wasn't something she was into.

Her route usually took her through a couple of parks, but at the moment her favorite was under construction. "Park improvements," they said. "Your tax dollars at work," declared one sign. The trail around the park remained open for joggers like her. It was not that long, but a few laps still made for a great workout.

Andrea chose to run in the morning, not only because it was her favorite time of day, but simply because she knew herself. If she did not exercise in the morning, the likelihood she would hit the trails or the gym at night after a long day's work was slim.

And she prided herself for being in pretty good shape for a woman in her forties. She was single and liked it that way. She liked to do most things alone. Frequently, she wore a diamond on the ring finger of her left hand, not from some previous marriage but one she had purchased for herself. It kept guys at bay in bars, restaurants, coffee shops, and all of the other places they tried to pick women up.

Most men were scum. She could feel it when their eyes crawled over her, not wanting anything from her but that one single thing. They couldn't see her mind, her wit, and most never would. She wouldn't even let them get close.

That included running. All of her friends told her it was dangerous to go alone especially this early in the morning. The homeless problem in Sacramento was no secret even though she'd never had an issue herself. So, she carried pepper spray, never put in both headphones at the same time, and kept to well-lit parks and trails for the most part. She'd also taken a women's self-defense course and been a star pupil.

Of course, she had. Andrea had secrets. Things in her past that no one knew.

Ahead, she thought she saw movement beside the trail. She slowed and reached into her pocket to stop the music coming through her headphones. When she did, she heard rustling in the brush, and shifted into a walk, but didn't stop. Her heart rate, instead of slowing, sped up, and she could hear her breath follow suit. There was a new smell, a whiff of musk of some kind, or maybe...

Something was there. Or someone. The air was still, suddenly sticky even in the cool morning.

Andrea found herself walking instead of running.

Then she felt it. Something brushed her pony tail, something behind her. Before she could turn to see what it was, something stretched around her throat and pulled tight. She couldn't breathe.

Her first reaction was panic. How had she let this happen?

She tensed the muscles in her neck and managed a small hiss of air. Her attacker must have heard it, because whatever was around her throat tightened further.

Her instincts kicked in. Unable to look down, she picked up her right foot and stomped backward where she assumed a foot would be.

Hit! The blow hurt her heel, even through her running shoes.

Next, she threw an elbow backward, toward the attacker's midriff.

She struck something hard and unyielding.

Her vision narrowed to a small tunnel. Every sound around her seemed large and powerful. She swung with her balled fists, striking nothing but air. She switched tactics, clawing at her throat, trying to get at whatever was around it. It was made of cloth but didn't stretch and she couldn't work her fingers under it.

She couldn't see, taste, or smell. There was no air for that. She tried to shake her head, trying to somehow manage to get some oxygen in her lungs.

She threw her head backwards in one last desperate maneuver.

The back of her head struck something, and she heard a crunch. For a second, she snuck in a breath, but it wasn't enough. She needed more.

She threw her head back again, and this time struck something hard and sharp. The thing around her throat loosened some more.

Andrea gasped, trying to fill her lungs, holding on to what oxygen she could. The air tasted cool and sweet, but her throat stung and burned. She kicked out backward instinctively and struck something else.

The thing around her throat disappeared. Something fell to the ground. She tried to spin, and kick out at her assailant, but she was simply too dizzy. All she saw was a shadow.

"Hey! What are you doing?" she heard a voice from far away yet, she hoped close enough to make a difference. She swayed. The shadow ran.

Andrea fell toward the side of the trail, and landed on her side, hard. What little breath was in her lungs fled.

Andrea tried to scream. In front of her lay a woman, eyes open, rolled back into her head. Long brown hair lay splayed out on the grass beside the trail. One headphone remained stubbornly in her ear.

The woman's mouth was open, but she wasn't breathing. Bruises around her neck revealed why.

Andrea drew in a ragged, painful breath and tried to scream again. Instead, she started panting.

She heard a rushing in her ears. Her vision wavered again. She tried harder to slow her breathing, but it only sped up.

She felt hands on her shoulders, felt herself being rolled over, and heard a voice.

"Over here! She's still alive!"

She saw a kind looking, but frightened, man's face peering down at her.

*I'm safe,* she thought. Then, letting her mind go, her thoughts raced backwards into darkness and Andrea passed out.

**1**

---

# CALL OF DUTY

**N**ick took one last look around his hotel room in Salem. He had everything. He was sure. Nothing left in the bathroom, the small closet, or the hotel safe.

Heading for the lobby, he stopped briefly to check out, and grabbed two extra copies of the Salem paper on the way out. He was proud of his contribution to solving the case at the old Oregon State Hospital and his photos that the local paper had published. However, he was not sure yet who he would share the story with.

He didn't really want to tell his parents. His mother was already worried about his year-long trip around the country to photograph state capitol buildings for *Travel USA* magazine. She thought it would likely have an adverse effect on his freelance career and the business he had built in Seattle.

He didn't need to add that he'd been chasing down murderers, too.

His friend Gerry, the social media manager for *Travel USA* magazine and the reason he had landed this gig in the first place, already knew, at least, part of the story. And his editor, Emily?

Well, she already knew too, and didn't think of him as a hero as much as a slacker, butting his nose in where it did not belong. Luckily, his photos impressed her, but he had the feeling he'd better be careful.

His bag already felt heavy, his legs weary of travel, especially his right one, the one he'd injured in college. That was the one thing that had kept him, once a star athlete at Boston College and now a free-lance photographer, from getting into the NBA.

Walking from the dim hotel lighting into the sun, he popped the trunk of his car and tossed his bag inside. He took his laptop and camera bag up front with him and set them gently in the front seat. His laptop battery had nearly quit on him in Olympia and he wanted to make the computer last as long as possible. He'd hoped it would take him through this entire assignment, but had his doubts so Nick was being extra careful.

Next came his camera bag. Inside was an Olympus EM1X, but not the latest version. He lusted for a new camera as well, but this one actually worked just fine, especially on this assignment.

As he got in the car and connected his phone, setting the route to his hotel in Sacramento into his GPS, his phone rang. He pressed the button on the dash to answer.

"Hey, Gerry," he said.

"Hey, Nick. Saw the paper this morning. Very cool of them to use your photos."

"I thought so," he said. "I hope Emily shares your enthusiasm."

"Me, too," she said. "I bet you never thought your red-headed self would be famous for photography instead of basketball."

"Life does take strange turns," he said. "Thanks again for this assign-ment. I feel like it is really stretching me and doing me some good."

"Absolutely," she said. "I trust you and so does Emily. She can be gruff, but she loves your work so far."

"That's good to hear." Gerry was a good friend and never would be more than that, not because Nick didn't find her attractive, but because she was a lesbian. He missed her company though.

"How are you doing?" he asked. "Keeping busy?"

"Of course."

"Maybe you could fly over one of these times and spend a few days with me in one of these capital cities."

"That would be great. We need to plan ahead. Maybe we can even get Emily to pay for my ticket."

"Don't hold your breath," Nick said. "I would love to see you though."

"You driving down to Sacramento today?"

"Yep. It's a long drive, but I am going to do this one all in one shot."

"Drive safe," Gerry told him. "Text me when you get in."

"Will do," Nick told her.

Nick merged on to I-5, and then cancelled the directions on his GPS. It was a long drive, just over eight hours, but a simple one. He'd be on the same interstate the entire time.

A few hours later, Nick pulled into a gas station in Redding for snacks and some gas. When he got back into the car and back on the freeway, his phone rang again.

"Hey, Nick." It was Emily, his editor.

"Hey, Emily," he said, somewhat cautiously.

"Where are you today?" she asked.

"Redding, headed south," he told her. "I should be in Sacramento in just a few hours."

"No side trips, no mysteries this time?" she asked. At least, it sounded like a question. Or maybe an order.

"Straight on task this time."

"Great photos in Salem," she told him. "Good job."

"Thanks."

"And congrats on the newspaper byline. I know you're a freelancer and every bit of publicity helps."

"You're right about that," he answered. "I appreciate your understanding."

"As long as you keep doing your job, I am fine with it," she told him. "But don't get sidetracked and don't fall behind. This book is on a tight deadline, and that comes from higher up than me. The marketing guys are excited, but once we set a release date, we have to meet it."

"It will be tough, but I can do it," Nick answered. *I hope,* he added in his head.

"Keep it up," Emily said. "Let me know if you need anything."

The call ended. He wanted to talk to his parents, but not right now, and with the time difference between California and Boston where they lived, by the time he got in tonight it would be too late.

He'd have to call in the morning. Technically, tomorrow, Sunday, was his day off anyway. He'd probably do some picture taking and scouting like he had in Salem.

Maybe this week, if he kept his nose clean and on task, he could finish early and head to Carson City.

The rest of the drive was a quiet one. Soon the rolling fields of the agricultural sectors of California gave way to the outskirts of Sacramento. Nick had arrived at his next destination.

He decided to check in and grab some supper somewhere close to his hotel. Preferably something more nutritious than the road food he'd eaten all day.

2

___________

## A ROUGH START

As he exited his car, the first thing Nick felt was the heat. It was warm here, warmer than Salem, but not too humid. The sun was nearly ready to set, and his entire body ached from driving all day. He instantly regretted not leaving earlier in the day, so he could have gotten here sooner.

He popped the trunk, grabbed his luggage, and walked into the welcoming chill of the lobby.

"Hi there. Nick O'Flannigan," he told the desk clerk.

The clerk looked up at him, and kept looking up, even though he was standing behind the counter at his computer.

"Can I help you?" he asked.

"Yes, I have a reservation. I'll be here for the next week taking some photos of the state capitol building." He patted the camera bag hanging from his shoulder.

"Do you have a floor preference?" the clerk asked as he quickly typed on his keyboard.

"Something with a view, if possible," Nick said. "I work from the room often when I am not out taking photos."

"Okay, fill this out for me please, including your license plate number. I'll put you in 405."

Nick scribbled his now-memorized information onto the form. "Is there a place I can grab a light bite to eat that is pretty good and close by?" he asked as he finished.

"We have a restaurant here in the hotel," the clerk said. "They're known for their excellent food, and they have forty craft beers on tap."

"Sounds great," Nick said. He made his way up to his room, deposited his stuff inside, and headed for the lobby and the restaurant. He knew if he sat down in the room, he would lie down, and then he would not end up going out at all. Just in case he felt like taking a walk and a few photos before he came back up, he took his camera bag with him.

When he walked into the restaurant, Nick found the place surprisingly crowded. Nearly every table was full, and the smells in the room were amazing. Tables were well-spaced, covered in white tablecloths, and designed to seat either two or four. There were intricate centerpieces with candles in the center, and most of the diners were dressed in business casual attire. Nick was happy to be wearing, at least, a polo and khaki shorts, so he didn't feel completely out of place.

"Can I help you, sir?" a hostess asked.

"Sure. Just here for dinner," he said.

"Will it be just you dining this evening?"

"Yes."

"Table or bar? We have the full menu available there as well."

Nick looked over toward the bar and saw there were a few open seats. There were two next to a pretty attractive brunette who sat, legs crossed, staring into her drink.

"Bar, please."

"Go ahead and choose any seat you like. Let your bartender know anything you need." The host handed him a menu, and Nick made his way through the tables to the large oak island flanked by well-lit shelves filled with bottles.

He sat down with a seat between him and the brunette and pushed the stool back to make room for his long legs. He hung his camera bag on a hook under the bar made for purses, but it served his needs just as well.

The brunette glanced over, looked up at him, and then looked back down.

"What can I get you?" the bartender asked.

"I'm normally a porter or stout guy," Nick told him. "But with this heat, I was looking for something lighter. What do you recommend?"

"If you are a fan of sours, we have a great Blackberry Parfait from Fieldwork Brewing. They are local and do a good job. We also have their Fantastic Ideas pale ale on tap."

"Can I try a sample?"

"Sure," the bartender told him. "Be right back."

"Their Morning Time is a great coffee stout," Nick heard from his left. He looked and saw the brunette staring at him. "As long as you don't want to fall asleep anytime soon."

"It's been a long drive," he said. "So maybe I will try that tomorrow afternoon. I'm Nick, by the way."

"I'm Andrea, " she said. "Nice to meet you."

"Same," he said. "Thanks for the recommendation."

Andrea was pretty, with a delicate but straight nose and not-too-high cheekbones, green eyes, and a soft chin. Around her neck, she wore a loose scarf that seemed out of place even though the bar was cool. She wore a short-sleeved blouse and a longish skirt with a tie-dye pattern.

"Sure," she said. She smiled and went back to her drink.

Nick picked up the menu and looked at the soup and salad section. The burgers looked amazing, but he needed to stay with something light that would let him sleep but not put him into a food coma.

The bartender returned with his samples. The pale ale was almost too mild for his current taste, but the Blackberry Parfait seemed perfect.

"What do you think?" the bartender asked.

"I'll take the blackberry," he said. "And the grilled kale salad with a side of prawns."

"I'll get that in for you," the bartender said, and hurried away.

"The kale is an interesting choice," Andrea said. "I pictured you as more of a burger guy."

"I usually am," Nick answered, turning to face her. "It's been a long drive."

"Where from?" she asked.

"Salem," Nick said. He watched her and saw her eyes dart to the door, and then toward his camera bag. Something was off about her, he felt it. He just didn't know what.

"Sorry," she said, shifting in her seat. "I don't usually just talk to strange men in a bar."

"It's fine," he told her. "Things can get kind of lonely when you're traveling."

"Is that a camera bag?" she asked.

"Yes," he told her. "I am a freelance photographer on an assignment to visit each state capitol building in one year, taking photos for a new book."

"Oh. What do you shoot with?"

"An Olympus EM1X. It's a great camera, even though I'd love to have a newer one. This one is a few years old."

"I'm a bit of an amateur myself," she said. "I'd love to see your work sometime."

"Check out macrophotography4u.com," he told her. "Feel free to drop me a message sometime."

"Thanks," she said, and drained her drink just as Nick's beer arrived. "See you around."

She left, and a moment later, his salad and prawns arrived as well.

Nick dug in, finishing the food quickly, and sipping the beer as he went. As he ate, the restaurant and bar slowly emptied, other patrons finishing up as well.

It was a Saturday night. People were either headed home or headed elsewhere for more fun he supposed.

He drained the last of his beer and paid his tab. Grabbing his camera bag, he decided to go try to get some night shots of the city, maybe something unusual he could use on social media or his blog.

He took the camera out, fitted it with his standard lens, and slung the bag back over his left shoulder.

His right leg could use the walk and the stretch.

He left the hotel and took a right, heading toward downtown and the capitol building. Streetlights lit the sidewalk, and across the street, there was a park filled with grass and trees.

He took off at a brisk pace but was only a short distance down the sidewalk when someone ran into him, nearly knocking him over. All he saw was a masked face and pair of green eyes.

"Hey, watch it!" he said. But before he could react, a knife slashed out, cut his camera strap, and his attacker was running down the street taking the camera with him. The man was tall like Nick and his long legs carried him away quickly.

"Not today," Nick said as he secured his camera bag and ran after the would-be robber. He surprised himself by starting to close the distance between them.

As he ran, he pulled his phone from his pocket and dialed 9-1-1.

"What's your emergency?" the mechanical voice on the other end asked.

"Someone stole my camera," he said, panting. "He's running parallel to the park, headed north I think toward the capitol. I'm running after him." The sentence took longer to say than he wanted it to. He was out of breath already.

"Okay, stop chasing him," the voice said. "He may be armed and dangerous. We'll send a unit as soon as we can."

"I'm keeping him in sight," Nick told her and kept running.

He had been closing in on the thief. But his leg started to ache, and his camera bag, even sans camera, weighed on his shoulder with the lenses inside. He slowed as the man ducked into an alley up ahead.

Just then, a squad car pulled up, lights flashing. An officer got out. Nearly six feet tall, he was exceptionally lean, and locks of red hair poked out from under his cap. He wasn't young, but not old either, probably in his early 30's.

"You the guy who had his camera stolen?"

"Yep, that's me," Nick managed.

"Which way did he go?"

Nick pointed, panting. "Into that alley up there."

The officer spoke into a radio at his shoulder, and while he did so, Nick caught his breath. He heard sirens all around and glimpsed a police car moving rapidly down the street a block over.

"What's your name?" the officer asked.

"Nick O'Flannigan."

"What's your address?"

"I live in Seattle, not here. I'm just traveling through." He gave the officer the name of the hotel where he was staying and his room number, along with his cell phone number.

"Officer Terra," the cop said.

Nick shook his hand, and for the first time noticed his piercing green eyes, very similar to the ones of the man he had been chasing.

"Here's my card. If you think of anything, give me a ring. We'll be in touch, Mr. O'Flannigan. Don't worry."

But Nick was worried. If he didn't find his camera soon or replace it, he'd be behind and possibly out of a job. He shook his head in disgust and headed back to his hotel room.

# 3

## BEST LAID PLANS

Nick paced the room. He hadn't slept well, and he was up early, thinking. He held his cell phone in one hand and had his laptop open on the small desk provided.

His camera was gone, and despite the assurances from the police, he didn't hold out much hope of getting it back. The last thing he wanted was to call Gerry or Emily, his editor, and tell them his camera had been stolen.

But he couldn't just take photos with his phone. Even with the latest cameras, a pro could quickly tell the difference. He worked only with pros, and there was no way the photos would be high resolution and quality no matter what kind of talent he had.

Equipment mattered.

Maybe he would send them a reassuring email. One that promised the police were on it, and that he had a backup plan.

*What backup plan?* he thought. *What if the police don't find it?* Sure, he had been lusting after a new camera, but he didn't have the three thousand bucks to grab a new one, and he really didn't want to borrow the money, even though he probably could borrow it, either from his bank or from his parents.

Nick shuddered at that thought. They were already worried

enough about his adventure across the country. They certainly did not need to know he had been the victim of a crime.

He needed to call them anyway, but it would have to wait.

The first thing that needed to happen was Nick needed to figure this out.

So, he sat down and opened his laptop. At the same time, he turned on the television to the news, more as background noise than anything else.

As he looked down at his keyboard, he saw a card there, sitting askew over the keys. It was Sandra's, the photographer he had met in Salem.

Her cell number was right there. She had said she would love to travel, and he liked her.

*I wonder if she would come here and let me use her camera.*

*Bold move, Nick.*

He picked up the card between his long, thin fingers and looked at it. Felt the edges on his skin as he spun it around.

It might be too early to call on a Sunday. But if he was going to do something, he needed to do it sooner rather than later. Technically, it was still a travel day and his day off, but if he was not in touch soon, people would start to worry, and call on their own.

He opened his cell phone to dial, and froze, staring at the television.

"Woman Escaped Strangulation, Suspect Sought," the tagline underneath read. But he wasn't looking at that.

It was her. The woman who he'd met in the bar last night. She was on TV, the victim of a crime.

He turned up the volume.

"Saturday morning, a local woman narrowly escaped being strangled by what police are calling 'The Sacramento Strangler.' The woman would have been the fifth victim in as many weeks."

A police detective's face filled the screen. "What's unusual is that another victim was found at the same time. We think this victim must have come upon the killer just as he was leaving. Anyone who has seen anything unusual in the parks and elsewhere around Sacramento, please call the tip line on your screen."

"Do you have a description of the assailant?" the news anchor asked.

"No, unfortunately, the victim did not get a good look at him," the officer said. "But we do know he is a little over six feet tall, slim, and has green eyes. One witness said she thought the man who fled was wearing a mask."

*Sounds like the guy who stole my camera,* Nick thought. *And I met his escaped victim in the bar? What is going on here?*

He set Sandra's card aside. She would be his next call.

First, he called the tip line.

"Sacramento police tip line," a mechanical voice said. "All of our operators are currently busy. Your current wait time is estimated to be..." there was a pause. "Seven minutes. If you do not wish to hold, leave a call back number, and we will call you as soon as we can."

Nick followed the prompts and did just that but still he was anxious. He didn't have a tip per se, but he needed to know who the victim was, find her, and find out if she had anything to do with the theft of his camera. Her meeting him right before it was taken seemed too much of a coincidence. So was the description of the suspect.

In the meantime, he pulled out the card the officer had given him the night before and dialed the number.

"Officer Terra, I'm not available right now. Please leave a message, and I will get back to you as soon as I can."

Nick left him a message as well.

His frustration mounted. He knew who had taken his camera. Sort of. But he could not reach anyone. He could call the non-emergency police number.

*Think, Nick,* he told himself. *You have left two messages already. Patience.*

It was hard to have patience when his livelihood was on the line.

He needed a shower, but he did not want to miss a call back. It was still early, but it was Sunday. He would just leave a message for Sandra.

He grabbed her card again and dialed the number.

"Hi, Nick!"

"Sandra?"

"Yes. I was hoping you would call. Did you get to Sacramento okay?"

"I did," Nick said. "Thanks for asking. I have had a setback, though."

"Oh no. What happened?"

Nick took a few minutes and outlined the crime to her.

"Well, I would not hold out much hope for the camera," she interjected.

"Normally, I wouldn't either. But I know who took it, maybe."

"What?"

Nick explained seeing the woman on television, and the similar description of the strangler to what he glimpsed of the thief.

"That makes no sense. Why would a woman who has just been the victim of a crime be a part of another crime the next night?"

"I don't know," Nick said. "I've left messages for the police."

"I have an idea, if you are open to it," said Sandra. "It may sound a bit forward though."

"I'm listening," Nick said.

"I can take a couple of days off. If you can swing covering my hotel room in Sacramento, I will come down, bring my camera, and help you get some photos. You can use my gear."

"That's very generous," Nick said. "Let me see what I can do to get you a room where I'm staying. I really appreciate the offer."

"Hey, by the time I have to head back here, you will either have your camera back, or you will have that new one you have been wanting. Don't worry."

"I do worry," he said. "But thanks for offering to help. I'll call you as soon as I have the hotel information."

"It's a long drive. I won't get there until tonight, so I will head out now. Text or call when you have details."

"Thanks, Sandra. I barely know you. You certainly don't have to do this."

"It's my pleasure," she said. "I'm happy to help."

Nick hung up and sighed. He had a plan. Sandra would be here before he really had to start taking photos. He called the front desk, and easily secured a second room for her on the same floor where he was staying. He texted her the information and got a thumbs up emoji in response.

He should call his parents and Gerry, and leave out the camera theft and that story, at least until he had more information.

Then, he actually might go take some photos today with his phone while he waited. He could get the idea of some of the setup for some shots.

He would take some at the capitol, but he would also go somewhere else, maybe McKinley Park. It looked beautiful.

Besides, he might find some clues. Once again, despite the promises he had made himself, Nick was involved in another mystery. This one was his own though.

**4**

---

## MOTHERLY ADVICE

"**M**om?"

Nick only heard rustling sounds when she picked up the phone, then a heavy clunk.

"Nick!" she said with excitement. "Your father and I were just talking about you."

"All good things, I hope."

"Of course!" she said. "How is your new little project coming along?"

He made the decision right then. Until he had to, that was if he ever had to, Nick would not be telling them about his missing camera. No way.

"Everything's fine, Mom. Things are going great," he sighed. "How are you guys?"

"What was that sigh, Nick? I know my little—I mean big—boy."

"Just a minor setback last night, Mom. Things will be fine."

"What happened?"

So much for not telling his parents. Nick could leave a lot out when he talked to them but lying, he could not do. Besides, he wasn't good at making up stories on the spot. Not a wordsmith, he was much better with photos.

"My camera was stolen," he told her. "But the police are on top of it. And I have a friend coming tonight with one I can borrow in the meantime."

"Do they know who took it?"

"Yes," he said. It was only a little white lie. He had called the tip line and left his number, and the police would know as soon as they called him back.

"What's going on?" he heard his father yell in the background.

"Someone stole Nick's camera!" his mother yelled without talking the phone away from her mouth. Nick winced.

"What? We're buying him a new one!" his father's deep voice responded, now closer. He was yelling, too, though not directly in to the phone.

"No, the police are trying to find it!" his mother answered.

Nick held the phone at arm's length as he listened to them argue.

"We're buying him a new one and that is final!"

"No, we're not! Not until we know if they found his old one."

"How can he do his job without a camera? He's a photographer!"

"He has a friend with one he can borrow."

"Why didn't you say that?" his father must have been closer, his yelling much louder. Both parents appeared to have forgotten that he was on the phone.

"I was. You didn't let me finish."

"You paused!"

"You never let me finish!"

Nick heard the familiar ping of a call trying to ring in, and saw it was a Sacramento number on the screen.

"Mom!" he yelled into the phone. "I have to go. I have another call. I will call you back later."

"What?" he heard, just before he pressed the red button to end her call, and the green one to accept the new one.

"This is Nick," he said.

"Hi, Nick. This is Officer Gluch from the Sacramento police department. You have a tip for us?"

"I do," he said. "I'm not sure how helpful it will be."

"Okay. What do you have?"

Nick took a deep breath and told the story of the theft of his camera the night before. "I'd describe the man who took my camera the same way you did the suspect on TV. Tall, over six feet but shorter than me, with green eyes. He was wearing a mask."

"He stole your camera?"

"Yes. I filed a report with Officer Terra last night."

"Okay. Let me look it up. In light of this, he may want to follow up with you sooner rather than later. Would that be okay?"

"Sure. This is my cell. He can call me anytime."

"Perfect. Thanks for your help, Mr. O'Flannigan."

Nick ended the call, tossed the phone on the bed, and paced back and forth. It would be hours at best before Sandra was here, and he hated just waiting.

He'd go down to McKinley Park, grab a bite to eat, and take some photos with his phone. It wasn't ideal by any means, but he would be doing something.

His stomach growled, and he realized he also needed some more coffee. He was sure there would be someplace worthwhile nearby.

He grabbed his phone and checked the distance to the park. It was a twelve-minute drive, maybe a bit longer with the construction he'd seen around downtown, plus time to find parking.

Tiferet Coffee House was right around the corner on H Street. Then he noticed, in frustration, they were closed on Sundays.

But there was the Original Mel's Diner, a local chain that looked like they had pretty good breakfast, or in this case, brunch. And coffee. They had coffee.

Nick headed down to his car and left the hotel. It was going to be a long day, and he might as well start it out with some good fuel.

# 5

## CAPITOLIZATION AND SANDRA

The Original Mel's Diner was as advertised. American diner style food, good coffee but nothing fancy, and a simple atmosphere.

Nick clearly stood out from the crowd, but he usually did. The red hair combined with his height was both a curse and a blessing. No one who met him ever forgot his name, but on the down side, anyone who had met him would recognize him on seeing him again.

The one thing this travel assignment offered him was some brief moments of anonymity, and he enjoyed those when they came.

He folded himself to fit onto one of the stools at the bar.

"What can I get ya'?" the waitress was short and round, only a few inches taller than Nick when he was sitting. She wore a pink dress and a white apron and pulled out a small notebook and a cheap pen to take his order.

"I'll try your bacon, egg, and cheese bagel."

"How do you want those?"

"Scrambled."

"Hash browns okay, or you want to substitute something else?"

"Hash browns are fine."

"You got it. Anything besides coffee?"

"Water," he said.

"No problem. Be right up, hon."

Nick smiled. He looked up at a TV in the corner and saw the local news and the woman's photo on the screen.

"I better have some answers soon," he said to himself.

A few moments later, his food came, and Nick took a quick overhead shot of the simple presentation, posting it to his Instagram. He added the hashtags #phonepic #AmericanBreakfast.

He dug in and finished in just a few moments.

He paid the bill and then headed for the park at a brisk pace.

He could immediately see why people liked the park. A giant cedar sat in the center of a grassy area, and kids played noisily on a playground just behind it. A well-marked, paved trail circled the park and even though it was pretty warm, joggers wearing headphones passed him as he walked down the trail. Gorgeous roses decorated the path, and he occasionally glimpsed the lake in the middle of the park through the trees.

Nick didn't know exactly where the strangulation attempt and the actual strangulation had occurred, but he assumed that would be obvious. There would still be crime scene tape and markers he also assumed, and maybe even an officer watching the scene.

*I mean, the criminal usually returned to the scene of the crime, right?* he thought to himself.

The police would expect that and be watching.

Except, of course, this was not your typical criminal. How many strangulations had there been? "Four in five weeks," the news had said. Andrea would have been the fifth.

This wasn't even a serial killer. This was more of a spree killer, at least from what little he knew.

*Why are you getting involved, Nick?* he asked himself.

*Maybe it's related to my camera,* he answered. It was more than that though, and he knew it. First in Olympia, then in Salem, he had helped solve local cases, and if he admitted it to himself, he liked playing at detective and was proud of how his eye for detail made him good at it.

As he rounded one corner, he saw it. Clearly, the crime scene tape had once stretched across the trail, but now it was just around one area of bushes beside the trail. There was no one guarding it, but there was a sign attached to the tape.

"Keep out, by order of the Sacramento Police Department."

Nick pulled out his phone, opened the camera app, and made some adjustments to the settings.

He walked around the scene, carefully avoiding the tape, but shooting photos as he went, several at a time.

He even knelt and, using the new portrait mode, blurred the background and focused on the crime scene tape. It would make a great shot for his social media profiles.

"Hey buddy, can't you read?"

Nick stood and turned toward the voice. A slim, uniformed cop looked up at him.

Nick put on a smile to hide how nervous he felt.

"I didn't go inside the tape. I'm just taking a few photos. I'm a freelance photographer."

"Hey, if you are a member of the press, take it up with the PR department. You're taking photos with your phone?"

"My camera was stolen last night. I'm waiting for it to be found."

"Oh really? Did you file a report?"

"Yes, sir."

"What's your name?"

"Nick O'Flannigan."

"Wait right there, Mr. O'Flannigan."

The officer stepped a couple of feet away and spoke into the radio mic at his shoulder. He was clearly athletic, in good shape, and wore some kind of boots that looked pretty comfortable, even in this heat. Every cop he'd met here seemed well-trained and polite. Nick could hear tinny voices but not make out the words.

The officer walked back over. "You're free to go, Mr. O'Flannigan. Please don't take photos of a crime scene without permission, though. Technically, I could confiscate your phone. Dispatch told me that you might have given us a lead on the perpetrator, and I understand your frustration. But don't come around again, not without a media pass from the department."

"Understood," Nick said. "Have a great day."

He turned and walked away but could feel eyes on his back. He checked his watch. It was only two. Sandra would not be here for another few hours.

He walked back toward the diner and where he had parked his car, and then got in and drove toward the capitol building. He might as well walk and look around the mall area rather than go back to the hotel to sit and wait. As he turned the corner onto P Street his phone rang again. It was Gerry this time.

"Hi, Gerry," he said with a sigh.

"Nick, you alright?"

"I could be better." He told her what was going on.

"Don't worry, Nick. You have time. You just got there. Give the police time to do their jobs. Now, tell me about this Sandra."

"She's nice."

"You said that, Nick. Tell me more."

"I don't know much more," Nick said. "I'm on the road for a year. I like her, but I'm not looking for a relationship if that is what you are implying."

"Oh, Nick," she said. "You are so naive. She's coming from Salem to help you?"

"Yes."

"Why do you think that is?"

"I don't know."

"She likes you, Nick. She's hoping you feel the same."

Nick sighed. "I don't need any drama, Gerry."

"Don't worry about it. Just go with the flow."

"I plan to."

"If something sparks, don't be afraid to pursue it. Who knows, maybe you could partner up at some point, and help each other out."

"We'll see," he said.

"And you'll find your camera."

"Or mom and dad will buy me a new one," Nick told her. "Thanks for cheering me up. I just hope you are wrong about Sandra."

"I'm not. And you actually don't want me to be wrong. Hope your week gets better. I have a feeling it will."

"Thanks, Gerry. I think."

"Oh, were there any photos on the memory card?'

"A few. Nothing really important."

"Well, my friend told me about a new app. She's a bit of a computer geek. It lets you recover deleted or damaged files from the card even if someone intentionally or accidentally deletes them."

"Sounds cool. Send me the information, and I'll download it. Might be a good idea anyway."

"Of course. Talk to you later."

"Wait!" he yelled into the phone. "Please don't tell Emily. Not yet."

"I won't, Nick. I have your back."

Just as the call ended, he turned onto G Street and saw a parking space. He took it. This would be close enough for now, and he really could use the walk to clear his head.

Maybe he was hoping Sandra liked him after all. At least for this week, he would have some company.

He wandered toward the capitol building and found that his phone took some pretty great photos once he got it set up right. He took his time going through the area around the capitol mall, even taking photos of all the interpretive signs in the park. There was a lot of history in this small area. Sacramento had been a boom town, and from the look of things, was still a thriving metropolis.

These weren't photos he would use for the book, at least probably not, but for his social media, they were perfect. The hours passed quickly, and as he was setting up for a wide shot of the capitol from the south side, his phone buzzed in his hand.

It was from Sandra. "Just got into town," the text read. "Where are you?"

"Downtown by the capitol building," he typed back. "Meet you at the hotel in fifteen."

"I'll get checked in," she replied.

Nick looked at his phone and smiled. Twenty-four hours in town, and finally something was going right.

It took him a few moments to walk back to his car, and then a few more to drive to the hotel. Once inside, the clerk greeted him.

"Your guest has arrived," the tall man, wearing a name tag that said, "Walter," told him.

"Thank you, she texted me. Any good spots to eat nearby? I tried the hotel restaurant last night but had a bad experience afterward."

"So I heard, Mr. O'Flannigan, and on behalf of the hotel staff, I am sorry about your camera. I do hope it is found."

"Me, too," Nick answered. "The restaurant?"

"Binchoyaki is great for Japanese cuisine. The Empress Tavern is also quite impressive. Both are appropriate places for a date."

"Oh, we're not dating," Nick said. "We're just—"

"We're what?" Sandra said from behind him.

"I'm. I... We are just, or rather I am..."

"Yes?" she asked, cocking her head. She smirked. Sandra was wearing a summer dress with a V-neck, cut low, but not too low. She wasn't too petite, but not overweight either. She was taller than Nick remembered, unless...

He looked down, accidentally checking out her legs as he looked at her shoes. Nope. No heels. Sneakers in fact, sensible ones. Good attire for a photographer.

"We're friends," he managed. "And I am taking her to dinner because she is generous enough to let me borrow her camera."

"How nice of you, ma'am," Walter said. "And good evening to you both."

"So, Japanese or American?" Nick asked once they moved toward the lobby doors.

"Japanese, please," she said. "And it doesn't have to be your treat."

"Thanks," he said. "We'll take my car. Shall we?"

Sandra looked up at him. "We shall."

He followed her out of the hotel and toward his car.

Dinner was great. The food was amazing. The conversation was even more so. Nick had forgotten how much he enjoyed female company. It had been a while since he had been on a date, and while he tried to convince himself this wasn't one, it certainly felt like one.

They talked about family, and she laughed when he described his parents and their desire to buy him a new camera.

"Maybe it's not a bad idea to have a spare," she said, echoing his thoughts from earlier that day. "It almost makes sense."

*What are you doing, Nick?* he asked himself as they headed back to the hotel. *You're on a year-long trip around the country that, really, just started.*

"What's wrong?" Sandra asked. "You just looked a little troubled."

"Just thinking about my camera, and this week," he lied.

"Don't worry. I'm here to help," she said, and brushed his arm as he drove.

It felt good. He liked it.

"Thanks," he said. Maybe he liked it too much.

The rest of the drive was quiet.

When they got to the hotel, he walked Sandra to her room and told her goodnight.

"I'll see you in the morning?" she asked.

"Of course," he said. "We can get started then."

When he got back to his room, Nick fell into bed right away. He dreamed of a photo shoot in a tropical location. Sandra was with him and they were happy. The sun was warm and he wasn't worried about a thing.

## ANOTHER MANIC MONDAY

Nick's phone rang, and he sat up in a panic. Still dressed in his clothing from the night before, and lying on top of the covers, he struggled to remember where he was and what happened.

Sandra. Sandra was here.

They had gone to dinner.

He fumbled for his phone. It was Emily, his editor.

"Good morning," he said, trying not to sound groggy.

"Good morning, Nick, I hope you're ready for a great week?"

"I am."

"No mysteries so far this week? No dead bodies, missing persons, anything I should know about?"

Nick paused, and he knew the pause was a mistake. But he wasn't a good liar. There was no way not to tell her without somehow bending the truth.

"Really, Nick?" she said. "You've been there for a whole two days, and already you are involved in something?"

"Okay, Emily," he said. "Saturday night, my camera was stolen."

"Stolen? Nick, that's terrible. How did it happen?"

Nick outlined the events for her, trying to tell her only what he had to. Yes, he'd contacted the police. Yes, they had a description of who might have done it. He realized about halfway through the explanation that he really had to pee. He got up and started pacing as he talked.

"Do you need a loaner camera? Is this going to put you behind?"

"I'll be—"

"Because if it is, that is okay. This is a valid excuse. Oh, I'm so sorry, Nick. This must be awful for you."

"Emily, it is okay. I have a friend who has a camera I can use. I'll get the photos and get them on time. If the police don't find my camera soon, I'll get a new one. My parents have already offered—"

"Good, good." Emily did not even let him finish his sentence. "That is good news. Maybe we can get you some traveler's insurance or something. I'll look into it. Everything else good? Computer? Car?"

"Yes, it's fine," he said. He thought briefly of the blue screen scare in Olympia but decided to leave that tidbit out. If the tenant subleasing his apartment continued to work out, maybe he'd get a new computer, too.

*Maybe letting mom and dad buy me another camera wouldn't be so bad after all.*

"Okay. Listen, sorry about giving you a hard time. I just get concerned, you know. Deadlines and all that. Marketing is up my butt already to get some early shots from some of the places you visit. We may want you to start blogging at some point."

"Okay," Nick said. His urgent need was starting to override all thought and even the ability for him to make conversation. "Can we talk about this later, Emily? I have something I really need to take care of."

"Sure," she said. "We'll talk later. I'm looking forward to your photos. What will you be shooting with?"

Now he was really pacing, getting closer and closer to the bathroom door. There wasn't much room to move in this suite, so his route was limited.

"A Canon, I think. I'll know more in a couple of hours. Talk to you later, Emily." Nick ended the call and then burst into the bathroom, barely making it.

As he completed his quite urgent task, his phone rang again.

"For the love of—!" he exclaimed. The screen read "Gerry."

"Good morning, Gerry," he said.

"How'd last night go?"

"It went fine. We're going to take some photos today."

"Okay, do you—"

"Gerry, don't start." Nick was getting irritated. "I'm not in the mood. I've got to figure this out."

"Okay, Nick, I just want you to be okay. And to be happy."

"Don't worry about it. I am perfectly happy."

"You don't sound like it. What has gotten into you?"

"Look, my camera was stolen. My parents are being, well, my parents. Emily is almost too helpful and clearly anxious. I have a 'friend' here to help me who clearly wants to be more than a friend, but I am on the road for a year. I am only in the third city. It's just a lot, Gerry. A lot."

"I get it, Nick. I really do. I won't press any more. About the girl, or anything."

"Look, I'm sorry—"

"I'm sure you will feel better later. Talk to you then."

Gerry ended the call, and Nick just stared at his phone. As he did, it rang again.

"Damn it," he muttered, but answered the Sacramento number.

"Hey, Mr. O'Flannigan, Officer Terra here."

"Hi there," Nick said. "I hope you have good news."

"I do and I don't."

"Okay."

"Thanks to you we have a lead on the killer and your camera thief, maybe."

"Maybe?"

"Yes, sir. With your description, we were able to compare video footage outside of your hotel with the footage of people entering and leaving McKinley Park, and we found a possible match. We don't have a good description of his face, just his eyes, similar to what you described. But we do have an idea of his build and height."

"That's the good news?" Nick was exasperated, and he knew his irritation showed through in his voice, but he couldn't hide it.

"We also saw something unusual. The suspect was with a woman."

"A woman?"

"The footage is grainy, but she appears to match the description of the latest victim, the woman you talked to in the hotel bar."

"That's great! Why don't you ask her who he is?"

"Because the address she gave us is wrong. Turns out she doesn't live where she said she did, and we can't find her. The number she gave us has been disconnected."

"How is any of this good news, Officer Terra?"

"We're making progress, Mr. O'Flannigan, and you may be able to help."

"How, exactly, would I do that?"

"Keep an eye out for this woman. We have no idea why a victim might be working with the man who tried to strangle her, but that appears to be exactly what is going on. If you see her, call this number. The one I just called you on. It's my cell. I'll have it on all the time, until we solve this case."

"Okay. Any leads on my camera?" Nick felt stupid and selfish as soon as he said those words. They were talking about a killer here, and some weird things going on. But those things did involve his camera, and that camera meant a lot to him. Photography was not only his job, but his life.

"Nothing at local pawn shops. We're looking, Mr. O'Flannigan. The theft, the murders, and the woman you met? They all seem to be related. If we find the answer to one, we'll find the answer to them all."

"Thanks," Nick said, and ended the call. He saved the number to his phone under Officer Terra, and then looked around the room. He pulled off his shirt from the night before, sniffed, and tossed it toward his bag. His pants followed.

*First a shower. Then breakfast. Then a simple day of taking pictures. It's only Monday. I have time.*

He shaved before jumping in the shower, something he would often skip, but Sandra was here, so he wanted to at least seem like he cared. The water felt good. He had to duck to wash his hair, but hotel showers were rarely tall enough for regular people, let alone a six-foot-six former basketball star. It could have been much worse. Some would hit him in the navel, and he would practically have to kneel.

The towels were adequate, but since he would be traveling so long, he had considered getting his own. Hotel towels were often too small, and usually they were cheap, meaning rough material often ineffective at drying.

He wrapped the towel around his waist, a job it was barely adequate for, and went to pick out his clothes for the day. As he did, there was a knock on the door.

He looked out the peephole and saw Sandra standing there.

"Just a minute!" he called out.

So much for taking his time deciding what he would wear.

# 7

# PICTURE THIS

The Capitol Mall was crowded. There were a few joggers, some business people passing through on their way to work, but there were also at least four classes of children walking around, looking excitedly at signs, and talking loudly to each other.

In fact, he and Sandra had circled several times looking for parking. The buses took up four spaces each, and they were scarce anyway. The parking problem was compounded by ongoing construction.

Sandra had a nice Canon. The EOS R was comparable to the EM1X Nick usually carried, with some exceptions. It took a few shots for him to adjust, but she was very helpful at giving him direction.

They took turns shooting. All four sides of the capitol building were equally photogenic in unique ways. While Sandra had the camera, Nick snapped a few shots with his phone just to see what it would capture and do some comparisons later.

She had a great macro lens and Nick snapped some shots of the flowers outside, and various other objects with the capitol building in the background or as part of the shot. Sandra watched as he did so, fascinated.

In one case, he took a photo of one of the traffic pillars on the north side, the posts that kept cars from driving onto the sidewalk. The state seal decorated the top of it, and it made a great shot. He switched to his phone and took a pretty good shot he thought would work well for a social media post.

As they headed toward the capitol steps, Nick knelt and took a shot of the state flower, the California Poppy, sometimes known as the "Cup of Flame," growing in a cluster of others nearby. He got the steps in the background, and even a glimpse of the shot on the tiny camera screen told him he had a winner.

Just as he was about to head inside, a huge class, or rather, a group of classes crowded onto the steps. A guide stepped in front of them with a PA system of some sort and started to talk.

"Welcome to our state capitol building," she said. "I'll be your guide. Please stay together and don't wander from the group. We are going to start on the second floor, go downstairs, and then up to the top floor and talk about the capitol dome."

As the guide droned on, Nick felt a hand on his arm.

"They are going to be a while," Sandra said. "And it will be a real challenge to get the shots you want."

"You're right," Nick said, handing her camera back to her. He'd been on a roll, but the large group of students killed his vibe.

"Why don't we grab some lunch?" she said. "My treat. We can come back this afternoon, or even tomorrow to get some inside shots. Maybe we can get some night shots tonight?"

"Good idea," Nick said. "Maybe we can kick around old Sacramento for a while, even do some sightseeing."

As he said it, Nick realized just how tired the morning of shooting had made him. His shoulders ached, he was both hungry and thirsty, and he felt the start of a stress headache coming on. The whole point of this assignment, and of his life really, was to enjoy what he was doing. He needed to slow down, to remember that.

"There's a Starbucks across the street. Let's grab a coffee while we decide where to eat," Sandra suggested.

His stomach growled and Nick just nodded. The caffeine would help his headache, and he was hungry.

Sandra put her camera back in its bag, zipped it up, and they headed across the street.

The coffee shop was not too crowded, and they got their order right away. The two of them sat together at a corner booth and went through the photos on Sandra's camera, studying them on the small screen.

"I should have brought my laptop," Nick said. "I'm a little off my game."

"That's understandable. Once we get some lunch, we can head back to the hotel and upload them if you need to."

"I'll get them done tonight," he said. "There is no reason to rush. There is plenty to see here in Sacramento. We might as well enjoy the town. It's my first time here, and I know I won't be back anytime soon."

"That's not a bad thing," she told him. "You're going to see some pretty cool stuff over the next year."

"True," he said. "I just want to make sure I make the most of this assignment."

"You will," she said. "Shall we search for restaurants?"

"Sure. I was hungry before. Now, I am starving."

He opened the maps app on his phone and entered "restaurants near me."

"Firestone Public House is close," he told her. "They just opened at 11."

"Sounds good," she said after looking quickly at his phone. "There are plenty of others to try. We have an entire week."

She stowed the camera again, and they walked down the street, pointing at various things they saw long the way.

"Maybe we can hit some museums this afternoon," he told her once they were seated. "Do you have a spare memory card?"

"Of course. Why do you ask?"

"In Salem, I uploaded some photos to the magazine cloud server that were not exactly on point with the assignment," he told her. "My editor was less than thrilled. I'm trying to avoid accidentally doing that again."

"Great idea," she said. "I'll load it after we eat."

Nick ordered a beer and dug into the Rueben he'd ordered. Sandra ate a steak salad, and even offered him a taste. He gave her a bite of his sandwich. Both were excellent.

The afternoon passed quickly. Old Town Sacramento and the railroad museum were both spectacular. Nick started to relax, even feel better about the way things were going. He would get his photos. Even if they did not find his camera, he would get a new one.

Things were going to be fine. He didn't think about the strangulation victim or the theft at all that afternoon.

"I need to head back to the hotel," he finally told Sandra. "I'll upload the photos from this morning and change before we go to dinner."

"We're going to dinner together?" she said, a twinkle in her eyes.

"Well, I assumed…" Nick trailed off. "Would you like to have dinner with me?"

"I'd love to," she said. "I'll pick the place."

"Sounds good," Nick told her as they arrived at the hotel.

"Here's the memory card from this morning," she told him, handing it over. "I'll text you when I am ready. Is an hour enough time for you?"

"Sure," he said, and took the card from her.

When he got back to his room, Nick opened his laptop, plugged in the memory card reader, and opened it.

The card was blank. There was not a single photo on it or even a single file.

# 8

## SECONDS AND SECRETS

The blank spot in the screen stared back at him. A morning's worth of work, somehow gone. They had looked at the photos at the Starbucks, and, at some point, Sandra had switched the memory cards. Hadn't she?

Nick was sure she had. He hadn't seen her do it, but he was pretty sure.

He picked up his phone to text or call her, and then hesitated.

If the photos were not still in her camera, or if she had not given him the wrong card, he would probably be furious. Maybe even unable to enjoy dinner with her.

There had just been too many setbacks on this trip already. Too much had already happened. On the other hand, he wanted her to like him, see him as cool headed for a red head, which he normally was.

He took a deep breath.

*Calm, Nick. Calm. Either way things will be alright.*

He decided to call. He pressed the phone button next to her name.

"Nick?" she asked. He could hear water running in the background.

"Uh, sorry to interrupt," he said. "The SD card you handed me was blank. Can you check—"

"Oh my God, Nick. I think I forgot to switch it out. Hang on."

The phone clattered to a surface. Nick could still hear the water running, and for a moment could picture Sandra in a towel or robe, opening her camera bag, looking inside. He didn't want to picture the scene but could not stop himself. He felt uncomfortable.

"They're here!" he heard in the background, then she picked up the phone. "They're here, on the camera still!"

"Oh good," he said.

"You want to come get them?"

Again, the image of her getting ready for the shower, or maybe a bath, swam into his mind.

"No, no. Go ahead and get ready. So will I. Text when you're done, and we can meet in my room before we go to dinner."

"Sounds good," she said. "So sorry, Nick."

"No problem." He ended the call.

He headed for the shower, tossing his clothes aside as he went. He would need to do laundry or drop his off somewhere sometime this week.

Then he thought of Sandra. She got to go home after this, back to Salem. This was a little vacation for her.

For him it was a long vacation and a lot of work. He thought of Seattle, his apartment, and home as he showered. He stayed under the hot water longer than he really needed to.

Just as he got out, his phone dinged.

"You ready?" the text read.

"Ten minutes," he replied. Then he hurried through dressing and brushing his teeth to make sure it was true. He wore khakis and a casual button up shirt, something he hoped would pass for wherever Sandra chose for them to go.

Promptly ten minutes later, he heard a knock. Nick took one last look in the mirror and then answered the door.

She looked gorgeous. A blue shimmering dress flirted with the tops of her knees. She wore heels, but not ones that were too high.

Gaps in the sleeves exposed her shoulders, and her dark hair was tied back in what Nick assumed was a "messy bun" that hid its length.

Sandra handed over the memory card. "You look nice," she said. "How about Mulvaney's B & L?"

"I've heard good things. Did you call for reservations?"

"It's a Monday night, how busy can they be?" she asked. But she opened the search app on her phone.

Nick turned and slid the memory card into his computer adapter. Personal photos were mixed with the capitol building ones, and he carefully separated them into folders on his hard drive preparing the right pictures for upload to the cloud file he shared with his editor.

"Well, not busy at all, it turns out." Sandra showed him her phone, pointing out that the restaurant was closed on Mondays. "But I made reservations for tomorrow night through their online system if that's okay."

"Sure," Nick said, running his hands through his hair. It had already been a long day. "What would you say to staying in tonight, ordering some Chinese, and just relaxing? We can look through these photos and I can get at least the outside pictures edited?"

"Sure," she said. "Your room or mine?"

He saw it was meant to be a joke and laughed. It felt good to relax.

She kicked off her heels and flopped on to the small couch in the suite portion of the room.

"I'll make the call."

Once the food arrived, they spent the evening going over photos, uploading some to the cloud, and a few to his website. He would post some to his social media profiles, and watermark and keep others exclusive to his site. The television played some shows from a local channel, but neither one watched. It was just background noise.

Sandra watched in fascination. "You make a living at this?"

"A decent one," he said. "Nothing extravagant. Don't you?"

"Sort of. I have an inheritance. Some investments. While I do need to make some money, I don't need to make as much as many people do. It frees me up to pursue my passion without too much worry."

"Very nice," he said. She leaned close over his shoulder and pointed at the screen.

"That's a great one," she said.

He smelled her perfume and found that he liked her being close. Her presence in his personal space gave him an odd comfort, something he hadn't gotten from anyone in a long time. He smiled up at her and their eyes met for just a moment.

Nick broke eye contact and looked at the photo of the state flower with the steps in the background. It was pretty good. He put it in the magazine file rather than the one for his website.

He did a quick double check of that folder, and then clicked to move it to the cloud.

"Fortune cookie?" she said as Nick turned around.

"Sure," he said, taking one and breaking it open.

The small piece of paper fluttered to the ground, and as he bent to get it, he saw the television had switched to the local news.

"Breaking News," the banner at the bottom of the screen said. "Sacramento Strangler Strikes Again" was in smaller letters under that.

Over the news anchor's left shoulder was an artist's sketch. He scrambled for the remote and turned up the sound.

"—another victim, this time found by the river, appears to be a victim of the Sacramento Strangler. A warning. The next few photos are graphic." A few photos flashed on the screen along with victim's names.

"Although one victim did manage to escape, she has not been seen since she reported the crime, and police are worried for her safety." Another photo appeared on the screen, showing the woman he had met in the bar, but without the scarf. He could clearly see bruising on her throat. But it looked...

Nick spun back to the desk and opened a browser on his laptop. He typed in the website for the channel they were watching.

He clicked on "Streaming Live Video."

A hand touched his shoulder and he jumped.

"Nick, what are you doing?" Sandra asked.

"Something is different. Something is wrong with the bruises on the woman who lived. They don't seem like the others."

"How can you tell? And if that is true, I am sure the police noticed, too."

"I need to be sure they did."

"And that's the woman you met before your camera was stolen?"

"Yes. I'm sure of it."

"—police fear the killer is escalating. Runners are encouraged to stay in groups whether in the morning or at night, or to simply avoid exercising outdoors during the following times." A graphic appeared with various times of day blocked out in red.

"Nick, this could be dangerous. This isn't—"

"It isn't my job, I know. But it could lead to my camera, too. I'm just going to make a couple of calls."

"Um, okay, I suppose," she said. "I guess we'll talk in the morning?"

Nick just nodded. He was rewinding the video and stopping it the various victim photos, taking screen shots of each one.

He heard the door to the hotel room click as Sandra let herself out.

# 9

## SUSPECTS

Nick woke with a start. He was still at the desk in his room, still in his clothes from the night before. He'd slumped over, head on his arm, and fallen asleep. A puddle of drool decorated the desktop and part of his sleeve, and his neck was sore and stiff.

He rotated his head, cracked his spine as he stretched, then looked at his screen. His computer had long gone to sleep, and when it woke it up, it prompted him for his password. After typing it in, the screen opened on two isolated images, his screenshots from the night before.

On the victim who escaped, two largish bruises decorated the front of her neck. However, they did not extend to the sides of her neck at all.

On the other victim, her neck was bruised on the sides, and less in the middle. It was almost as if there were two different killing methods, two different killers.

He opened his browser, and found he needed to connect to the Wi-Fi again. He did, and a webpage loaded.

"Strangulation Methods and their Telltale Signs," the headline read. It was a white paper, an academic piece by a coroner from New York.

There were two pencil diagrams early on the page, both from different types of strangulation. He didn't remember opening it last night, or of even doing the search, but it proved what he was thinking.

Why didn't he remember? Had he blacked out? Slept that hard?

He should tell someone. The question was, who? He didn't know anyone at the local paper, the *Sacramento Bee*. He could call Officer Terra, but with what information? His suspicions about a couple of photos?

*How did that work out for you in Salem, Nick?* he asked himself.

"Not well. Not well at all."

He looked at his watch. 8:30. He could call the police station, hoping maybe Officer Terra was in and would take his call. Just a simple heads up, a text or email of the pics, and that would be it. He could at least say he had done something.

Then he could shower and get in touch with Sandra so they could go finish taking photos.

Sandra.

She'd been here, and then...left.

He looked around and saw scattered food boxes, the little white ones.

Chinese.

A date that had turned into staying in and looking and photos, and then...

Then, he couldn't remember. The local news came on, and she left when...

When?

Nick didn't know. Had he really gotten so absorbed in the mystery and what he was doing that he'd simply ignored her?

It was one of the many hazards of being alone and single for a long time.

He picked up his phone up to call her, but as he did, it rang, showing a Sacramento number.

"Nick O'Flannigan," he said.

"Mr. O'Flannigan, it's Officer Terra, Sacramento Police Department."

"What can I do for you, officer? Any news on my camera?"

"We may have a suspect in custody," he said. "But we haven't found the camera yet."

"Okay. That's something, I guess."

"He's also a suspect in last night's strangulation. I'm sure you saw it on the news."

"Yes. I was actually going to call you this morning. I noticed something—"

"Can you come down and do a possible identification?"

"I can," Nick said. "I didn't really get a good look—"

"Mr. O'Flannigan, you are one of our only leads since the victim who escaped has disappeared. We can't stress how important this potentially is."

"Okay. Give me a few minutes to get ready. I also—"

"A car will be there in ten. We can only hold this guy so long." The call ended.

Nick looked at the phone. He had been trying to tell the officer something important, and now he felt like he was just being used. What if their suspect wasn't the right guy? Would the police be angry at him?

He darted into the bathroom, brushed his teeth, applied some fresh deodorant, and five minutes later sat on the edge of his bed pulling on a clean pair of socks.

He called Sandra's number. It went straight to voice mail. She must be sleeping in with her phone turned off.

He texted her. "Sorry about last night. I have to run an errand. I'll explain when I can. Brunch?"

He hoped it was enough for now. As he ended the message, his hotel room phone rang.

"There's someone here for you, Mr. O'Flannigan," the desk clerk said as soon as he picked up. The voice sounded nervous.

"It's okay. I'm expecting them." As he said the words, Nick understood how it sounded.

"O-o-okay," the voice said.

"Tell them I will be right down."

A few moments later he was in the front seat of a police cruiser. Shortly after that, he was seated in a waiting area not unlike a doctor's office.

A large officer, balding, with only wisps of gray hair clinging desperately to his scalp, walked in. He was bursting from his uniform, the buttons strained to unreasonable limits.

"Right this way," he said.

Officer Terra stood in a room looking into what Nick assumed was one-way glass. He'd read about this, but never been a participant in a real lineup.

"Hi, Mr. O'Flannigan. This is one-way glass. You can see those on the other side, but they can't see you. Just do the best you can to pick out the person who took your camera."

"Okay," Nick said. He considered sharing his thoughts with the cop, but surely, they would have seen what he did? Even if not, it seemed like this was all business, and he doubted they wanted to hear his theories now.

*You're a photographer, not a detective, Nick,* he thought.

"Bring them in," Terra said into a microphone.

A line of five men walked in, some shorter than others. Three of them had red hair. All of them had green eyes of various shades.

As the third one in line turned toward him, Nick's breath caught in his throat.

"Does one of them look familiar?"

"Number three," Nick said. "That's him."

"You're sure?"

"I'd know those eyes anywhere."

"Step forward number three," he said into the mic.

The man did.

"Turn to the left."

"Now, to the right."

Nick studied the man carefully. The build was right, and so was the height. The eyes though. They were what gave it away.

"Thanks, Mr. O'Flannigan," Officer Terra said. "That will be all."

"Can I talk to you for a few minutes?" Nick asked.

"Can it wait?"

"I'll be quick."

"Sure, let's go down to my office. But make it fast." He turned.

"Take them out," he said into the mic. "Put number three into Interrogation One."

He spun on his heel and gestured for Nick to follow. Two doors down was a small office, and the officer stepped inside and turned around.

"What is it?" he asked. His voice had a hard edge. "We're doing our best to find your camera and I know it is important to you. I'll let you know as soon as we have something, but as you can see, we are pretty busy."

"It's not that," Nick said, clearing his throat. "I saw the report on the news last night and I noticed some things in the photos. There were some differences between the victims, and it got me thinking—"

"Are you a detective?"

"No, but please, just look. You probably already know but look at the difference between the marks on the victims' throats." Nick turned his phone around, showing the officer the first photo he'd saved to the cloud, and swiping quickly to the second.

"These are just screen shots," he continued. "But I'm sure you and the media have better photos."

Officer Terra's eyes widened, but quickly went back to normal. If Nick had not been watching closely, he wouldn't have seen it. There was also something different about the detective's eyes today, but Nick couldn't put his finger on it. He seemed to remember them being a different color.

"I'm sure the coroner and others have already noticed this. But I will mention it to them if it will make you feel better."

"They're so different, I can't help but think it is two different types of strangulation."

"Possible, Mr. O'Flannigan, but leave the detecting to us, okay?"

"Sure," Nick said. "I just wanted to make sure I said something."

"Thanks for coming in. Let me show you out."

A few minutes later, Nick was outside in the sun. It was already warm. He looked around, and the officer who'd brought him stood by a cop car, waiting.

"Are you ready, Mr. O'Flannigan?" he asked.

"Hey, thanks for the offer. I'll hang out around here and take a cab or walk back to my hotel."

"Whatever you'd like, sir."

Nick walked down the sidewalk. Before he got to the next corner, his phone chirped a text message.

It was Sandra.

"If you're not busy, I'd love brunch."

"I'll call you in a few moments," he typed back, then opened his maps app.

He was further away than he thought from both the hotel and the capitol mall. He searched for restaurants nearby and found there was hardly anything.

He better find something spectacular for brunch to make up for the night before. He walked back toward the police station intending to ask someone. Cops and taxi drivers always knew the best places to eat.

As he did, he saw the suspect he'd identified walking down the steps. He put on a pair of sunglasses and walked the opposite direction. Nick considered following him, instead, he headed back inside.

# 10

## ALIBI(S)

As he opened the door, Officer Terra nearly ran into him. "Excuse—oh, it's you."

"What happened?" Nick asked.

"He has an alibi."

"For the camera theft?"

"No, you dolt. For the strangulation last night. It wasn't him."

"Oh, I'm sorry."

"You're sure that is the guy who took your camera? The one you saw outside your hotel?"

"Yes."

"Then the two incidents are not connected at all. It's a coincidence that he looks like the perp in the murders."

"Maybe."

"You wasted my time. My department's time. Whoever is doing this is still out there."

"I'm sorry."

"Just stay out of this, okay? If we find your camera, we'll let you know. Until then, do your job. I'll do mine."

"Okay. Again—"

"Excuse me. I have places to go. And Mr. O'Flannigan?"

"Yeah?"

"I wouldn't hold out too much hope for the camera. Don't you have some kind of insurance?"

"I'm working on it."

"Good luck." The police officer walked away, and Nick watched him.

He headed back down the steps. He wasn't going to ask about restaurants now. He hit the phone icon next to Sandra's name.

"Hi, Nick. Are things better this morning?"

"Is it still…" he looked at his watch. "Not really. I'm down at the police station. Can you meet me? I'm happy to take you to brunch."

"Sure. Any word on your camera?"

"Nothing good, I'm afraid. I'll explain while we eat."

"Okay. I am about ten minutes away."

Nick walked down the sidewalk and back again, first in the direction he'd headed in the first place, and then the other way, the way the suspect had headed.

He paced and thought.

First things first. He needed to patch things up with Sandra. It was already hot. Maybe they could do something fun this afternoon, and finish taking photos of the inside of the capitol building tomorrow. Second, he needed to accept that he might never get his camera back. It was time to talk to his parents.

*Later today,* he thought to himself.

Sandra pulled up and he climbed in the passenger side of her car.

"Hi, Nick," she said with a smile. "Do you know where you want to go?"

"Not yet." He explained what had happened that morning, and why he'd taken off so abruptly. He ended the story with the suspect walking away.

"Nick, I'm sorry," she said.

"No, I am," he said. "About last night…"

"You're a good guy. You were trying to solve a problem."

"That doesn't excuse my behavior."

"Listen, I'm used to being alone, too. I get it. You could have handled it better, but so could I. This means a lot to you, and I get that."

"I hope they really do see the patterns I see," Nick said.

"You did your duty. You showed them. The rest is up to the police."

"I get it," Nick said. "I do."

*It doesn't stop me from wanting to make sure,* he told himself. *I can follow up from a distance.*

"So, food?"

"Right," he said. "Let's see what's downtown."

As she drove, he looked over restaurants near Sacramento downtown. "Ink Eats & Drinks looks good," he said, and they headed that way.

The interior was tattoo themed. There was a full bar, and Nick imagined the place would be hopping in the evening. The atmosphere was casual, and their waiter was friendly and prompt.

As they talked, Nick started to relax. Still, in the back of his head, was his need to figure out his camera situation and what would happen after Sandra left, but for a few minutes he tried his best to let things go. If things like this kept up on this trip, he would have to start meditating or something, but for now, Sandra's company was enough.

"What's your plan?" she finally asked.

"Plan?"

"For getting the rest of the photos. The rest of the week, you know."

"I thought this afternoon we could relax. Just do something chill or something. We can get the rest of the interior photos tomorrow."

"Sounds like a good idea. What's your camera plan after this week?"

"Well, unless you can take a year off, I guess I will have to get a new one," he told her. "My parents have offered to front me the money. Maybe you can help me pick what I should carry next."

"Probably Olympus, since you already have lenses. Theirs don't always play well with others."

"True. I don't want to have to start over."

"We can look at some over dinner. Or afterwards, if you can keep from watching the news."

"Sounds good."

"So, where do you want to start?"

"How about the Crocker Art Museum? Maybe we can walk along the river after it cools down."

"Sounds good."

Nick paid the check and they left. They arrived at the museum a little while later. That museum led to another, and another. They took photos of the exterior of the buildings, but for most, they had to check Sandra's camera at the front door. Still, Nick snuck a couple shots of various things with his phone, not from any desire to break the rules, but because he wanted to have some memories of this afternoon. By the time they walked out of the fourth of the day, the Wells Fargo Museum, Nick was hungry again. He looked at his watch and saw it was six-fifteen.

"Ready for some dinner?" he asked her.

She put her arm in his, and Nick resisted the urge to check his phone. If something had happened or someone wanted to get in touch with him, he would have heard it.

Besides, this was a nice break from reality. He reminded himself that, as urgent as this project was, it was supposed to be fun, too.

This was fun. It had been a long time since he'd been out on a date with a woman he actually liked.

A date? Is that what this was?

Just as they headed down the sidewalk toward Sandra's car, his phone rang again. It was Emily.

"Sorry, I have to take this," he said.

"Nick!" Emily said as soon as he answered. "How are things going? I saw some great photos last night. Nice job!"

"Thanks, it's going as well as can be expected. I'm hoping to have an answer on my camera soon. But it isn't looking great." He felt like their last couple of conversations, she'd been especially cheery. Either his photography was that good, or she was just excited he was not involved in some kind of other criminal investigation.

"Okay. Well, let me know what you need."

"Will do. We'll take more exterior photos tomorrow. Then we'll finish up on Thursday or Friday. By then, I should know my next move."

"Great!" she said. "Keep up the good work."

Maybe the unspoken part of that was "keep your name out of the paper, at least, out of the crime section."

Nick didn't care. He'd done his duty and identified the man who took his camera. He'd told the police what he noticed about the victims, and everything he knew about the one who was missing. There was no stake for him other than finding his camera, which seemed less and less likely by the minute.

"Your editor?" Sandra asked after he ended the call.

"Yep," he answered. "She seems pretty happy with things overall."

"Good," she said. "We'll get some great shots tomorrow and keep her that way."

As she said it, she stretched up on her tip-toes and her lips brushed his cheek. Nick blushed and smiled.

"Let's go eat."

Their food choice of the evening was simple since they already had reservations at Mulvaney's. The restaurant was nice, and the food came in excellent portions. It was well worth the reservations and the money, and they even had room for dessert, although a shared one. When they were finished, Nick paid the bill and they headed back to the hotel.

"Should we go to my place this time?" she said. "I'll keep the news turned off while we look at photos from today and look at new cameras for you."

"Sounds good," he said. He was insanely curious about any developments in the case today but decided to resist the urge to look. One night with no news and no television would not kill him.

"Okay, follow me," she said.

Nick trailed behind, and once inside, they set up his laptop on her desk. There was only one chair, but they pulled up a little vanity stool and sat side by side.

Sandra pulled up the photos she'd taken that day, all around the museums and even of the entrance to the restaurant.

She clicked through them one by one, taking time to look at each and only keep the best of any duplicates. Her arm brushed his from time to time, and she smiled at him, a lot. Dimples decorated her flawless cheeks. Her pale blue eyes sparked.

Then she got to a few she'd taken outside the Wells Fargo Museum, their last stop.

"Whoa! Stop!" Nick said.

"What?"

"There. Stop. Let me see."

Nick slid the laptop over and zoomed in. There, on the sidewalk, a short distance from the museum door, a woman sat on a bench.

She wore sunglasses and a colorful scarf around her neck.

It was her, the victim, the one he'd met in the bar.

Also, around her neck was a camera. He couldn't be sure, but he was almost certain it was his, or one just like it.

The woman was staring right at them. There was no mistaking her.

Nick had found the missing woman and his camera, both in the same photo.

He reached for his phone, but Sandra's hand suddenly covered his.

"Not yet, Nick. Tell me what's going on. Let's think this through together."

"That's her," Nick told her. "The woman I met in the bar. And that," he pointed. "That camera around her neck is mine."

"So, what are you doing?"

"Calling the police."

"And telling them what?"

"What do you mean?"

"You're going to tell them I took a photo this afternoon of the victim who disappeared? And that she had in her possession what you think might be your camera?"

"That's exactly..." Nick stopped. He began to understand.

"And it was how many hours ago?" Sandra looked at her watch. "Six?"

"Okay, okay, I see your point."

"Think, Nick. Whether you tell them now or tell them in the morning, there's no difference, right?"

"I suppose."

"Besides, I think I have a better plan. You want the police to pay attention to what you told them, right?"

"Yeah, but—"

"No buts about it. Let's give them something to pay attention to."

"What? What in the world do you have in mind?"

For the next twenty minutes, Sandra outlined her plan. Nick nodded, asked a few questions, and in the end they agreed on a course of action.

"Tomorrow will be an early morning then," Nick said.

"It sure will," she replied. "You better go get some sleep."

Nick closed his laptop and put it away. He stood, and Sandra stood with him.

"Well, goodnight," she said, and held her arms wide, looking for a hug.

"Goodnight," he said. She stepped into his embrace, looked up, and their lips met for just a moment.

"See you in the morning," she said, letting go.

"Yep. I'll set my alarm for five."

Nick turned and left, but he wondered as the door closed behind him what would have happened if he asked to stay.

He turned back around and almost knocked on the door but stopped himself.

Instead, he walked down to his own room, opened the door, undressed, and dropped into bed as soon as he set his alarm.

This might be a horrible idea, but either way, he needed to be alert and ready in just a few hours.

11

―――――

## ALARMED

F ive o'clock came early, and although he didn't remember doing so, he must have set a pretty obnoxious ringtone for his alarm, one he couldn't ignore, because he sat straight up as soon as it started.

Sandra's plan was a bold one, but it might also be a horrible one. Only time would tell.

Nick pulled on a pair of pants, his shoes, and a light shirt. Sacramento had been hot during the day, and even this early it wasn't what he would call 'cool' outside.

A second after he dressed, he heard a light knock on his door.

Sandra wore sweats, a light hoodie, earbuds, and her camera bag slung over her shoulder.

"Ready?" she asked.

Nick nodded. His one concern was his leg. Sometimes he limped a little, but most of the time he could run for short distances. A longer jog would probably wear him out quickly.

"You know this is a crazy idea, right?"

"I know. We have no idea which park the killer will strike in next, if that will be today or next week, and what that will look like. But we can try, right?"

"Sure," he said.

They left the hotel and drove to the park she'd selected, Discovery Park, at the northwest end of the American River Parkway. There were several trails and it was gorgeous. The drive was silent until they reached a parking area.

"Okay. I'll work as the spotter. I'll warn you of joggers coming, you take the photos and be ready to chase them if you if you need to."

"I get it." Nick took her camera and fitted it with a telephoto lens, adjusting it for low light conditions. It would be hard to run with it, or even jog even with two perfect legs, and he hoped he would not have to. As an afterthought, he pulled out his phone and adjusted its camera too, getting it ready for low-light conditions. He turned it to 'vibrate.'

"Okay, let's go. I'll call if I see something. If I need to, I'll use my phone to take photos, but if I call, you come running, okay?"

"Sounds good."

Sandra started off down the path at a quick walk, and Nick looked for a good place to position himself where he had a long view of the running trail. There wasn't a great one, and so he decided to follow it but gave Sandra a long head start first.

Sandra had been right. From the photos they'd seen online, the trails offered great shade, which also meant great cover for someone hunting others.

That's exactly what this killer was doing.

Nick moved as fast as he could, setting up to see sections of the trail when possible and even snapping a few photos. He scanned the area near the trails, looking for movement, concealment, anything suspicious. A couple of times, other runners came the opposite direction, and most were being pretty wary. They eyeballed Nick so he feigned taking photos of the river and lake when they did.

The breeze was cooler than he anticipated, and he wished he'd worn something a little heavier. It was probably the proximity of the water.

As he rounded one corner, the smell of dead fish hit him in the nose. He remembered that smell in Seattle along the Puget Sound and he battled a sudden pang of nostalgia.

His phone started to buzz and he looked down at it. It was Gerry, not Sandra, and he reluctantly hit the ignore button. He'd have to call her back after this was over.

*Why was she calling so early?*

He looked up, and saw a dark shadow moving through the trees toward the trail.

Nick stopped and knelt. Often his height offered him an advantage, but not when trying not to be seen. He snapped off several photos, shooting as fast as he could. In one hand, the person held something red, and Nick tried to focus on it.

He backed out the zoom for a wider shot, and then saw something. A jogger was coming down the trail toward him, but she did not see him or the shadowy figure yet.

His phone buzzed in his pocket at the same time.

*Do something, Nick. Do something!*

The jogger got closer. The dark shadow closed in on the jogger.

Nick crept forward, snapping a few last photos. It needed to be clear to the police what the man was doing.

Then he saw it. The shadow leapt forward.

Nick stood. "Hey!" he shouted.

The jogger stopped only ten feet away looking directly at him. She reached for something at her belt.

Behind her, the shadow turned and ran back through the trees.

Everything moved in slow motion. Nick saw Sandra coming down the trail, a look of concern on her face.

Then the jogger's hand reappeared and came up.

"Oh, shi—"

Nick didn't finish. His face erupted in fire, his eyes watering, and he fell to the side, blind. The scent of pepper overcame his ability to breathe.

He heard shouts. Sandra's voice, then a new one. Running footsteps followed, the sound moving away from him.

He wanted to rub his eyes but knew that was the worst thing he could do.

Holding his hands out to his side, he sat up the best he could. Snot ran from his nose to his chin. Drool mixed with it, and he struggled to draw air into his lungs. Every tiny bit that hit his throat burned. Only a few seconds later, he could no longer hear. Instead a loud ringing filled his world, then stopped in favor of utter silence.

He couldn't see or hear at all. His eyes seemed to be covered with a gel that moved and pulsed, only revealing glimpses of light and color. The only thing he could smell or taste was sharp and painful.

He felt the breeze on his hands, coming from his left, so he turned that way.

A second later, water cascaded over his head, and he tried to duck away. Some went in his mouth, and it tasted cool and sweet, taking some of the burn down his throat with it. His ears popped at the same time.

"Don't swallow it," he heard Sandra say. "Spit it out. Turn your head up, so I can wash out your eyes."

"Is he going to be okay?" another female voice said.

"I'm sure he will," Sandra said. "I'm just glad he didn't drop my camera."

"I thought he was the bad guy."

"He's not great with his approach to women," Sandra said. The water stopped flowing and started again a few seconds later.

Nick turned his face first one way and then another, trying to get the water where things hurt the most.

"How did you meet him?" the voice asked.

"He picked me up in a bar," Sandra answered as the water stopped.

Nick blinked. He couldn't see, yet, but things seemed to be getting better. Either he was getting used to the pain, or it was going away.

His taste buds seemed better, too, but he wanted more water, some to swish, some to drink.

"Wat—" he tried to say, but his attempt to speak ended up in a coughing fit that hurt.

"We'll get more in a minute. Think you can walk if we guide you?"

Nick nodded between coughs and felt himself being pulled to his feet.

"Wow, he's tall," the new voice said.

"A good thing, most of the time. Hey Nick, you're going to have to help us here. We won't be able to support you, but we can direct you which way to go, okay?"

"Sur—" he tried to say, starting another coughing fit.

"Don't talk yet," Sandra said.

*What about the shadow?* he thought to himself. *Did he get away?*

He stopped and tried to gesture down the trail even though he could not see which way that actually was.

"We called the cops. Hopefully they will find something," she said. "Now let's get you to the parking lot. We may need to have you checked out."

Nick resigned himself to half-blind stumbling between his two guides. As they went, his vision cleared a little, but not entirely.

After what seemed like endless minutes, he heard another female voice.

"You the ones who called the ambulance?" he heard.

"Yes. He took a shot of mace in the face."

"How did that happen?"

"It was me," the first woman said. "I'm Victoria. I was jogging, and I guess he was trying to warn me of something, but I didn't see it that way."

"Easy mistake. He's a big guy. What's your name?" the new voice asked.

"Nick," he managed to croak without coughing.

"You rinsed with water?" she asked and he nodded.

"Okay, Nick. I am going to give you some wipes to use. They'll be much more effective than just water. Then I have some stuff for your eyes."

Nick took the wipes he felt pressed into his hand and used one in each hand to wipe his face. Everywhere they touched, they provided awesome relief.

"Thanks," he croaked.

"You swallowed some, huh?"

Nick nodded.

"Drink some milk. Let me see if I have a small carton in the van. A couple of hours and you will be as good as new."

"Thanks," he said again.

"Be right back."

He felt a hand stroke his back. "So sorry, Nick. The cops will be here soon."

"I'm sorry, too." Nick could make out a shape he assumed to be Victoria.

"It wasn't the most thought-out approach," he said. Talking still felt like scratching glass across his throat.

"Here you go," the paramedic's voice broke in. "Drink this."

Nick did, and the milk instantly cooled both his throat and mouth.

"Now sit down and tilt your head back."

He felt hands guide him until he was sitting on what he assumed to be the bench of a picnic table. He heard the sound of someone climbing onto the actual table. He tilted his eyes toward the brightening sky.

Fingers held his left eye open, and as liquid flashed through it, he found he could see better and better.

"Now the other one," he heard, and the process repeated.

He looked straight ahead, blinked, and was surprised with nearly normal vision blurred by some tears.

"Your face is as red as that hair," he heard, and turned to see an attractive woman in an EMT uniform. Her blond hair was tied back in a tight bun, and dark rimmed glasses framed blue eyes resting on a well-tanned face. "But you'll be fine soon. Just take it easy today."

"I will," he said.

"I'll make sure he does," Sandra said.

The paramedic left.

Nick and Sandra walked toward the parking lot arm in arm, Victoria walking beside them. A police officer approached.

"Are you the ones who called?" he asked.

"Yes," Sandra answered. "My friend and I were in the park, and he saw someone wearing dark clothes near the running trail approaching this woman," she said, indicating Victoria.

"What's your name?" the officer said, turning to Nick. He was not a small man, but still stood four inches shorter than him. The officer was wider at the shoulders and looked like he'd spent some time in the military. He probably spent time at the gym, too.

"Nick O'Flannigan. I'm a freelance photographer who—"

"Has been talking to Officer Terra. Now I know who you are. What were you doing here?"

"Taking an early morning walk."

"Uh-huh. Not doing some investigating of your own?"

"No, sir." Nick knew the officer saw the answer for what it was, a lie, and he felt bad. But if he answered truthfully the police would not take anything he said next seriously.

"We're going to need to take this camera," the officer said, indicating the Canon.

"That's mine," Sandra said.

"Is this where the photos are stored?"

"I can give you the memory card."

"Our techs will get them off of it, and then you can have your camera back."

"You can't take it with you. I need that." Sandra's hands went to her hips.

"I can actually. It contains evidence in an ongoing investigation. I'll give you a receipt and our team will give you a call when we're done with it. You can pick it up downtown after that."

"Fine. Nothing better happen to it," she said.

"We'll be careful, I promise."

The officer returned to his cruiser and filled out a receipt form with all of the data from the camera. He brought the piece of paper back over and handed it to her, then turned to Victoria.

"Are you the one the strangler was targeting?"

"I guess I am."

"Can you come downtown with me and answer some questions?"

"Sure. I didn't see anything real clearly."

"You might remember more than you think. Come with me, please."

Victoria turned and waved. "Sorry again, Nick."

"No problem," he said. "Really, my bad."

She nodded, and the officer looked at him and Sandra. He nodded, too.

"Have a nice day, folks. Thanks for helping out."

When they walked away, Nick turned to Sandra. "What do we do now?"

"We wait," she said. "Let's get you back to the hotel."

# 12

# FOUND

Nick got into the shower as soon as he was back in his room. His stomach growled as he soaped up, and he felt like a fool.

It was Wednesday, and thanks to Sandra's idea to stake out the park, neither of them had a camera to take photos with today.

He'd brought his clothes into the bathroom with him because Sandra, true to her word to the paramedic, was waiting in his room. She'd promised to take him to breakfast but made him promise not to drive today.

Nick sighed as he shut off the water. Sandra was a good person. He liked her. Maybe liked her too much.

It had been a long time since someone other than family and his few close friends was so concerned about his well-being.

Still, something bothered him about what had happened this morning. There also seemed to be something he was forgetting.

He heard his phone ring through the door, and debated hurrying to answer it when he heard Sandra say, "Nick's phone."

"Oh, hi, Gerry! I've heard a bit about you. What's going on? He's in the shower. He's had an adventurous morning. I will let him tell you about it. What's that?"

Sandra laughed. "Oh, yes, he is. The photos? Actually, we may have to finish taking them tomorrow. Thanks to the morning's adventures, Nick may be out of commission most of the day."

There was a pause.

"Well, I do have to feed him. I'll have him call you when he's done, before we go to breakfast, more like brunch now."

Another pause.

"He is indeed. Nice meeting you by phone. I look forward to that, too."

Nick looked at his pile of clothes and pulled on this underwear and pants before turning the water on to brush his teeth.

Once done, he finished dressing, hung up his towel, and left the room.

Sandra sat at the desk, looking through her phone, probably her social media.

"Gerry called," she said. "You're supposed to call her back."

"I heard," he said. "I need to call my parents, too."

"About the camera?"

"Unless mine shows up today."

"Okay. It would be exciting to get something new."

He nodded. "You and Gerry have a good chat?"

"We did. I'm looking forward to meeting her."

"Meeting her?"

"Of course," Sandra said. "I can't wait to meet some of your friends."

Nick looked at his bare feet and then back up. "I suppose I should call her back."

"Did I say something wrong?" Sandra asked.

"Not at all," he said. But it was wrong. He liked her, but he knew he would disappoint her. He was no catch, at least not in his own eyes, and he certainly could not ask a woman he'd just met, even though he loved the time they were spending together, to wait a year for him. She certainly could not take time off and travel for a year with him, nor would he ask her to.

For the moment, he pushed those thoughts aside and called Gerry.

"Hey," he said when she picked up. "You rang?"

"Yeah, I was just checking in. On the camera and the...you know."

"I do. Things are going well."

"She mentioned an adventure this morning."

"Yes. I got pepper-sprayed. Long story."

"Okay. I look forward to hearing that one. Any word on the camera?"

"Not yet. I'm talking to my parents today."

"Bummer. I know you loved that one."

I'm sure I will find another one I like," he said. "I'll keep you posted."

"And she's sweet, Nick. I know you can't talk right now, but she seems nice."

"Yes," he said carefully. "I'll call you tonight."

He looked at Sandra. "Let's go eat," he said.

They left the hotel and went back to the Original Mel's Diner, Nick considered it worth a second visit. The portions were large, and he was hungry.

When they finished, he decided before he called his parents, he would do some camera shopping. That would give him an idea of price and what model he really wanted. Besides, he wanted to give police one more day to find his original camera.

Until he used Sandra's Canon, he didn't realize how used to his camera's interface he'd become.

He looked for shops on his phone, and besides the big names like Fry's and Best Buy, there was a local shop called Mike's Camera. The large stores might not have what he wanted in stock. Not many people walked in there looking for his kind of high-end camera gear. If he had to order something, having it shipped to his next destination could end up delaying his trip.

In fact, Mike's did have some great cameras and new lenses he would love to try. He picked up everything from Canon to Nikon models to a nearly \$10,000 Fujifilm body that he knew he could not afford but lusted for anyway.

They spent about an hour and a half there, talking to the salesman, trying various models and lens combinations, and talking about what Nick was doing. Sandra even looked at some newer Canon models with what appeared to be serious interest.

As they stepped out of the store into the sunlight and heat, Nick's phone rang.

"It's Officer Terra," the voice on the other end said. "We found your camera."

"Great!"

"You can pick it up this afternoon. Along with the one that belongs to your friend. I heard you were...jogging this morning."

"I—we were."

"I see. Well, once you have your stuff back, you can leave the policing to us, right?"

"Of course," Nick said. "I never intended—"

But the call had already ended.

"Well, good and bad news. They found my camera. Which, after looking at new ones, is mixed news at best. You can have yours back, though. We can pick them up this afternoon."

"Sounds like mostly good news, Nick."

"Yeah. I can get back on track tomorrow, and you can..." he stopped himself. He didn't want to say it.

"I came for the week Nick," she said. "I'll leave Friday or Saturday when you do."

He smiled. "I'd like that. It will be a while before I am back in this area of the world."

"I know, Nick."

They decided to grab a quick bite to eat again and stopped in at a sandwich shop they spotted while walking toward the car. They would then head downtown to the police department to get their cameras.

The lunch had been good, and Nick sipped on a water he'd

refilled as they left. While they walked, Sandra held his hand in hers. He let her. It felt good.

When they reached the car, he reluctantly let go, and got in to the passenger side.

It was a quick drive. They could have walked, and Nick was feeling completely normal after his morning adventure. But she was being protective, something he found cute, comforting, and a bit annoying. Mostly the first two though.

It was a shame he would be leaving in just a couple of days.

When they walked into the police station and once they had passed through security, Nick went to the reception area to ask for Officer Terra.

They were directed to sit in some plastic chairs.

A moment later a door opened, and Officer Terra invited them through and ushered them into a side room.

"Wait here," was all he said. He seemed cold, and as if he was rushing them. Nick felt uncomfortable.

The officer came back carrying both cameras by the straps. Nick cringed as they both swung back and forth, narrowly missing each other.

He looked at the cop's hands gripping the straps and saw a bandage on one of them. There seemed to be some blood seeping through, as if the wound was fresh.

"Here, let me take those," he said, and quickly grabbed both by the straps, but gripped them closer to the camera body and held them, wide apart, so they had less room to swing and were less likely to hit each other.

"The lens was gone from yours, Mr. O'Flannigan. The thief must have pawned it at a different shop. But we found the body at a downtown pawn shop."

"Did they have video surveillance?"

"Yes. Unfortunately, it loops over every twenty-four hours, and by the time we got to it, the footage was erased. We do have a description of her though."

"Her?"

"Yes."

"But my camera was taken by a male, I'm sure of it."

"It may have been an accomplice who pawned it. Anyway, you have it back."

"Thanks." Nick turned it over in his hands. There didn't appear to be any damage, just the missing lens.

"And for you, ma'am," he said to Sandra. "Here is your camera back. Thanks for letting us take the photos from it. Everything should be just as you left it."

"As if you gave me a choice," she said. "But thanks."

"What did you do to your hand?" Nick asked.

"Oh, this? I fell and cut it while I was on a run this morning."

"Ouch," Nick said. "I hope it heals soon."

"Me, too."

Officer Terra turned to leave the room, and as he did, he hit the back of his hand, the one with the bandage, on the door jamb.

"Ahhh!" he grabbed it and bent over double. "That freaking hurts!"

"Are you alright?" Nick asked and moved closer. He glanced at Sandra, who stood there staring.

"Fine," he said. He wiped his other hand over his forehead and then rubbed his left eye. "Just, damn, that hurts."

"Are you sure it isn't broken?" Sandra asked. "It looks swollen."

"I'm sure," he answered, and looked up at her. Nick saw it then. There was a small, brown blotch that looked almost wet on the back of the officer's hand.

While one eye was a pale brown, the one he'd just rubbed was piercing green.

Officer Terra looked at his own hand, and then dropped it to his side, closing the green eye. "Now I have something in my eye. Excuse me. And good luck with the rest of your trip," he told them.

"Thank you for finding the camera," Nick said. "I do appreciate it."

Officer Terra showed them out, and when they got outside, Nick turned to Sandra.

"We have to get back to the hotel and look at the photos on your camera that I took this morning."

"Why?"

"I think I know who The Strangler is. I just have to prove it."

# 13

# A THOUSAND WORDS

Nick powered on his laptop with shaking fingers. Sandra held out the memory card.

Carefully, he placed it into the adapter on his computer.

The file icon came up when it loaded, and he clicked on it while holding his breath.

There was one folder on the card, and it was empty. There were no photos on it at all.

"Come on, come on," he whispered, clicking out of the single folder one more time. There had to be a way.

*Why would the police delete the photos before giving the camera back to them?*

*They wouldn't,* he told himself. *Only one person would. The Strangler.*

"Let me see," Sandra came behind him, and clicked in and out of the same folder. Still nothing.

Then, he remembered the app Gerry had told him about, the one for recovering deleted files. She'd sent him the link but in all the excitement, he hadn't installed it yet.

Nick searched his email and found the link. One click opened his browser, and he waited impatiently while the site loaded and the download started. He clicked on the icon, and opened the app.

Clear instructions told him what to do, and he imported the empty folder into the program window.

Files appeared, first one, and then several.

It was working.

Once done, there were 77 files, all photos.

He opened them in the photos application and clicked through them. The first few were of the empty trail and the river, the cover photos he'd taken.

Then he saw, toward the end, the first of the photos where he'd focused on the red item in The Strangler's hand. With a few clicks, he highlighted those and moved them to a new folder.

He then opened his heavier duty photo editing software. He cropped the first photo, and zoomed in, but not too far.

The photo was good for a shot without a tripod. Both of The Strangler's hands were visible.

The left one was gloved and he held a red scarf in it.

The right one was bare, with a fresh, deep gash across the back.

Sandra gasped from behind him. She must have made the connection at the same time Nick realized he'd verified his suspicions.

Officer Terra was The Strangler.

"It's him!" Sandra said.

"It is," Nick said. "And this is the proof. The question is, who do we tell?"

"He's off duty by now, right?" Sandra said. "He's been working all day."

"We can hope so."

"Call the tip line? Did they have an email for tips, too?"

"We can ask."

Nick looked back in his phone, and realized the number was quite a way back. His phone rang way too often lately.

He clicked on it and the phone on the other end rang.

"Tip line, Officer Terra speaking."

Nick hung up.

"He's there," he told Sandra. "He's volunteering. Watching."

"Intercepting the best tips," she said. "Now what?"

"We offer someone else the tip. If he is manning the tip line, someone else must be at the station."

"You're right," she said. "Let's go."

They left the hotel one more time that day. Nick felt incredibly tired and exhilarated at the same time. He looked forward to one thing: this ordeal being over.

They both were armed with their cameras and Nick had his laptop and the SD card. They drove in silence until they had almost reached the police station.

"What if they don't believe us?" she asked.

"I don't know," Nick said.

The doors were locked and reception was deserted, with a phone on the outside wall next to a sign declaring it was the way to reach someone after hours.

Nick picked it up slowly and dialed zero as instructed.

A male voice answered. "Officer Jesper, how can I help you?"

"We need to speak to someone about The Strangler case."

"One moment. I will send someone out."

A full three minutes later, an officer came out and walked toward the doors. He opened one and gestured for them to set their cameras down and step through security. Nick emptied his pockets and did so.

"Follow me," the man said once they were clear.

They went through the door into the hallway and turned right into the room where they had retrieved their cameras just a few hours before.

"Wait here," they were told.

Another few minutes passed. Nick fidgeted, then got up and paced the short room. Sandra sat, bouncing her leg and chewing her lower lip at the same time.

"What's taking so long?" she asked.

"I don't know," Nick said. "But I'm about to go find out."

He reached for the door when a large man walked in. He wore a rumpled suit, and the jacket, which clearly had once been able to button over his now-generous gut would not even come close any more.

"Have a seat," he said looking up at Nick. "Mainly, so I don't get a crick in my neck looking up at you. How tall are you anyway?"

"Six-six," Nick answered automatically.

"Ever play ball?"

"High school and college. A leg injury kept me out of the pros. But that's not—"

"Why you're here," the man finished for him. "I get it. It's late. What do you have for us?"

"Well, this morning, we were out running and saw The Strangler about to strike, so we took some photos."

"Ah, you're the big fella that got pepper sprayed by that little jogger. I saw your photos. No face in them though. Too bad."

"The face doesn't matter," Sandra said. "It's something else."

"What else?" he asked.

"Show him, Nick."

But Nick was already ahead of her. He spun the laptop around with the photo zoomed in on the hand filling the screen.

"Hey," the cop said. "Officer Terra has an injury just..."

"Yes, he does," Nick said quietly.

"Um, I. Uh. I'll be back." The cop's chair clattered backward as he stood, striking the wall and falling over. He moved more quickly out the door than Nick thought possible, and it clicked shut behind him.

"We have to wait again?" Sandra said. "What is wrong with these people?'

But the wait this time was only a minute. Two men came in this time, the large one and a thin one who, if he'd stood sideways could've hidden behind a flag pole.

"Show him," the large one said.

Nick hit the trackpad, and the screen lit up again, revealing the photo.

"That wasn't in the group we saw earlier today. Where did that come from?" he asked.

"These were deleted before I got them back," Nick said. "I used a program to restore them."

"Really?"

"Yes, really," Sandra said. "Where is Officer Terra now?"

"Right here," he said from the door.

Everyone turned to look. Officer Terra's figure filled the doorway. His pistol was out of its holster, in his hand, at his side.

"Hold it, Terra. Put that gun away," the thin one said. "No one is saying anything because of this yet."

"Not yet, but they will," he said, raising the gun slightly.

"No!" Nick said, seeing what was happening.

Time slowed again. This time, Nick propelled himself toward the officer, grabbing for his gun hand, which was slowly coming up, nearly pointing the gun at his own temple.

Just as Nick struck him in the stomach with his shoulder, the officer's gun went off. Nick felt something brush the back of his hair, and he was falling. He felt the body under him, heard the grunt that meant the officer was alive, and he felt his head hit something sharp and unyielding. Then there was nothing.

# 14

# SEE YOU LATER, NOT GOODBYE

The fog lifted to reveal pain. His head really hurt, and even though he felt like he was lying down, the room seemed to spin for a moment before orienting itself in some semblance of order.

"Where am I?" he said, as a hand holding a glass of water with a straw in it appeared in front of him.

"Drink," Sandra said.

He did, and the cold water felt good going down his throat. He smelled some kind of chemicals in the room. A hospital. He'd what? Hit his head?

"Is Officer Terra okay?" he asked.

"Yes. He's in custody and offered a full confession. It's all over the news."

"What time is it?"

"Two in the afternoon, Thursday. You were out all last night, and most of today."

"What? When can I get out of here?"

He tried to sit up and fell back on to the soft pillow. He found himself wearing a hospital gown and an IV tube ran into his arm.

"Not now, that is for sure. You took quite a knock to the head. The doc will come in soon and fill you in, but they'll probably watch you one more night."

"What about the photos? I still have to photograph the inside of the Capitol, and then get on the road."

"Don't worry about it. I took some for you. You can look them over later and make sure they are good enough."

"Thanks for doing that. I'm sure they are good, but—"

"I know. You're supposed to take them. Gerry and Emily have both called already. Your little adventure was on the news. I told them you would be fine and mentioned I could help by taking some photos."

"Thanks. If I get out early enough tomorrow, maybe we can go take some more."

"We will, I promise. Why don't you rest some more and we will talk later, okay?"

Nick nodded and found that although he'd only been awake for a short period of time, he was already sleepy.

When he woke again, it was dark in his room. There was no window, only the sterile shapes of metal tables and two padded, wooden chairs for guests to sit in. They were both empty.

A steady beep told him his heart was good, and his head really did feel better. Beside the bed, just within reach, was a water glass and a pitcher of water.

On the bed next to him was a remote of sorts, one that controlled the television and apparently the lights, too. There was a nurse call button.

His stomach growled. It had been a long time since he'd eaten anything.

He pressed the button and a nurse appeared.

"Good to see you awake, Mr. O'Flannigan. How's the head?"

"Better," he told her. "I am hungry though."

"Well, the kitchen is closed, but I can rustle something up for you."

"That would be great," he said.

She disappeared and he turned on the TV. The news was on.

"The Strangler, a now-former member of the Sacramento Police Department, will appear before a judge on Monday. Sources say that he's plead guilty, and any trial should be more to determine sentencing than anything else. Apparently, when confronted, the suspect tried to take his own life, but was stopped by this man, a free-lance photographer working on a travel assignment for *Travel USA* magazine who somehow became involved with the investigation."

Nick smiled for a moment. Emily would either love or hate that. A photo of him appeared on the screen behind her and Nick groaned. It was his least favorite head shot, but probably one that was on his website.

"During the scuffle, the photographer suffered a concussion, but is expected to make a full recovery. Now, over to Scott for the weather. How long is this heat going to continue?"

The newscast went on, but Nick quickly changed the channel to a wildlife show. The nurse came with a plate of food and he scarfed it down quickly.

When he was finished, Nick stayed awake for a while. He sipped on his water as the television droned on in the background. Eventually, he fell asleep again.

The next morning, he left the hospital around ten a.m., after he had breakfast, got dressed and was discharged. Sandra was there, and took him to his hotel. He actually felt pretty good, all things considered.

"Let's look at those photos you took," he told her, and they sat at the desk and opened his laptop. He had to admit, they were pretty good. He selected most of them and uploaded them to the cloud folder.

"Do you have time to go take a few more?" he asked her.

"Sure. I plan to head home this afternoon. I'm going to go about halfway and spend the night with some friends, but we can certainly go take some photos for a couple of hours."

"I'm sorry to see you go, Sandra. If I wasn't traveling for the next year, things would be different."

"But you are, and that's fine," she said. "You have a job to do."

"I do," he said. "And it's a great opportunity."

"Let's go," she said and grabbed her camera.

They made their way down to the Capitol building. Surprisingly, it was quieter than it had been on Monday, with fewer tourists and school children. They were able to get some great shots.

"Let me get a photo of you," he said. She posed near the railing on the second floor, and he snapped a few great photos, zooming in on her face. Portraits had never been Nick's strong suit, but he thought he did pretty well capturing her.

"My turn," Sandra said. "We need to replace that awful head shot on your website." He posed, and followed her instructions to the letter, turning his head, tilting his chin, and placing his arms this way and that.

"You look good. I'll transfer these to your laptop, and you can do whatever you want with them."

"Thanks," he said. "It will be good to have some new photos online."

She just smiled, and he held out his arm. She took it, and they walked back outside. When they got back to the hotel, they sat and transferred the photos they'd taken to his computer.

Finally, Sandra stood. "I have to get going, Nick."

"I know," he said, and stood with her.

She hugged him, and he returned the hug, resting his chin on the top of her head, then lightly kissing her hair.

"See you later, Nick. This isn't goodbye." She left quickly, and Nick looked around the room. He missed her already, and she was barely gone.

It wasn't fair, to him or to her. The timing, the feelings he had and that she clearly shared.

*You'll figure it out,* he thought to himself. He looked at his phone, almost texted her, but stopped himself.

*Too soon.*

Instead, he decided to go down to the hotel laundry, wash some clothes, and then get ready to go.

He mapped out his route to Carson City, his next stop, deciding to take his time and do the trek in two days instead of one.

He went to the hotel restaurant after his last load of clothes finished and was folded then put away in his suitcase. He didn't feel like venturing out tonight at all.

He sat there, wondering about the victim who had escaped The Strangler and how she had done so. He wondered who had taken his camera and made a note to replace the stolen lens even though he had a similar one.

It was too late to call his parents, too late to call Gerry and Emily. He'd have to catch up with them soon.

There were mysteries still unsolved in Sacramento. There were still some photos left untaken, and there always would be. He glanced down at his phone, hoping for a text from Sandra, but she must still be driving. Sipping the last of his drink, he stood, paid the bill, and headed up to his room. One more city down. Only forty-seven more to go.

**THE END**

# FACTS ABOUT SACRAMENTO

Here are some fun facts about Sacramento, California:

Sacramento is located where two rivers, the American River and Sacramento River converge. As a result, there is a lot of waterfront area.

Sacramento covers an area of 100.105 square miles.

Sacramento was not the first capital of California. There were five others, including Monterey, San Jose, Vallejo, Benicia, and San Francisco. Sacramento was the capital by 1862, but a fire destroyed the capitol building and for a brief period the capital was temporarily San Francisco.

The Pony Express that stretched from Sacramento to Missouri originated in Sacramento in 1860.

Sacramento has had several nicknames over the years including Sactown, the Big Tomato, River City, City of Trees, and Camellia Capital of the World.

Sacramento's Discovery Park, where some of this book takes place, is submerged in the winter to help control flooding.

In Old Sacramento tourists can ride paddle steamers and steam-hauled trains.

In Old Sacramento, the streets are cobblestone and there are many buildings dating back to the 1850s and 1860s. If you are in Sacramento, it is a great place to visit. Plan to spend some time there.

Sacramento is home to the California State Railroad Museum, which houses 21 restored locomotives. It actually takes some time to get through them all, and many are pretty spectacular.

The only city in the world with more trees than Sacramento is Paris, France.

Despite being an inland city, Sacramento has a thriving port, accessible via the San Joaquin Delta River and Sacramento River.

There is a large tunnel network under the city of Sacramento, but it became evident that the city would have to be raised to deal with flooding, and the tunnels were abandoned.

Sacramento is home to the art museum The Crocker, which is the oldest art museum in the western U.S. It also houses some amazing art.

The Sacramento Zoo was founded in 1927. School and other groups can have a sleep over in the zoo to experience nature and the zoo at night. Besides the Capitol building, it is one of the most common school field trips in the area.

The biggest almond processing plant in the world is located in Sacramento. It is the Blue Diamond plant, which processes as many as 12 million pounds a day during harvest. Is it just me, or does that sound just a little nuts?

The climate in Sacramento is Mediterranean, with mild temperatures and lots of sun.

Don't forget to visit Folsom Lake, which is a recreational area with 75 miles of shoreline. It's beautiful, and even on hot summer days, it is nice down by the shoreline.

Sacramento is home to California's largest 'Certified Farmers Market'. There are at least 50 farmers markets in the city thanks to the climate and ability to grow produce with high yields. There are many crops grown in the surrounding area, including a huge sweet potato industry just south of the city in Central California.

# DECAPTIATED IN CARSON CITY

BOOK #4 IN THE CAPITAL CITY MURDERS
SERIES

# PROLOGUE — BOX

"I've never had so much fun at a VFW convention," Bud said as the two former MPs exited the convention center. "Taxi or walk to the hotel?"

"Walking is fine with me," his friend answered. A stocky 5' 11" and 245 pounds, Tom still gave off the impression he was not a person to be messed with even though he was now approaching the age of fifty. That outward persona was just a show, however, as he was a soft teddy bear at heart, and there was nothing he wouldn't do to help others.

"It's almost like being in Vegas or Reno with all the lights."

"Yea," Tom replied. "But once we leave Carson Street, it'll be back to deadsville."

"Why'd they pick this place for the convention? There are certainly more exciting places to bring a bunch of old farts than a place named after Kit Carson. This is the fifth one I've attended, but there's not much to do here but attend the meetings and go on the bus trips."

"Number eight for me, joined right after I retired." Bud said. "Figured it would be a good way to keep in contact with some of the old Army buddies. Never thought I'd run into you again," he added as the two men suddenly stopped as a car sped around the corner without even slowing down.

"Where's the fire, pal?" Tom yelled out. "Try your lights, too." The car was already down to the next block where it swerved around a stopped car and continued south on the main road out of town.

The two men turned left on the dimly lit East Proctor Street. "Not the most glamorous hotel or the prettiest street in town," Bud started. "But at least it's a lot closer to the center than that hotel where we stayed last year. Great hotel with beautiful views, but not close to anything at all." Bud stopped suddenly as they reached an alley.

"What is it?" Tom asked.

"I think I hear something in there," Bud whispered.

"You've got better hearing than I do," Tom replied. "I wouldn't be able to hear a thing if the VA hadn't given me these hearing aids. There's still some stuff I can't pick up, but it's certainly better than before."

"Sounds like someone's moaning," Bud said as he took one step after another into the alley.

"Are you sure?" Tom asked.

"Come on," Bud said. "We've headed into worse than this before."

The two men continued in the direction of the sound. The light escaping from the occasional window pane provided some illumination, but not much.

"There it is again, the moaning," Bud said. "Probably up there near that pile."

"Wish we had our old flashlights," Tom said.

"We've got our phones. Just use that."

Tom stopped, reached into his pocket, pulled out his phone, and tapped the screen to turn on the light. The alley was no longer dark.

"Box," came the faint moan up ahead of them.

"Up there," Bud said. "Shine your light up there," he added as he pointed to a pile of cardboard boxes on the left side of the alley.

"Box," they heard again.

Bud took long confident strides toward the pile as Tom followed, the beam of his light bouncing all over as he tried to keep pace.

"Box," the old man moaned as Bud approached.

The old man's right arm quickly shot up and then his forearm covered his eyes from the bright beam from Tom's phone, the dirty sleeve of his tattered coat blocking the light.

"Point it down," Bud told Tom.

Tom shifted the focus of the light from the man's face to the pavement and then to the pile of cardboard boxes that were the old man's temporary home. Was he just here for the evening, or was this where he lived?

"Box," the old man said again.

"What about a box?" Bud asked. "These are boxes here. Are these your boxes?"

"Box," the old man said again as he pointed to his right. "Box."

Tom aimed his light where the man was pointing; it was a large TV box. "Is it that box?"

The old man nodded repeatedly. "Box."

Bud walked over to the TV box and slowly pulled it away from the pile. Tom approached from behind and aimed the light inside the box, but it was empty. Bud pushed it away.

"Box," the old man moaned again as he pointed once more to where the TV box had been.

Tom turned his light back to that area. The light revealed a small puddle of dark liquid on the ground. The two former MPs walked over. The flashlight beam revealed a reddish-brown substance.

"Blood?" Tom asked, and Bud nodded.

Drip. A drop splashed into the small pool.

He moved the light up toward the source of the liquid, stopping when the light hit the corner of a 12x12x12 box sitting on top of a stack of others. Its corner was dark with moisture. Another droplet formed at the corner.

Bud reached over the wet area on the ground and grabbed the box by opposite corners, lifted it, and set it on the ground. He slowly opened the lid.

Tom stepped forward and aimed the light inside. A man's severed head was lying on its side. A thin line of blood extended to the corner of the box.

"Maybe the crazy driver we saw dumped this, and that's why that car was driving away so fast," Bud said as he let go of the box flaps and stood up. He and Tom carefully stepped over the blood and returned to the old man who kept saying "Box" over and over again.

"Yes, that was the box," Bud said as he pulled out his phone and dialed 9-1-1.

"9-1-1. What is your emergency?"

"I'm retired Military Police, and I'd like to report two emergencies. One is a possible homicide. And the other is an elderly gentleman in the same area who needs medical attention."

"What is the nature of the homicide?"

"We found a severed head inside a box in an alley off East Proctor," Bud said calmly. "The old man appears to be homeless, somewhat delirious."

"We have someone on the way. Can you stay on the line until they get there?"

"Sure," Bud said, calmly answering the operator's questions as Tom knelt down next to the old man.

"You'll be fine, sir," Tom said as he put his arm around him. The man responded by leaning his head against Tom's shoulder.

The sound of sirens increased and soon red, white, and blue lights decorated the once-dark alley.

1
———

## LAKE TAHOE

**N**ick checked out of the Sacramento hotel, put his suitcases in the car, and set his camera bag in the front seat with him. He topped off the car's tank at a nearby gas station where he bought an energy drink for the day's relatively short trip. One more drive down Ninth Street past the capitol building, and Nick was soon on eastbound U.S. 50. The weekend traffic was rather light as he headed toward South Lake Tahoe, a popular weekend destination for many in the greater Sacramento area.

He saw that the exit for Folsom State Prison was two miles ahead.

Should I go and see if I can get some photos? he asked himself.

As Nick pondered his decision, he saw the sign, "Folsom State Prison NEXT EXIT."

No. Emily might not like it. I just made her happy with the photos I got this past week despite some real obstacles. And that was an understatement. It was a good thing he'd had his new friend Sandra's help.

The traffic increased as he entered Eldorado National Forest. He switched off the cruise control and slowed to a comfortable speed behind a line of cars in the right lane.

Nick pulled off the highway at a Rest Area since the energy drink had worked its way through his system. The morning sun angling through the tall trees created alternating shafts of light and shadow, perfect subjects for some black and white photos.

Nick got out his camera bag and tried some different lenses for different shots. After the ordeal in Sacramento, he was just glad to have his own camera back. His head nodded up and down as he reviewed the digital images.

I'm no Ansel Adams, but these are pretty good. Maybe I can create an "à la Ansel Adams Across the USA" book. Emily didn't say I couldn't take pictures for my own benefit.

He got back in the car and resumed his drive north along Highway 50. Traffic slowed to a crawl as Nick neared South Lake Tahoe. *Patience,* Nick told himself as he knew he still had eleven months to go on his assignment. He followed the line of cars turning right at the fork for the continuation of U.S. 50. Most of the traffic in front of him peeled off into the various casino parking lots once they crossed the state line into Nevada. "In two and a half miles, turn left onto Zephyr Cove Drive," his phone's mapping app announced.

Nick followed the app's instructions and turned left four minutes later. He pulled into the parking lot of the *The Zephyr Queen*, grabbed his camera bag and a light jacket from the back seat. A few heads turned and looked up toward Nick favoring his right leg as he walked to the ticket window. "May I help you, sir?"

"Yes," Nick replied. "I'm on a photography assignment from *Travel USA* magazine, and I was wondering about your professional media rate."

"Our media rate is thirty dollars, half the normal ticket price. Do you have your media badge?" the young lady asked as she bent her head back to look Nick in the face.

"Shoot," Nick said. "I have a card since I'm a freelancer, but," he paused. "But it's in the car, and I'm parked at the back of the far parking lot," Nick said as the edges of his mouth curled into a light smile.

The young lady looked right, then left, then back to Nick. "That's okay," she said softly. "Just don't tell anyone on the boat."

"Of course," he replied as he got out his wallet, and handed his credit card to her. "Thanks," he added.

She ran the charge, and handed the card back to him. "Here's your ticket and a brochure of *The Zephyr Queen*. Enjoy your tour, sir."

"Thanks," Nick replied as he put the card back into his wallet, took his ticket and headed toward the landing. The two-hour cruise went by quickly but Nick was able to get some amazing photographs in Emerald Bay, including the old Tea House and some sailboats silhouetted against the pines near the water's edge. His growling stomach told him he should have added the cruise's lunch option to his ticket. It was getting closer to dinner time, even though it was still a little early.

As the boat returned to the dock, Nick stopped by the ticket booth to thank the young lady, but she was gone. His phone rang as he was walking up the hill to the parking lot. "Hey, Gerry," he said as he stopped in the shade of a tall pine. "What's up?"

"That's funny," she replied. "I was going to ask you the same thing."

"What?" he asked quizzically.

"How'd it go with you and Sandra?"

"Oh, that. Um, it went okay. We got some great photos, I got my camera back. And thanks to that app you told me about, we were able to recover deleted photos from her memory card that revealed who the killer was."

"And?"

"And nothing," Nick answered. "She's on her way back to Salem, and I'm in Lake Tahoe right now. I'm sure we'll keep in touch." He paused. "But we're just friends, kind of like you and me."

"Yea, well we're a little different than you and her."

Gerry's not-so-subtle reference to being gay wasn't lost on Nick. "That's true, but just friends for now."

"That's cool. Heading into Carson City tonight?"

"No, going to spend the night here in Tahoe. Maybe see a show ..."

Gerry cut in. "And do some gambling?"

"I'm not much of a gambler. Perhaps a little Black Jack if they've got a cheap table."

"Okay, just don't go too crazy."

"Crazy? Not me."

"Sure," she said. "Well, take care and be good. I'll call you later in the week."

"Sounds good. Thanks for the call. Catch ya' later."

"You bet. Bye, Nick."

"Bye, Gerry," he said as the call ended. Nick closed his eyes and his mind replayed the feel of Sandra's parting kiss. It was brief and gentle. But it was a kiss. His lips broke into a smile as he walked to his car.

He went to the hotel, checked in, and took his bags to the room. Even though he wasn't going to be there very long, he knew better than to leave his camera gear in the car. The flashing sign on the casino next door shone through his room window. "Dinner & Show Special $45," it announced.

A quick look at a brochure on the end table showed details of the offerings this evening.

*Perfect*, Nick thought as he grabbed his jacket and headed next door. Dinner turned out to be a buffet, but there were plenty of choices and the price included two glasses of wine or beer. Nick chose the Porter. He enjoyed the variety show except for the comedian whose material was a bit raunchier than it was funny. The light applause at the end of his act reinforced Nick's opinion.

Nick looked at his watch; it was only 7:30, so he walked through the gambling area. He saw a five dollar Black Jack table, pulled three twenties out of his wallet, and sat down in the middle position. Nick's preferred places at the table, First Base and Third Base, were already occupied. "Good luck, sir," the dealer said as he took Nick's money and pushed twelve red chips in his direction.

"Thank you," Nick replied. He looked to his right, and then to his left. Both men had a bottle of Bud Light. "Hey, guys," he said them. "How's the table tonight?"

"It's green like it always is," First Base chuckled as he took a big gulp of beer.

"New to the area?" Third Base chimed in.

"Just passing through," Nick replied as he pushed a five-dollar chip into the betting circle.

"Thought so," Third Base said. "Didn't recall seeing your carrot top in here before." He finished his beer and clumsily managed to find the inset holder in the table. He looked across the table to his buddy. "Your round or mine?"

"Expect me to remember? You're the smart one," First Base replied.

"You bought the last one," the dealer said, pointing to Third Base.

"Then I guess it's my turn," First Base slurred. "Buy you a beer, Red?"

Nick smiled and paused before he responded. "No, thanks."

"If we don't have Mister Manners here," Third Base interjected. "You don't have to get all uppity with us just because you're passing through. We live here, not you, and we deserve some respect."

"No disrespect intended," Nick said as he looked down at his cards, 10-8. "Stay," he said to the dealer.

"Sounds like disrespect to me. Whataya say, Jim? Does he need some learnin'?" Third Base said as he stumbled getting out of his chair.

As Jim also rose, Nick pushed his chair back and stood.

"Oh, shit," Jim said as his scrawny five-nine frame was towered over by Nick's. Sensing possible trouble, the pit boss headed to the table.

"Okay, guys," he said to the two drunks. "You've had enough, and you're not going to start anything tonight. Go call a cab or crawl home, I don't care, but you're done here."

"We just ordered another beer," Third Based stammered as he rocked back and forth.

"You're done," the pit boss repeated. "Now, get out. I'm sure you're not too drunk to find the way," he added and pointed to the main door.

The men staggered as they made their way out. Third Base grabbed Jim by the sleeve as he turned toward the slot machines. "This way, buddy. We're outta here."

"My apologies, sir," the pit boss said. "They're locals who get a little carried away on the weekend. May I buy you a drink?"

"Not a problem," Nick said as he sat back down. "Sure, a dark beer, please. Thanks."

"Player wins," the dealer said as he dealt himself a seven to go with the King-five already showing.

# 2

## NOTHING BUT THE HEAD

The short drive from the Tahoe hotel to Carson City was punctuated with numerous photo stops along the way. There were many pullouts along the windy road through the mountains and Nick took advantage of several spots to stop and take pictures.

I can always sort them later, he thought.

The brown desert view across the plain as he headed out of the mountains contrasted with the lush green forested area he'd just come through. Was that how it was going to be from now on as he headed east through desert areas?

LED displays had replaced the original flashing neon lights that typified most Nevada towns, especially the gambling meccas. In addition to being more cost-effective, the new lights were as visible during the bright sunlight as they were at night. "Sunday Champagne Brunch Special $14.95" flashed the sign at the Double CC Casino and Hotel. Nick pulled into the parking lot, put all of his bags into the trunk, and locked the car.

"Good morning, sir. May I help you?" the tuxedoed doorman asked as Nick stepped into the air conditioned lobby.

"Restroom first," Nick answered. "And then the champagne brunch."

"Of course, sir. Restrooms are just over here to your right, and then the brunch, best in the city I must add, is back to the left. Right through the archway."

"Thank you," Nick said as he headed that way.

The brunch layout contained a large variety of meats, fruits, cheeses, vegetables, and desserts. There was the champagne, of course. Nick had just returned from the desserts display when the waiter came by. "More champagne, sir?"

"Is beer also included, or is it just the champagne?"

"Just the champagne, sir."

"Okay. More champagne then," Nick responded. He saw a television on the wall as he leaned his head back slightly to take a sip. It looked like a news program. There was an image of a box, perhaps a cardboard one. The wording was hard to make out, so Nick got up and walked closer. "Head in Box," the title said.

Nick stood there as the reporter continued her story. "Carson City Police are investigating a possible homicide with the discovery last night of a human head inside a cardboard box. The rest of the body has not yet been recovered. The box was one of several cardboard boxes in an alley off East Proctor Street. It appears there was a homeless individual who might have witnessed something. One person is currently in custody but the Police have not yet said if that person is a suspect or simply a person of interest. We'll continue to update this story as we get more information."

"Nice story to have on while everyone's eating," Nick said to an elderly couple who'd put their utensils down on their plates.

The gentleman waved down a passing waiter. "Can you either change the station or turn down the volume? We don't need to hear that."

"My apologies, sir," the waiter said as he stepped to the TV, picked up the remote, and pressed the Mute button.

Nothing but the head. That's pretty gruesome, Nick thought as he returned to his table. East Proctor Street, I saw that on the directions to the hotel. It's gotta be close by.

He got up, paid the check, left the casino, and went to his hotel, just two blocks from the capitol building. After checking in, he made his way to his room, unpacked his bags, and plopped down on the bed to watch NBA replays on ESPN, something Nick really enjoyed. He closed his eyes during a commercial, and the image of Sandra's kiss was there again. He opened his eyes, rolled over toward the nightstand, hit the mute button on the TV remote, and picked up his phone.

"Call Sandra," Nick said into the phone.

"Hello," the female voice said after two rings.

"Hey, there. It's Nick. Make it back to Salem okay?"

"Oh, hi, Nick," Sandra replied. "Yes, it was an easy drive, especially since I broke it into two days. How's Carson City?"

"Definitely not Vegas, but it seems okay."

"That's good. What did you do on the way over from Sacramento?"

Nick told her about the boat ride in Tahoe, the two drunks at the Black Jack table, and the stunning scenery on the way from Tahoe to Carson City. "Oh, and you won't believe this. On the news was a story about a man's head being found in a box. Just the head."

"You're not getting involved in that, are you, Nick?"

"No, no. It was just a bizarre item that came on the TV while we were eating. It was found in an alley off a street that's just a couple blocks from here."

"We?" she asked.

"It was a Champagne brunch at one of the casinos."

"Okay," she said. "Have you told your parents that you got your camera back?"

"No, I'm planning to call them tomorrow."

Good idea." There was a slight pause. "Well, I need to take care of a few items since I was gone most of the week."

"Right," Nick said. "Thanks again for helping me out. I don't know what I would have done without you."

"That's what friends are for," Sandra replied.

Friends. Is that what we are? Nick thought.

"Well, thanks again. Maybe we can meet up again somewhere along the road. Or should I say roads. There are a lot of them still to go."

"I'd like that, Nick. Maybe I could fly in and meet you someplace."

"Sounds great," he replied.

"Oh, did you have a chance to upload a new headshot to your website?"

"Oops," he replied. "Yea, I do need to do that, don't I? Thanks for the reminder."

"Of course. Umm, I gotta go."

"Yep," Nick said. "Bye for now."

"Bye," Sandra said as she ended the call.

Nick unmuted the TV and continued watching the game. East Proctor Street, it's not that far from here, he thought. Maybe I could take just a quick look, a few photos. But not tonight.

3

___

# THE APARTMENT

After breakfast the next morning, Nick grabbed his camera bag and walked the short distance to the capitol building. The eastern sun draped the main entrance in shadows so Nick walked through the trees to the northern and southern sides of the building to take some oblique pictures. Photos of the front façade would have to wait until the afternoon when the sun would be at his back. Nick went in the front entrance, picked up a brochure, and went on the offered self-guided tour, taking photos as he walked around.

The main door to the Governor's office was open so he went inside.

"Good morning, sir. How may I help you?" the secretary asked as Nick entered.

"Good morning, ma'am," Nick began. "I'm on assignment from *Travel USA* magazine to photograph each state capitol building, and I was wondering if I could make an appointment to meet with the Governor, take some pictures, and maybe get a few words from him about what makes this city and the state so great."

"Well," she began. "He's quite busy the first few days of this week. How long are you in town?"

"Until Friday or Saturday, ma'am, and I'll work with any time he has available."

She clicked her mouse a few times. "How about Thursday morning at 11:40? He'll only have about fifteen minutes."

Nick pulled out his pocket notebook and wrote down 'Thursday 11:40 Guv.' "That's perfect. Thank you, ma'am. My name is Nick O'Flannigan. Here's my card." he added handing one to her by stretching his long arm over her desk.

"Thank you, Mr. O'Flannigan. We'll see you Thursday."

"I'll be here. Thank you so much," Nick said as he turned around and left. He was walking up the stairs to the second floor when his phone rang. It was Ben, his renter.

"Hey, Ben. What's going on?"

"Hey, Nick. How's the trip going?"

"Pretty good so far. In Carson City right now. What's happening in Seattle?"

"Not much, just staying busy with work. But the garbage disposal went out a few days ago. It just stopped working. Should I call Mr. Lam or what?"

"Yeah. Call him first. He'll send Phil, his maintenance guy, over to check it out. He's been pretty responsive in the past. His number is on the refrigerator. Anything else?"

"No, it's been pretty quiet here," Ben said. "Oh, yea," he added after a slight pause. "I deposited the rent check. So you should be able to see it in your account now."

"Awesome," Nick replied.

"One other thing. My manager said he might be sending me on an assignment back east. He said it could be three or four months, or maybe even longer. Maybe even permanent."

"Uh," Nick groaned. No other words came to mind.

"I told him I'd signed a year-long lease, and going back east would create a hardship. Not just for me, but also for you."

"Yea," Nick muttered. "Well, buddy, you do what you have to do," he added as he closed his eyes and shook his head back and forth.

"I know," Ben replied. "I'll keep you in the loop."

"I appreciate it."

"Well, have fun in Nevada, and I'll let you know when I have more information."

"That's good," Nick replied. "Let me know how it turns out."

"Sure will. Thanks, Nick."

"You bet. Take care, Ben."

"Yep, talk to you later, man," Ben said as the call ended.

Nick put his phone back into his pocket and continued up to the second floor to view some of the historical exhibits there. He picked up brochures for some other places to visit in the area on his way out of the capitol. He looked at the shadows and saw that he still needed a few more hours before he could get really sharp pictures of the front of the building.

*Guess I'll have to come back later,* he thought as he walked back to the hotel. Once in his room, he called his parents.

"Hello."

"Hi, Mom. How's everything in Boston?"

"Nick," she yelled into the phone. "We've been worried since we haven't heard from you."

"Sorry, Mom. It's been a little crazy. But I did get my camera back." He left out the part about the missing lens.

"He got his camera back, Patrick," she yelled. Nick pulled the phone away from his ear. She always yelled, and right into the phone, whenever she was relaying information to her husband.

"That's good," Nick could hear his dad yelling back. "So he doesn't need us to buy him a new one?"

"Tell him I don't need a new camera, Mom. It would be nice to have a spare one, just in case. But thanks anyway."

"He doesn't need one. They found his old one, but he wouldn't mind having an extra one anyway," she yelled.

"Tell him we'll buy him another one if he needs one," Patrick yelled.

"I heard that, Mom," Nick said. "I'll think about it."

"So where are you now?"

"Carson City, Nevada. It's my fourth stop. I've been to the three states on the west coast, and now I'm starting to head east."

"How is everything else? The car? Is it still okay?"

"It's fine, Mom. Oh, yea, my renter called and said he might be moving back east. So I might have to find a new one." Nick pulled the phone away from his ear as he knew what was coming next.

"His renter might be moving," she yelled.

"What can we do to help him?"

"What can we--" she started.

"I heard him, Mom. I'm fine for now, but I'll let you know."

"Okay, you just be careful, and don't pick up any hitchhikers along the way."

"I won't, Mom. Love you, and tell Dad I love him, too."

"I love you, Nick. Be good now."

"Always, Mom. Bye-bye."

"Bye, son."

Nick ended the call, opened the maps app, and entered East Proctor Street.

*That alley should be easy to find,* he thought as he saw that it was only a few blocks long. He swung his long legs off the side of the bed, and stood up. "Ouch," he mumbled as a shooting pain in his right leg forced him to sit back down on the bed. *Not today,* he thought as he put the phone on the nightstand. He never made it back to the capitol as he got too involved with a Netflix movie. *There's always tomorrow; I've got the whole week.*

4

———

## THE VIDEO

"Oh, not the most comfortable bed," Nick groaned the next morning as his outstretched arms extended past the bed's sides and his feet hung over the bottom edge. The barely adequate curtain kept some of the light out, but the brilliant morning sun forced its way into his room through any open space it could find. "Note to self," he muttered. "No more rooms on the east side of a building."

He got out of the bed and stretched his body every way he could. *Crack, pop,* his body responded. "I've got to hit the gym," he said as he went into the bathroom to splash water on his face. He dressed in his gym clothes, went downstairs, and worked out on the few pieces of equipment the hotel had.

I'd better check out the facilities a little better in the future, he thought as he sat down to cool off.

After showering and getting dressed, Nick went back downstairs feeling much better. He picked up a copy of the *Carson City Courier* as he entered the breakfast room. He noticed several guests gazing up at him as he walked in. He'd gotten used to people staring at him because of his height many years ago. He sat the paper down on an empty table and retrieved a tall glass of orange juice and a cup of coffee.

He took a sip of coffee and opened the newspaper to see the headline, "Police Seek Clues in Head Case."

*Head Case?* Nick thought. He read the first few paragraphs and got the answer to his question. The case was about the human head that was found in the alley. *The alley off East Proctor Street. I should be able to find it. No sweat. And it won't take much time.*

The paper lay flat on the table and Nick looked at the photo as he ate scrambled eggs, hash brown potatoes, and a few strips of soggy bacon. He stood up to get more orange juice when something in the photograph caught his eye. "A security camera," he said loudly, and others in the room looked his way. "Sorry, folks. I thought I was just thinking to myself."

"No problem," came one response.

"That's okay. I do it all the time," another person said.

"Thanks," Nick said, nodding. So the security camera on that building should have captured what happened and who did it.

Nick grabbed the paper, forgot about the orange juice, took a banana, and headed up to his room. He looked at the front page article again. *East Proctor Street isn't that far from here,* he thought as he finished reading the story.

He put the paper in his camera bag pocket, picked it up, and headed out. He was at the entrance to the alley ten minutes later. The entire alley was empty except for a few remnants of yellow police tape stuck to the sides of the buildings on the left side. Nick walked in slowly and saw an area that had been recently cleaned.

*Must've been the blood,* he thought as he saw one scrubbed area about two feet in diameter, and then over a dozen scrubbed areas leading out of the alley. *Alternating from one side to the next. Could've been shoe prints of someone walking. Maybe the killer?* He looked up to his right and saw the security camera on the brown brick building. He pulled out the paper. *Yep, same camera.* A gum wrapper blew by him as he put the paper back into the bag and went around to the front of the brown brick building.

Nick walked up the five steps to the front entrance of an apartment building with no name on the front. There was a bank of locked mailboxes and a buzzer above each. He looked at every name but didn't see a name or buzzer for a manager or building supervisor. He stepped to the front door and tried to open it. It was locked. Then he saw a small label, "Manager 702-555-1744."

He took out his phone and dialed the number. "Hello," said the curt voice on the other end.

"Good morning, I'm a photographer and I saw that you have a security camera on the back of your building that appears to be aimed in the direction of where the cardboard boxes were in the alley. Is that camera active?"

"If you mean, does it still work, yes it does. We already told the police that. Who are you again?"

"My name is Nick O'Flannigan. I'm a photographer from Seattle, Washington. Did your security camera pick up any activity in the alley that might show anyone putting a box there, such as the one they found with that head in it?"

"The police already asked that, but the camera's on a twenty-four hour loop, and so anything happening in the alley was already overwritten."

"Is there any way--" Nick started. He was thinking of the app he'd used in Carson City to recover deleted photos. Maybe it could do the same for video.

"Sorry, but I have other things to do. Bye now." The manager ended the call.

"Thank you, sir," Nick said automatically. Too bad the police didn't check the tape earlier.

Nick returned to the alley and took some photos. He zoomed in on the security camera. *Not much security if it writes over itself every twenty-four hours,* he thought as he left the alley. *I'm sure the police already thought of trying to recover any deleted files.*

He pulled his phone out and opened his banking app. *Yep, Ben's check is there. Oh, I hope he doesn't get transferred.*

# 5

# FROM MINT TO MUSEUM TO CURIOSITY

Nick put the phone back into his pocket and left. Back on Carson Street, he took his camera out of the bag and hung its strap around his neck. There were some interesting signs that would make great contrasting photos with shots in the daytime and then at night. He walked along the pathways in the trees and shrubs of the State Capitol Complex, snapping photos as he went. The three main buildings—the Legislature, the Supreme Court, and the capitol building—all created different images as he framed them through the eyepiece. Built at different times with different architects, each building had its own distinct footprint, shape, and style.

He sat down on a bench near the Law Enforcement Memorial, primarily to look through some of the brochures he'd picked up in the capitol, but also to rest his right leg. He wasn't used to doing so much walking every day. He rubbed it, bringing minor relief. He'd have to find a way to get a few days of pure rest sometime on this trip, and maybe this was the week for it. *Maybe even a visit to the chiropractor.*

As he looked through the brochures, the State Museum looked interesting. The building was the site of the former Carson City Mint, popular among avid coin collectors. The "CC" mint mark on the Morgan Dollars or the Liberty coins of the 1870s were prized possessions, typically commanding a significantly higher premium than similar coins of that era.

Nick opened his mapping app and typed in "Distance to Mint." The Mint Hotel and Casino was a half mile up Carson Street, and the old mint, now a State Museum, was a little further. He stood up and realized that his sore leg wasn't up for much more. He opened the Uber app, saw there were several drivers in the area, and he entered "State Museum." His ride would be at his location in two minutes, and it would cost him $4.75. *Well worth it, even for such a short trip.*

The drive to the museum took just a couple minutes. Nick and the driver exchanged a few comments about basketball, and then they arrived. The Uber driver pulled to a stop and turned his head around to the right. "Here's my card," he said to Nick. "I'd be happy to pick you up anywhere and take you anywhere. And maybe we could talk a little more about basketball on a longer ride."

"Thanks," Nick said as he reached into his shirt and pulled out one of his cards. "Here's mine. And thanks again. I'll give you five stars," Nick said as he opened the car door and swung his long legs out to the sidewalk and exited the car.

"Nice air conditioning," Nick said as he showed his media card to the older man selling tickets.

"The thick blocks help out a lot," the man said. "It'll be half price, four dollars. Standard rules. No video and no flash photography."

"That's fine," Nick replied as he handed the man four ones. "Elevator?" he asked. "Bad right leg."

"Right over there," the man said as he pointed across the hall.

"Thanks," Nick said.

Nick looked around as he stepped out of the elevator on the second floor. He looked at a few of the exhibits featuring the old mint. He bent over to look at some of the old coins with the famous "CC" mint mark. "Nice," he said as he nodded his head and moved on.

"The History of Capital Punishment," the sign said. "Interesting," Nick muttered out loud. He stepped back and took a photo of the replica of the gallows at Carson City's Nevada State Prison. "Wow, some strange methods here," he said to a man wearing a VFW hat. "They built a shooting machine to replace the firing squad."

"Yep," the man said. "A little bizarre."

"More than a little bizarre, I'd say," Nick replied. "But speaking of bizarre, did you hear about the head that was found in a box in an alley?"

"Of course," the man said. "It was Bud over there who found it," he added as he pointed toward a man. "We're here for a VFW convention."

"Really?"

"That's him."

"Thanks," Nick said as he walked over to the group. "Excuse me," he said in Bud's direction as he pulled a card from his shirt pocket. "I'm a freelance photographer, and I know it sounds really strange, but how did you happen upon the box in the alley?"

All heads turned in Nick's direction, and then they all looked up. A few mouths opened wide at the sight of the six-foot six man with a bushy head of orangish hair.

"Tom and I were walking down the street when we heard some moaning in the alley, and we went in to see what it was," said Bud, the previous center of everyone's attention.

"What did the head look like?"

"Are you into some sort of macabre photography?" Bud asked.

"No, just curious," Nick replied. "The alley is close to my hotel, and after reading about it in the paper I went by there this morning, and it looks all scrubbed down now. The boxes are gone, and there's just a little bit of crime scene tape left."

"It was pretty shocking. All I can say is I hope the man was already dead before his head was removed. The cut looked ragged, and pretty ugly."

"I bet," Nick replied. "And what about that homeless person who was reported in the area?"

"I think he might've seen something, but all he could say was 'Box' when he found him," Tom interjected. "Whether he was shocked by the situation, or he had some other trauma, he was in sad shape. I sat down next to him while the police were on their way, and he just leaned his head against my shoulder. And I thought to myself, 'It's probably been a long time since someone cared for him or held him close.' It broke my heart."

"I can imagine," Nick said. "How's he doing?"

"He's in the hospital," Tom said. "We took up a collection at our convention, and gave it to the social worker who was taking care of him. A few of us are going down to see him tonight."

"That's nice," Nick said. "Thanks for sharing with me. Sorry for interrupting your tour."

"No big deal," Tom said. "We were happy to help, and sad about the circumstances."

"I feel the same," Nick said. "I hope the rest of your convention is good, and uneventful."

Each man shook his hand, and then turned back to their group.

Nick went back to the capital punishment display. He shook his head as he read stories of botched executions as well as really awful ways of carrying out the death penalty. He walked around some more, and toured the first floor, and then pulled out the Uber driver's card and called him.

"Be there in four minutes," the driver said. And he was.

Back in his hotel room, he took out his laptop and opened a browser window. He typed "decapitation methods" in the search bar and pressed Enter. Over two point seven million entries. *This could turn into a long day and night.*

He first read some of the history, where an axe was used to kill murderers and traitors in England. But the executioners didn't always hit the right spot, sometimes missing the victim entirely. The invention of the guillotine was considered a more humane method as it would always hit the right spot. But if the blade wasn't sharp enough or heavy enough, it might not completely sever the head from the body.

*Wow,* Nick thought. *And Bud said that the head in the box was crudely cut off.* He continued reading various articles, many of them with graphic drawings and pictures.

He looked at his watch and realized he'd spent the past five and a half hours reading about this gruesome method of killing someone.

Am I liking this too much? he thought to himself. Is this how real detectives get sucked in to solving mysteries?

And now he was hungry. Nothing on the rare side tonight.

# PHOTOGRAPHY EXHIBITION

Nick went back to his hotel room after dinner and was going through the day's photos when the vibrations on the desk told him his phone was about to ring. He picked it up and looked at the Caller ID. It was Emily, his editor.

"This is Nick," he answered.

"Hey, Nick. It's Emily. How's everything in Carson City?"

"It's great here," he replied. Did I upload some wrong photos again?

"That's good to hear. I'm getting some good feedback on your photos. The quality is fantastic. Happy to have your camera back?"

"Yeah. The Canon I used was great, but this is so much better."

"Good. Did you replace the lens you lost yet?"

"No, but I have a similar one for now.

"Good to hear. There's only one issue with the pictures so far," Emily began.

Uh-oh.

"Your photos are starting to look a little repetitive. They're all great shots, but we need to mix things up a bit. Maybe some contrasting shots taken in daylight and then at night. Or perhaps color as well as black and white of the same image."

Nick chuckled. "That's funny because I was thinking the same thing as I looked at some of the old original neon signs here in town. Most of them have been taken down and replaced with LED ones."

It was funny. He'd been thinking the same thing. How was he going to keep the creativity going for fifty states? There were only so many angles, so many ways to take shots. Each would have his unique eye and style, but he had to be careful not to get stuck in a rut.

Nick closed his eyes as he created the picture in his mind. "Picture a four-image window all of the same sign. Bottom left is daytime black and white. To the right is night time black and white. Then at the top left is night time color and completing the frame on the right is daytime in color. Now most people would put those four images in a different progression, but I think this way makes you think. It's not just the everyday pattern."

Nick's creativity was on a roll.

"I was also thinking of some reverse images where the background is highlighted and the main image is secondary. And--"

Emily cut in. "Sorry to interrupt, Nick. I like all those ideas. They're great. We still need some of the regular shots, so don't use up all of your ideas just in Carson City. You've got a long way to go. I just wanted you to tap into that creative box inside your brain that Gerry told me about. After all, that is one of the main reasons we hired you. Anyone can take photos. In fact, it would have been a lot cheaper for us to hire a photographer in each city, but that would have been too run-of-the-mill. And we do want some consistency with your style."

Nick leaned back in the desk chair and stretched his long legs. He closed his eyes, nodded his head and smiled as Emily continued to talk. *She likes my work. Awesome!*

"Are you getting involved with anything there?" she asked, catching him off guard.

He bolted upright in the chair. "Involved with anything? What do you mean?"

"You know what I mean, Nick. Getting involved in police cases. With strange women you met in bars. Sticking your nose where it doesn't belong. Anything like that?"

"No," he replied emphatically.

"Good. We certainly wouldn't want you to get detained and not be able to stay on schedule. Right?"

"Of course, Emily. I'm working one hundred percent for you." The desk chair squeaked as Nick nervously rocked back and forth.

"I like that answer, Nick. It's okay to have some fun. After all, you are going to be gone from home for a full year. We just don't want you to lose sight of the big picture. The magazine and our readers, even though they don't know it yet, are really counting on you." Emily paused as the pace of the squeaking increased. "You have any questions?"

Nick stopped rocking. "No," he said.

"Okay, then," Emily said. "Keep up the good work, and we'll talk again soon."

"Thanks," Nick answered. "Thanks for calling."

"You're welcome, Nick. Take care now. Bye."

"Bye," he said as he closed the call and put the phone into his pocket.

I can sort these later. I think I'll scope out some places for some really unique combinations of shots that'll blow Emily's mind.

Nick shut down the computer, slipped his camera bag over his left shoulder, and grabbed his pocket notebook. He took the elevator down to the lobby where he noticed a new poster near the entrance to the breakfast room. The bright colors got his attention first, but it was the large picture of a camera that really caught his eye. "PHO-TOGRAPHY EXHIBITION" was the headline. He read further. "Thursday 7:30 PM at Western Nevada College. Free Admission."

Nick turned to the desk clerk. "Was this poster here this morning?"

"No," the young man replied. "Two students from the college came in about thirty minutes ago and asked if they could put it up."

"Western Nevada College," Nick said. "I've never heard of it."

"It's not bad for a small school," the clerk responded with more enthusiasm. "I'm taking night classes there working on a Business Management degree."

"Good for you." Nick looked back at the poster, and then back again toward the clerk. "So, do you know anything about this photography exhibition? That's what I do for a living. Do you think it would be worth my while going, or do you think it will be a fairly low-level thing?"

"I honestly don't know," the clerk replied. "But the college usually puts on some pretty good cultural exhibits. It's not that far of a drive. Since it's free, if it's not that good, you can always bail. No great loss."

"Good point. Thanks," Nick said as he pulled his phone out and took a picture of the poster Then he headed out to scout for some new photos Emily would absolutely love. The aromas coming out of Red's Old 365 were too tempting, even though he'd already eaten. But it had been a light dinner. Nick went inside and was quickly enveloped with the smell and smoke of real barbecue.

"Help ya', hon?" the waitress said as she craned her neck back to look up at him.

"Just one for dinner," Nick answered.

"Table, booth, or the bar?"

"Where ever you'd like me."

"Sorry, I'm on the clock. But if you're free later..." she said, winking and smiling up at Nick.

Nick blushed at her comment. "Sorry, I didn't mean. . ." He stopped. "A booth would be great, if you don't mind."

"Sure," she said as she led Nick to an empty one near a window. "Will this work?"

"Looks perfect," Nick said as he stuck his long legs under the table and slid in on the wooden bench.

"Anything to drink?" she said as she set a menu in front of him.

"What beer goes best with the ribs?"

"A lot of the locals drink Bud or Coors, but I'd recommend a nice lager."

"Sounds good, pick one for me," Nick said as he smiled up the waitress.

In her early thirties, Nick thought

"Sure thing, hon. I'll get you the Smoke Maibock, it's a Bourbon barrel-aged lager from Tahoe Brewing," she said as she headed toward the bar. "It's one of my favorites."

Her recommendation was spot-on as the crispness of the beer didn't overpower the flavor of the tender and juicy baby back ribs. He didn't want to stop eating and wipe his hands and mouth, so he just nodded his head when she asked if he wanted another beer. He finished the ribs and beans and coleslaw, took the last sip of the beer, and went to pay his check.

As he paid at the register, his waitress walked by.

"I'd check you out myself," she said. "But I already did."

Nick blushed, she laughed, and he waved before heading outside.

He shook his head. The electric signs were coming to life.

*Time to get to work,* Nick, he told himself. Now he could get some of those contrasting shots he mentioned to Emily.

# 7

## SIZE 14 SHOE?

Nick hit the exercise room and then the hot tub the next morning. The pulsating stream of the bubbles and warm water felt good on his leg. It was finally starting to feel a little more normal. All the driving and sitting around wasn't good for him. He leaned his head back as his long legs stretched to the other side. "Hmmm," he sighed as he briefly dozed off.

"Mind if I join you?" The voice startled Nick and he sat up, pulling his legs back from the other side of the hot tub.

"Sure. Sorry," Nick said as he looked up to see a short man with protruding belly standing nearby. "I was about to get out anyway."

"You don't have to leave on my account," the man said as he pulled up on the waistband of his baggy blue swimsuit.

"Not at all," Nick replied. "I've been in here a while, and I really do need to get a start on the day."

As Nick stood up in the hot tub, with his feet on the bottom, his head was up to the man's shoulders. The man's mouth opened as he watched Nick's long stride step out and stand next to him. "Are you here for that basketball exhibition?" he asked as he leaned his head back and his gaze extended upward.

"No," Nick said as he wrapped a towel around his waist and began to dry off. "I didn't even know there was one."

"I just thought," the man began. "You know, your height at all."

"Used to play, but my bum leg took me out of the game," Nick said as he patted his right leg. "Enjoy the relaxing water," he added as he turned toward the exit.

"Have a good day," the man said.

"You, too," Nick replied as he left the area, went to his room, showered, dressed, and went back down for breakfast.

Nick picked up the last copy of the local paper as he entered the breakfast room. A few new heads turned to stare as he walked by.

New faces, he thought. Didn't see them yesterday.

He got a large glass of orange juice and a cup of coffee and headed for an empty table near the window. He put the drinks and the paper down, and took a seat. Nick unfolded the paper as he reached for the glass of juice. He took a big swig as he looked at the headline. *A scandal in Reno, not a real shocker there.* He flipped the folded paper over. "Why Him" was the title that sat above a photo of a happy looking thirty-something man.

"Excuse me, sir," came a voice from his right side.

Nick looked up from the paper and saw a uniformed hotel employee. "Yes?"

"We'll be closing the breakfast area in about fifteen minutes. Is there anything I can get for you?"

"Oh, my," Nick said. "I didn't realize it was so late. My apologies." He stood up and looked around. "There's plenty here, thanks. Thanks for letting me know."

"You're welcome, sir."

Nick got a plate of food and a banana to go, and returned to his table. He started reading the article below the photo. It was about the decapitation victim. The whereabouts of the rest of the body were still unknown. *"Johnny was everyone's friend,"* said the Maintenance Manager at Western Nevada College. *"He was always on time, was a great worker, and wouldn't hurt a soul. Such a shame."*

The article continued onto the next page. Nick ate some his

breakfast before turning the page. There were more comments about Johnny being *"a good family man"* and someone who'd *"give you the shirt off his back."* An anonymous person familiar with the investigation said that a bloody boot print looked to be about size 14. "That's my shoe size," Nick mumbled to himself as he pushed the chair back and looked down at his large feet. He did, indeed, wear a size 14, fairly common for someone his height.

Nick finished breakfast, folded the paper under his arm, and grabbed the banana. He went to his room, put the Do Not Disturb sign on the door, and sat down at the desk. He opened the computer, logged on to the network, and opened a browser window. *Google certainly knows; it knows everything.* He typed in the Search bar: "number Carson City residents size 14 shoe."

"Shoe Size Conversion Chart" was the top response. Nick scrolled down the page. Nothing about the residents. Just articles on how to measure shoe sizes, and what a size 14 in the U.S. was in the U.K. He went to the next page, and the next, and the next. "Wow," he said out loud. "There is actually something Google doesn't know."

Nick tossed the paper into the trash. *Oh, well. I told Emily I wouldn't be digging into any more police cases, and I shouldn't be. I'm a photographer, not a detective.* He went into the bathroom and saw his wet bathing suit. *That guy down at the hot tub mentioned a basketball exhibition. I'll bet some of those guys wear a size 14, or close.*

Nick went back to his computer, re-opened the browser window and typed in "Carson City Police Department." Articles about the department, its Facebook page, a map, its address and phone number were quickly displayed. He picked up his phone and dialed 7 7 5...8 8 7...2 5 0 0.

"Carson City Police Department. How may I direct your call?"

"Yes. May I speak to one of the detectives working on that decapitation case?"

"Please hold."

"Homicide. Detective Jones speaking."

"Good morning, Detective. My name is Nick O'Flannigan. I'm a photographer from Seattle on assignment here in Carson City, and I noticed something in the article in this morning's paper. It mentioned a large boot print, maybe a size 14."

"I don't know where that came from," was the gruff reply.

"Yes, sir. I understand. But what I was thinking was that as a former college basketball player, I wear a size 14 shoe."

"So?"

"Well, I heard there was a basketball exhibition in town, and I'm sure that most of those players also wear a large shoe size, say 14 or so."

"What did you say your name was?"

"O'Flannigan. Nick O'Flannigan."

"May I have your phone number, please?"

"7 8 1 … 5 5 5 … 8 4 2 3."

"Well, Mr. O'Flannigan. Let me ask you this since you used to play basketball. How tall are you?"

Nick smiled. He was helping out. "Six-six."

"What about your stride? Do you take long steps?"

"Of course. Most people my size automatically take long strides, even longer when we're in a hurry."

"So, then would you say that someone wearing a size 14 shoe or boot would most likely then have a long stride?"

"Of course," Nick nodded. I knew they'd like my help.

"What I'm about to tell you," the Detective began slowly, "is confidential. If it comes out, then I'll know who said anything about it, so this is off the record, just to satisfy your curiosity. There was more than one boot print. Right, left, right, left, and so on. The distance between each of those prints was no more than two feet from one to the next. So, I'd be willing to bet my next paycheck that the person wearing the boots was not a tall basketball player."

"Oh," Nick sighed dejectedly.

"I appreciate your interest, Mr. O'Flannigan. Do give us a call if you come up with something else, perhaps a little more substantial."

"Sure," Nick said as he disconnected the call. *It seemed like a perfect fit.*

He scanned through the photos of the capitol he'd taken. *That's a good selection, and some of the ones of the signs will be good too. Adding photos with the Governor will definitely be the cat's meow.* Nick smiled as he shut down his laptop. He grabbed his phone and headed downstairs and outside.

The smells coming from the buffet were quite enticing as he entered the casino across the street. *Breakfast here tomorrow.* There was one Black Jack table open, and it had one player. Nick sat down at Third Base, and put two twenties on the green felt. The dealer nodded as he took Nick's money and swapped it for eight red chips. "Forty dollars," he said without taking his eyes off the table.

"Thank you," the pit boss said.

The other player at the table was nursing a bottle of Bud Light. He looked up at Nick and Nick smiled at him. "How's it going?"

"I'm about even, so not bad."

"That's good," Nick replied as he pushed a chip into the betting circle. He won some, lost some and finally looked at his watch. *Thirty minutes. Up ten dollars. Not exciting.*

"Thanks," he said as he put one of the red chips near the dealer's area, wiggled out of the tall chair, and headed to the Cashier. He went to the slot machines, sat down at a quarter machine and put a twenty into the slot.

Zero credits. That's what the machine showed. *How long have I been sitting here?* He looked at his watch; it had been thirty minutes. *I don't remember that much time passing. I must've zoned out.*

He got up and headed back outside when his phone buzzed. It was a text message. "Disposal fixed; was old. No word on possible move. Ben."

Back in his room, Nick looked back through some of the photos for the magazine, and then washed up as he got ready to head out for dinner. *Those ribs were great. I just might have them again tonight.* And he did. And the lager was nice and cold. The waitress was different, however. He wasn't sure if that made him happy or sad.

8

___

## TREE TRIMMING

Thunderstorms and rain prevailed throughout Wednesday night. Nick left the window open so he could listen to the sounds of the thunder and the rhythmic patter of the rain. He'd been able to take most of the photos he wanted to get. There wasn't a specific number he was supposed to submit from each city. It was his artistic draw to capture the scenes and the contrasts, but he knew he could only do what nature would allow him to.

But the weather was not cooperating with him or anyone else who wanted to be outside. The drizzling rain was present when he awoke, and the prediction for the day was that it would stay that way all day, or even worse. His online calendar sent a pop-up reminder that he had an 11:40 meeting with the Governor. It would be short, the secretary had told him. *Gotta be on top of my game.*

Nick grabbed his camera bag, umbrella, a light jacket and went to the casino across the street for breakfast. The country fried steak and gravy completely filled one plate. Two pancakes, two eggs, and two sausage links filled another. Fork in his right hand, he scrolled through photos on his camera with his left. Occasionally he needed both hands to use the fork and the knife. *Good photos, Emily will like them. And the lighting today is great for black and white ones.*

After breakfast he went out looking for opportunities for some nice grayscale black and white photos. Holding the umbrella in his left hand, he steadied the camera in his right as he captured shots of birds silhouetted against the clouds. He was framing the capitol building's portico between two tall trees when a couple turned and walked toward the building. Nick snapped several frames of the couple holding umbrellas in their outside hands while walking hand-in-hand, not knowing that they were creating some beautiful photographs that would someday be seen all over. There was nothing identifying about these shots since he couldn't see their faces, so Nick knew he didn't have to get their permission.

As he walked along Carson Street, Nick raised his camera to take a photo of an old neon sign where the letter S was flickering. *Didn't see that before*. He snapped the photo just as a bolt of lightning darted down from the sky and stopped right behind the sign. *Lightning shocks sign* might be the name for that photograph.

The ensuing thunder was nearby, just a few seconds after the lightning. Sensing a heavier rain, Nick stowed the camera in the bag, secured the top, turned around, and briskly walked back to the hotel. He was just inside the lobby when more rumbling thunder crashed down. He looked outside and saw heavy rain and even some hail coming down.

"Is this typical?" Nick asked the desk clerk.

"Well, not really," the clerk answered. "The good news is that storms usually move through rather quickly. But predicting the weather around here is always a guessing game."

Nick looked at his watch. "As in thirty minutes or so?"

"Yea, that's about right," the clerk responded. "But if it's still around in thirty minutes, it'll be here all day." The clerk looked around and saw no one else. "Why, did you have some plans for outside?"

"Kind of," Nick responded. "I've got a meeting with the Governor in a little over an hour, and I don't want to go in there looking like a soaked rat."

"Let me see what the Weather Channel shows," the young man

said as looked down at the computer screen and typed away on the keyboard. He nodded his head as he looked at the results. "You should be in luck. It looks like a fast-moving storm that should be out of there in twenty minutes or so. There might be a little drizzle a little later, but nothing heavy like last night or what's out there right now."

"That's good news. Thanks, man."

"No problem. Still going to that photography exhibition at the college tonight?"

"Sure am. You have a class?"

"Nah, I'm done for the week. At least for classes." The lobby doors opened, and another guest entered.

"Thanks for the information. I need to go up and change," Nick said as he stepped away from the desk.

"Any time. Good luck with the Governor. He seems like a pretty good guy." The clerk turned his attention to the new guest as Nick headed toward the elevator. "Good morning, sir. How may I help you?"

Nick went to his room and transferred the photos from his camera to his computer. He sent a quick email to Gerry, and he scanned social media for anything requiring his attention. A few followers from his MacroPhotography4U website had responded to his posting of the exhibition he was going to tonight. "Hope you find some cool ideas," one post said.

"They should have YOU as the expert," said another. Nick clicked the Like emoji for those posts and a few others.

He looked at his watch, 11:05. He did a quick calculation. His appointment was at 11:40, and he wanted to be there ten minutes early. Planning on ten to twelve minutes from the room meant he should leave about 11:15. *Time to change.*

As he left the hotel with his jacket, umbrella, and camera bag and walked to the capitol building, Nick's long stride made him think of his conversation with Detective Jones. He'd never actually measured his own stride. He looked down at his footprints on the wet sidewalk. The steady drizzle made it hard to actually see them so he stepped to a crack in the sidewalk, and then took a couple steps. He extended both arms. *Two steps a little over seven feet.* He quickly brought the umbrella back over his head.

The security guard recognized Nick, as did most people who'd met him, when he entered the capitol. "How are you today, sir? Staying dry?"

"I'm trying to," Nick answered. "Sure glad the heavy part of the storm moved through quickly. I wasn't sure what I was going to look like had it kept up." He set his camera bag on the moving belt as it made its continuous loop through the scanner.

The guard was too entranced with Nick's height and his stature to even look at the monitor as the bag was scanned. He looked at his clipboard. "11:40 with the Governor?"

"Right," Nick replied. "I'd like to get some outside shots with him. I mean photos," he corrected, realizing how that sounded. "But clearly this isn't the day for it, and his schedule is quite tight." Nick retrieved his bag and slung it over his shoulder. "I'm just happy to get any time with him. The magazine is going to love it."

"Good luck, and break a leg," the guard said as Nick headed to the Governor's office.

"Did that already," Nick said as the guard's comment seemingly triggered an ache in his right leg.

Relax. You can do this. You're okay.

Nick regained his composure, and walked confidently into the Governor's suite of offices. "Good morning," he said to the secretary.

"Good morning, Mr. O'Flannigan. Quite some weather out there."

"Yes, ma'am. But at least it has slowed to a drizzle. Are we still on track, fifteen minutes?"

"Yes," she replied. "But if you could cut it two or three minutes short, that will help, and maybe we could arrange something in the future, perhaps hiring you as a special events photographer. It would have to be much later as he's out of the office all day tomorrow and then the first part of next week."

"Of course, ma'am. Not an issue at all, and I appreciate the offer," Nick said even though he didn't expect anything to actually come from it.

The time with the Governor went by quickly. Nick was able to take several photos, including one that focused on the Governor framed in the large window behind him. It was still raining outside, albeit lightly, and there was someone out there trimming the trees. *I guess they're used to working in the rain given how unpredictable the weather is.*

"Thank you for the time, Governor. I appreciate you meeting with me," Nick said as he extended his right hand.

"Thank you very much, young man. I appreciate your flexibility. I used to freelance in my younger years, but in a completely different type of business, and I know how hard it is to meet your time schedules when you're depending on others. Do give my office a call if there's anything else you need while you're in the area."

"I certainly will, sir. Thanks again."

Nick left the Governor's office, thanked the secretary, and walked outside. He did manage to get a few more black and white photos in despite the little drizzle. He heard a small electric motor running and he looked to see that tree trimmer again. The short man was using a step ladder to gain access to the limbs of the tree.

What an industrious fellow.

# 9

# PHOTOGRAPHY EXPERTS

The rain stopped mid-afternoon, and the gray clouds gave away to a bright blue sky and brilliant sunshine. With his hotel window facing east, Nick saw the clouds and the rain moving toward the central part of the state. The afternoon sun was "behind" him, and the sun's rays bouncing off the rain created a full semi-circle rainbow. *What an amazing shot if I could get it to encircle the capitol.* He knew the rainbow wouldn't last long so he hurried to the rooftop terrace and snapped at least a dozen photos of the rainbow, using various camera settings to create different images. He turned his back to the rainbow, held the camera at arm's length, pointed it at himself, and took a photo. The selfie was perfect, a rainbow looking like a vertical halo over his head. He hit the web button on his camera and texted the selfie to Sandra, with a note, *"Thinking of you."*

After dinner he grabbed his camera bag and headed to the Photography Exhibition. He typed Western Nevada College into his phone's mapping app, plugged it into the car's USB port, and followed the instructions. When he arrived, he found it was not a large campus, but there were large posters and signs pointing the way to the Arts Building so he found it easily.

The exhibition contained more than just photographs. There

were demonstrations of various tools and programs for enhancing images, some of the same things that he'd discussed recently with Emily. He was intrigued by a demonstration by three of the students and their professor. They had developed a program called "Reveal-It!," and were giving demonstrations of how it worked. The basic idea of the program was that it could remove "image layers," even ones that the user didn't know existed, to reveal what was behind them.

"One of the uses of this new program," one of the students was saying as Nick approached, "is to eliminate unwanted or distracting layers in an image. For example, here's a photograph I took outside today during the rain. As you can see, the rain and the haze blur out what's farther back in the shot. But with just a little manipulation," and he paused to type in a few computer commands. "The rain and the haze are gone, and now the image is bright and we can see what's in the background much more clearly."

"That's interesting," Nick said. "But doesn't Photoshop already have that feature?"

"Good question," the professor intervened. "While their methodology has been the standard for image editing for many years now, what we've developed is based on an entirely different set of algorithms that are completely user-controlled. So, for example, you don't have to remove layers based on their relative position within the image. You can remove, replace, or modify entire layers or even parts of a layer."

"As a freelance photographer, I'm sure I could find many good uses for that application. Is it available to the public?"

"Not yet," the professor responded. "We've filed various patent applications, and we've been advised by our attorneys, or should I say the college's attorneys, that we shouldn't release it until we have a definitive ruling from the Patent & Trademark Office."

"That's too bad," Nick replied. "But you're showing it here. Doesn't that damage the filing process?"

"I'm just a professor, and the attorneys said it was okay to demonstrate it. We just can't sell it or even release it for beta testing yet."

"Makes sense," Nick answered.

"Do you have an image you'd like to try it on?"

"Hmm. Hadn't thought of that," Nick said as he switched his camera on and went through the images on his SD card.

"Nice rainbow shots," the professor said as he also looked at the camera's display. "Even the selfie," he said, chuckling.

"I was lucky I was able to get to the hotel's rooftop in time before it faded away." Nick continued scrolling through the images. He came to the one at the capitol where the Governor was framed by the window in the background.

"Nice composition," the professor said. "Notice how the view out the window is quite faded? You can barely see the trees."

"Yeah, the rain," Nick replied.

"Right. But, if you don't mind, let's put that image through our software and see what else we can see out there."

"Sure," Nick said as he switched the camera off, popped out the SD card, and handed it to the professor.

The professor handed the card to the student at the computer. He put it into the card slot, and a folder opened with Nick's images. The student found the right image and made a copy of it. He then opened the image in their program, identified various layers, and selected two of them. A clearer image was now on the screen.

"You see how it's as if there is no rain at all?" the professor asked. "Much sharper and clearer now, don't you think?"

"Definitely," Nick replied. "Can you zoom in on the tree trimmer there?"

"Sure," the student said as he manipulated the image some more.

"Holy crow," Nick exclaimed.

"What?" the professor asked.

"The tree trimmer," Nick said.

"Oh, yes. They work in all kinds of weather here. It's amazing that one hasn't been electrocuted or shocked. They run all sorts of equipment no matter what it's doing outside." The professor looked at the image some more. "Hey, that's Manny. He used to work here at the college. Something happened and he was let go not long ago. But he's such a hard worker for such a short guy. Look at him on that ladder using a Sawzall to trim those thicker limbs." He paused for a moment.

"Why's he using a Sawzall to trim branches?" one of the students asked.

The professor shrugged his shoulders. "Good question. He always talked about his chainsaw when he was here, and how he kept it so sharp it could cut through anything."

"Maybe he didn't want to risk ruining it in the rain," Nick added as he looked up and saw another student nearby in a cowboy hat. "Nice hat."

"Thanks," the cowboy student replied.

"Good possibility," the prof replied.

"But even a battery operated machine like the Sawzall is more dangerous in the rain than gas powered," the student at the computer replied. "My dad got a bad shock that way once."

Nick continued to look at the image. Something caught his eye. "Can you save that image on my card? I'd like to look at it some more."

The student raised his eyebrows and looked up at the professor.

The professor paused. "We're not supposed to," he said.

Nick pulled a business card out his pocket and handed it to the professor. "Here's my card. I think this image might be very important, and I promise I won't say anything about your software. If you give me your contact information, I will let you know if my theory pans out right away. It might even be tomorrow."

"Excuse me, fellows," the professor said to his students as he motioned for Nick to follow him to an area to the side where they would not be overheard.

The professor outlined something for him, and Nick agreed. After they shook hands, they returned to where the student was at the computer.

"Go ahead and save that image on his card," the professor said. The student pressed a few buttons, ejected the card, and handed it to Nick who re-inserted it into his camera.

"Thanks again, professor, gentlemen. Nice job. I hope you get your approvals soon and get this out to the market. You'll not only make a lot of money, but you'll make certain types of photography easier to do, and a lot more fun. Take care," he added as he turned away. There was more to see, but he wanted to get back to the hotel and look at that enhanced image again.

# 10

## RAIN, RAIN, GO AWAY

Nick was awakened the next morning by the sound of thunder and the rain pounding against the hotel room window. His work was essentially done here in Carson City. All he had left to do was to finalize his selection of photos for the magazine and upload them to the Cloud. Then he could have a relaxing rest of the day as he planned out his trip to Boise, Idaho.

He had planned to go to the breakfast casino buffet, but opted to stay dry at the hotel. He grabbed a newspaper out of habit and then got some orange juice and a cup of coffee. He set those down along with the paper and went back to the buffet. When he returned to his table he unfolded the paper. "El Niño and the Rain" was the headline. *So that's why so much rain here.* "Good for the reservoirs," the article went on to say, but flash floods were causing problems at the base of the mountains.

The buzzing in his pocket told him his phone was about to ring. He pulled the phone out, it was Gerry. *Why would she be calling this early in the day?* "Hey, Gerry," he said quietly into the phone as the call was connected. "What's up?"

"Hey, Nick. How's it going there?" Her normally effervescent voice was a bit placid.

"It's all okay here. It's been a good week, in spite of the weather trying to throw curveballs at me every so often. You know I love your calls, but this is a bit early even for you. Everything okay?"

"Emily asked me to call and give you a heads up that the payroll system has gone on the fritz, and your check for Sacramento won't be deposited into your account today like it was supposed to be. She's sorry about that, but she wanted you to know that we're all in the same situation. They hope to get it back up and running over the weekend so checks can be deposited on Monday. If that's a problem, I can go take some money out of my savings and put it into your account to cover for the weekend."

"You're sweet, Gerry, but I'm fine. My credit card payment isn't due for another couple weeks, and I have some money in savings too. A few more days won't matter, but thanks for the offer, and tell Emily thanks for the heads up."

"Will do. Emily said you two had a good chat earlier in the week. That's always good news."

"Yea, it was. She liked my ideas for mixing up some of the photo styles. Oh, and last night I went to a photography exhibition at the local college. A few of the students and their prof developed a new photo editing program that is really sharp. It can pull out layers and other properties so you can focus on what are otherwise hidden details. They did it on a photo I took in the Governor's office and looking out the window. The detail that it brought out was amazing. Uh," Nick realized he was telling Gerry too much about something he wasn't even supposed to be involved in. "Anyway, it's pretty sharp."

"How's everything else there?" she asked.

"Great," he replied. "I'm finalizing the rest of the week's photos and uploading them to the Cloud. Looks like a long drive to Boise, but I should be able to get an early start in the morning."

"That's great. Have you heard from Sandra?

"Yeah, we exchanged some texts last night."

"Cool. Safe drive tomorrow."

"You bet. Thanks for the call, Gerry."

"Bye, Nick."

After another hotel breakfast, Nick went to his room, and separated the photos into the "Magazine" and "Personal" folders on his computer. He reviewed the photos for the magazine, and when he was satisfied, he took one final look at them before sending them to the magazine's Cloud folder. He didn't want to make the mistake of uploading some his personal photos again. *Once was certainly enough.*

"Let's look at that image again," Nick mumbled as he opened the "Personal Photos" folder. He double-clicked the image from last night's exhibition. The gardener, Manny is what the professor called him, was so clear in the edited image. The professor didn't think there was anything wrong with Manny working in the rain. It was common according to the professor. Nick zoomed in. The professor said he was short, so maybe five-four or five-six. As he brought the magnifier down the man's body, his boots looked out of place.

For a short man, the boots looked big, really big. Nick grabbed some note paper and marked off the length of the boots, and then compared that with the length of his legs and his arms. The boots were definitely too large. He'd never heard of any "short people" having such big feet.

Was that possible or even likely? And what was it that Detective Jones said about the relatively short stride for such large boots?

He copied the image to a thumb drive, went downstairs and printed the image. That's all he would take with him.

# 11

## STILL NO BODY

**B**ack in his room, Nick looked online for the address of the County Morgue. He wrote it down, grabbed his phone, the printout, jacket, and umbrella. He entered the address into his mapping app, and followed the directions. It seemed only fitting that the rain was still coming down as he pulled into the parking lot. It was much lighter now, barely a drizzle. Not a very lively place on the brightest of days, the dark and gloom outside was an indicator of what it was typically like inside.

He shook as much water off his umbrella as he could before entering the morgue's main lobby. He strode confidently up to the counter where a uniformed member of the Sheriff's Department had today's desk duty.

"May I help you, sir?" the deputy asked.

"Yes. Good morning. I'm a freelance photographer from Seattle in town on a magazine assignment." He paused as he pulled a business card from his wallet and handed it to the man. "I had a meeting with the Governor yesterday, and I told him that I had some information that could be helpful in that decapitation case." At least the first part was true.

The deputy's eyes opened wider and when he stood up, his eyes were even with Nick's chin.

"Anyway," Nick continued, "he suggested that I come talk to the coroner about it. He said you could call him to verify. But I only have today as I have to leave tomorrow morning for another assignment. Is Doctor Larson available?"

The normally unflappable deputy, himself a solid six feet tall, seemed taken aback by Nick's confidence. "That is outside normal procedures," the deputy said. "But let me check with the Coroner."

"Of course," Nick said. He remembered that the Governor's secretary said he would be out all day today, so even if the deputy called, there would be no way to verify or disprove what Nick had told him. He felt a little awkward about the lie, but he felt like it was a good cause. He stepped away from the desk although he could still overhear the deputy's side of the conversation.

"Excuse me, sir," the deputy called to Nick. "The coroner said it would be okay. Do you have any weapons, knives, guns, anything like that?"

"Nothing; just my cell phone."

"That's okay, but no photographs without the coroner's permission."

"Of course," Nick replied.

"I still need to wand you," the guard said as he stood and ran the wand up and down Nick's front side and back.

A side door opened, and an elderly man in white scrubs appeared. "I'm Doctor Larson," the man said.

"Good morning, sir," Nick said as he handed him a business card. "Thank you for seeing me. I'm sure the Governor will appreciate your courtesy just as much as I do." The old man led him through the door.

"So, Mr. O'Flannigan, exactly what is it that you have that made the Governor so sure I'd want to hear from you?"

Nick cleared his throat. "Well," he began. "My specialty is macro photography. I focus on small details that most people overlook." Nick switched from being on the defensive to being on the offensive.

"Now before I go into what information I have, I would like to ask you something." He did not pause. "What was the apparent method of decapitation?"

"We've not yet released that information, but in deference to the Governor, I'll tell you our preliminary findings. But you are to hold this in strictest confidence. Do I have your word?"

"Naturally," Nick replied.

"It couldn't have been a pretty sight, not that many beheadings are. It was a rough jagged cut, and our initial speculation is that it looks consistent with the cutting patterns of a chainsaw or something similar. Obviously, what we don't know, given that we don't have the rest of the body, is if the victim was already dead when the head was removed."

"Ooh," Nick said. "That does sound ugly. Now, I'm more familiar with cameras and photography paraphernalia than I am with power tools. In your experience, why would someone cut off a man's head with a chainsaw?"

"Why? Good question, but it is easier than other methods. Axes and other chopping methods are messier. A chainsaw is fast and fairly clean. A sharp sword is better, but that takes more skill. But as for the real why, that's for the police to figure out." He paused. "Now, what was it that you said you had that might help?"

Nick pulled the printout from his pocket, unfolded it, and slid it to the coroner. "Here is an enhanced image from a photo I took when I was with the Governor yesterday. Here's the gardener, his name is Manny I was told, using a Sawzall to trim the trees. A professor out at the college said that Manny had been a gardener there, and that he was very proud of his chainsaw. So the professor thought it was odd that he was using a Sawzall in this photo."

"Good point," the Coroner said. "Perhaps he just had some small limbs to clean up and he didn't feel he needed the extra power."

"Those limbs look pretty thick though. It could be he didn't want to use it in the rain and perhaps ruin it," Nick added. "I'm no expert, but I would think using an electric saw, even with just the battery, would be more dangerous than using a gas-powered chainsaw. And look at those boots. They are much bigger than any man his size would normally wear. I chatted with a Detective Jones down at the Police Department, and he said that the bloody boot prints showed a short stride. That's not normal for someone wearing a size 14 boot. Normally, the person wearing them would be tall like me, I wear a size 14, and it would be a long stride. So here's a man using a Sawzall instead his chainsaw, wearing large boots that look about like a size 14, and he's a short man."

"Hmmm," the coroner said. "That's some pretty good figuring, and a good guess. But I know what the police are going to say. They'll want to know what the motive was, and where the weapon is. Using a Sawzall instead of a chainsaw on the tree is pretty circumstantial."

"I know," Nick said. "But it seems strange that he would wear those large boots and that there would be more than one short man wearing them here in town. Don't you agree?"

"Actually, I do. I'll call them and offer the information. Just don't get your hopes up." The coroner picked up a phone and placed a call.

"Yes, this is Doctor Larson at the County Morgue. May I speak with Detective Jones in Homicide please?"

# 12

# WHAT'S IN THE SHED?

Two marked police cars pulled into the Capitol Maintenance parking lot. Nick arrived a few minutes later, having stopped by the hotel to grab his camera bag. Detective Jones said that he could tag along, but that he had to stay back a "safe distance." A junior officer was assigned to stay back with him and "keep an eye on the photographer."

"Don't they need a warrant?" Nick asked.

"No," the junior officer had told him. "It's a state building, so a search warrant isn't necessary. Besides, we brought in the State Police, and they can search anywhere on their property. Since the maintenance shed and the tools belong to the state, not the suspect personally, at least they can have a look."

Nick put his longest telephoto lens on the camera as he stood next to his car. Two officers went around the building to the rear entrance, the one with the large roll-up doors for the machinery. Detective Jones and his partner slowly approached the main office door. Jones motioned with his left hand for his partner to open it, which he did, and the door remained open as the two men stepped inside.

Nick saw the Detective's hand motion through the camera and

used it to his advantage. "He signaled for us to come on," Nick said to the officer waiting with him, and slowly started walking forward.

Nick approached with caution and kept looking through the camera's telephoto lens. He could see that Manny was talking with secretary when the officers entered. Manny turned and disappeared from Nick's view. He increased his pace as he heard Jones yell.

"Manny!" yelled Jones. "Go after him," he yelled to his partner who was already heading through the rear door in pursuit.

"Suspect heading into back of building," Jones said into his shoulder mic.

"Roger," an officer replied.

"Be careful," Jones responded.

"Will do. Two officers moving in stick formation."

A side door to the building flew open, and Manny came running out.

"There he is," the officer said.

Nick raised his camera, snapping photo after photo. The young officer with him was absorbed by the action too, and didn't stop him. Even at this safe distance, Manny's small frame filled the telephoto lens.

One of the officers from the back of the building sprinted after Manny who started running in the direction of Nick and the officer. Nick kept snapping away, and the young officer stepped forward, his hand on the butt of his weapon. Manny saw them and turned around. The officer was closing in on him, and another approached from the opposite direction.

Manny appeared to be trapped. He turned back around and ran to the front of the building just as Jones appeared in the doorway.

"Manny, stop!" Jones yelled.

But Manny kept running. His short stride and baggy overalls slowed him down, and Jones quickly caught up, tackled him, and wrestled him to the pavement.

Nick caught the action with his camera, including Jones cuffing Manny and pulling him to a standing position.

"Why were you running?"

"I don't trust you," Manny replied. "You didn't help me at the college. Why would you help me now?"

"But if you didn't do anything, why would you need our help?" Jones asked as he held the cuffed hands with his right hand. "Those are rather large boots, aren't they?"

"I like them," Manny replied. "Keeps my normal shoes and my clothes clean."

"It's okay, fellas," Jones hollered to Nick and his guard and motioned for them to approach.

Manny stared at them.

"I wonder what's in the shed," Jones said to Manny. "Shall we go see?"

Detective Jones, the two officers, and Manny walked toward the shed that looked like an old building that had been abandoned decades ago. Jones's partner and Nick walked briskly from the front of the building as the others converged on the shed.

"Damn, that's a long stride," Jones's partner said as he struggled to keep pace with Nick even with his slight limp.

Nick smiled. "Six-six and size fourteens."

Detective Jones waited until everyone was right there. "Everyone put gloves on, don't touch anything unless instructed to by me, and watch where you step. We don't know that it's a crime scene inside, but we need to protect it just in case."

Gloves on, Jones turned the handle on the shed door and slowly pushed it inward as the hinges shrieked from dust and neglect. He looked at his hand, something was on it. Something dark red. Rust? Blood? It was dark inside. He pulled the flashlight from his belt, turned it on, and shone it on the light switch next to the door. There was more of the dark red stuff on the switch plate. And what was that stench coming from inside?

"Flannigan," Jones called out.

"You mean O'Flannigan?" Nick responded as he replaced the telephoto lens with the standard one.

"Whatever," Jones replied. "Come in here and take some pictures," he said as he flicked on the light.

The second officer led Manny through the door as Nick snapped pictures of the shed and Manny's entrance into it. Nick stepped inside, took photos of the light switch and plate, and turned to see a crest-fallen Manny. Snap. Snap.

"That's awful," one of the officers said as he turned around and stepped back outside to the fresh air.

The overhead light did little to illuminate the shed. Jones used his flashlight to follow a trail of blood. It led to a wooden box. "Over here," he said to Nick who took pictures of the blood on the floor, and then carefully walked around it. More photos of the wooden box.

"What's in the box, Manny?" Jones asked.

"Tools. Stuff."

"Why the blood?"

Manny shrugged. "I must have cut myself." He looked down to the floor.

"Open it," Jones said to the first officer.

Nick snapped more pictures as the box was opened and flies escaped into the small room. A horrific smell also leapt out of the box and smacked them in the face.

"Whoa," Jones said as the smell of the headless body made him cough. "Whew, that's bad. Get some photos if you can, but this is where we call Coroner Larson in."

Nick coughed as the smell was unbelievable. "My god, that's horrible," he said as he snapped only a few photos before he couldn't take it anymore. He turned around and quickly got outside. As soon as he smelled the fresh air, he doubled over, spitting and coughing. No matter what he did, it didn't seem like he could get the cloying smell from his nostrils and the heaviness out of his lungs.

After a few deep breaths, he was finally able to stand. This was an experience that would stay with him for a long time.

He was quickly joined by the officers and the handcuffed Manny.

"So, Manny," Jones began. "Why'd you do it?"

"He was out to get me from the very beginning," Manny said in a soft voice.

"What do you mean?"

"Ever since I started at the college, Johnny never liked me. Accused me of seeing his wife when he was out of town. That's all a lie. Then one day a piece of equipment was missing and he said I stole it and sold it to some developers up in the mountains. I was the last one who'd used it, so they believed him. And I was fired. I told him I'd get even with him some day. It's a shame the bar is bent on my chainsaw. But it was worth it."

"I wouldn't worry about that, Manny," Jones said as he read him his rights. "You won't be trimming any more trees where you're going."

# 13

# TIME TO SAY, "SO LONG, NEVADA"

Nick watched as Doctor Larson and the junior officer carried a body bag out of the shed and put it into the van. Both men had masks over the nose and mouth. Nick took his pictures from about fifty feet away. Even so, the foul smell lingered in his nose.

He got back into his car, drove to the hotel, and took a long hot shower as soon as he got to his room. The warm spray helped relax him and clear the smells from his body. But he couldn't get the image of the headless body out of his mind as his body shook uncontrollably. *Is this how soldiers feel when they kill someone or come upon a corpse?*

Tears rolled down Nick's face. He was a photographer who normally took pictures of beautiful things. Today he took pictures of a headless body, a man who'd been murdered and then brutally decapitated. How would he get that image out his mind?

He'd encountered the darker side of humanity, the side few saw or wanted to see. He was suddenly glad he was not a detective, not a police photographer. He vowed then and there to stay out of police business from then on.

Nick dried off and opened up the photos app on his phone. He found a couple photos of Sandra. Her image calmed him down. He smiled at her. *Oh, to kiss her again. Even if for just a second.*

He took his Western States map downstairs with him as he went to a different casino buffet for what he hoped would be a quiet dinner. He knew he had a long drive ahead of him tomorrow. The Friday night crowd wasn't that big, so he got his wish for a more subdued evening. As he waited for his main course to arrive, he looked at the route he was planning to take: up to Reno, then to Winnemucca, then up to the Jordan Valley and some small towns before getting on the Interstate that would take him the final leg into Boise. The legend showed him it would be about a four hundred fifty mile trip. And he would lose an hour as he crossed into the Mountain Time zone.

*Better get an early start tomorrow,* he thought as the plate of T-bone steak with potatoes, gravy, and asparagus arrived. It smelled great, and the taste matched.

As he got back to the hotel, he saw that Breakfast hours on the weekend started at 7:00; *perfect.*

He went to his room, went through a few more photos, uploaded them to his personal account, and even a few to social media. He'd promised Detective Jones that he would send some to him, so he emailed six photos of the encounter with Manny and the arrest earlier today. The ones of the headless body still repulsed him. He was sure he could still smell that body just by looking at them.

Nick packed up his clothes and camera gear, although he did put the battery into the charger so it would be one hundred percent in the morning. He plugged in his cell phone, set the alarm for six, and slipped into bed. It had been a long day, and a long week. Tomorrow would be a calm relaxing drive. *Hopefully.*

# SOME FACTS ABOUT CARSON CITY AND THE STATE OF NEVADA

The State Capital since Nevada's 1864 statehood, Carson City was named after Kit Carson.

Numismatists, aka coin collectors, know Carson City as the place where silver and gold coins were minted with the rare "CC" mint mark. The mint building now serves as a state museum.

Nevada was the first U.S. state (and the first in the world) to adopt the gas chamber as its method of carrying out death penalty executions in Carson City. The metal chair used in the gas chamber has been loaned to "The Mob Museum" (the National Museum of Organized Crime & Law Enforcement) in Las Vegas.

Carson City is the smallest of the United States' 366 metropolitan statistical areas.

While California is known for its Gold Rush, Nevada is called the 'Silver State' because of the discovery of silver first in 1859. Called the Comstock Lode, it was the largest silver find in the world.

Nevada gets its name from a Spanish word meaning "snow-clad," an oddity given that most of the state is desert land. There are some mountains and mountain ranges that have snow for half the year.

Speaking of mountain ranges, Nevada has more of them than any other state.

The longest Morse code telegram ever sent was the Nevada state constitution. It was sent from Carson City to Washington D.C., in 1864, the year Nevada became the 36th U.S. state.

Guinness World Records point to Carson City as the site for the 1988 Women's International Bowling Congress Championship tournament which attracted 77,735 bowlers over 96 days in 2004. This event represents the most participants in a women's sporting event ever.

Mule deer are year-round residents in Carson City and other Nevada towns.

# BURIED IN BOISE

BOOK #5 IN THE CAPITAL CITY MURDERS
SERIES

# PROLOGUE — MISSING PERSON

"Today marks the one-year anniversary of the mysterious disappearance of Jennifer Langsford, wife of a local businessman who is pleading with anyone with information about her to please come forward. Welcome to our Sunday Focus on the Valley Show. I'm Sandy Johnson filling in for Kerri Wilson who has the weekend off." The cameraman pulled back as the close-up of the fill-in news anchor turned into a broader view of the news desk and the team of reporters. "We start tonight with a special report from Angelá Martinez."

The camera swung right and zoomed in on the young Boise State University graduate, born and raised in the Treasure Valley, whose goal was to become a news reporter, and maybe someday an anchor at a local station. "Thank you, Sandy," Angelá began. "Yes, today marks one year since Boise businessman Malcolm Thornton reported his wife Jennifer missing, and she hasn't been heard from during that time. We were able to interview him at their home where he shared with us more about Jennifer and what it's been like living without her this past year."

The picture switched from the somber news reporter to a video inside the Thornton residence. "It's been difficult," the husband said as he walked through the living room. "She would sit here and play such beautiful melodies." He pointed to the upright piano against the wall next to the brick fireplace. "Friends would come over for Christmas and we'd sit in front of the fireplace and sing carols as she played. Or we'd just sip a warm drink and listen. She was magical. Her presence would light up a room the way she lit up my life."

Malcolm turned and walked through the dining room to a sliding door leading outside. "You've not heard anything from her in the year?" Angelá asked as they stepped out on the patio.

"Nothing."

What have the police told you about their investigation?"

"Hmm," he sighed and then swallowed hard. "There's been no activity in her accounts, checking, savings, cell phone. Nothing. The only thing was a nine thousand five hundred dollar withdrawal from her savings account they day before she disappeared."

"That's a rather large amount. Was that typical?"

"No, but it was her money from her inheritance. Sometimes she would tell me when she was taking money out, and why, but I never asked."

"Our viewers might wonder why you waited two days to report her missing. Can you tell us about that? Did you try calling her? Or contacting any of her friends?"

"I did. I called her cell phone and left messages until the mailbox was full. I called her friends, her sister out of state. No one had heard from her."

"But you thought she was somewhere even though her car was still here in the garage?"

"Yes, that is crazy, I know. But sometimes a friend would pick her up or she would take an Uber. She would often take trips with a friend for a day or two. That didn't seem completely unusual."

"I know this is a bit sensitive, but were you two having any troubles? Anything with your marriage or your business that might have triggered her to just leave?"

"No. My business is solid. We're not rich, but we're comfortable. She's never had to work, although she's been contacted by several ensembles when there's been an opening for a pianist. She could do it, but she liked playing for fun. She said that the enjoyment might disappear if it became her job." He blinked his eyes and small tear drops began to roll down his cheeks. "Sorry," he added as he sniffled and wiped the tears with the back of his tanned hands.

"That's okay," Angelá offered. "I understand she was really into flowers. Which ones were her favorites?"

The scene cut to the back yard where planter boxes lined the back fence. Malcolm stopped in front of a low one teeming with white hydrangeas and turned toward Angelá. The sun shone brightly on his face, and he squinted his eyes as he took sunglasses out of his pocket and put them on.

"Jennifer was very active in the Garden Club, something she wasn't able to do much where she grew up in Boston. She would occasionally hold a meeting here, and the women would share tips on planting and growing and getting the best from each variety. She even took notes."

"Can you tell me about these flowers and why they meant so much to her?"

Malcolm turned to his left and reached down to cup a large globe in his hand, and the camera followed. "The color is so pure, and they grow so easily. One of the things that she liked about these is the fact that they can change color based on the soil composition." He released the flower and stepped to the next box.

"These are interesting flower boxes," the reporter said, stepping back and looking at the mix of box heights and wood combinations.

"Jennifer wanted something different, so I told her I would create a skyline of planters for her."

The camera panned out to take in a wide shot, and then tightened back in on the reporter.

"They look nice, and I like the way you have the taller bushes in the lowers ones, and the short flowers and herbs in the taller ones."

Malcolm smiled as he reached into the flowers and held one of them. "These are intriguing. They were new last year, originally pink, but they have slowly changed to blue and lavender. Maybe I'll see what the ladies in the Garden Club think about that the next time I see them."

"Did she spend a lot of time out here?"

"As much as she could when she wasn't involved with other activities."

"I can imagine, it's a beautiful area. What other activities was she involved with?"

The scene cut to Malcom and the reporter sitting at a patio table under a cover. The cameraman had been able to choose a better angle this time.

"She was always into social activism, and that was one of the many things I loved about her. I think that's perhaps even why she kept her maiden name. It was her identity, and her way of saying she wasn't a conformist. She cared for other people, especially those who were not always treated fairly by society. She used some of her inheritance to start a Hispanic Asylum Center in rural Canyon County."

"I know all about that place," Angelá said. "I was born and raised in that area. My dad worked the farms, and he told me when I was very young, and kept telling me every year, that I was going to college so I didn't have to work with my hands the way he did. It's a great cause. For our viewers who aren't aware of the Hispanic Asylum Center and what it does, would you tell us a little about it?"

"Of course."

1
———

## LONG DAY'S DRIVE

**A**s he ate breakfast in the Carson City Hotel on Saturday morning, Nick thought about what happened the day before. He'd photographed a headless body, and he was hit with a putrefying smell that he hoped he'd never encounter again. He couldn't help but pick up a newspaper. The story was there, right on the front page, including one of the photographs he'd sent to Detective Jones. He quickly scanned the article. *Phew, no mention of my name,* he thought. *Now maybe I can forget that this ever happened. And maybe I can wipe that horrible smell from my memory.*

After eating another predictable and less-than-exciting hotel breakfast, Nick went upstairs and did a second check of his room before he checked out at the front desk.

"Enjoy your stay, Mr. O'Flannigan?" the clerk asked.

"There were great parts, and then there are parts I'd just as soon forget."

"Did you see that article about the headless body? Wow!"

"Yeah, I did," Nick answered. *I was trying to forget about that,* he thought as the clerk typed away and then handed Nick his copy of the bill. "Thanks," Nick said.

"Thank you for your business. Heading home today?"

"I wish," Nick sighed. "On my way to Boise."

"Hope you have good air conditioning. You're crossing a lot of desert."

"I saw that. Well, I'd better get going. The staff here was great. Thanks again," Nick said as he extended a long right arm across the counter to shake the clerk's hand.

"Take care," the clerk said.

Nick climbed into the front seat of his car, fastened the seat belt, checked the mirrors, started the engine, and looked at the fuel level. *Plenty to make it to Reno,* he thought, *but then I'd have to get off the freeway.* He headed north on Carson Street, stopped at a gas station, filled up, washed the rain spots off all the windows, bought an energy drink, and hit the restroom one more time. *It might be a long drive,* he thought.

He'd entered his Boise hotel into the mapping app on his cell phone and plugged it into the car's USB port. "453 miles to your destination," the display showed. "Continue north on North Carson Street," the app instructed. Nick pulled out of the station, turned right, and followed the directions until he was on Interstate 580, heading in the right direction. He lowered the windows a bit as he wanted to enjoy some fresh air before he was forced to turn on the A/C. *Almost all freeway for the rest of the trip,* he thought as he set cruise control, and enjoyed the fresh air circulating through the car.

Heading north toward Reno, Nick turned on the radio, but heard nothing on FM that appealed to him. He switched to AM and scanned until he found a talk show that sounded interesting. He closed the windows so he could hear the radio, and he turned on the A/C. The sun was coming in the other side of the car, but Nick could feel its warmth on his right side. The cold A/C felt good. He listened to "Money Matters" through Reno, where he joined I-80, and then the show ended shortly before he reached Winnemucca. He switched off the radio, and enjoyed the quiet for the last thirty or so miles into the small Nevada town.

Nick pulled off the freeway and stopped at the first gas station. The energy drink had kept him alert, but it had also worked its way through his system. As he swung his long legs out the car door open-ing, his right knee popped. "Ow," he said automatically as he reached down and rubbed the knee. "I've still got a long way to go. I need to stop and stretch more often." He filled up before heading to the attached convenience store. He drew stares as he limped slowly, favoring his right leg.

"Hi," a young woman said as she opened the door to exit the store.

"Hi," Nick replied as he tried to smile through the pain.

Noticing the grimace on his face, she held the door open for him. "Are you okay?" she asked.

"I am, thanks," he answered. "I've got a bad leg, and I've been driving for almost three hours. I just need to stretch it out some."

She looked down at his leg, and then all the way up, smiling as her eyes scanned Nick back down from head to toe.

Nick turned to go inside as she held the door for him.

"I've got some really strong pills that'll take away that pain."

Nick stopped, thought a moment, then replied. "Thanks, but no thanks. I'll just get some aspirin or something."

"No worries. I just hate to see a nice guy like you suffer."

*A nice guy like me?* Nick thought. *How would she know? Time to move on.* "Thanks," he said again. "Have a good day."

"Pain medicine?" Nick asked the idle clerk.

"Third aisle, left side," the clerk answered. "Basketball?"

"Used to," Nick replied. "Injured my leg, ending my plans for an NBA career." Nick walked by the third aisle and went into the restroom. As he came out he found the pain medicines and picked a box of Extra Strength Tylenol. He grabbed an energy drink and a couple bottles of water. "Any great burger joints close by?" he asked the clerk as he took his items to the counter.

"I'm partial to the fries at Burger King, but if you want a really good burger, I'd go to Wingers. It's at the far end of town, but you can't miss it. You go by it, and you're out of town."

"Thanks," Nick said as he paid for his items. He opened the box, then a bottle and popped three pills into his mouth, chasing it with the entire contents of a bottle of water. "Recycle this?"

"Sure. I'll take it and the box too."

"Appreciate it," Nick said as he let out a big sigh.

"Where you headed?" The clerk looked outside and saw that the young woman who befriended Nick earlier was still standing outside by her car.

"Boise. What do you think? About another five hours?"

"Yeah. Five with stops. Four if you just push through."

"Did that coming in from Carson City. I don't imagine there's much along the way, but I definitely need a couple stops."

"That's a smart idea. Also watch out for the cops in Oregon. They love to get speeders, especially if you have out-of-state plates."

"Thanks for the heads up."

"Sure," the clerk replied. "That gal out there, the one who held the door for you. Her name's Judy, and she's no good. She'll probably offer to fix you lunch but that's not all she has in mind. I'd avoid her if you can."

"Trouble is certainly something I don't need," Nick replied as he grabbed the bag and headed out the door.

Nick forced himself to walk without a limp as he headed straight to his car. He saw her approaching from the side, but he didn't slow down.

"Hey, there," Judy said as she got closer. "We're pretty neighborly here in town. How about I fix you some lunch?" She smiled at Nick as he looked at her.

"Thanks, but I'm kind of on a deadline, and I need to get going."

"A big guy like you can't go without lunch, can you?" Her eyes gave him the up-and-down look again.

"I'll be fine." Nick got into his car and headed down the road toward Wingers. He looked in the rearview mirror to see if Judy was following. She wasn't. At least he didn't see her.

He couldn't pass up the Garlic Breath Burger at Wingers. Just the name alone was enough to draw him in. The parmesan-garlic aioli & melted sharp cheddar cheese was awesome. He avoided the temptation to have a beer. *Not when I such a long drive ahead,* he thought.

As Nick walked out of the restaurant, Judy from the gas station was there. She had parked her car next to his. "I thought you said you had to get on the road. What's the matter? Is there something wrong with me?"

"No, you look just fine, and you're very kind. But I don't have time to stop here."

"This town doesn't have anyone like you. The guys here are all hicks, not studs." Judy walked up to Nick and put her arm around his waist. "And a girl like me gets lonely, if you know what I mean."

Nick stepped away. "No thanks," he said as he unlocked the car and sat down. His long legs were still outside, feet flat on the asphalt.

Judy followed him, reached down with her left hand and rubbed his right knee. "I can make that feel much better. And other things, too," she said in a soft voice.

Nick swung his legs inside the car, forcing her to pull her hand back. "Good bye, Judy."

"You know my name? Who told you?"

"It seems like everyone in town knows your name," he answered as he closed the door, hit the door lock button, and started the car.

She slammed her fists on his car as he pulled away.

Nick resumed the mapping app on his phone. "Head west on I-80 for three miles, and then turn north on US 95," it told him. Nick followed the instructions and headed out of town. The air conditioning was blowing cold air on him, but it felt like a bit too much and he turned it down.

About an hour out of Winnemucca, Nick found himself sweating and reached down to crank up the fan. But the air blowing on him wasn't getting any cooler. In fact, it wasn't cold at all.

"Crap," he muttered out loud. "Nothing I can do out here in the middle of the desert. At least it's not that hot outside," he added as he let the windows down. The rushing air felt good, even cooling him off a little as it evaporated his sweat.

He stopped at a gas station in McDermitt, a small town straddling the state line between Nevada and Oregon. He got gas, went to the restroom, and asked if there was anyone in town who could find out what was wrong with his car's air conditioning.

"Chuck usually can do it, but I think he's been in the bar most of the day," the station attendant said. "He's usually closed on Saturday."

"Is there anyone else besides Chuck?"

"Nope. Our town of 500 doesn't have many of those services. The closest would be in Winnemucca. Let me check your radiator to make sure you have enough coolant. You don't want to overheat."

"Thanks," Nick said. "And I just came from Winnemucca, so I don't want to head back that way."

"Where you headed?"

"Boise."

"That'd be your best bet, then. Let me give you a clean towel. Just keep that wet and use it to wipe yourself down. That'll help keep you cool." The man said as he retrieved a blue shop towel and handed it to Nick. "And if you're looking for water or snacks, the grocery right over there has the best selection." The man pointed across the street to McDermitt Grocery.

Nick went to the store, picked up some snacks, a couple energy drinks, two bottles of water, and went to the register. He set his items on the belt and smiled at the clerk with her heavily tanned and wrinkled face.

"Anything else, sir?" she asked.

"Yeah, do you have any of those things you get wet and wrap around your neck to keep you cool?"

"No, everyone around here just carries an extra handkerchief or washcloth to wipe down."

"Okay. That's all then," Nick replied as he paid, grabbed his things and headed back out. He opened a water bottle and doused the towel in it and wiped down his face.

*Feels good,* he thought. He got into the car, popped three more Tylenol capsules into his mouth and washed them down with water. He set the bottle in a holder for easy access, and continued his drive.

Shortly after he left the Jordan Valley area, he saw the sign welcoming him to the state of Idaho.

The next sign he saw said, "Entering Mountain Time Zone."

"Forgot about the time zone change and losing an hour," he said to himself. "Oh well, I should still be able to make it to Boise no problem."

# 2

## MUSIC FESTIVAL

Nick slept in Sunday morning after the rather long drive from Carson City. Not having air conditioning for the last four hours exhausted him, but at least the sun was mostly at his back. Before going downstairs for the included breakfast, he took the elevator to the roof top bar that he'd read about when booking online.

"Nice view," he observed as he stepped out of the elevator onto the roof at the Residence Inn on South Capitol Boulevard in downtown Boise. He'd picked the hotel because of its location—about five blocks directly south of the capitol building— and because Yelp had shown lots of restaurants and bars in the area. Plus there was a Trader Joe's just across the street.

"I can see why this place is a little more expensive than other hotels, but I think it's the perfect location," Nick added. He looked north and saw a reflection of the morning sunlight glancing off the large bronze eagle atop the capitol dome. "Emily is really going to love the photographs from here," he said, and then returned to the elevator and went downstairs.

As he passed through the lobby, Nick picked up a copy of the *Boise*

*Weekly.* Nick's height at six-six usually garnered attention, and his bushy orange hair solidified peoples' memory of him.

"Good morning, Mr. O'Flannigan. Did you sleep well last night?" the desk clerk asked as Nick walked toward the breakfast area.

Nick looked over to see the young man who'd checked him in last evening. "Yes, I did. Thank you very much." Nick continued on his way and then added, "Nice roof top view."

"It is, isn't it?" the clerk responded. "Since you're going to be here all week, you should check out some of the evening entertainment and specials we'll have up there."

"I will, thanks," Nick added as he let his nose guide him to breakfast. It was still the weekend, so technically it was a "travel day," but the view of the capitol building from the rooftop really jazzed him. He went to an open table and sat down, placing the paper to his left. He pulled out his phone and sent a text message to Emily, his editor at *Travel USA* magazine, the one who hired him for this year-long adventure to all fifty U.S. state capitals: "You're going to love the photos from Boise. I just saw a view of the capitol building from the roof top patio. It's absolutely spectacular."

He left the paper on the table and grabbed an assortment of eats from the buffet style breakfast.

*Nice assortment, pretty good flavor, definitely better than others*, Nick thought as he ate and thumbed through the *Boise Weekly* paper. Billing itself as "Idaho's only alternative weekly newspaper" and as "Boise's best source for news, arts and entertainment, classifieds and upcoming events," the paper's headlines highlighted the music festival that was ending today. "Boise Centre on the Grove," the article said. Guess I need to figure out where that is, he thought as he finished eating.

Nick cleared his table, grabbed the paper, and went back to the front desk. "Yes, Mr. O'Flannigan?" the clerk said as Nick approached.

"The paper mentions a music festival at Boise Centre on the Grove," Nick said as he set the paper on the counter. "Is that close by?"

The clerk chuckled. "Once it gets started in about an hour, you won't need to know where it is. You'll hear it, and you'll feel it. But in case all the bands are on a break, it's one block north toward the capitol, and then it's behind the Grove Hotel on the opposite side of the street. Less than five minutes from here, and that's if you hit the red lights."

"Cool," Nick said. "Thanks," he added as he grabbed the paper and headed toward the elevators.

Nick spent a little over an hour managing activities on his macrophotography4u website, uploading photos, responding to comments, and answering a few questions. His north-facing window was open, open as much as hotel windows can be opened lately. He heard the guitar music and he got out of the chair and went to the window. *Hmmm. Yes, over in that direction,* he thought as he looked to the north-north-west. *Why not? I've got all day here and nothing else I have to do.*

He closed down and put away his computer, straightened the bed sheets and cover, and grabbed his camera bag. Nick was out of the hotel and walking north on Capitol Boulevard just two minutes later.

*A new pizza joint and Trader Joe's. Pizza plus wine for the room. I'm going to love Boise.* He thought as he stopped at the southeast corner of Front and Capitol and took out his camera. The colorful engraved image of a waterfall on the corner façade of the Grove Hotel was sparkling as the eastern sun bounced off the building. After snapping some photos, he turned slightly to his right and snapped a photo of the capitol building framed between the hotels and restaurants closest to him.

The desk clerk was right. Even if he didn't know where the music festival was, he could have easily found it just by following the sound. Nick crossed the street and followed the lines of people heading into the open area behind the Grove Hotel. Heads naturally turned toward him as he was definitely a head above most of the others. "Wow," Nick said as he entered the Centre on the Grove. "I thought Boise was this small sleepy town. Music stages, food stands, and lots of people. I'm glad I've got an entire free day here."

One of the advantages Nick's height gave him was that he could stand back and still see what was going on "up front." He walked toward the music stage that was active. He didn't have to be very close to hear the music. "Is this a regular thing?" Nick asked a couple young women who were nursing cups of coffee.

"This is the first year for this one. But there is a big indie music festival each year in early Spring. It's called Treefort and it last four or five days, and there have been some pretty good bands picked up from it." One of the gals replied.

"Thanks," Nick responded as he smiled and nodded. He turned back toward the stage, pulled out his camera started taking photos of the band on stage and of the crowd. He swapped lenses and used the telephoto lens to zoom in close on the band members. The lead guitarist was bouncing from one foot to the other, and there was a big smile on his face.

"Yea," the woman who'd spoken to Nick said to the other woman. "She came to my teller window and took out all that money, and she didn't want large bills. She said it was for one of her special amigos."

"Must be nice to have that much money you can just give it to anyone you want, especially her amigos," her friend replied in a loud voice competing with the band's volume.

"I agree, but that's what she said. I thought that was a little odd for her to use that word since she was from Boston, and I don't think she hung out with amigos back there. And, of course, her husband says he has no idea what happened to her."

"Boston?" Nick said as he snapped his head back to the women. "Someone from Boston? That's where I'm originally from."

"You don't know?"

"Apparently I don't. Know what?" Nick asked.

"A woman who was from Boston and married a businessman here in town went missing a year ago, and nothing's turned up since. There was a news special on the anniversary of her disappearance the other day. What I was telling Katie here is that a couple days before she disappeared she came into my branch and withdrew ninety-five hundred dollars, all in small bills."

Nick's bushy eyebrows lifted. "That's a lot of cash to take out. And right before she goes missing? That seems a bit suspicious, doesn't it?"

"Yep. But she was pretty well off. Some people have said that they think her husband did it to get his hands on her inheritance."

"But he seemed pretty grief stricken on the news," the other woman added.

"It could be an act," the first answered.

"Well, I just got into town last night. I'm on a year-long assignment to visit each U.S. state capital and take photos for a travel magazine."

"Hey, that's a pretty cool assignment," Katie said. "How long are you in Boise?"

"Just the week. I hope to be heading out on Saturday for my next stop in Helena."

"Not the most exciting place, but it does sound like a fun gig," the first woman said.

"You said she was from Boston. What's her name? Maybe I knew her."

"Jennifer Langsford," Katie replied.

"Seriously?" Nick replied as his mouth went wide open and his head rocked forward. "We had a couple of accounting classes together at Boston College. How bizarre!"

# 3

# GETTING INVOLVED

"What was that restaurant those gals mentioned?" Nick muttered as he was getting dressed the next morning. He picked up his phone and opened the Notes app. "Goldy's," he read. "And they said it's really close by." He did a quick search on Goldy's and found it, just a couple blocks north. *What a bonus,* he thought. He grabbed his camera bag, took the stairs down this time, and left the hotel. "Perhaps I'll try the pizza tonight," he said to himself as he walked past the pizza joint across the street from the hotel.

The line out the door on the next block up was a hint about where he was going. Goldy's Breakfast Bistro, one of the top ten TripAdvisor restaurants in all of Boise, was clearly a popular eatery. "How does this work?" he asked one person in line.

"You go in and sign in. Give them your cell number, and they'll call you when they have a spot ready."

"How long does it take?"

"Maybe twenty minutes tops," the man said. "Most of the people inside understand what the wait is like, and so they don't just sit and dawdle. Tables turn over fairly quickly."

Nick signed in, and then came back out to wait with the others.

The line moved forward as four people walked out. "We left some for you," the man joked as his group walked south. There were a few chuckles from some of those waiting.

"My first time here," Nick said to the couple in front of him. "Any recommendations?"

"It's all spectacular. If you're here for any length of time, you'll want to come back and try several combinations. They have so many choices you just can't pick one favorite. We come here every other week, and I'm sure there are things that we haven't tried yet."

"I'm getting hungrier just hearing you talk about it," Nick replied.

"Want to join us if we can get a table for three?" the main asked.

"Sure, thanks. Nick," he said as he extended his right hand.

"I'm Danny, and this is my wife Sue," the man said as Nick shook hands with each of them.

The line continued to move forward, and it was finally their turn. The three sat down at one of the larger tables downstairs shared with other smaller groups of patrons.

"There are booths upstairs. But they fill up fast," the man told him.

The others at the table, already eating, looked at the new arrivals and smiled. Nick scanned the menu and saw so many choices. "I'll just make it simple this first time," he said as the waiter came by. "I'd like the Chicken Fried Steak with eggs over easy, Corned Beef Hash, and the Cinnamon Raisin Walnut bread, please."

"Something to drink?"

"Orange juice and coffee with cream, please," Nick replied.

"Certainly, sir. And for you?" the waiter continued as he took the orders from Danny and Sue.

Nick looked around the small bistro. *There were maybe fifty or sixty seats,* he thought. The waiter headed toward the kitchen, and Nick turned back to his new friends.

"The A/C went out on my car yesterday as I was driving in from Nevada. I'd prefer to take it to an independent shop rather than the dealer. Do you know of a good place that won't rip me off?"

"That's easy," Danny said. "Tune Tech at Twelfth and State. Not more than a half mile, perhaps a little more, just north and to the west of here. I've been taking my cars there for years. And I never worry when Sue takes hers in. Tell them I sent you."

"Thanks," Nick said. The three of them continued to chat, and then their food arrived. "Oh, my," Nick said as the aromas from the huge plate rose to invade his nostrils

"Enjoy," the waiter said. And enjoy they did. There was no time for talking as the three of them focused on the magnificent food.

"Wow, that was great," Nick said as he finished his meal. "I'd better get the car into the shop," he added. "Thanks for the company and for the recommendation." He signaled the waiter that he was ready for his bill. Nick stood and shook hands once again with Danny and Sue, paid and left the restaurant.

As he walked back to the hotel, Nick looked up directions for Tune Tech. *Boise is an easy city to get round,* he thought. He went to get his car keys and went back downstairs. He drove to Tune Tech and went inside.

"What seems to be the problem?" The mechanic behind the counter asked. Nick saw the name 'Pat' in a patch on his chest.

"The A/C went out driving through Nevada. Just stopped blowing cold," Nick told him.

"Might just need a recharge, might be a compressor," a mechanic who had just stepped up to the counter said.

"We're kinda backed up on Monday morning," Pat said. "And we're short one technician. I would say maybe early afternoon until we can take a look. Then we can call you with a better idea of how long it will take to fix." the old man said as Nick looked at the certificates hanging on the wall. He saw Pat's name on many of them.

*The old man must know what he's talking about,* Nick thought. "I don't have much of a choice," Nick said. "Here's my card with my number."

"There's no charge for the diagnosis. And we'll give you an estimate before we actually start any work."

"Okay, thanks," Nick said and left the shop.

Outside, Nick looked around. The weather was pleasant, and

there was plenty of shade on the sidewalks. "I could take an Uber, or I can get a few photos of the capitol on the way back to the hotel. Yeah, I'll walk," he decided.

The walk was a little longer than he thought it would be, and his right leg was hurting by time he got back to the hotel. He'd gotten some good photos of the capitol building and the surrounding park areas, but he needed to rest his leg.

After taking a couple Tylenol and drinking another full bottle of water, he sat down at the desk area, opened his computer, and did some searching for his Boston College classmate, Jennifer Langsford. "So she's missing," he mumbled as the results appeared. The first page of results was all local stories, mostly in the *Idaho Statesman*. He read through them, and most were fairly consistent.

They detailed that the Boise Police Department was spear-heading the investigation. The only thing that stood out was that her husband didn't report her missing until she'd been gone for two days. "She might have taken an Uber, or gone with a friend. Did he really think someone would believe that story?" Nick said out loud as he shook his head.

"So she used part of her inheritance to found the Hispanic Asylum Center in Canyon County, wherever that is," he said as he read more stories. "And what was it that the gals at the music festival said? That she'd taken almost ten thousand dollars out for her amigos?" *That sounds fishy to me,* he thought as he looked up the Boise Police Department.

He got out his phone and dialed the Tip Line number.

"Boise Police Department, how may I help you?"

"Hi," Nick began. "I'm calling about the disappearance of Jennifer Langsford.

"Please hold while I transfer you to the detective in charge of that investigation."

Nick held for a few moments, and then a voice came on the other end of the line.

"Detective Russell."

"Hi. I'm a freelance photographer who went to college with that missing woman, Jennifer Langsford, and I was wondering if I could find out some more information."

"Can I have your name, sir?"

"I'd rather remain anonymous," Nick said, already regretting making the call.

"That's certainly your right. What type of information were you looking for?"

"Well, she was always a very responsible person in school. We were in Accounting classes at Boston College, and I don't think she'd just run off on her own. I was at that music festival yesterday and a gal there said that Jennifer withdrew almost ten thousand dollars, saying it was for her amigos. Was she involved with anyone out at that Hispanic Center she founded?"

"I can't comment on an ongoing investigation sir."

"Well," Nick responded. "What about her husband? He didn't report her missing for a couple of days. What kind of husband would wait two days?"

"No comment," the voice on the line said.

There was silence on the line.

"So you're not looking into the husband even a year later?" Exasperated, Nick blurted out, "She was a good person who deserves better."

"Anything else, sir?" The Detective sounded bored.

"I guess not," Nick said in a dejected voice.

"Thank you for your call, sir. You might check with the newspaper reporters who covered the story. They might be able to fill you in on some of the information we've already released to the public. Good bye."

The line went dead.

"What a bunch of crap," Nick said as he looked at one of the online stories that had a picture of Jennifer. "Just as beautiful as she was at school," he said in a soft voice as a tear began to roll down his right cheek. "Damn it. It's not fair." He exhaled deeply in frustration.

"Call Sandra" he instructed his phone.

"Hello," came the familiar voice after a couple rings.

"Hey, it's Nick."

"Hey there. How ya doing?" Sandra replied.

"Good. I'm in Boise. What a great city. I might even move here from Seattle when I'm done with this gig. But I'm frustrated."

"What's going on?" she asked.

"So this gal I went to school with in Boston married this guy here in Boise. She went missing a year ago, and I called police to ask for information about a withdrawal she made from her account the day before she went missing. They wouldn't give me any information."

"So you're getting involved in another mystery?"

"This is personal. I knew her. She was a good person. She founded a Hispanic asylum center. Her husband didn't report her missing for two whole days. They wouldn't talk to me about that either."

"Nick," Sandra said in a soft voice. "They look at things differently. You knew this person, she was a friend of yours. She's just a name to them, they have no attachment. Don't let it get to you."

"You're right," Nick acknowledged. "I know I shouldn't get involved, but Jennifer deserves better. A more thorough investigation."

"I know. Do what you can do, but don't lose sight of why you're there."

"I know," Nick said dejectedly. "It's just so frustrating."

"Hey," Sandra said in an upbeat voice as she changed the subject. "I can get away in a few weeks. Would you like me to come and spend some time with you? I've even got an idea for an awesome YouTube series we could start. What do you think?"

"Hmm," Nick answered in a noncommittal voice. "That might work. I'll be in Denver in five weeks. That's certainly a more exciting place than in the Dakotas or Wyoming."

"Might work?" Sandra replied as she let her disappointment creep into her voice.

"Sorry, my mind was somewhere else."

"I got it. Maybe we can talk about it later. Call me later this week?"

"Sure. Thanks for listening."

"Anytime, Nick. Good talking with you. Bye for now." Sandra's voice seemed different, and the call ended abruptly.

"Bye," Nick said to dead air.

It was late afternoon when his phone rang. "Hello, Mr. O'Flannigan. This is Pat from Tune Tech. I think we found the problem. You don't need a full compressor, but you do need a clutch. We won't have it until the morning. If you need the car now, you can come get it, and then bring it back when you can leave it for an hour or so."

"No, that's okay," Nick replied. "Just keep it and let me know when it's done."

"Will do," Pat said. "We'll call you tomorrow. But with the part and the labor, it shouldn't be over a hundred and seventy dollars."

"Okay, thanks," Nick said as he ended the call.

"It's a good thing there are a lot of restaurants nearby. Maybe I'll go have pizza tonight," he said to himself. He instinctively rubbed his right leg. *No pain, that's nice,* he thought.

# 4

## TIPS DON'T ALWAYS PAN OUT

Nick woke up the next morning, still upset at the rude treatment he got from the Police Department. "Those guys are wrong, and I'm going to shove it in their faces when I find out what happened to Jennifer," he said as he got in his workout clothes. He hit the gym and hit it hard. Sweat was streaming down his face, and he was breathing rapidly.

"Feels good," he said as he wiped his face, tossed the towel into the basket, did some relaxation stretching, and went back to his room.

The invigorating shower helped to get Nick in a mood to be very productive. "I'm going to kill it today," he said as he got his camera bag ready to head out after breakfast. *Goldy's was good yesterday,* he thought, *but I need to stay focused.* He dressed and went downstairs for the complimentary breakfast. The morning news was on the television as he filled one plate with fresh fruit, a couple hard boiled eggs, and a yogurt cup. He set it down and went back for a plate of hot food. The workout made him extra hungry. He looked up at the TV as he was taking a bite of the sausage patties.

"Our recent news story about the one year anniversary of the disappearance of Jennifer Langsford, wife of Boise businessman Malcom Thornton, has drawn a lot of tips," the news reporter began. "We reached out to the investigators, and they said that one of the callers was one of her college classmates, a photographer, who said her disappearance was out of character. He also questioned why they weren't looking more into the husband who didn't report her missing until two days after her disappearance. Police have refused to comment, again, as this is an ongoing investigation. Clearly even a year later, it has the attention of the citizens of Boise and even those who aren't from around here."

"What?" Nick exclaimed out loud as the story continued. "Those," Nick stopped before he said something that he'd regret saying out loud. He picked up his plates and moved to another table where he couldn't see or hear the television. He pulled out his phone, and typed a text to his friend Gerry. Gerry was a good friend in Seattle who was instrumental in his getting this plum assignment of traveling to each U.S. state capital city and taking photographs for an upcoming book. "How rude! I called the police and asked them some questions about an old college roommate who went missing a year ago. They brushed me off and then reported it to the news media. I'm pissed!"

Nick's face was turning red and he was breathing heavily. He finished his yogurt and his phone beeped. It was Gerry, she sent a reply text. "Hey, there. Don't let it upset you. Keep focused on your assignment. You're doing an awesome job. Emily really loves your work!"

"Thanks," he replied.

As Nick went to get a coffee refill, he heard the TV reporter continue, "And in a written response from the Hispanic Asylum Center when we reached out to them, they said that had not had any contact with or from Jennifer Langsford for several months before her reported disappearance, nor had they received any donations from her during that time or since. But in an exclusive interview we had with the Center, they did reveal that her husband Malcolm

Thornton had made four one thousand-dollar donations over the past year."

"I don't care," Nick mumbled as he put a lid on his coffee. "I'm going to find out what happened to her," he added as he went back up to his room.

5

———

## CITY OF TREES

B ack in his room, Nick took the lid off the coffee and slowly sipped it as he thought about what Gerry had texted. *She's right, it is the assignment I need to focus on.* He finished his coffee grabbed his camera bag, left the hotel and turned north on Capitol Boulevard.

"This building looks very similar to the U.S. Capitol," he said as he got closer and the entire building came into view. He waited for the crosswalk signal to indicate WALK and he stepped into the middle of the street and snapped several photographs of the capitol. Nick apparently took longer than he should've as a car behind him honked his horn. Nick hadn't seen that the light had changed.

He turned around and waved at the driver as he continued across the street. The driver turned toward Nick as she moved on. "Need a ride?" she asked in a lilting voice.

"I'm fine, thanks," he said as he smiled at her.

"Too bad," she muttered as she continued north.

Nick chuckled to himself. He'd read that Boise was a friendly city. "Almost too friendly," he said as he approached Bannock Street and crossed into a small park-like area that split the north-bound traffic into lanes to go around the capitol building. He recognized the person represented by the statue. It was Abraham Lincoln.

"Hmm," he said. "What did Lincoln have to do with Idaho?" He read the nearby plaque, "This benchmark preserved in recognition of Abraham Lincoln Land Surveyor 1834-1836."

"What? Lincoln in Idaho?" Nick mused. He took out his phone and searched for "Was Lincoln in Idaho?" Nick scanned through some of the results. "Lincoln never set foot in Idaho, but he did sign an act on March 4, 1863 to create the Idaho Territory."

"I'm curious now," Nick said as he typed in a new search. "So that's when it became a territory. When did it become a state?" He phone displayed the answer, July 3, 1890. He walked across the street into the park. The morning sunlight coming through the trees' canopies created shafts of light just like spotlights in the theater. *I can use some of these for my own portfolio*, he thought as he zoomed the lens in and out while looking through the eyepiece. *And some of these will also be perfect in black and white.*

Nick snapped various shots of the capitol building from the park, then he crossed back over to the grassy island and got some straight-on photos. *I bet some of these would pass for the U.S. Capitol if they didn't have the Idaho flag in them.* His phone rang as he crossed Jefferson Street where there was a replica of the Liberty Bell. He pulled out the phone, answering it. "This is Nick."

"It's Gerry. Are you doing better?" Gerry was gay, but that fact had no impact on their relationship. They were good friends, and that was all that mattered.

"I'm fine," he replied. "I'm standing literally at the steps of the capitol here in Boise. Here this?" he asked as he used a fist to hit the big brass bell.

"No. What is it?"

"I just rang the Liberty Bell replica that's here. There's a clapper hanging down, but I don't want to make spectacle out of myself."

"You kinda do that anyway with your height and your hair, don't you?"

"Wow," he replied.

"Sorry, that sounded bad," she said. "I didn't mean it that way."

"No worries," he said. "I'm learning some interesting things along the way in addition to all the photographs I'm getting. There's this statue of Abraham Lincoln here, and I read that it was Lincoln who created the Idaho Territory in 1863 even though it didn't become a state until 1890. This really is a pretty town."

"That's cool," Gerry said. "We know you're great at spotting details, that's one of the main reasons Emily hired you. Just don't get too wrapped up in this missing person thing. I'd hate to see that get in the way of what you're doing for the magazine."

"I know. I won't."

"Oh," Gerry interjected. "Emily said the payroll system has been fixed and we've all been paid. I asked her to confirm that yours was deposited, and she said it had been."

"That's great news," Nick answered. "Well, I'm going to climb up all these steps and go see what I can find inside."

"Okay," she said. "Have a fun time in the City of Trees."

"I will." Nick paused. "Anyway, thanks for the call and the good news about payroll."

"Any time, my friend," she replied. "Take care and keep the good work."

"You bet," Nick answered. "Bye now."

"Bye," Gerry echoed as she ended the call.

Nick ambled up the steps to the capitol's entrance on the second floor. He pulled out his phone and other metal items to put them through the metal detector. He looked around. "No security?" he asked incredulously.

"This is Idaho," a passerby said as he smiled at Nick.

"Wow," was all that Nick could say. By the time he had wandered through all five levels, the limp in his right leg was telling him that it was time to head back to the hotel. He looked at the camera display. He had taken one hundred twenty-seven photographs today. He looked at his watch, "Almost four hours? No wonder it hurts," he said as he made his way back down the front steps. The pain in the right leg was accentuated when he led with that foot, so he went slowly and gingerly down the steps.

His phone rang as he reached the bottom. He looked at the display, it was a 208 area code. "Hello, this is Nick."

"Mr. O'Flannigan, this is Pat from Tune Tech. Your car is ready, and I'm sorry it took so long. They sent the wrong part and so we had to have them rush the right one over. But it's ready any time you want it."

"What's your address again?"

"We're at the corner of Twelfth and State."

"Okay, I'll get an Uber and be there shortly," Nick responded.

"I could have someone deliver the car to you since it took longer than I said it would," Pat said.

"That's okay," Nick replied. "I'll make my way over. Thanks."

"You're welcome, sir."

Nick closed the call, opened the Uber app and typed in "Tune Tech State Street."

A shiny silver car pulled up three minutes later and took Nick to the shop, where he spotted his car in the parking lot and saw that it had been washed. *Outstanding service,* he thought.

Back at the hotel, Nick ordered some Thai food through Door-Dash as he wanted to upload photos to the Cloud for the magazine. *Emily's going to love these,* he said to himself as he scanned through exterior and interior photos. Looking straight up from the capitol's rotunda floor to the vaulted dome, shafts of light came through just like the ones he taken of the trees across from the capitol. *She'll like that comparison.*

Nick shut down the computer, took a couple Tylenol, and lay down for a nap. He yawned and he stretched his arms out. *It was a lot of walking and standing, but I got a lot done today,* he thought. *But I do need to rest up. I've got 45 more weeks to go.*

He awoke a few hours later, took a shower, and consulted the Yelp app. He found a nearby comedy club and nightclub that was running happy hour all evening "That sounds good," he said as he scanned through the menu. "An interesting name," he added. "It's only a block away, and now that I'm liquid, I might as well go to Liquid tonight. Seems appropriate," he said as he finished dressing and went out for the evening.

# 6

## BACK TO THE SHOP

After a good morning workout and long shower, Nick felt invigorated for the second day in a row as he got dressed. Yesterday had been a very successful photography day, and he rewarded himself today with a pleasant drive south of town to the World Center for Birds of Prey. Like many others, he'd heard of the California Condor. *I thought they were just in California, thus the name,* he thought as he listened to a raptors podcast on his way out of town.

The cool crisp air felt good as he got out of the car and looked around. He went into the Visitor's Center, picked up a brochure for the self-guided tours. The young lady behind the counter smiled and slowly leaned her head back as Nick approached. At six foot six, Nick was used to people looking up at him and remembering his bushy orange hair.

"May I help you, sir?" she asked.

"I'm a freelance photographer here in town on assignment for a magazine. Is it okay for me to take pictures and submit them to the magazine or even use them on my own site?"

"No problem," she answered. "The only restriction is in the enclosed areas that are darkened. We don't allow any flash photography there."

"That makes sense," Nick replied. "Do you recommend any particular sequence to going through the exhibits?" Nick said as he set the brochure on the counter.

"There's no particular order you should follow, except checking that board over there for times when there are live shows. It's best to arrive about fifteen minutes early for those, but we're not as crowded mid-week as we are on the weekends or when school groups come out."

She paused and started again just as Nick was about to say something. "The Flying Falcon demonstration is pretty spectacular. Try to get some video of that one if you can." She circled the location and the times for the falcons.

"Thanks," Nick said with a smile and a nod of the head as he picked up the brochure and headed toward the first exhibit. *They certainly didn't build these with tall people in mind,* he thought as he ducked his head just in time before running into a wooden cross beam. Nick was getting great photos of so many spectacular birds. *Emily's going to love these,* he thought as he was mentally separating them into ones for the magazine and ones for him.

The Flying Falcon demonstration was everything that the young lady inside had told him. What she didn't tell him, however, was that it was in the direct sunlight, devoid of shade trees so that the falcons had full freedom to fly. But Nick was able to get some great action shots with his high-speed settings. *Instagram winners,* he called them.

After a light lunch and a couple bottles of water, Nick climbed into his car for the drive back to the hotel. He turned on the air conditioning unit as the early afternoon outside air was heating up. He set the fan on High and turned the vents toward himself.

"Not again," he muttered as the blast of air coming out of the vents wasn't cold at all. In fact it felt as if he'd turned on the heater instead of the A/C. He reached down and switched it to Heater. Hot air there, also. Back to A/C, still hot air.

"Crap," he said as he turned the fan off and opened the windows for air movement through the car. "Tune Tech, here we go again," he grumbled as he headed into town and back to the repair shop.

"Hi, Mr. O'Flannigan," Pat said as he saw Nick open the door and enter the shop's office. "How's the car running?"

"I've got hot air coming out of the air conditioner," Nick replied as sweat rolled down his face.

"Seriously?" the owner asked. "I mean, I checked it out myself yesterday, and the air was almost too cold."

"I know, it worked fine for me when I picked it up. But I went out to the Birds of Prey and on the way back I turned it on. Nothing but hot air. I switched it to the Heater, and then back to A/C. Just hot air."

"I'm so sorry. Let me go take a look."

The two men looked like Mutt and Jeff as they went outside. Nick at six-six and muscular, and then Pat at maybe five-six and not-so-muscular. Nick followed Pat's instructions, releasing the hood latch and starting the engine.

"Now turn on the air and the fan," Pat hollered over the sound of the engine. "That's not good," he added as he stepped back. "You can turn it all off."

Nick turned off the air, the fan, and the engine as Pat walked to the driver's door. "The compressor's making a terrible noise, like a bad bearing, but maybe not. I'll get on it as soon as I can, but every bay is full right now. Can I have one of my guys drive you to the hotel and bring the car back, and then I'll call you as soon as I know what's wrong?"

"Don't have much choice, I guess," Nick said as he shook his head and shrugged.

"I'm really sorry. In fact, why don't you drive back to the hotel, and I'll play with the air controls and see if it seems like anything else."

"Okay. Let's go," Nick replied.

Pat closed the hood, got in the passenger door and the two men drove off. "Didn't hear anything else," Pat said as they arrived at the hotel four minutes later. I'll give you a call just as soon as I can," Pat said as Nick got out of the car. Pat walked around to the driver's side, got in, and adjusted the seat way forward. Nick grabbed his camera bag and went inside.

## A SIMPLE FIX, NO?

"**G**ood afternoon, Mr. O'Flannigan," one of the desk clerks said as Nick went through the hotel lobby toward the bank of elevators.

"Hi," Nick said as he turned and waved. *No going incognito for me,* he mused. He went to his room, opened up the laptop and downloaded the photos and videos from his time at the Birds of Prey.

"There are a lot more than I thought I'd taken," he said. But that was the advantage that digital photography had over film. You can take a dozen photographs of the same thing, going for that one that was just perfect. Delete the other eleven and it's as if you'd only taken that one great one.

He was sorting the photos into ones for the magazine and others for himself when his phone rang. "Hello, this is Nick," he said since he didn't recognize the 208 number.

"Mr. O'Flannigan. This is Pat from Tune Tech. It is indeed the compressor that's gone bad."

"So that wasn't the problem before?

"No, sir. Well, it might have been, but that wasn't the symptom. The clutch seal had gone bad, and that might have caused the oil to leak out of the compressor, causing the bearing to go too. I'm sorry, but I'm pretty sure that's what happened. There's no way we would have caught it the first time."

"Okay," Nick said haltingly when there was a pause in the conversation.

"Um, the compressor itself is eight hundred and eighty-nine dollars, and the labor to install it is another hundred and forty. But what I'm going to do is to refund the hundred and sixty-five you paid yesterday, so your net is going to be eight hundred and sixty-four dollars. I know that's a lot, but the new compressor comes with a lifetime warranty that is good at any place that services AC Delco parts. I'll order the part from the dealer, and then we'll get on it right away. It shouldn't be more than a couple hours."

"Ouch," Nick said as leaned back in the desk chair and exhaled heavily. "No choice, I need a car."

"Aside from the compressor, the car seems to be in really good shape. You said you were doing a lot of driving, so I'll have the guys top off all the fluids and check the belts at no charge while we're waiting for the part."

"Okay," Nick sighed. "Go ahead, and then call me when it's ready."

"Will do. Thanks," Pat said as he ended the call.

Nick tossed his phone to on the bed. "So much for making some money." He kicked off his shoes, flopped down on the bed, and picked up his phone. "Call Mom," he said into the phone.

The other end of the call rang twice before it was answered. "Hello?" his mom said into the phone. His parents hadn't emerged into the digital age so they didn't have Caller ID. Sometimes they wouldn't answer the phone because they were eating or watching a good TV show. "It's our phone and we pay for it, so we don't have to answer it if we don't want to," Nick heard them say many times when he was home.

"Hi, Mom. It's Nick," he said in a voice that didn't exude confidence.

"Hi. Where are you?" she replied.

"Boise, Idaho," he said.

"He's in Boize, Idaho," his mom yelled to her husband in the next room.

Nick grimaced as he pulled the phone away from his ear.

"It's Boise, Mom. It's an 's,' not a 'z.'" He knew that correcting her would not matter as she wouldn't catch the difference.

"So what's it like in Boize?" she asked.

"It's a nice place, sort of a laid-back atmosphere, but with a lot of great restaurants and very friendly people."

"Are you getting some good pictures?"

"Yes, Mom."

"How's the car?"

Nick hesitated before answering. "The compressor went out on the air conditioner, so it's in the shop getting replaced."

"His car's air conditioning broke down," she yelled to her husband Patrick.

*Maybe I'll just put her on speaker phone,* Nick thought.

"Does he need any money?" Nick heard his father yell back.

"I'm fine, Mom. It's a small setback, but I haven't had to do much on the car, so I look at this as deferred maintenance. Anyway, how's everything in Boston?"

"Not much change. Your father sits and argues at the television, says a few words, and then we go to church on Sunday, and it's all forgiven."

"Okay, Mom. I've got some more work to do. Tell Dad that I love him, and I love you, too."

"Love you, Nick. Be careful."

"I will, Mom. Bye," he added as he heard the line click.

Nick sat up, went to the desk and sat down. He looked at the pad of paper on the desk where he'd written down "Jennifer Langsford." He closed his eyes as he thought about when the two of them were at Boston College. She was very pretty, with rich parents, and so there were always lots of young men, really boys, hanging around her. He'd lost track of her after school. His cheerleader girlfriend Susan was very jealous, not that Nick had ever been all that interested in Jennifer anyway. *I've got to find out what happened to her.*

He got his phone and instructed it to "Call Ben."

"This is Ben," was the professional sounding answer. *Must be at work,* Nick thought.

"Hey, Ben. It's Nick. Catch you at a bad time?"

"No, it's cool. What's up? You in Idaho now?"

"Yea, pretty nice place." Nick paused and then continued with the purpose for the call. "I've got a favor to ask. Can you use your amazing software development skills and do some dark web research for me?"

"You bet. I love doing that stuff" was the enthusiastic response. "What do you need?"

"There's a missing person's case here that gets to me, partly because the woman who's missing is someone I went to school with in Boston. Her husband has a great story about why he waited two days to report her missing. I don't buy that. I think he's trying to hide something."

"Sounds fishy to me, too. What's his name?"

"Malcolm Thornton. The last name is t-h-o-r-n-t-o-n."

"Sure, let me look into it," Ben replied. "It might be an hour or so, but there are some pretty cool tools most people don't know about."

"Thanks, Ben."

"You bet, man. I'll talk to you later."

"Bye," Nick said as the call ended. He set the phone down, and went back to the bed to lie down. It had been a busy day so far, and he deserved a short nap.

A short nap is what it was. No more than thirty minutes later, his phone started vibrating on the desk and then it rang. He saw it was Ben. "Hey, Ben."

"Hey, Nick. You won't believe what I found on that guy. He had multiple affairs between two and five years ago. I've got photos of him with the other women, and it looks as if he's really enjoying their company. I'll send the photos over to you along with links to some of the stories."

"Will I be able to access the links if they're on the dark web?"

"Oh, yea. All you need is the URL. It's not encrypted and doesn't require you to logon. It's just a matter of finding the information, and then it's available for everyone to see. I think you're right about this guy trying to hide something."

"Like maybe his wife?" Ben offered.

"Sounds like it."

"Hey, thanks, man."

"Anytime," Ben added as he ended the call.

A minute later, Nick's email inbox began to ding as emails from Ben started arriving. He looked at the photos of Malcolm and the other women, and he clicked on the links to the stories about the affairs. "Dead to rights, buddy," he uttered.

One of the files he opened had PERSONAL in bold letters across the top. It was a Private Investigator's report to Jennifer about her husband and his affairs. Nick scanned through the pages; it was quite the detailed report. The P.I. reported that some of the affairs were while his wife was out of town, but others were while she was at home. "The guy's an A-1 creep," Nick said. The report included copies of hotel bills and bar tabs, most of them billed to his company. "Maybe I can report him for tax fraud. That should get the attention of the police or at least the D.A." The report concluded with the statement, "We found no evidence of affairs over the last eighteen months." The report was dated approximately four months before Jennifer's disappearance. Nick shook his head in disgust as he downloaded some of the files to his computer into a new folder labeled "Jennifer."

He leaned back into his chair and read each file from start to finish. The newspaper articles were essentially what he'd recently read. The police interviews surprised him. "How'd they get that information?" he wondered. An hour passed by until he was done reading everything Ben had sent him.

Nick called the Police Tip Line.

"Boise Police Department, how may I help you?"

"Detective Russell, please."

There was a slight pause. "This is Detective Russell."

"Hi," Nick began. "I called before about the disappearance of

Jennifer Langsford. I just uncovered some stories about her husband and the affairs he'd been having with other women."

"We know about him and the affairs," the monotonous voice replied. "We're trying to find out what happened to her."

"And what if she found out about the affairs, threatened to leave him, and he killed her? Don't you think that's a reasonable possibility?"

"I don't who you are, but what you've just said is Disappearance Investigating one-oh-one. Don't you think we'd look into that? He's got his alibis, so we're not looking into him anymore. If you come up with something else, something that actually helps us find her, then call us again. Otherwise, please go back to reading your mystery novels, and leave the real investigative work to us."

"What about tax fraud? He was taking those women to hotels and charging it to his business. That's illegal." The pitch in Nick's voice got higher.

"We don't deal with fraud," the detective answered. "You can call the D.A. if you want, but that's not our concern."

"That's it?" Nick's voice continued to escalate as his personal interest in the case was growing. "You're just going to let him get away with it?"

"Thank you for your call, have a nice day." Click.

Nick raised his arm, ready to throw his phone against the wall in anger. *Not a good move, Nick. You'd just have to buy a new phone,* he thought as he set the phone on the desk.

He typed out a quick text to Gerry. "Slammed by the police again! Maybe I should stop this." He included an angry face emoji.

His phone dinged as Gerry replied, "Don't take it personally; remember what your main job is." She attached a smiley face emoji with two red hearts for eyes.

"Damn, she's good," Nick said as a light smile appeared on his face.

8

———

## BOISE AT NIGHT

**S**itting at the hotel room desk, Nick looked at his watch. He knew the repair shop closed soon. *Am I going to get my car tonight?* he thought. The day had started so well, and then went downhill. His phone rang, it was that same 208 number. "Hello, this is Nick."

"Mr. O'Flannigan. This is Pat down at Tune Tech. Your car is fixed, the air conditioning is running great, and we've gone through everything. The only thing we didn't do was to rotate your tires. If you don't mind giving me your credit card number over the phone, I'll run it through and bring the car down to your hotel."

"Sure," Nick said as he pulled out his wallet and read off the numbers.

"Great," Pat said. "I'll be there in five minutes."

"Okay, thanks," Nick said. "I'll be down in front." He shut down the laptop, and headed downstairs. He saw his car approach and he waved to Pat, as if the man wouldn't recognize him.

Pat stopped the car, put on the flashers, opened the door, and put the seat back as far as it would go. "Sorry, my legs are little shorter than yours," he said as he stepped out.

"No problem," Nick replied. "I'm just happy to have it back.

Thanks again," he added as the two men shook hands. "Can I give you a lift?"

"Nah," Pat said. "It's time for a beer. I'd offer to buy you one, but I'd chase away all the girls. I'll just go where the old guys go," he said as he turned and walked south.

"Thanks," Nick said as the old man walked away.

Pat raised his right arm, waved his hand, and kept walking.

Nick got in the car, adjusted the seat and mirrors, turned off the flashers and drove around the block to park in the hotel's garage. He went upstairs, dropped the car keys on the desk, and went into the bathroom to freshen up. He changed into a sporty shirt, splashed on a little cologne, and headed back downstairs and stopped at the front desk.

"Good evening, sir. How may I help you?" The desk clerk was one that Nick hadn't seen before.

"Any particular suggestions for some lively spots tonight?"

"It depends on what you want. Sports bar, pub, live music, you name it, it's within ten minutes."

"A sports bar where there's some action, and not just a bunch of beer-drinking guys."

"Gotcha," the clerk replied. "Double Tap Pub is just two blocks away," he said. "Go out here, turn right to the first light at Broad. Cross to your left and it's a block down, just south of P.F. Chang's."

"Thanks," Nick said as he turned and left the hotel.

Music was coming out of many restaurants and bars as Nick walked as he'd been directed. Heads turned as Nick walked by. His long stride enabled him to get to the pub in just a few minutes. He heard music and laughter as he entered. He looked around and saw a lot of beautiful young women. Some looked to be about six foot tall, a couple of them even taller. He smiled as he made his way to the one open seat at the bar.

"Something to drink?" the bartender said as he approached.

"Yes, and do you have food too?" Nick replied.

"Of course," the bartender said as he grabbed a menu, and handed it to Nick.

"What's with uh, all the gorgeous women?" Nick asked.

"Volleyball tournament this weekend. Know what you'd like for a beer?"

"A porter or a stout?" Nick replied.

"Sure thing," the bartender said as he went to help other patrons.

"Find something on the menu?" the bartender said as he returned with a rich brown beer.

"The Kobe Beef Burger, please," Nick said as he lifted the glass and took a slow sip. "Mmmm," he said in appreciation of the richness of the ice cold brew. Nick pushed the stool back and stood up. He continued to sip as he scanned the room. One of the taller girls waved at Nick, and he nodded his head and smiled.

She turned to her friends, said something Nick couldn't hear, and then the group approached him at the bar.

"Hi," he said as he was suddenly surrounded by seven beautiful young women. "You don't look old enough to drink," he said to the one who'd waved.

"We don't have to be, we just need something that says we are," She replied as she sidled up to him and smiled.

"Are you here for the tournament?" one of her friends asked.

"No, I didn't know about it," Nick answered. "I'm a photographer on assignment to visit each U.S. state capital and take photos for a new book."

"That sounds like fun," the second girl said as she looked up at him with wide eyes.

"Here's your Kobe Beef Burger, sir," the bartender said as he put a plate on the bar.

"Why don't you come join us?" the first girl said as she slipped an arm around Nick's waist.

"Yeah," several of the girls chimed in.

"Okay," Nick said as he picked up his plate and followed the girls to where they'd pulled several tables together. "Hi, I'm Nick," he said to the group.

"Hi, Nick," a few said in chorus.

"Sorry to eat in front of you," he said. "It's been a crazy day, and I'm starving."

"That's okay," said one who was apparently shy. She'd been sitting silently while the others came on to Nick.

All of them were sitting, but this one seemed shorter than the others. "Are you on the team, too?" he asked her.

"No, I'm the team manager," she said.

"Well, hi team manager. Do you have another name?"

"Laura," she said.

"Nice to meet you, Laura," Nick said as he stood and reached his long arm over the table to shake her hand.

"Thank you, Nick. Nice to meet you, too."

The other girls giggled, watching her and Nick interact.

"So, Laura, why did you decide to become the team manager?"

"Well," she began slowly. "I wanted to play volleyball, but I wasn't tall like these girls, and plus I'm not terribly coordinated. Or as some people say, I'm coordinated terribly." A couple of the other girls giggled.

"I think being a team manager is a very important part of any team. There is a lot of responsibility that goes with the role, and you have a lot of work to do before and after a match," Nick replied. "I think it's just as important as being one of the players. Sometimes, it's even more important."

"Gee, thanks, Nick," Laura said. Nick saw scorn on some of the other girls' faces.

The players engaged in idle chit-chat as Nick took a few bites of his burger, juice dripping down his chin. He wiped it with a napkin, and his phone rang. He set the burger down and answered it without looking at the display. "Hello?"

"Hey, there. How's it going?" It was Sandra, but the background noise made it hard for him to hear.

"Fine," he said, still not knowing who it was. "How are you?" he asked as he pulled the phone away from his ear and looked at it. He covered the phone with his free hand. "Excuse me," he whispered to the girls.

"What's going on there?" Sandra asked.

"Just a pub in downtown Boise having a burger and a beer after a crazy day."

"Sounds like quite the party. Who are you with?"

"No one. I mean there are people here, but I don't know any of them."

"Sounded like a bunch of girls."

"There's a volleyball tournament this weekend, and they wanted to know if I played and if I had any pointers for them."

"I'm sure that's what they're looking for," she said sarcastically. "Well, I don't want to keep you from your fun."

"Hey now," Nick responded with some actual hurt in his voice. "The hotel recommended this pub and so I came here. I didn't know who would be in here. I'm just trying to eat a burger and drink a beer. That's all. I promise."

"Okay," Sandra responded. "I'll call you when it's a better time."

"Okay," Nick replied. "Take care."

"You, too. Bye," she said and the call ended.

Nick returned to the table, took a big drink of the beer and finished the burger. He wiped his mouth, and once again, turned his attention to the shy one. "So tell me, Laura. What do you find to be the biggest challenge of being team manager?"

The other girls looked at Laura and shook their heads.

Laura smiled as she explained.

# 9

## GARDEN SHOW

Nick picked up a copy of the *Idaho Statesman* as he walked through the hotel lobby the next morning. He headed back to Goldy's to have another of their amazing breakfasts. He thumbed through the paper as he stood in line. The headlines in the third section read "Garden Show Starts Today." Under the headline was a photograph of the featured landscaper and his wife. He started to turn the page when it struck him. *She was in one of the photos Ben sent me.* The truck in the background had a logo that was a little grainy, but it looked like it said "Integrity Landscaping."

The line moved forward, and Nick made it inside where his mind recalled the scrumptious breakfast he'd had previously. Nick sat at the counter and continued to read through the paper. "Surprise me," he told the waiter, "but I also want orange juice and coffee." Phil Robinson, Nick read, founded Integrity Landscaping ten years ago, after moving to Boise from Hawaii. His wife Amanda was born and raised in Boise, went to Boise State University, and was a nurse at one of the local hospitals.

"Here's your surprise, sir," the waiter said as he put a plate of three different Eggs Benedicts in front of Nick. "This one is Salmon;

this one is Mexican, and this one is Beluga Sturgeon," he added as he pointed out each one. "You made the chef very happy."

"They look great," Nick said. "I'm quite sure they're going to make my stomach very happy also. Thank you."

"You're welcome, sir. Enjoy. More coffee?"

"Yes, please," Nick answered as he looked at all three offerings, deciding which to start with and which to save for last. He ate them in the order they were described to him. Finishing breakfast with the Caviar & Eggs Benedict was a definite treat. *I need to know what sauce he used, it certainly wasn't Hollandaise,* he thought as he scraped the plate with his fork to get as much of the thick liquid he could into his mouth.

"Didn't like them, I see," the waiter said as he came by.

"Awesome," Nick said. "What's the sauce on the caviar?"

"It's one of the chef's secret recipes. I know he uses a little mustard and cayenne pepper, and then a little parsley. I assume you liked it?"

"I'd lick the plate if there weren't so many people watching. Loved it. Do tell the chef how good all of them were."

"I'll do that for sure," the waiter replied. "Anything else?"

"Just the check please."

"Right away."

The waiter brought the check, Nick paid it, and went back to the hotel. He tossed the paper on the desk, got his camera bag, and his phone rang as he was heading out the door. "Hello, Emily," he answered.

"Hi, Nick. How's it going in Boise?" His editor's voice was very pleasant and happy sounding.

"Much better now that I got the car fixed. Air conditioning problems."

"Oh, sorry to hear that. But I'm loving the photos you uploaded. I particularly like the comparison of light coming through the trees and then the capitol dome. Very creative. Did Gerry let you know about the payroll getting fixed?"

"Yes, she did. Thanks a lot."

"Oh, good."

"I also got some great photos yesterday at the World Center for Birds of Prey. This is an amazing area. I bet if it had a coastline and beaches, it would be just as popular as California. The people are so friendly that I truly think I'll miss this place when I leave."

"That's impressive," Emily said. "Have you gotten yourself involved in anything there?"

"You mean like in Sacramento?"

"Or Salem or Olympia."

"Nope. Gerry has helped me to stay focused. I really like her."

"She's gay, you know."

"So? She's a nice person and we get along great. Gerry and I think alike, and that's great."

"Sorry, Nick," Emily began to apologize. "I didn't mean anything by it. I wasn't sure if you knew."

Nick laughed. "She told me that in probably our first thirty minutes together. I think that's one of the things I really like about her. She's open and honest."

"Oh, that's good," Emily said with a touch of relief in her voice. "Well, keep up the good work, Nick. You're taking amazing photographs."

"Thanks, Emily. Talk later."

"You bet. Bye," Emily added as she ended the call.

"I can do the Train Depot and go see the blue turf tomorrow," Nick said as he looked at the newspaper on the desk. "How about Garden Show houses? I'll get lots of great photos I can use, especially close-ups for my website."

**10**

---

## SUCH PRETTY FLOWERS

Nick had seen beautiful arrangements of growing flowers before, but many of the flowers at the Garden Show houses were also very artistically arranged. Besides being pretty, there were also side-by-side demonstrations of the results of using special nutrients versus regular soil and standard off-the-shelf fertilizers. There was a significant difference in the flowers in one particular display.

"What's in those nutrients?" Nick asked the homeowner.

"It's a special blend of zinc, potassium, and lye," the older woman replied. "Quite unique, isn't it?"

"It certainly is," Nick replied. "I thought lye was bad for plants and flowers."

She smiled at Nick. "Young man, there are many things in life that people say are bad. But when used properly, they're actually beneficial. In this case, with the right combination of zinc and potassium, the chemical reaction with the lye boosts the plants' desire to grow faster and produce more color."

"Oh, wow," Nick responded. "That's interesting. Thanks."

# 11

## CHEMISTRY 201

Nick continued his self-guided tour of some of the Garden Show homes. One of the homes on the tour was that of Malcom Thornton. *Really?* Nick thought. *This could be interesting.* The signs in the yard indicated an entrance through the side fence gate, and Nick went through. There were about a dozen people back there looking at the flowers and chatting. Many seemed to know each other. Nick was the outsider here, something he was getting used to on this trip.

A man he recognized from his photo in the paper came up to him. "Hello, welcome. My name is Malcolm Thornton. You like flowers, I take it?"

The two men shook hands. "Yes, I do," Nick replied. "I'm a photographer on a magazine assignment, but I'm more interested in taking some photographs for my own use. May I?"

"Sure," Thornton replied. "Do you have a card so I can say I knew you before you were world famous?"

Nick chuckled. "Don't know how likely that is, but here's my card. The name's Nick," he said, handing him a card. "I like the interesting arrangement of the flower boxes. Looks like a city skyline."

"You've got a good eye, young man. That's exactly what they're there to represent. My wife wanted something to remind her of Boston, so I said, 'Why not a city skyline?' She loved the concept and the result."

"I can see why, they look great," Nick said as he raised the camera, removed the lens cover and snapped a lot of photos. He grimaced as he knelt down to take some ground-level shots. "Ouch," he mumbled as he forced himself to stand back up. He moved to various locations and took straight-on shots of some of the boxes.

Thornton had gone back to chatting with others and Nick was ready to move on, so he just hollered a "Thank you, sir," and waved as he went back out the gate to his car. "Seemed pretty casual and normal for a man whose wife is still missing," Nick told himself as he got in the car. He went to a few more houses and then grabbed some lunch on his way back to the hotel.

He downloaded the photos to his laptop and then did some research on gardening. The first woman had told him that she was using zinc, potassium, and lye to make her plants more productive. And she was right according to the first online article he found. *"When mixed in the proper ratios, potassium, zinc, and lye can greatly stimulate the propagation and coloration of certain types of flowers."* His eyes opened wide and he leaned his head closer to the computer as he read another article. "Seriously?" he exclaimed. *"While accelerating the growth mechanisms of flowers, a recently discovered mixture of potassium, zinc has been shown to increase the decomposition of the human body, even the bones, making any detection virtually impossible within two years."*

"Holy crow. That's why he was so calm. He killed her, buried her in the planter box so the flowers grow beautifully while at the same time decomposing her body. Quite the clever fellow. No use, though. I've tried calling the authorities already and they've just blown me off." Nick rocked back in the chair as he considered his options.

He opened the folder for the photos he'd just downloaded. He was particularly interested in the ones at Thornton's house. He went through them, one by one, until he came to one that looked different from the others. The flowers were more brilliant in one of the boxes than in the others. He zoomed in and saw a brass plate on the side. He zoomed in some more. The plaque said, "Integrity Landscaping."

That name rang a bell, and he grabbed the newspaper. Right there on the front page was that photo with the landscaper and his wife—one of the ones that Thornton had an affair with—and the truck that said "Integrity Landscaping" on it. He panned across that planter box and saw white spots, *bone chips?*, peaking through the wood openings. He knew that was a stretch, but what other option was there?

Nick copied a few files to his thumb drive, went downstairs, and printed them at the business center.

He went back upstairs, stuck the printouts and the newspaper section in his camera bag, and drove back to Thornton's residence. "He was calm because he didn't do it," Nick said to himself as he stopped in front. The gate was still open, and Nick took a deep breath and went into the backyard. The only person there was Malcolm Thornton.

"Hi there," Thornton acknowledged as Nick entered. "Did you forget something?"

"No, sir. May we talk?"

"Sure," he replied slowly. "What do you have in mind?"

"I want to show you something. May we sit at the table?"

"Of course."

Both men sat down as Nick set his camera bag on the ground. "You know I took quite a few photos here today. With your permission, I might add." Nick began.

"Yeah. I told you that was okay."

I was looking through them back at the hotel, and I noticed that one of the boxes here has a brass label on it. It's from Integrity Landscaping. What can you tell me about them?"

"That's simple. My wife wanted some new plants in the boxes I made for her, so I contacted them to replace the soil and plant some new flowers. Just like she wanted."

Nick pulled the paper out and showed him the picture. Do you recognize him?"

"Of course, that's Phil Robinson and his wife Amanda."

"As in the Amanda Robinson you had an affair with?"

"Hey, what's all this about?" Thornton stood up, his anger clearly showing in his eyes. "My wife found out about the affair, and forgave me."

"Relax, please," Nick said. "Maybe she forgave you, but maybe Phil didn't." Nick pulled out the photo printouts. "See these white chips? What do they look like to you?"

Nick waited, and continued when Thornton didn't answer. "They look like bone fragments to me."

"Bone fragments?"

"Let me try to put the pieces together for you. Phil finds out about the affair, and is definitely mad. But he's not as mad at his wife as he is at you and at your wife for forgiving you. In his mind, she let you get away with it. Then you call him and ask him to do some land-scaping work for you. He fills the boxes, puts his plaque on one of them, and leaves. When did you have this work done?"

"It was a little over a year ago. Phil and I agreed on a date, and." Malcolm stopped mid-sentence as his mouth opened wide and his jaw dropped. "That's right, he did the work the day after Jennifer went missing. I didn't think anything about it at the time. I just thought it would be a nice surprise when she came home."

"How well did he know your wife?"

"We were acquainted socially, although we did not see them much after..."

Nick stayed silent, letting the man make his own connections.

"Jennifer did say something. I can't remember what. I don't think I even mentioned it to the police. It's part of why I didn't call sooner. She said something about meeting one of her amigos to talk. I thought she meant someone from the Amnesty Center.

"Do you mind digging up some of your wife's favorite flowers? I think we might find something interesting in that flower bed."

Thornton went into the shed and returned with a shovel. He care-fully moved Jennifer's prized hydrangeas into a wheel barrel and then thrust the shovel down into the dirt. Almost immediately it struck something hard, and he got down on his knees. He began pulling away the dirt with his bare hands. "Oh, my God!" he cried out as he buried his sobbing face into his muddy hands. His legs were wobbling as he tried to stand.

Nick wrapped his long arms around to steady him.

"He buried Jennifer's body here. You were right," he wept uncontrollably as he leaned into Nick.

"I'm sorry," Nick said as he saw the grief spread from the man's face to his shaking arms and hands. Nick walked him back to the patio where he sat him down.

Nick pulled out his phone and dialed 9-1-1. As the call rang through, he pressed the Speaker button.

"9-1-1, what is your emergency?"

Tears formed in Nick's eyes as he looked at the distraught husband. "I'm at the house of Malcolm Thornton, and we've discovered a dead body buried in one of the planter boxes. Mr. Thornton is here with me, and we believe it is the body of his missing wife. We also believe we know who did it."

"What is your name, sir?"

"Nick O'Flannigan. I'm a freelance photographer from Seattle."

"Please stay on the line as we send authorities. I'll put you on hold and then be right back."

# 12

## DO MORE LANDSCAPING?

"Thank you for holding. The police are on their way and should be there in a few minutes," the 9-1-1 operator said. "Is there anyone else there or is anyone in a dangerous situation?"

"No," Nick said as he watched Malcom's head shake on his crossed arms. He'd helped him to a chair, and the man sat and continued to weep.

The increasing pitch of the sound of sirens stopped, and four uniformed police officers came trotting into the backyard through the open side gate. "The police are here," Nick said softly to Mr. Thornton who slowly lifted his head.

Nick stood as the officers approached. He told them about his theory, and what he'd found out about flowers and decomposing bodies.

"Pretty good detective work, young man," one of the officers said.

Nick then laid out his plan to lure Phil Robinson back over to the house under the pretense of more work while detectives looked for evidence at his landscaping business.

"Think you can make that call, Mr. Thornton?" an officer asked.

Malcolm nodded his head. "Anything for Jennifer," he mumbled.

"Give me a couple minutes to clean up and compose myself," he added as he went inside.

The officers went to the planter box. "Definitely bone fragments," one of them said. The other officers shook their heads in disbelief.

Malcolm Thornton returned to the patio, looking calmer although grief was still written across his face. "I'm ready," he said as pulled out his phone and Phil Robinson's cell phone.

"Integrity Landscaping, this is Phil."

"Hey, Phil. It's Malcolm Thornton. Say, I know it's last minute, but I have another landscaping job I'd like you to come over and give me a quick quote on. I've got to catch a flight in a few hours, so I'll gladly pay extra if you can come over now, and then take care of it while I'm gone." Malcolm fought hard to hold back his emotions. He did just what Nick told him to say and to do.

"I'll do it, Malcolm, but I'll have to charge you double 'cause I'd have to push out some other jobs. I hate to do that, but otherwise my schedule is really full."

"That's okay. It's a high priority for me, so I'll gladly pay."

"Okay, I'll be there in about twenty minutes," the greedy landscaper replied.

"Good job," Nick said.

Both men hung up and one of the officers also made a call. "Yep, look for a wood chipper and any sign of blood splatter or bone fragments. I know it has been a year, but it's worth a shot."

"We're all set," the officer said. "Meet him at the front door, and keep him occupied so he doesn't know we're here."

"Let's move the cars, two other officers said as they trotted back out to the front.

"That's easy. I'll offer him a drink first and we can chat about old times. Let's do it."

"He's on the way," one officer told them. "Let's get out of sight," he said to the others.

"Our officers are on site. If there is something for them to find, they'll find it," he told them.

Few minutes later, Robinson pulled into Thornton's driveway. He appeared not to notice the unmarked sedan parked down the street. The landscaper went to the front door and rang the bell.

Thornton answered the door with a cocktail in his hand. "Hey, Phil. Join me in a high ball before I have to bug out?" he said as he raised the glass in the air.

Ten minutes elapsed before the back door to the patio slid open. "Come on out, Phil, let me show you how Jennifer's Hydrangeas are doing." He intentionally slurred his speech, and Phil followed him outside. Thornton reached back and closed the door with a slam. "Oops, sorry about that."

"Hey. What happened there?" Phil questioned as he saw the dug up flower box.

"Police. Hands in the air!" one of the officers exclaimed as they rushed toward an astonished Robinson.

"Keep them in the air and don't move," the second officer yelled as Robinson began to turn away. He started to run, but Thornton stuck out a foot and tripped him. His glass fell to the patio and shattered into pieces as the landscaper fell into the broken glass.

"Good job, Mr. Thornton," the officer said as the second one bent down, put a knee in Robinson's back, and pulled his arms back to handcuff him.

"We found the lye, and the old wood chipper you tried to hide under the tarp at your shop," one officer told him. "We'll have to verify the DNA, but turns out you were a bit sloppy, Mr. Robinson."

"I swore that thing was spotless," he said. "You can't prove a thing."

"Not yet," one officer said. "but we have enough to hold you while we do."

"You," Robinson said, pointing at Nick. "You're that nosy photographer who needs to learn to mind his own business."

Nick left as the officers led Robinson out front where the two marked cars had been brought back. Back at the hotel, Nick uploaded his final photographs to the magazine's Cloud folder. "I can pack after dinner," he said as he walked out of his room to go have his last dinner in Boise.

# 13

# PRETTY FLOWERS NO MORE

Nick thought about going to Goldy's for breakfast again, but decided he would get something on the way out of town. He picked up a newspaper in the lobby. The headlines read, "Landscaper Arrested in Langsford Disappearance." The sub-heading was more graphic, "Bones Found in Planter Box Lead to Arrest." He read the article. There was no mention of his name, just a recap of the timeline since Jennifer's disappearance.

Nick left the hotel and drove by Malcolm Thornton's house one more time. There were several unmarked cars, plus a coroner's van nearby. Nick pulled over and parked a couple houses away and sent a group text message to Gerry and Sandra. "They Got Jennifer's killer!" Nick started the car and put it into gear when he saw two men removing a section of Thornton's side fence and a backhoe being driven into the backyard.

A tear ran down Nick's cheek as he thought about Jennifer. "She didn't deserve that," Nick said as he breathed deeply, pulled away from the curb, and headed toward the freeway. He looked down at the mapping app on his phone. 486 miles it showed. *It's a long way to Helena,* he thought as he let the cool air hit him in the face.

·  ·  ·

**THE END**

# SOME FACTS ABOUT BOISE AND THE STATE OF IDAHO

- Boise is pronounced with an "s," not with a "z."
- The 44 counties are designated alphabetically. Ada County (seat of the state government and home to Boise) is 1A, and Washington County (W) is the last. There are ten counties that begin with the letter B.
- The area of Ada County is only 1.3% of the total area in Idaho, yet its population is about 23% of the state's total population.
- Two of the "characters" in this story are real people who volunteered to be included. Their roles are clearly fictitious, but thanks to Judy (from Lincoln, CA) and to Laura (from Boise, ID) for being such good sports. You, too, can volunteer to be a "character" in one of our books. Go to the website capitalcitymurders.com and find the link under "The Books."
- When we've mentioned "Boise, Idaho" to people around the world, two responses were usually given: "Idaho potatoes," and "Blue football field." Yes, the Boise State Broncos are well-known for the blue turf, first installed in

1986. The Broncos also have the best winning percentage (0.841) of any football program from 2000-2018 (197-38).

- Several major companies are either headquartered or have/had significant presence in Boise. Albertsons grocery store was founded in 1939. Micron Technology was founded in 1978. The former Morrison-Knudsen Construction Company was founded in 1912. Hewlett-Packard began its Boise operations in 1973, becoming the home for its laser printer business. J.R. Simplot is credited with inventing the frozen potato fries and becoming their main supplier to McDonalds.
- Speaking of potatoes, Idaho provides almost one-third of all of the potatoes grown in the United States.
- At 7,900 feet deep, Hell's Canyon is about 1,800 feet deeper than Arizona's Grand Canyon.
- The Idaho state seal was designed by Emma Edwards Green, and it is the only U.S. state seal designed by a woman.
- New Year's Eve ceremonies in Boise include the "Dropping of the Potato" at midnight.
- Boise is home to the largest Basque community outside of Spain.
- Idaho native Brandi Sherwood is the only person to have held the titles of Miss Teen USA and Miss USA.
- Boise consistently rates very high (sometimes #1) in "Best Places to Live" studies.
- National forests occupy nearly 40% of Idaho's land area.

# ABOUT THE AUTHORS

Troy Lambert and Stuart Gustafson are each successful authors in their own rights. As residents of the Great State of Idaho (Troy lives in Meridian, and Stuart is in the capital city of Boise), they have teamed up to bring to you, the reader, this new and exciting series of novelettes **set in each capital city** of the United States of America!

And yes, a total of fifty states means a total of fifty novelettes. Are you ready?

**Troy Lambert** is a full-time writer and author. Having written over two dozen mysteries and other novels, Troy is well-versed in story creation, and he knows what it takes to make a fictional story real! Troy's hobbies and pastimes (when he's able to break away from the computer) include hiking into the mountains of Southwest Idaho, fishing in a fast-rushing stream, and going for a drive where his mind can work on creating that perfect twist to the book he's currently writing. A native of Idaho Falls, Idaho, Troy and his wife live in Meridian, Idaho. You can find his other works, including his latest book, *Harvested*, at fictionupdates.troylambertwrites.com.

**Stuart Gustafson** took early retirement in 2007 to spend more time traveling (he's been to 55 countries and 155 cruise ports) and writing (four novels, nine non-fiction books, lots of travel articles). Speaking on cruise ships in many parts of the world has been a great "post-retirement gig," as some have put it. He has leveraged some of the experiences from those travels to insert reality into a few of his mystery novels set in exciting locations around the globe. A native of Southern California, Stuart and his wife live in Boise, Idaho. The majority of his books are available at stuartgustafson.com/books.

# NEXT: HANGING IN HELENA

*One cried 'God bless us!' and 'Amen' the other;*
*As they had seen me with these hangman's hands.*
*Listening their fear, I could not say 'Amen,'*
*When they did say 'God bless us!'*

—*Macbeth*

He used the name Harry Hickman, although it was not his.

The hammer felt good in his rope-calloused hands. He performed the task the same way he always had, the way his father had, and his father before that.

Measure twice, cut once.

Create the joint on one end of the board, then the other.

The custom created stool stood below the strongest limb of a tall oak tree at the edge of a meadow. It was just the right height, and a nearly finished set of steps led up one side. The back of it had a handle, one just the right size of Harry's large hands. This was not the Hanging Tree, the one of Helena legend. That one had been cut down long ago, and the legends about it were far from true.

Of course, there were other legends and facts around hangings in Helena, Montana, and they made Harry happy to be here. The true Hanging Tree in Helena had been cut down by Methodist ministers in 1875. Most of the time, using a tree limb to execute someone this way ended cruelly, with the victim suffering for long minutes before they died. There were legends of another hanging tree south of town, but he knew them for the lies they were. His great, great grandfather had overseen hangings at the Jefferson County Courthouse in Bishop, albeit for a brief time. Those hangings were legal, but such methods of execution were frowned upon now.

Harry didn't know why. The death he wrought was instant and

merciful. An eye for an eye, a crime for a crime, but the Lord never intended for those who violated his laws to suffer on earth. Their suffering would come after death, at the hands of one much crueler than he.

He merely provided a service. Everyone knew the American justice system did not always work. When it failed, certain key people often hired him to make things right.

He balanced the newly created stool carefully. He would burn it after this, for it was the worst of luck to carry around anything used in such work with him. Once, he'd reused a stool, and it had broken under the weight of the criminal before Harry had been able to get the rope just right. He'd been forced to shoot that man to put him out of his misery, something he despised doing. Guns were for hunting, and hunting people was also cruel.

He fingered the sign, the sign that would hang around his charge's neck, written on white cardboard. It too would burn.

MURDER

A life for a life.

He finished setting the small set of steps he'd created next to the tall and overly large stool. Grabbing a coil of rope, his swift and practiced hands laid it out on the surface in first a "C" shape and then that of an "S". Pinching it together, he began to wrap, then completed the knot and pulled it tight, studying the eight coils. Perfect. The rope slid through the knot, but not too easily, making the loop easy to adjust while not leaving it loose.

A practiced toss put it in place over the limb. Harry was just over six feet tall, his muscles hard, his aim true, and he had practiced this act dozens of times, not counting the number of times he had assisted his father.

Harry looked at his watch. Just in time. His arms ached, but in a good way, from the work of getting things ready. It had been worth it. The man's last view would at least be a beautiful one.

In the distance, he saw three men making their way up the rocky trail toward the cliffs.

Harry inhaled the scent of wildflowers and pine. He looked

around at the soothing landscape, felt the brisk wind on his skin, drying the sweat formed by his hard work. The sun was about to set, and no clouds were present in the big blue sky this state was famous for. Maybe when he was done, he could hang around Helena for a few days. It had been a while since he was here, in what had been his home for a brief time, and no one would recognize him anymore. Certainly no one would know who he was or what he did now.

# THE "CAPITAL CITY MURDERS" SERIES

"Introduction to Nick"

Book # 1 "Overdoses in Olympia"

Book #2 "Slaying in Salem"

Book #3 "Strangled in Sacramento"

Book #4 "deCapitated in Carson City"

Book #5 "Buried in Boise"

Compilation #1: "The Wicked West"

All the books in the "Capital City Murders" series are available at www.CapitalCityMurders.com and your favorite e-book seller.

9 780988 727021